D1617061

FRANTIC!

Andrew D. Malloy

Raider Publishing International

New York　　　London　　　Cape Town

Cover images courtesy of istockphoto.com

ISBN: 978-1-61667-175-4

Published By Raider Publishing International
www.RaiderPublishing.com
New York London Cape Town
Printed in the United States of America and the United Kingdom

FRANTIC!

Andrew D. Malloy

1

July 2007— Miami, Florida, USA

It was an exceptional day in the city. He was sure that he had heard the local radio station's weather girl mention something about the hottest day in twenty-five years. The only comfortable way to travel in the heat was by air-conditioned transport.

The cab driver was doing his bit for the tourist trade, extolling the virtues of the resort. The words were falling on deaf ears, however— his passenger planning activities perhaps not to be found in the *What's On In Miami* guide.

Tall, dark and black suited, the man was still able to convey an intimidating presence, even in his fifties; like some kind of cross between the Devil and a sadistic tax inspector— or maybe an ex-FBI man. The cab rolled up into the setting-down area in front of the five-star Park Keys Hotel. Almost before the wheels stopped spinning a friendly hotel hand was pulling on the back door, eager to please, as befitted such a prestigious organisation.

The big guy stepped out into the ubiquitous splendour, squinting uncomfortably as the sun flooded his eyes.

Neatly manicured lawns, towering palm trees, majestic fountains sprayed huge plumes of water into the cloudless sky; their falling misty droplets picked out giant shimmering rainbows.

In the distance, the beautiful blue-green shades of the

Virginia Keys stretched out into the Atlantic Ocean and beyond.

As he stood there, hands on hips, drinking in the opulence, the cab driver and the bellhop teamed up to transfer the visitor's bags to the hotel reception.

Ten minutes later, the checking-in procedure was complete. The bellhop was suitably tipped, the big man finally left alone in the most expensive suite at the Park Keys.

He laid down his perfectly laundered jacket on the arm of the sofa and wandered out onto the glorious sun terrace, surveying all from his top-floor position.

He sat in the sumptuous easy chair on the terrace, closing his eyes for a few seconds. Down below, at street level, he could just about make out the spontaneous sounds of the busy traffic on the arterial roads around that area of the city. He was feeling so comfortable and relaxed at that precise moment that he almost forgot the reason for his trip.

As well as the small matter of some pressing business that had to be taken care of, Miami had been among his front-runners for a retirement destination and he hoped that he might make some time to check out the town.

Sighing wearily, he stood and returned to the cool of the apartment. He wiped away the sweat from his forehead, bent and reached under the king-sized bed— a stunning showpiece in the centre of this huge suite.

It is here. Just as they said it would be.

He pulled out a slim, shiny, black leather case, laying it carefully on top of the bed. Still on his knees, he reached under once more, this time producing a cylindrical leather bag, zipped to the top. He opened it and peered inside.

A minute later, the man appeared back on the sun terrace, bag over his shoulder, carrying the leather case in his free hand. In the other hand he was clutching a small bottle of carbonated mineral water, plundered from the room's minibar.

Around his neck dangled a pair of powerful binoculars— sleek, black, and expensive.

He blew away gathering sweat from under his nose, rolled up his shirt sleeves and towelled his hands and arms dry. There was no margin for error in this business. *Let me see now. Hotel Parkhurst Lodge.*

The binoculars swept from the left, moving up and down with the varying heights of the neighbouring hotels. After a few moments, the name Hotel Parkhurst Lodge came into view.

Bingo!

The hotel was around half a mile away and stood twenty-one storeys high, resplendent in the Florida sunshine.

The seventh floor.

The binoculars were now trained on the desired level.

Sixth apartment.

The man counted from the left under his breath. His eyes, still as sharp as ever, were now firmly focused on the small balcony of the sixth apartment. The sliding door to the inside was open, indicating that the occupant was home.

In recent weeks, a number of hotel guests in downtown Miami had returned to find their rooms ransacked, apparently by daredevil, human-fly-type cat burglars. It was a common occurrence among the Florida skyscrapers. The thought of real money could drive a man to do extraordinary things. The hotels, without exception, would strongly advise their guests to slide over the terrace doors before leaving their apartments.

He continued to observe, finally identifying a mark— an object— more often than not, bright in colour. This mark would allow the observer to return quickly to the area without having to re-count storeys and apartments. In this case, the mark was a red beach towel, hung out to dry on the balcony of the room above.

*   *   *

The man was sitting on a small bar stool at the edge of the sun terrace. He had earlier set up the tripod stand before clipping the body into the designated point.

Studying the picture of a man of about forty, fair haired, with a thick moustache, the man's face was a vision in concentration. Printed under the picture were the words: 'Wilbur T. Masterson, President of the Licensing Board of Las Vegas, Nevada'.

Minutes later, on the balcony of the sixth apartment from the left— on the seventh floor of the Hotel Parkhurst Lodge— a sandy haired man, around forty years, was standing stroking his thick moustache.

A relaxed Wilbur T. Masterson casually leant forward against the top railing of the balcony. At that moment the whole package— the weather and the salubrious setting— made him feel like the luckiest man alive.

*   *   *

Half a mile away, a finger caressed the trigger of a high-powered rifle. Half a mile away, a man held his breath, and squeezed. A split second later, the bullet struck Wilbur T. Masterson high on the forehead, snapping him back on his heels. The crimson spray from the exit wound spattered the whitewashed wall behind him, leaving bizarre, unruly patterns. Wilbur staggered forward, before violently somersaulting over the safety railing.

The shooter watched as the limp body fell through the floors like a rag doll, finally crashing head first onto a huge awning, set up over the entrance to an expensive diamond jeweller's shop. The resultant screams of the customers in the store could be clearly heard— even at that distance.

The man picked up the binoculars, still around his neck. He studied his handiwork. Wilbur T. Masterson was lying face down outside the entrance, legs and arms twisted beneath him. Blood began to pool around his head.

Masterson's bravery in resisting a mob application to open a new casino— an obvious front to launder money— had ultimately cost him his life. The Las Vegas crime cartel would now be free to promote its very own 'yes man' to the board.

It was time for Jack Feltham to make himself scarce. His first visit to Miami was going to be even shorter than he had earlier envisaged. Thoughts of retirement would have to be shelved— for now!

Los Angeles, California— two days later

Sam Giancarlo sat rather impatiently in the back of his Rolls. He was not used to waiting around for the hired help. The fact that the driver was also his useless nephew would certainly not be enough to save the boy from his uncle's venomous wrath.

"Where the fuck is that jerk?" The mobster's fat belly was telling him that he was going to be late for a dinner date at his favourite restaurant. "So help me, I'll put a slug in his head!" Giancarlo reached into his inside pocket, grappling for his angina pills.

"Calm down, boss. He's here." One of the dark-suited heavies opened the driver's door of the limousine. Poker faced, he shook his head in exasperation at the lad for stirring up the foul-tempered old man.

Sam Giancarlo was in his mid sixties, and was overweight as well as bad tempered. His prostitution, gambling and drugs empire, ruthlessly built up over the years, had seen his stock rise steadily among the other families. The old man had trodden on a few important toes along the way, however, and someone, somewhere among the faces, had decided that it was time something was done about it.

Giancarlo had got wind of the threats, but had always felt protected behind the security gates at his country estate. Unfortunately, the thought of dinner at Luigi's had tonight proved to be too much of an attraction. His two favourite bodyguards had been assigned the task of babysitting their boss for the evening.

"Sorry, Uncle Sam. I was…"

"Don't wanna hear it, Angelo! Just fucking drive!" Giancarlo cut in, easing back into the leather seat. His face was like thunder.

Angelo clicked his seatbelt into place, wisely choosing to do as he was told.

The Rolls purred down the drive, pulling smoothly into the early evening traffic.

Fifty yards up the road, the driver of a black Cadillac was on his mobile phone, issuing final instructions.

*　　*　　*

The Rolls slipped into Giancarlo's private parking space near the front door of Luigi's on Sunset Boulevard. The two monkeys got out, checked all around for any potential threat to their boss' life.

"Okay, boss. We're clear." The poker-faced guard opened Giancarlo's door before hustling him safely into the restaurant.

"Meester Giancarlo! So good to see you again." The telephone call that had made the dinner reservation had prompted Luigi himself to greet his best customer.

"Hello, Luigi. What's the special tonight?" Giancarlo's bloated face lit up when the scrumptious, cooking smells wafting in from the kitchen filled his nostrils.

"Too many to mention. For you— anything, Meester Giancarlo." The host pulled back a cushioned chair for his esteemed guest and handed him a detailed menu.

As he made himself comfortable, Sam couldn't help but notice the beautiful girl sitting alone at an adjoining table.

Whoever stood her up must be nuts, he thought. *Could be my lucky night!*

The girl returned his smile, with interest.

Sam Giancarlo sat back happily in his chair, fit to burst, having over indulged— as usual. In addition, and for good measure, he had downed a good few glasses of his favourite wine.

The pretty girl at the next table had been giving the old man the eye throughout the meal. Sam was not naïve enough to believe that it was because of how he looked. He knew she was only interested in him because he was a powerful man— a rich man.

Who cares? Never look a gift horse in the mouth. The girl had just risen to visit the ladies' room. Giancarlo left instructions with the obviously younger, fitter Angelo to invite her back to the mansion when she returned to her table.

Standing up a little unsteadily, the strong wine taking hold, Giancarlo made for the gents, flanked by one of the two bodyguards.

"Just a minute, boss." Poker-face put his hand on Sam's shoulder, urging him to wait at the door of the toilet while he checked inside.

The toilet appeared to be empty, apart from one locked cubicle. Poker-face stood for a few seconds, waiting.

"Come on, for fuck's sake! I need to pee!" Giancarlo brushed past the bodyguard and walked over to a urinal, fumbling with his flies.

Poker-face's gaze never left the door of the cubicle. He quietly drew his handgun.

This guy should be out by now. Where the fuck is he? Poker-face's attention was slightly distracted by the main door to the toilet opening again, directly behind him.

The pump of the silencer instantly made Sam Giancarlo wet on his shoes in shock. The silenced bullet had slammed into the back of Poker-face's head; the spotless, white tiles on one of the walls were suddenly lashed with arterial blood spray. The bodyguard nosedived to the floor in a sickening, gurgling heap, deep red creeping across the tiles. His gun clattered noisily into the corner.

Sam Giancarlo turned to face his assailant only to see familiar eyes staring back at him— pretty eyes, unsmiling eyes. The girl squeezed off the second round, catching the mobster flush on the cheek, directly below his right eye. Giancarlo crashed heavily to the floor next to his guard.

She delivered another round to each body to be absolutely certain, and replaced the gun in her handbag.

Walk, don't run! Quickly composing herself, she was back at her table to collect her jacket, expertly side-stepping the attentions of the dead man's useless nephew.

By the time bodyguard Number Two had realised what had gone down, the pretty, but extremely dangerous assassin, was climbing into the black Cadillac. The car slowly disappeared into the night.

Chicago, Illinois— Two days later

"Okay. Let's try it again, Honey. Remember, take a breath, hold it, then squeeze." The big Texan's deep drawl sounded like melted honey over a freshly baked bagel.

His student was trying her hand at long-range

marksmanship; half a dozen ripe melons on sticks provided the targets.

They were standing on a piece of waste ground on the outskirts of Chicago.

Jack Feltham, otherwise known as the Master, was attempting to recreate the conditions leading to the assassination of Wilbur T. Masterson in Miami. Again, it was an exceptionally sunny day. Feltham had meticulously paced out for half a mile, before driving the melon lollipops into the hard, dusty ground. A cool breeze could be felt today in the windy city. He figured this would almost replicate the high altitude conditions of that top-floor apartment at the Park Keys Hotel.

The girl stood, arms folded, slightly irritated that the Master should still treat her like a rookie. After all, Sam Giancarlo had been her third contract.

Two days earlier, she had calmly exited Luigi's restaurant in LA and jumped into Feltham's waiting Cadillac. She tried to explain to him the rush that she felt on completion of this particular job, her first solo run.

Jack Feltham had looked into her eyes as she gleefully ran through the fine details of the hit. He saw something there that worried him. Jack had always done the job purely and simply for the money. There was absolutely no emotional content. He did not feel remorse or pity for his targets, nor did he feel antipathy towards them.

It was all about making sure that the job was done properly and efficiently and getting handsomely rewarded for it.

This girl seemed to actually like the killing. For the first time, he wondered if he had made a mistake in agreeing to train her in the first place.

Almost exactly a year before, Feltham had first come across the twenty-five-year-old waiting tables in a New York diner. It was clear to him straight away that Kelly

Martin was one of those worldly-wise sorts; a survivor, no matter what life would throw at her. She had left her home some years before, running to escape the pain of a failed relationship. The unmistakable draw and sexy reputation of the Big Apple had led her to try to make a new life there.

A self-confident individual, Kelly had sweet-talked the manager of the diner into taking her on. It would pay the bills until she figured out her next move.

The beautiful brunette and the seasoned assassin had hit it off immediately, despite the difference in their ages. Feltham found himself drawn to the girl; his visits to the local eatery became more and more frequent.

The unlikely partnership would be strictly non-sexual, however, Jack Feltham far too much of the Southern gentleman to be involved in that kind of nonsense. That said, the girl was good for him in other ways— kept him thinking positively— and that was crucial for a man in his line of business.

At that particular time, Jack had based himself exclusively in New York. Crime was on the up there and that was good for business.

Inexplicably, he found himself confiding more and more in Kelly Martin, interested to hear her views on anything and everything. Inevitably, one day the subject on the agenda would be the art of killing.

Things progressed rapidly from there, and the Master suddenly discovered that he had unwittingly signed up to educate another student.

Jack was sure of one thing— if he did as good a job on Kelly Martin as he had done on former protégé, Brodie Metcalf, she would make one hell of a killer.

Don't get angry! Don't get angry! Deep breaths. One of the melons exploded into a thousand pieces. Reload. Seconds later, Number Two was destroyed.

"Much better, Kelly. Now let's see if you can hit one

of the wooden poles." Feltham shot her a mischievous look. "Better still, why don't you try it, Jack?" She beckoned to him to take over.

Sometimes it's good to bring them back to Earth, Jack thought. He concentrated. The shot cracked into the distance, splitting the slender pole neatly in two.

"Humph! If you can't be good, be lucky!" Kelly declared, her face eventually breaking into a smile.

Jack Feltham wasn't smiling. About a mile down the little dirt track, a car had left the main road and was winding its way up towards them. Feltham picked up his binoculars, the relief only etched on his face when he recognised the driver.

"Who is it, Jack?' Kelly asked.

"Someone I think it's time for you to meet." He walked over to greet Brodie Metcalf as he stepped from the car.

"Thought I'd find you up here, old man. Old habits die hard, eh?" Metcalf recalled the numerous visits to the area, practising the long-distance stuff.

Feltham nodded, then turned to take Kelly's arm.

"Brodie, I'd like you to meet Kelly."

"Heard a lot about you, Kelly." Metcalf leant forward to shake hands. "Although, Jack forgot to mention just how beautiful you are."

She smiled shyly.

"Thought you were in Detroit?" Jack asked, changing the subject to deflect her embarrassment.

"I was. Job done. I just took on the next one."

"A glutton for punishment. Anyone we know?" Jack turned to dismantle the rifle and tripod. He had decided that their session was over.

"Yeah, I'm looking at him," Metcalf replied, his tone darkening.

Jack froze. He kept his back to Metcalf, his hand slowly reaching for the tiny derringer strapped to the inside of his left arm. Metcalf, the pupil, of course read the move.

"Steady, Jack. You know the drill. Two fingers. Throw it over here."

Feltham did as he was told. He had no choice, a 9mm Glock pointed at his face.

"What's going on, Jack?" Kelly asked, obviously confused.

"Let her go, Brodie. This has nothing to do with her," Jack said calmly.

"No can do. The last thing I need is another shooter on my tail, hell bent on revenge. Sorry it has to be this way, Jack."

Metcalf never took his eyes off the Master. He, more than anybody, knew the skills and craft that his mentor possessed. One moment of indecision could prove fatal.

A sudden movement to his left, a bird taking flight, distracted Metcalf for a micro-second; enough time to allow Feltham to withdraw a knife from a holder between his shoulder blades.

Kelly Martin had managed to grasp her handgun, but was unable to pull the trigger in time. Brodie's first bullet hit her upper body, knocking her off her feet. From there she tumbled backwards thirty feet down a steep gully, crashing against rocks and bushes on the way.

Brodie turned back to feel the blade catch him just below the shoulder bone. He screamed in agony, but was somehow able to bring his gun up to meet the advancing Jack Feltham. The next bullet ripped into the Master's chest, tearing out through his back. The bullet had pierced the heart, the life literally draining out of Feltham as he fell roughly on top of his former student.

Dying determination made Jack grab the handle of the knife, still stuck deep into Metcalf's shoulder. He roughly worked the blade from left to right. Brodie howled in agony, before somehow gathering the strength to push the older man away from him. Jack Feltham flopped onto his back, facing the sky, now unable to move. He drew his final couple of breaths.

Brodie Metcalf struggled to his feet; indescribable pains shot through his body with every movement. He peered over the edge of the gully, taking care not to stumble over, especially not in his present condition.

At the bottom, Kelly Martin was lying flat on her back, lifeless. Her body was partly masked by a large rock. Brodie took shaky aim, the pain making him narrowly miss his target with bullets three and four. The fourth made a deep gouge in the dirt next to her head.

He was forced to succumb to the agony and sat watching her for a few minutes, until he was sure. There was no way he could climb down in such pain.

Satisfied that Kelly Martin had breathed her last, Brodie eventually staggered to his car.

This would be one time he couldn't have given a damn if he messed up the interior of his beloved Pontiac.

2

One year later— Osaka, Japan

Typically, the rain seemed to get heavier as she pulled up outside the tall building on the outskirts of the city.

She checked the address.

This is the place.

Osaka, Japan's second city, has a population nearing three point seven million and is widely regarded as the nation's kitchen and the Mecca of gourmet food.

Whoever decided on these culinary labels had obviously not sampled any of the delights of this particular area.

The young woman could smell the mouth-watering aromas emanating from a series of snack vans parked along the road. The scene could have come straight out of a street in a rundown part of New York, westernised hot dogs and beefburgers— both with onions of course— now firmly part of the staple diet of the young Japanese.

The vans were waiting patiently for the nightclub brigade to tumble out of these seedy establishments; spend the rest of their hard earned cash trying to clog up their arteries.

The girl stole a final look at her watch— 1:35 a.m. She got out of her car before reaching through the open rear window into the back seat. She smiled as she grasped the weapon, holding it up in front of her. A sudden noise to her right quickly prompted her to conceal the blade under her full-length raincoat. She blew out her cheeks with relief as she watched a spooked cat shoot into the shadows.

The rain began to really rattle the road at her feet, bouncing two feet in the air. A short sprint up the steps to the rain canopy, set above the outside door of the building, allowed her to stand for a minute to gather her senses. She slipped off her raincoat, letting it fall at her feet. Grasping the handle of the sword, she withdrew the full length slowly, making sure to clear the end of the scabbard. Resting the scabbard carefully against the door standard, she pushed her way into the apartment building.

She immediately noticed that most of the lights on the ground floor were out. She shuddered, sensing a huge shiver travel all the way up to the nape of her neck.

All part of the plan, she mused.

Keeping the sword pointing safely away from her body, she slipped past the elevators, heading for the emergency stairwell.

Within minutes, she had arrived at the door leading to the third-floor landing. Looking through the little half-window of the fire door, she noted the absence of sufficient lighting there as well.

Flat Number 7.

She sensed a movement at her shoulder. The blade whistled past her neck, literally missing by millimetres. The full impact was met by the wall at her head; a huge lump of concrete crashed to the floor at her feet.

The girl swung around, easily parrying the next attack; the sparks from the clashing weapons lit up the gloomy landing area.

She grabbed at the door handle, shoving it with all of her might at her attacker, catching him full on the shoulder. He yelled out, tightly clutching his injury.

The Japanese man quickly regrouped, following his prey onto the landing. No sign. He glanced along at the target apartment— Number 7. The door was open; light streamed out from the narrow hallway, illuminating part of the landing area.

He brought the samurai sword up to about waist height, silently gliding towards Number 7. Almost as if sensing the air displacement, the man ducked the attack from the other side of the landing; the sword bounced from the wall onto a fire extinguisher. The concrete walls and ceiling echoed loudly as the extinguisher was ripped from its housing, splitting and bouncing frantically across the floor. White foam spewed up under pressure against the ceiling, raining down onto the pair.

The man swung his weapon around in defence, deflecting the woman's next attack.

The pair traded a further half a dozen blows as the fluid from the extinguisher began to fizzle to a conclusion. The floor was now a creamy mess; the vinyl surface below became transformed into a slippery skating rink.

The inevitable Bambi moment came almost simultaneously for both of them; the sheer physical effort required to swing their weapons unbalanced them, contributing to their downfall.

Both blades clattered into separate corners as their owners fell heavily onto their backs among the treacherous crap.

Japanese martial arts instructor, Takashi Tagaya, watched intently as his pupil attempted to get to her feet. Three times she tried; three times, she landed right back on her rear, the last time bursting into gales of laughter.

Tagaya laughed along with her— until he felt the sensation of cold steel against his throat. The point of her dagger barely broke the skin.

The little Japanese swallowed hard.

"Congratulations," he announced. "You've passed."

3

April 2009— Glasgow, Scotland

The dirty curtains were so long that they trailed at least two feet too heavy over the carpet. The tenant of this particular flat did not exactly believe in privacy. His drapes lay open wide to the world all day, every day.

Apparently, he did not much believe in hygiene either; his cesspool of an abode had become legendary amongst the neighbours in these upmarket, executive apartments, deep in the heart of middle class Glasgow.

Indeed, the campaign to have Longthorn Reeves Baltimore III evicted from the building had gathered momentum over the past three months. This was a direct result of the former all-American college boy's drug habit spiralling mercilessly out of control.

The solution to the problem was to present itself very soon.

Longthorn's extremely wealthy parents had long since disassociated themselves from their wayward son; only underlying feelings of guilt compelled Longthorn Baltimore II— the father— to grudgingly cover the cost of the luxury apartment near Glasgow's city centre. For good measure, Dad also wired a hefty weekly allowance straight into the lad's bank account.

The rich friends of the country club back home in Chicago regularly asked after the Baltimore's only son and

17

heir. The answer was always the same— Longthorn was really big in the city, nurturing investment trusts, managing millions for multimillionaires.

The boy's special love affair with marijuana and coke, allied to his strong liaison with the local drug dealer, had often considerably lightened the old man's pocket. Numerous private investigators and expensive rehab treatments later, had finally forced the father to admit defeat.

The goody-goody brigade hadn't been a lot of help either, stating politically correct phrases directly from their handbook that his son would, 'need to want to help himself,' along with the strikingly similar: 'change would have to come from within'.

The problem was that Lonnie liked taking drugs. He never wanted to stop. As long as his father was funding, he would be using.

The constant pressure from Lonnie's parents, combined with drug-fuelled paranoia, was to ultimately drive the boy from the country of his birth.

His choice of living in a small European country called Scotland had been bizarre to say the least; Lonnie's favourite film of all time— Mel Gibson's *Braveheart*— a deciding factor in his selection.

To be fair, the tall, blond Yank had initially tried to control his drug abuse, even managing to hold down a decent job in a small, West End accountant's office. He had dated a couple of gorgeous, respectable girlfriends, one the daughter of a well-heeled, local councillor. Longthorn's parents visited twice, leaving with renewed hope each time.

Unfortunately, both relationships and the job were doomed to failure by his descent into what could best be described as heroin hell.

Two short years later and the millionaire's thirty-year-old son was a suppurating, shambling wreck, firmly addicted to the drugs that he found himself pushing for the local Glasgow Mafia.

Repeated warnings from the bosses of the organisation were losing their impact. Something had to be done about the constant skimming of the profits.

* * *

A hefty hand thudded against the door of the flat, the reverberations rolling up and down the communal areas of the building. A simple pressing of the doorbell would normally have sufficed, but on this particular occasion the visitor was there to deliver an extra-special message to the occupant.

"Who's there?"

"A friend."

The visitor heard a movement on the other side of the door. He could sense a drug-fuelled eye watching him through the peephole.

A key turned slowly in the lock. The sliding bolt and door chain backup system slipped across slowly and deliberately.

"Fuck's sake, Lonnie! How many times have I got to watch you in this state?" the visitor asked, exasperated at the sorry mess standing in front of him. He brushed past the unsteady American, screwing up his face in disgust. The putrid stench of the place attacked his nostrils.

Dirty clothes were strewn all around; plates of uneaten food, green and crisp around the edges, lay in every corner. The man shook his head at the extent of the squalor. It was all he could do to stop his stomach retching. He composed himself before continuing, "Simpson's no' happy. I told you the last time."

"Cool it, man. I'll pay for the stuff. I have the cash." The former American jock stood in front of the man, hunched, looking at least fifteen years older than his thirty.

"Hah! You have the cash? Since when?"

"I'm waiting for money from the old man. It'll be here Tuesday."

"It'd better. Simpson wants two grand. And no more pilfering. This is your last warning." The man poked a finger in Baltimore's face.

"Two grand! Aw, come on, man. Maybe five or six hundred pounds. No more, man. No more." Lonnie Baltimore shakily lit up a joint, slumping down on a chair laden with stained clothes.

He drew carefully on the joint, his body immediately reacting to the drug; more and more worries and anxieties seemed to disappear with every exhale.

Although the shakes had left his body for now, Lonnie's eyes sank deep into his skull— like piss holes in snow. The man gave him time to settle himself down before reiterating.

"It's two grand to make it go away, Lonnie. Okay? You want me to write it down?" he asked, sounding more than a little patronising. The man walked over towards the door. He'd had enough of the stinking hellhole.

"No way, man. No way. Simpson's not getting that. Stuff's crap, anyway." His red-rimmed eyes were testament to that fact. The combination of heroin, cocaine and marijuana had changed his personality; it had given Baltimore an uncharacteristically petulant demeanour.

The visitor stopped dead in his tracks, turned around to face the upstart; a look of venom crossed his face.

"What did you say?" he hissed.

"I said the stuff's fucking crap and I'm not paying for crap!" Lonnie leant back in the chair, his eyelashes fluttering with self-induced tiredness.

The visitor made fists in his pockets, the rage stoking up inside him, trying to find an outlet.

"Okay, I'll pass that message on to Simpson. I'll tell you now, Lonnie. You'd better buy yourself a fuckin' crash helmet," he said through clenched teeth. He wasn't kidding.

"I don't give a runnin' fuck for a rollin' doughnut, man!"

Longthorn Reeves Baltimore III dismissively waved away the words. Seconds later, his heavy, rhythmic breathing signalled unconsciousness.

A weighty brass figurine— ironically, an expensive gift from his parents some time before— flashed under the harsh centre light in the room.

Lonnie never felt any pain; the dusty ornament crashed into his skull. Small pieces of brain and bone showered the room. The shock of the blow made the young American instantly jump to his feet. Like a headless chicken in its final moments, pure nerves keeping it alive for a few seconds, he moaned loudly; then he staggered two or three steps to be met with a second crushing blow to the face. Lonnie's nose exploded like a ripe melon, hosing copious amounts of blood over the filthy Persian rug in front of the fireplace. The limp body slumped forward, face down onto the floor. A few short gasps later and Lonnie Baltimore was still.

The visitor stood over the corpse for a few seconds, apparently congratulating himself on a job well done; he stuffed the bloody figurine into a plastic, supermarket bag before leaving the dingy flat.

The bag was no doubt bound for the bottom of the River Clyde— once he had put some distance between himself and the murder scene.

4

The Parthenon Nightclub, Renfield Street, Glasgow

"Fuck's sake, Martin! You no' got a home to go to?" Vic Simpson asked, surprised at the appearance of his lieutenant in the attic office of the mobster's main city centre earner.

In his mid fifties, the gangster's face had seen better days; his purple, bulbous nose and craggy complexion told tales of an over indulgence in most excesses— especially alcohol.

Simpson had recently undergone tests for a variety of conditions: cholesterol, sky high; blood pressure, off the scale; body mass index, morbidly obese.

In this particular criminal's case, Sod's Law would dictate that he would probably live longer than he deserved, unless one of his many mobster rivals had other ideas.

"I could say the same about you, boss. I came in to see you, anyway," Martin Anderson replied.

He pulled up a little, black plastic chair, muttered something about how fucking uncomfortable it was and flopped down in front of the main man. Martin loosened his tie, rubbing his palms over the back of his neck, working out the kinks.

It was gone eleven-thirty in the evening and the cleaners had just left the nightclub. They had been asked to put in an extra shift to prepare the place for the special club night the following evening.

Simpson had dropped in to check the books, giving his manager the night off. He knew deep down that he needn't have bothered as there was no way any of his managers would steal as much as a peanut from him. Vic still liked to check, though. He reckoned it kept everyone on their toes.

He was just getting ready to call it a night when Anderson's face appeared at the outside surveillance camera.

*   *   *

Martin Anderson was in his late twenties, tall, dark and well built with an evil temper. A deep scar on his right cheek, courtesy of a rival teenager during a gangland fight, detracted slightly from his obvious good looks. He had suffered unenviable abuse from his father during his earlier life, finally taking bloody revenge one night when the old man foolishly decided to have a go at his beloved mother. The young killer calmly selected the family's longest, sharpest kitchen knife and speared it deep into Robert Anderson's throat, completely severing his windpipe.

Three years later, Martin Anderson walked free from the young offenders' institution, right into the clutches of a local gangster by the name of Victor Simpson. Simpson had people on the inside at these institutions, their job to identify new, up and coming talent. Martin's official record would indicate that he had behaved impeccably during his stay at Her Majesty's establishment. The truth, however, was vastly different, and would show that he had been one of the dominant males, constantly involved in numerous power struggles for supremacy among the strongest of the teenagers. Anderson had unwittingly passed the tests with flying colours; the fact that he also managed to do it with stealth and secrecy made him a prime candidate to join

Simpson's team.

Vic hadn't been disappointed. The young lad had been with him for ten years, showing an intense aptitude for racketeering. The fact that he could also play the heavy, when required, had served to make his role doubly important within the business— until now.

Martin had considered not telling Simpson of the demise of one of their many drug dealers until the following morning. It was only because he happened to be passing the club later on that night that he had decided to pay a visit.

The killing of the young American was considered by Anderson to be no big deal in the grand scheme of things. It would not be the first or last time that the organisation had had to violently retire a rogue pusher. The way Simpson's many business interests were set up was through either pure raw fear or a simple tier of command system, providing anonymity unlimited. It would take some kind of a special genius to pin as much as a parking ticket on Vic Simpson.

Martin Anderson hadn't really given the Baltimore incident another thought. He had been very careful to conceal his identity and get rid of the murder weapon. Also, the guy was a foreigner— no close relatives; Anderson had never heard Baltimore mention any recent visits by his family. No ties; as far as Anderson believed, this should be another case consigned to the unsolved pile; merely society ridding us of another worthless junkie.

* * *

"I'm tired, Martin. I need to get to bed. What's happening?" Simpson was beginning to get a little fractious, a consoling bottle of malt no doubt waiting for him at home.

"I went to see Lonnie Baltimore. To straighten him out."

Vic Simpson lifted his head from a petty cash book that he had been checking; a hint of concern flashed across his face.

"What d'you mean, straighten him out?" he asked impatiently.

"You know he's been fleecing us, boss. I looked at the figures earlier. He's done us for hundreds, Vic. I told him we wanted two grand. What's the big deal, anyway?" Anderson had noticed the unusual expression on the face of his boss. If he didn't know him better, he would have sworn it was a look of fear.

"Who told you to go an' see him?" Vic's voice was hushed.

"What? What d'you mean? Did you no' hear me? He was fleecing us."

"I said who the fuck told you to go visit the bastard? Can you no' give me a straight answer?" Simpson's tone was becoming much stronger.

"Vic, what's the matter? I... I just went to see him to straighten things out."

A look of real panic replaced concern on Vic's face. Simpson had witnessed his hotheaded colleague's 'straightening out' procedures many times. He had a sinking feeling about this one.

"What happened, Martin? What did you do?" Vic Simpson already knew the answer, but had to ask.

"Baltimore said he wouldnae pay the two grand. Said we'd only get a few hundred quid. That was it!"

"Fuckin' hell, Martin! What happened?" The older man was, by this time, getting really exasperated.

"He really pissed me off. You should've heard the stupid bastard! I picked up an ornament and thumped him across the head. Instead of goin' doon, he got up. I cracked him again. Doon he went that time."

Silence.

"Is he dead?"

"Vic, what is the…?"

"Is he fuckin' dead, Martin? Can ye no' just tell me?" Simpson's eyes were literally popping out of his head.

"I… I think so. I don't really know. What the fuck is so important about him, anyway?"

Several deep breaths over twenty seconds or so managed to break the silence.

"Vic? What is it?" Martin Anderson was getting really spooked by this time.

"Longthorn Reeves Baltimore the Third."

"What? Who?"

"Longthorn Reeves Baltimore the fucking Third!" Simpson shouted this time, for maximum effect. "Son of a fucking millionaire— naw— a fucking billionaire! We're dead meat, son! Fucking dead meat! The father's a nut job! He's gonnae go fucking ballistic!"

"How… How d' you know, Vic? Surely it cannae be that bad?" Anderson was trying desperately to calm his boss down.

"This guy's got Mafia connections. I'm tellin' you, we're planted!"

Simpson rested his head on the back of his chair, closing his eyes. "Think! Fucking think!" He held up his hand in front of him, stopping Anderson before he uttered another word.

A few seconds later, the mobster's face lightened; his expression immediately appeared less strained. "Okay. This is your pigeon, Martin. If this guy, Baltimore, turns up here, you're explainin' to him what happened to his boy. You got that? You fuckin' sort it!"

Martin Anderson had no choice but to nod in agreement. He would have to think— and fast!

5

They say that girls mature quicker than boys; that they are generally smarter, more willing to adapt to any situation. In the case of Molly and Jack Munro, those particular notions would certainly appear to hold more than a grain of truth.

Molly's vocabulary had developed much more quickly than that of her identical twin; the three-year-old practically tied the boy up in verbal knots— chattering, commanding, and dominating.

"Come on, Jack, we have to go upstairs now. We have to play with my dollies." The little girl was grasping her brother's hand, hauling him out of the lounge and into the hall.

Sheepishly, he followed, like the proverbial collie dog.

Unwittingly, the pair had attracted the attention of a doting admirer.

Will Munro had been relaxing, for once, on his plush, green, leather sofa, chuckling silently at the antics of his children.

"Okay, dinner will be in twenty minutes, guys! Your mum will be home soon!"

He flicked off an extremely boring afternoon-TV chat show and rose to go into the kitchen to check on his latest concoction— pasta shells served with a Dolmio™ sauce, tuna chunks and chopped tomatoes— more than enough for everyone.

The words of the twins' mother were still ringing in his

ears. *Make sure she sits at the table to eat.*

Mary Munro was referring to their latest attempt to get their lightweight, but otherwise healthy, daughter to eat a bit more than her usual sparrow's portion.

No such coaxing would be required for their chunkier, heavier son. He would normally be downstairs in a heartbeat at the mere mention of food.

Mary had earlier sent Will a text message saying that she would be home an hour later than usual; something to do with a last minute meeting at the National Childbirth Trust.

It was Easter Monday and the bank holiday had forced Will into volunteering to look after the kids while his wife took full advantage of her chance of freedom, deciding to make a day of it.

Full-scale morning assaults on selected high-street shops were on the agenda, followed by lunch at Buzzy Wares in Princes Square for Mary Munro and her best pal, Leah Vieri. Leah's three-year-old kids, Josh and Mia, attended the same nursery school as the twins.

In a kind of bizarre, parallel life, both mothers had been admitted to Glasgow Royal Infirmary to have their babies on the same day; both had had twins within hours of each other; both boys weighed in at four pounds five ounces; the girls tipped the scales at four pounds exactly— both of them. At the time, the story had hit the front page of the local *Evening Times*; experts calculated the odds of such a collection of coincidences at around one hundred and forty million to one— about the same as ten major lottery wins.

Then, unbelievably, Mary and Leah enrolled their children at the same private nursery on the same day.

The two mothers had finally decided that it must have been their destiny to become best friends. Two and a half years later, they were still best friends.

In another bizarre twist, their husbands, Ben Vieri and

Will Munro, also ended up as best friends.

Ben and Will were both twenty-nine years old; Leah and Mary? Yes, twenty-six— both of them.

* * *

The two guys had done really well for themselves; Ben had just recently become a junior partner in the very prestigious, city centre, criminal law firm of Martin, Martin and McCreevy.

Will earned the corn from a very successful career as a chartered accountant, taking over the business from his retired father around a year and a half ago.

The abundance of cash coming in to their homes meant that both families would be more than comfortable. This allowed the women folk to indulge in their usual middle class merry-go-round of charity work, shopping sprees and endless city centre lunch dates.

Home for the Munros was a very comfortable, four-bedroom, detached house in the Bearsden area of Glasgow. The house had been built in the forties and, in keeping with properties of that time, it benefited from huge, sprawling garden areas.

Climbing frames, swings, chutes and slides adorned the rolling lawns at 59 Roman Road.

It was a perfect, almost idyllic existence for the family. Life couldn't possibly get any better for this, not so stuffy, accountant.

It could, and would get a whole lot worse.

The phone call that was about to turn Will Munro's world upside down would be the start.

"Dinner's out, kids. Come on, let's roll. That'll be Mum on the phone checking up on you."

Jack was already at the table, fork in clenched fist, preparing to attack. Molly appeared at the bottom of the

stairs looking decidedly uninterested, audibly muttering at
the untimely interruption to her play routine. She glared at
her father on her way to the table.

"Hello."

"Will? Is that you?"

"Who is this?" Munro's heart lightened in his chest, a
familiar voice exploding into his brain.

"It... It's me. Penny." The girl barked out the words.

Will noted that her breathing was strangely laboured as
if she had been running; either that or the words had been
borne out of fear.

Will couldn't decide which— for now. He was far too
engrossed in trying to figure out exactly what he should say
to his ex-girlfriend. It had been five years since they had last
seen each other; a huge, blazing row signalled the end of that
stormy episode. The girl's wandering eye had eventually
made Will Munro's mind up. Unfortunately, at that time,
the tall, leggy brunette had worked her way into Will's
heart; the break up caused him many more sleepless nights
than it did her.

Luckily for Will, he had met his future wife, Mary,
within six weeks of the split. This was undoubtedly a major
factor in saving him from crashing and burning.

Will could feel his heart quickening.

*What the hell could she possibly want from me after all
this time?*

He would tell her exactly where to go. She was bad
news and he tried to remember the words that he had
rehearsed in his head a million times, should they ever meet
again. Now he had his chance.

He tried to launch into the tirade, but the words seemed
to stick in the back of his throat.

"Will? Please, don't hang up. I need to talk to you."

"Why are you calling me now, Penny? I..."

"Just let me talk, Will. I know you loved me."

"I'm married now. I have children, for God's sake."

"I know. But I need your help, Will. As a friend. Please?" Her voice was laced with large dollops of panic-stricken emotion.

Will had never before been aware of that particular trait coming from his ex. He clenched his teeth tightly when he realised that he was about to relent. Again! She had done it again!

How many fucking times?

"What do you want, Penny? What's wrong with you?" Will asked with stiffening resolve, almost as if he shouldn't.

"He's going to kill me, Will."

The words didn't register with him at first. When they did, Munro wheeled around to check on his kids, as if to confirm reality.

Molly and Jack Munro were tucking into their pasta dishes. Well at least Jack was. Molly was pushing pieces of pasta shells around her plate, completely bored by it all.

As if by well-worn habit, her father clicked his fingers at her. The ritual always managed to galvanise the little girl into action. She screwed up her face, a mouthful half-heartedly disappearing down her skinny neck.

Penny Richards had really surpassed herself this time. *What kind of game is this?*

"Penny, what are you talking about? Who's trying to kill you?" Munro knew he should have hung up. The girl's power, though waning, was still working away inside Will Munro's head, lurking just below the surface.

"I didn't know where to go. I…" She began to cry.

"Okay. Calm down. Where are you?" he asked reluctantly.

"I… I'm hiding. He's going to get me."

"All right. Stay where you are. I'll come and get you."

"No! Meet me at the café. I'll be safe there. He doesn't know about it." Penny was referring to 'their café'. The place they had met— love at first sight and all that. It had been the venue for all of their anniversaries and poignant moments— the scene of their declaration of undying love for each other.

"Okay. I'll be there in thirty minutes. Just stay calm."

"Thanks, Will. I knew you would help me. See you then."

The phone went dead. Munro hung up and rubbed his face, vigorously, with both hands as if trying to rub some sense into his thick skull. He was expecting the worst.

What an idiot! But then, what if she is telling the truth?

Penny Richards was right. He had loved her at one time. The big softie— Mary had often referred to her husband in that manner— would never have forgiven himself if something had happened to her and he had done nothing to help.

It was a no-brainer. He had to go.

Will Munro did not feel comfortable with it; not one iota.

"Mummy!" Two little voices rang out in unison at the sight of their mother coming in the front door, laden with designer bags, the very weight of them digging the string handles into her fingers. The posh shops always used string bags— the more uncomfortable, the better. Mary Munro just managed to jettison the load before she was swamped by her twins.

"Hold it! Just let me get my shoes off. My feet are killing me!" She had an arm around each child, guiding them over towards the sofa.

Mary turned around; the three of them disappeared into the inviting leather chair. Molly and Jack hugged their mother tightly, competing for her attention in the way that only twins would. She kicked off her very uncomfortable high heels— the price of high fashion, and measuring only five-foot-two— and bent over to rub her tired feet.

"Hi, love. You had a good day?" Will leant over and kissed his wife tenderly on the forehead, at the same time pulling on his jacket.

"Aye. I'm knackered, though. I need a good strong cup of tea. Where are you going, anyway?" She frowned deeply, assuming that her man was once again having to go in to work to carry out a menial task that one of the plebs in the office should already have done. "Not again, Will. That's two nights in a row."

"Sorry, love, I... er... forgot that I had to email some end-of-year documents to a client. I should only be a couple of hours. Dinner's still in the pot. Just need to heat it up. I'll get mine when I come back. See ya in a bit, kids." Will turned and made for the door before his wife could think of an awkward question; she was usually so good at it. He waved at his children like a three-year-old, relieved at his relatively painless exit.

Will was already planning the best course of action to take when he met his old flame.

Sharp pangs of guilt racked his body, even though he knew that nothing could ever happen again between himself and Penny Richards.

"Big softie," Mary Munro muttered.

6

It was 5:30 p.m. Will Munro's shiny new black BMW X3 drew up outside The Loving Cup café at Byres Road in the West End of Glasgow.

Will craned his neck trying to get a look at the occupants in the dimly lit café. He could just about make out a dozen or so diners; there was no sign of Penny Richards.

What do I do? Sit here and wait for her? Go in? Maybe she won't show. That's it. One of her sick jokes. Typical!

The car purred smoothly into a parking space just beyond the café; Munro contemplated whether or not to take off again. Subsequent events would compel him to wish to God he had.

It was unusually dark for an early April day, overcast and threatening a downpour. The bank holiday had certainly eased the normal Glasgow rush-hour traffic; the journey from Bearsden, over the Switchback Road to Anniesland Cross and along Great Western Road, took less than fifteen minutes. At the wrong time of day it could sometimes take more than an hour.

Munro sighed deeply, checking out passing cars and pedestrians; no movements yet, in or out of The Loving Cup.

He tapped his fingers loudly on the steering wheel, whispering oaths under his breath. He hadn't seen Penny as he passed the café. What if she was sitting in the corner? He couldn't just drive away. He'd never be able to live with himself. Penny had treated him disgracefully, but in a perverse kind of way, he was excited at the prospect of seeing her again.

Will shook his head, berating himself for thinking such thoughts.

"Ah, fuck it! Let's get it over with." He swung his legs out onto the pavement, straightening to his full height of six-foot-two. The door of the BMW electronically locked as he closed it. One or two deep breaths later and he started the few yards to the front door of the café.

Will Munro couldn't help feeling like the male widow spider, doomed to meet a horrible end at the hands of his partner. The heavy, glass-laden door swung to the wall, bumping lightly off the rubber doorstop on the slate floor. Will Munro hadn't been near the café since the split with Penny Richards. He was a fairly superstitious character and figured that making further visits would have been a damned unlucky choice to make, given the history.

The decor looked much the same as before; maybe it had been freshened up a little using the same colour scheme— magnolia. Wall to wall plants seemed to be the unique selling point for the present owners.

The sound system was softly playing a seventies' compilation CD. Judging by the number of people in this tiny establishment they were obviously doing something right.

There were around thirty punters in the main customer area; a couple of short-skirted waitresses bustled about, setting down coffees and sandwiches.

Will studied the faces. He did an immediate double take on a tall, platinum blonde girl who stood from the shadows when he entered. Checking out her lithe frame, he found it near impossible to take his eyes off her. There certainly was something familiar about her.

Andrew D. Malloy

Penny Richards threw her slender arms around her ex's neck. Although he could recall almost every inch of her perfect body, Will had genuinely not recognised her as she walked towards him. Brunette had given way to blonde— a move that she had often threatened during their time together— and a few shallow lines around her eyes and mouth had aged her ever so slightly. A little more make-up than normal had been used to try to combat time.

"Oh, Will. I'm so glad you came," she whispered in his ear. "I'm sitting over here. Remember we used to sit there all the time?" She pointed over to 'their spot'; Munro experienced a fluttering of the heart when she looked deep into his eyes.

Don't look at her, for Christ's sake! Remember, you're only here to see if you can help her out.

"Can I have another two coffees, Marco? Still milk and two sugars, Will?"

"Just one sugar, please," he addressed Marco directly, turning stern faced towards his ex-girlfriend.

They sat next to an already drained cup. He figured that she had been there at least half an hour. She continued to give him the doe eyes. Will tried to visualise a point on her cheek, unwilling to allow her to manipulate him the way she used to do.

Aye right! Have I not already been manipulated?

He reckoned the best plan of action would be to simply get to the point. Any feelings of sympathy that he had earlier felt had vanished, dispersed by the girl's present unruffled demeanour.

"All right, Penny. You don't exactly seem upset right now. What's going on?" he asked tersely.

The girl's face then underwent a familiar change. Like the flick of a switch, she seemed to suddenly remember exactly why she was there.

Inevitably, tears began to flood her cheeks.

Don't look into her eyes! Too late!

Just as in some kind of fable, the wicked fairy seemed to be casting her spell on the unsuspecting prince.

Will Munro, the big softie, was about to be hypnotised.

"Oh, Will. It... It's my boyfriend. He... He tried to kill me." She sobbed softly.

Marco drew Will the dirtiest of looks, obviously choosing to blame him for upsetting his friend.

"Okay, just calm down." Munro patted the back of her hand. He lowered his voice, drawing his chair around the small table until they were sitting side by side. "Now just take it from the start. I'm here for you. Remember that." He was powerless to stop the consoling words.

Penny Richards produced a kind of squinty smile, calmly drew in a long breath, and began the story.

"About two years ago, I met this guy in a nightclub. He was really nice; bought me a couple of drinks."

Will found himself already prickling with jealousy.

What the hell is going on?

"Anyway, we met up a few times. He took me to dinner. Everything was cool. I liked him and he seemed to like me. After a few months— maybe four— he asked me to move in with him. I said it might be too soon, at first. But he was persistent, kept asking. A bit later, we had been out for a Saturday lunch. I'd had a few drinks, got a little light headed. Anyway, he asked me again and I said yes. I was back staying at my friend, Joanne's. You remember her?"

Munro nodded, tight lipped. He hated the opinionated cow.

"Well, I was fed up with her bossing me about. Y'know, trying to run my life for me?"

He nodded again. Any criticism of that particular female was fine by him.

"The next week, I moved out, and in with the guy.

Everything was fine. He treated me well. I was happier than I'd ever... eh, I'd been in ages." She was quick to correct the *faux pas*.

He hadn't noticed the reference to their relationship.

"Anyway..."

Will smiled at her still-constant use of the word.

"He was working late at the office one night. He was very secretive about his work. I never knew exactly what he did. Anyway, it was our six-month anniversary and I decided to surprise him. I went down to his office, expecting him to be working late as always. When I got there the place was in darkness, apart from the security guy at the door. He said he hadn't seen Martin— that's his name, Martin Anderson— since four o'clock. It was about half past seven by that time, and I was on my way back home when I saw his car parked outside some new flats near his house. I thought, *yeah... okay. Who the fuck is she?* Anyway, I got out of my car and walked around to the back door. I thought I could maybe get in a service entrance or something. I tried the door. Couldn't open it. I was really pissed off by that time. Y'know, wanted to cut off his bollocks or something."

Munro smiled ruefully, recalling her foul temper.

"Anyway, I heard raised voices coming from the ground-floor flat. I... I moved over t-to the window..." She struggled to continue.

"Go on, Penny. Take your time." Will was totally hooked by this time.

" W-well. I looked in. Martin was in there. He was arguing... shouting at this other guy. I couldn't hear what they were saying. Then... Martin picked up an ornament f-from a table. He... He hit the other guy, hit him so hard. He... fell to the floor." Penny buried her face in her hands. Her shoulders were rising and falling with loud sobs.

Host, Marco, looked as if he would jump over the

counter at any moment and attack Will Munro.

Hugging his former lover close to him, Will suggested they leave as the scene was beginning to attract curious stares from the rest of the people in the café. She agreed, propping against him on the way out. Will slapped a tenner on the counter. He wasn't going to wait about for any change.

"Where's your car parked?"

"I... I was frightened to use it in... In case he spotted it. I've been using public transport... and taxis."

They were standing outside Will's Beemer. Penny shivered in the late afternoon's cool air, and he suggested that they sit inside. Munro started up the engine as he concentrated on trying to sort out the mess.

"Okay, Penny. What happened after this guy went down?"

She swallowed hard, her body beginning to warm up in the gentle airflow of the BMW's expensive heating system.

"When he fell, he hit his head hard on the floor. I felt the thump through the wall. He... He wasn't moving. I think he was... He was dead!" She threatened to lose it again, somehow managing to compose herself.

"Are you sure it was your... er... boyfriend?" He felt uncomfortable saying the words; all kinds of familiar feelings for her flooded back into his body.

"No doubt. I saw his face. I'll never forget the look. It was as if I didn't recognise him. He looked so cold, so cruel. Anyway, I ducked under the window in case he saw me, and sneaked back to my car. I just drove around and around. I didn't know what to do or where to go. It was a nightmare."

"You're sure he didn't see you?"

"No, I... I mean yes... At least, at that time I didn't think so."

"What do you mean?" Munro asked, more than a little

puzzled.

"Well, I tried to work out what to do next; go to the police; go back to my previous digs. I was scared he would find me. I couldn't get that look on his face out of my head. Anyway, I decided to pretend it didn't happen. I got back to the house before him, shit-scared to the soles of my feet, but managed to carry it off. As the days and weeks passed, I even convinced myself that I hadn't seen anything; imagined the whole thing."

Penny visibly jumped when a pair of rowdy teenagers brushed past her door, roughly shoving each other and shouting the odds in broad Glaswegian. Munro glared at them, shaking his head at their silly antics. "It's okay. Just a pair of idiots." He patted her gently on the knee, glowering at the pair.

She responded with a half smile and continued, "Two nights ago, we went out for a quiet meal. In the city centre— Hope Street, I think. I can't even remember the name of the place. It was quite dark. I... I felt safe. Anyway, we were walking towards his car. Because it was a lovely mild night, we had parked along in the Ingram Street car park. Y'know where I am?"

Munro nodded.

"After the meal, we walked down Buchanan Street, across Royal Exchange Square and into Ingram Street. He was talking to me about football or something. Something to do with Rangers. He's a big fan, like you." Penny bravely tried to smile.

Will didn't like the way this was going.

"Anyway, we reached the car park. It was really dark and..." Huge tears had welled in her eyes. She blinked hard, sending the tears careering down her cheeks. "And we walked across to the car. We had to dodge the potholes. I... I heard footsteps at my back. I turned around and two men grabbed me. I went to scream, but one of them put his hand over my mouth. The other was taping my hands behind my back. I... I tried to..." She clenched her teeth tightly, determined to finish the story. "I tried to call to Martin, but he just turned and walked away. He... He jumped into the car and drove off." Penny buried her face in the strong shoulder of Will Munro.

He felt a protective rage rise up inside him.

He sensed the tightening of his fingers as the temper made him fashion a fist. She straightened up again. "The men dragged me over to a car sitting at the back of the car park. They taped my mouth and legs. One of them opened the boot. Th-they threw me inside. I... I must have hit my head against the edge of the spare wheel. Knocked me out cold!"

Will Munro sat there listening carefully. He could hardly believe his ears.

This kind of thing just doesn't happen here. No way! What is this, New York or something?

In a selfish way, he began to wish he hadn't picked up the phone that afternoon. His eyes began to glaze over. The girl seemed to be speaking, but he was somehow unable to process the words. He was finding it difficult to accept the situation that he now found himself in.

I have a new wife and two lovely children. All this has nothing to do with me!

The words were turning over in his brain, again and again.

"Will? Will?"

Firm words snapped him back to his senses. It took a moment for him to gather his wits. "S-sorry. I... er... Please, go on, Penny! I'm listening." He put on his finest, chartered accountant 'listening to client' expression.

"I was just saying that, when I woke up, I was aware of the movement of the car. It took a few seconds to come to my senses. I... I thought I was going to die. Funnily enough, when I was lying there, I began to feel quite calm, resigned almost. The next thing, there was an almighty crash. They must have run into something, another car maybe. I was thrown up against the inside of the boot— against the back seat. I managed to stop myself with my hands; tried to soften the impact. I was a bit shaken up, but okay. Then, there was silence, weird silence.''

"I had seen a programme on television the night before. A car crashed. There was a spark. The petrol leak made the car burst into flames. I panicked, and started to bang on the metal back of the seat. After a minute or so, I heard someone fiddle with the boot lock. I just prayed that it wasn't one of the guys. Anyway, the boot flew open. The light from a street lamp shone in. I... I couldn't see the man's face. He hauled me out of the boot— lowered me to the ground. I didn't know if he was pulling a knife out to kill me or free me. He cut the tapes around my hands and feet, and peeled the strip from my mouth. I was free! I somehow wriggled out of his arms, kicked off my shoes and just ran— like the wind. I didn't look back. Didn't stop until I hit the bus station. I jumped on the first bus I saw. Should've seen the looks I got, sitting there with no shoes on. Anyway, I ended up in Stirling. I didn't care, though. As long as it was as far away from him as possible. I had enough money with me to check into a Travelodge hotel at the motorway services in Stirling. Bought a cosy jumper and a pair of shoes from one of the outlet shops, and sat tight until this afternoon." Penny glanced sideways, trying to gauge the reaction that her predicament had provoked.

Will Munro sat there staring out at the passing traffic. He was obviously shell shocked.

What a mess! What the hell do I do?

"I'm sorry to land this on you, Will. You don't deserve it. It's just... I had nowhere to turn." She threatened some more misty-eyed emotions.

Will sat quietly for a few seconds. He was a firm believer in not rushing into rash decisions. That particular ploy had served him well, until now at least. Eventually, he reached into his jacket pocket for his wallet. He unbuttoned it and peeled off some twenty-pound notes. Penny instantly worked out his intentions.

"No, Will. Please. I can't take any money from you."

"Look, it's fine. I'll get you checked into a hotel. I have a friend, a client. He owes me a favour. Take the money. I expect you to pay it back, you know."

The statement drew a brave smile from the girl.

"I'll pick you up in the morning. You'll have to go to the police. You know that, don't you? It's the only option."

"No! He'll kill me. I can't!" she replied, shaking with fear.

"He won't get near you, I promise. I'll go with you. How's that?" He tried his best to reassure her. Will slipped the bundle of notes into her pocket and drew out of the parking space, heading for the safety of his chosen hotel.

After making sure the girl had settled in, he left for home, expecting a rollicking for being late. Will was not worrying in the slightest about that. Something was gnawing away in his head, telling him that he had much more serious things to consider.

7

Strathclyde Police Headquarters, Pitt Street, Glasgow

"Can I help you, Sir?" the beefy desk sergeant asked. He was peering over his glasses at the couple in front of him. In typically chauvinistic fashion, he addressed only the man.

"We're here to report a possible murder." Will Munro answered, nodding supportively at his companion, Penny Richards.

She looked slightly annoyed at being ignored by the cop.

The sergeant seemed to freeze for a couple of seconds, as if he was hearing something he wouldn't normally hear on an ordinary Tuesday morning. His big, round face appeared even bigger and rounder when he took off his glasses. Replacing them carefully on his red, boozy nose, he picked up a pen, and prepared to complete yet another form— in triplicate. Firstly, he had to clarify the last statement.

"To report a *possible* murder, Sir?" He invited Munro to elaborate.

"We think... Well, Penny thinks... That is, she saw it happen." Will suddenly developed a nervous stammer. He could hardly believe the way in which he had delivered the last line. He attempted to repair the damage, only succeeding in digging himself in even deeper. "Er, she... eh... We, yes, we need to talk to someone." Will lowered his eyes, feeling more than a little embarrassed.

His inherent childhood fear of all things authoritarian, dormant for long years, had resurfaced. He didn't know if there was a word for a fear of uniforms.

As a young boy of around eight, while on a family holiday in Spain, Will had seen a man beaten nearly to death by two policemen. He didn't understand why at the time, only finding out from his father much later that the man had stolen some fruit from a local market trader to feed his children. Even at that age, the compassionate young Will Munro had been horrified. He had treated uniformed police officers a little warily ever since.

"This lady saw the... incident, Sir?" Sergeant Chauvinist spoke again, as if Penny Richards wasn't there.

She could stay silent no more. "This lady is neither brain damaged nor invisible. She did, indeed, see the incident and she is ready to give you her details. Are you ready?" Penny asked, putting yet another guy firmly in his place.

"Name?" the sergeant responded tersely.

* * *

Will Munro was sitting in the small, sparse waiting room at the police station. He checked his watch— 11:25 a.m. It had been almost two hours since Penny had gone into the interview room.

What the fuck is happening in there?

Blowing out his cheeks in frustration, he reached into his pocket for his mobile phone. Will had an appointment with an important client at twelve o'clock and it looked odds on that he was not going to make it.

"Irene? Hi, it's me, Will. Listen, I'm not going to make the appointment with Roger Green at twelve. Can you call him and explain that I've been unavoidably delayed? Tell him any time tomorrow."

There was a long silence. Munro checked if he was still connected.

"Will, this is one of our most important clients. You can't just call off."

"Just do as I ask, please, Irene. I know how important he is, but it just can't be helped. Okay?" Munro replied in exasperation and completely out of character.

"Of course, Will. Are you all right?"

"Aye. It's just... eh... something came up. Irene, I'm sorry, I'll explain later." The line went dead. "Idiot!" Munro berated himself for the way he had spoken to his loyal personal assistant.

Irene Walters had worked tirelessly for Will's father for most of the last fifteen years. She was the best in the business, and he was the luckiest bugger in the world that she now worked for him.

The problem was that he didn't quite feel like the luckiest bugger in the world at that moment.

What the hell is going on in there?

He made a mental note to phone Interflora to order flowers for Irene Walters, when the door to the waiting room creaked open. An office worker— no uniform, probably a member of the police administration staff— entered the room, an armful of glossy brochures in his hand. He nodded politely at Will, neatly laying out the bundles on the small table in the middle of the room. Munro tilted his head like a curious hound, trying to read the large print on the front; anything to relieve the boredom. His curiosity deserted him when he realised that the brochures merely contained simple do's and dont's when confronting bank robbers.

Run like fuck in the opposite direction. That's a definite do.

He chuckled as he imagined one of the brochure's bullet points.

Will's expression changed when he looked again at his watch. Twelve noon. He began to wish that he hadn't promised Penny Richards that he would hang around until she emerged from Interview Room One.

Oh, Jesus! Come on! How much longer?

Counting the carpet tiles for the millionth time, he felt instant relief at the sound of voices outside the door; more specifically, the sound of Penny's voice. Will opened the door to face a tall man in a sharp blue suit. The guy was almost bald, a little band of dark hair stretching from ear to ear. Will was a big fan of seventies cops shows. He swore the guy standing in front of him was a Glaswegian version of Haskins, the chief from the popular show, *The Sweeney.* He recalled Haskins as being the polite, well-spoken head honcho of a gang of London-based ragamuffins known as the flying squad. This particular version was to destroy that recollection when he spoke.

"Will Munro?" he asked, gruffly. He looked Munro up and down as if he despised all human life forms.

"Yes."

"Ah'm Detective Sergeant Tam Watson. Ah need tae ask ye some questions."

Munro immediately recognised the accent as coming from the Western Isles. His father, Lachie Munro, had originally hailed from Stornoway.

Will developed a stiff knot in his gut. Something was not right here, and he had a feeling that he was about to find out exactly what.

The DS had piercing blue eyes and seemed to be cruelly training them like a laser, burning deep into Will Munro's brain.

Munro, on the other hand, was craning his neck to look over the cop's shoulder. He was looking for Penny Richards.

"The girl I came in with? Where is she?"

"The lassie gave us a statement. She had tae go. Somethin' aboot a doctor's appointment."

She never said anything about a doctor's appointment. I would definitely have remembered that. Will kept the thought to himself.

"If you come wi' me, Mister Munro," DS Watson said, lightening up a little.

Munro did as he was asked, following the cop into Interview Room One.

"Take a seat. Ah'll be back in a minute." Watson shut the door at his back.

Will Munro's stomach did cartwheels when he heard the key turn in the lock. He looked in vain for the two-way mirror on the wall, concluding that he had probably watched far too many American crime movies.

His mobile phone kicked in.

"Hello?"

"Will? Where are you? I tried the office. Irene couldn't tell me where you were. I thought that was unusual. She knows when you need to pee before you do!" Mary Munro said with a hint of sarcasm. She didn't really like Irene Walters, and would have been annoyed had she realised that she had actually just paid her a compliment.

"Hi, Mary. Listen, I've had a bit of trouble with the car. I'm sitting at the side of the road. The thing's just packed in."

"That's what you get for buying cheap German crap, dear! Where are you, anyway? It's really quiet. Are you on a side street?"

"Er… I'm down on the south side. Pulled into a little lane when I felt the power go. It's okay. I phoned the RAC. They're on their way." He stopped when he heard movements outside. A key went into the door. "Oh, that's the guy from the RAC now. I'll call you later, honey." Munro cut his wife off before the two officers entered the room.

DS Watson had returned with a colleague in tow. Detective Sergeant Mick McMenemy strode into the middle of the room, his cheery disposition so obviously designed to immediately put the interviewee at ease. He looked like the alter ego of DS Watson— short, fat and hairy. His round face had a kind of permanent grin all over it; the cheeky Geordie accent helped to convey the general feeling of friendliness to all around him.

"I'm Detective Sergeant McMenemy, Mister Munro. Please take a seat. We'd like to ask you a few questions, if you don't mind," McMenemy shook his target's hand, smiling broadly.

Will Munro sat uneasily at one side of the table, Little and Large at the other.

DS Watson, the bad guy of the pair, produced a small bundle from his pocket. He proceeded to tear off the cellophane wrapper from the packet, carefully laying two audio tapes on the table. He peeled two white labels and stuck one on each tape.

Watson marked the tapes A and B before placing one in a small recorder selected from another pocket. He laid the machine in the middle of the table next to tape B— used to produce a transcript of A— and leant back in his chair, waiting for his more amiable colleague to commence the interview.

Will Munro was remarkably calm, despite his situation. His uniform phobia was in check, due to the fact that there were none on view.

Pressing record, DS McMenemy began.

"My name is Detective Sergeant Michael McMenemy of Strathclyde Police force. Also present is Detective Sergeant Tam Watson of Strathclyde Police force. For the purposes of an investigation, this interview is being taped. For the record, I would ask the interviewee to confirm his name, address and date of birth." The DS nodded towards Munro.

Will Munro stared straight ahead, calmly maintaining his silence. McMenemy smiled and Watson rolled his eyes skywards. The tape recorder was switched off, and the three men sat for a few seconds, each waiting to see who was going to take the initiative.

"Sorry, guys, but this is the part where I need to ask you if I can make my phone call. You know, the one allowed by law?" Will thanked the Lord that he had actually digested some of the endless streams of legal information that his best friend, lawyer Ben Vieri, often spouted.

The two cops glanced knowingly at each other; DS Watson then calmly rewound the tape recorder the few seconds to the start of the tape.

"Gentlemen. I need to know if you're going to keep me here or not— if you intend to charge me with anything."

*   *   *

Five minutes later, Will Munro was out on the street, free, complete with the 'don't leave town' instruction from the police ringing in his ears. After receiving an extremely worrying, unobtainable message when calling Penny Richards' mobile phone, Will found himself pressing 'one' on speed dial.

"Ben? I need your help," he shouted at Ben Vieri over the early afternoon traffic, on the way to his BMW.

8

Crime Scene, West End, Glasgow

Detective Sergeants Tam Watson and Mick McMenemy managed to negotiate the apartment's door buzzer entry system. A rather unhelpful occupant of one of the first-floor flats in the complex had only reluctantly agreed to let them in when he heard the word 'police'.

His initial thought was that they were there to do something about the useless article on the ground floor.

Lord knows he had complained enough, as had everyone in the complex; maybe it was going to be party time this weekend!

"This is the one," DS McMenemy said.

The two cops were standing outside the door of the flat in question; the one that Penny Richards had described earlier.

Watson nodded in agreement. The door chime could be heard ringing inside the flat. A few seconds later, Watson again tried the bell. Still there was no sign of life.

McMenemy, the shorter of the two, bent and opened the letter box.

"Jeesuus!" He exaggerated each syllable; a noxious odour filtered ominously into his nostrils. "Fuck me, I hope that's not what I think it is!"

DS Watson's recent bout of gastro-enteritis had left him with a decidedly dodgy stomach. He bolted for the outside door when the stench reached him.

"I... I'll hae a look in the windae oot here," Watson blurted to his partner as he disappeared.

McMenemy chuckled to himself when he heard the heaving sounds from outside.

The pair had been work partners for the past two years. Mick had tried so hard to like the tall man from the Western Isles of Scotland. The fact that he was an ignorant swine with absolutely no sense of humour had not helped his case.

The two men were around the same age, though a million years apart in their perception of the meaning of the phrase 'good police work'.

Mick McMenemy's philosophy was about cooperating with the public, listening, helping; the accent was definitely on being friendly.

Tam Watson, the dinosaur, seemed to be more intent in blasting those values to pieces.

Mick had long since given up on his colleague, satisfying himself with the fact that he was there, at the sharp end, keeping a watchful eye on this man, ready to nullify any indiscretions. He also hoped that his partner would soon develop a hankering to return to his roots.

The Western Isles will suffice; New Zealand would be better but beggars can't be choosers.

* * *

Tam Watson, relieved of his early dinner, was peering through the window of the flat. The lights were out, but there was a little shaft of moonlight entering the living area. Watson shook his head in frustration; the light shone only into an insignificant corner of the room.

Tam knocked on the outside door, his big ugly mug pressed against the glass panel. For a second, McMenemy contemplated leaving him there.

"Ah couldnae see anythin' through the windae," Watson mused. "We'll need tae kick the door in!"

"We need to get a warrant, Tam. You cannae just do that!" Mick complained.

"Who cannae? Watch this!"

Launching the sole of his boot, Watson crashed locks and bolts in one strike; the door thumped against the wall on the other side.

"Fuck me!" Tam thrust the sleeve of his jacket across his nose, an unbelievable stench now unleashed on the pair.

Mick immediately whipped off his tie, holding it to his face. The smell of the silk material provided some welcome relief in the midst of the onslaught.

Both cops ventured tentatively into the flat; Watson grappled for a light switch.

After the light came on, the policemen instantly wished that it hadn't.

The untidiness was one thing; the filth and squalor was another.

In the middle of the floor, face down, lay the body of Longthorn Reeves Baltimore III. Congealed blood matted his dirty blond hair. Fragments of skull and brain littered the carpet around the body. Tiny white worms— maggots— cavorted among the blood and bone at the back of the skull.

Despite the extremely stressful situation, McMenemy was somehow able to recall an episode of his favourite television programme, *Crime Scene Investigation*. In it he had noted that, if maggots were encountered at a dead-body crime scene, there would be no flies on or around the body for at least another couple of days.

But then, how long has this guy been dead?

The smell could never be a guide. They would have to call for help.

"Come on. We'll call this in. There's nothing we can do here, anyway. The experts can take over," Mick McMenemy said. He was referring to the forensics department at Strathclyde Police.

Uncharacteristically, a smile as wide as the River Clyde flashed across Tam's normally sour face. He was happy to let someone else crawl around in this particular morass.

"Aye, let the geeks handle it. Gie the lazy bastard's somethin' tae dae!" Watson replied, a smug look crawling across his face.

Mick McMenemy frowned at the bastard's lack of respect.

"I'll let Blackwell know,' he said, already dialling.

* * *

"Cordon off the main entrance. Anyone entering or leaving the building has to use the back door, okay? I've already posted Constable Murphy out there. Only residents and police get in." The police inspector issued implicit instructions to the rookie constable. "After that, stand guard at the door of the flat. Don't let anyone in here unless you clear it with me first. Strictly no press. They have a habit of wriggling their way into a crime scene. Still happens to the best of us, unfortunately. Got that, son?" Detective Inspector Blackwell smiled reassuringly at the young cop, who nodded an acknowledgement to his superior officer. The experienced man patted the constable on the shoulder before turning to enter the death flat. He was already wearing non-powdered, latex gloves and blue shoe covers— both police issue— as instructed. So was everyone else at the crime scene, even Tam Watson.

Blackwell believed in playing everything by the book. His philosophy was simple— stick to the rules and respect the system.

It's not perfect but it'll do until somebody comes up with something better.

Mason Blackwell could definitely be classed as new police.

At thirty-two, he was one of the youngest police inspectors in Britain. The son of a Dundee carpenter, Blackwell had been a brilliant student, graduating with a first class honours degree in Law.

Ever since he was a young kid, the inspector had always wanted to be a policeman.

His rise through the ranks had been swift, from the beat in his local Dundee, to a plain-clothes commission among the good people of Dunfermline in the Kingdom of Fife.

A brief posting in Aberdeen, where Blackwell had been the main man responsible for bringing a brutal serial rapist to justice, had led to a top job in Scotland's premier police force in Glasgow.

The chief constable of Strathclyde never tired of informing top brass of the absolute certainty of his young inspector's eventual promotion to the number-one position in the UK— chief constable of the Met in London.

For the past couple of years, Mason had even harboured the notion of going into politics. The tall, good-looking cop had something going for him that most politicians could only dream of— the likeability factor. Happily married with two young children, this articulate, clean-cut, solid, upstanding pillar of the community would be an excellent choice of candidate.

Luckily for the force, he intended to stay and right a good few wrongs before considering a career in the pantomime that is Westminster.

"Kenny, nice to see you again. How's the wife keeping?" Blackwell asked Kenny Tilton, head of the team of forensics experts on the scene— the geeks, as some of the less than cultured officers would refer to them.

"She's doing really well now, Sir. Thanks for asking."

Mason didn't just ask for the sake of it. He really meant it. The inspector was polite to everyone— policeman, general public, even villain. He didn't see the point in making enemies for the sake of it. People would be much more co-operative if they were treated with respect.

DS Mick McMenemy had decided from early on that he would observe closely the actions and procedures of his superior officer. Mick was an intelligent guy, not so much academically, but definitely in a street-wise fashion. He had identified the inspector as the type of officer that he aspired to be. So far, the practice had worked a treat; McMenemy enjoyed a promising career, popular among both subordinates and superiors.

DS Tam Watson, however, didn't trust the young inspector, assuming that he was continually working an angle to benefit his own ends. Tam couldn't see the good in anybody if it hit him squarely between the eyes. The twisted copper seemed to delight in pissing off everyone.

The crime scene gathering at the stinking flat consisted of Blackwell and McMenemy, together deep in conversation, Watson standing alone on the periphery, and three swarming CSEs— Crime Scene Examiners. In the middle of the living room lay the star of the show— the battered body of Longthorn Reeves Baltimore III.

The forensic people, two men and a woman, were dressed from head to foot in white, disposable jumpsuits. They spent their time bagging and tagging evidence, scraping and swabbing Baltimore's body with Q-tips, and flashing endless photographs from every conceivable angle.

"The girl's information was spot on, Sir. This guy's had his brains bashed in." McMenemy was only confirming what they already knew. He gritted his teeth in anguish at delivering such an obvious statement, especially in the presence of his mentor.

CSE, Kenny Tilton, carefully took hold of the corpse's shoulders, gently turning it over, face up. The corpse's eyes— wide open, lifeless, soulless— seemed to follow them around the room like a great painting.

The three men screwed up their faces in disgust at the sight of Baltimore's smashed face. The nose had almost completely disappeared, in its place a mashed up void filled with congealed blood, splintered bone and squirming maggots.

All the individuals on the scene had somehow managed to acclimatise themselves to the room; the invasive stench became almost bearable the longer they stayed. However, putrid gasses began to filter from the body with the movement; the room again filled with a not-so-fresh threat to the lungs.

"Looks like two blows; one to the back of the head; the next flush in the face. No sign of the murder weapon anywhere," DI Blackwell said, by this time holding a large handkerchief tightly against his nose.

McMenemy copied the actions of his boss, nodding in agreement. Kenny Tilton, obviously more used to such experiences, chose to tough it out, unaided. "What a way to live." The inspector shook his head sadly. "Do we know who this guy is yet, Mick?"

"His name's Lonnie Baltimore, Sir. He's an American. I was talking to the next-door neighbour earlier. He said that he hardly ever saw him. Everyone was up in arms about the state of the place. There was even a petition to get rid of him."

"Ah, well. They won't have to worry about that now. Do we know anything about him?"

"Not yet, Sir. I called the details in. They're running them back at HQ just now."

Tam Watson, standing at the window, turned when he heard the sound of a motor pulling up outside.

"That's the vultures here." He sneered. The guys from the coroner's department had arrived to pick up Baltimore's corpse for autopsy.

Mason Blackwell ignored Watson's comment, walking out of the room to greet the vultures at the door.

"Sir! What about the suspect? Can we bring him in?" Mick McMenemy called after the DI.

"He'll keep till morning," Blackwell replied. "Tam! You come with me. I want you to talk me through your procedures for entering this flat tonight."

McMenemy suppressed a slight smile; his colleague reluctantly followed the boss to the door.

9

The Muscular Arms Public House, Bearsden, Glasgow

"Hi, Will. A pint of Guinness, mate?" Ben Vieri stood at the bar, a rather worried look on his face.

He had received what could best be described as a bizarre phone call from his great friend an hour earlier. Ben felt only slightly better when he saw Will come in; the requested meeting took place at a venue that they were both used to and comfortable with.

The young accountant nodded tentatively. Ben had never seen his pal look so distressed. The two men lifted their pints and retired to a quiet corner.

Will Munro took a long breath, and began.

During the story, a couple of young women, sitting at a nearby table, were trying every trick in the book to attract the attention of either of the two hunks.

After ten minutes, the girls realised that their moves were doomed to failure, declaring that 'this pair of gays were welcome to each other!' They left to try their luck in another bar.

Ben was like a Latin version of the Scandinavian-featured Munro.

The tall Italian–Scotsman was the resident heartbreaker in the law firm where he was rapidly making a name for himself. Women of all ages, shapes and sizes regularly threw themselves at Vieri. This annoyed him slightly, as he

59

desperately wanted to be appreciated for his skill in front of a jury.

Really, really deep down though, he was just a little chuffed at the attention. That did not mean that he would ever dream of cheating on his lovely wife.

Leah, a gorgeous former model, had provided them with two wonderful, precious children, and there was no way he would endanger any of that for a quick roll on the office carpet.

Ben and Will absolutely doted on their kids, and could be seen regularly revisiting their childhood with them in the local park at weekends. Sunday afternoons were usually then concluded at McDonalds, where they would all tuck in to regular fries and chicken nuggets, washed down with milkshakes.

Will Munro finished the story and leant back in his chair, hoping for a helpful reaction from his friend.

The initial silence indicated that he probably would not get one. Ben Vieri had jotted down some short notes during the conversation. He was carefully going back over them before opening his mouth. He had assumed that Will would probably want to hear something positive and encouraging, at least at first. Ben wanted to make sure that he was aware of the facts before he started. After what seemed like an age...

"Right. Let's analyse what we have." Vieri gently tapped the pen on his lips. "The girl, Penny? You haven't seen her for five years? No contact whatsoever?"

"None."

"And you say that she's now vanished into thin air? Her mobile phone number is coming up unobtainable?"

"That's right."

"What about an address?"

"She was staying with a girlfriend. I went around there earlier. Couldn't get an answer."

Ben screwed up his face, puzzled.

"You didn't tell Mary where you were going? Why not?" The lawyer had an extremely strong relationship with his wife. He couldn't understand why Will had not come clean, especially when he had nothing to hide.

"I thought that I could take care of it. I didn't see the point in saying anything. You know how jealous Mary can be, Ben." Munro was trying to justify his actions.

"Okay. We can't do anything about that. You have to tell her now though, Will. You know that?"

Will nodded. He had already prepared himself for that experience.

"The police? They started to interview you. How far did they get?"

"Not very far. I remembered what you had said about not volunteering information without a lawyer present."

"Good. That was the right thing to do. Tell me, Will. Did they introduce and run a tape at any time?"

"Yes. The wee guy— McMenemy, I think it was. He set it up."

"Mick McMenemy?"

"Aye, that was his name. Do you know him?"

"I've met him a few times. He's straight as far as I know. A good cop, I think. Er... the other guy, was he kind of tall, bald, bad-tempered look about him?"

"Aye, a right miserable bastard, called Watson."

"Tam Watson. He's a real scumbag; hates everybody. We'll need to watch him. Will, was there a head honcho there? A guy called Blackwell? He's a DI."

"No, just the other two guys. Why?"

"Just wondering. Mason Blackwell is a really good policeman, but he's as wily as a fox. We'll need to keep our wits about us when he gets involved." Vieri paused for a minute. He was in his element, his mind doing triple somersaults, trying to work out strategies, piece together a case. "Right. What do we know? The police tried to hold an official taped interview. That means you're a suspect in some kind of investigation. That's bad. On the other hand, they weren't able to hold you pending questioning. That means they don't have enough evidence, and that's good." He smiled, encouraging his mate. "Now, the girl said that she had witnessed a murder. Did she say where?"

"I... I don't think so. All I know is that it happened in a ground-floor flat. God knows where."

"Okay. Let's think. The killing of this guy must have something to do with all this. The boyfriend; what was his name?"

"She said that she wasn't sure about his business. Very secretive. I'm sure she said... Anderson. I think it was Malcolm or Martin or something."

The words stopped Ben dead in his tracks.

"Anderson? Martin Anderson?"

"Aye, Martin. That's the guy."

"Fuck's sake, Will! Martin Anderson! Fuck's sake!"

Will was taken aback. His friend had never been a man to curse frequently, except maybe in the heat of a Rangers v Celtic football match.

"You know him?"

"Know him? Fuck's sake! Have you never heard of him?"

Munro shrugged.

"He's the Glasgow equivalent of Sonny Corleone. A real hot-headeded bastard!" Ben referred to the fiery James Caan character from the film, *The Godfather.* "He's Vic Simpson's right-hand man. These bastards spend their lives breaking every rule in the book." He accentuated each word.

Munro had most certainly heard of Victor James Simpson. The major-league crime lord was notorious within the Glasgow area. From drug trafficking to prostitution to dodgy nightclubs. You name it. If it was rotten to the core,

Vic Simpson would probably be involved in it.

The news was slowly sinking into Will's brain. His face grew paler by the second.

"What should I do, Ben?" Will's eyes pleaded for guidance.

"Nothing. Sit tight. Go home and tell Mary. Kiss the kids for me." He lowered his voice. "Look, Will. You've done nothing wrong here, remember that. You probably won't hear anything else. This girl is just looking to cause trouble. After all, you didn't exactly part on good terms, did you?"

"No, I suppose not." Munro conceded. "But... But why... after all this time?"

"Will. If we could just figure out the workings of the female mind, we'd all be better off for it!"

Will nodded at his pal, the hint of a smile on his face.

"Another pint?" Ben asked, preparing to stand.

"One more. I'll get them in. Thanks, Ben. You're a good friend." Will nodded appreciatively at his best pal.

"Where do I send the invoice?" Ben joked.

"Will a pint do instead? I'm a bit short right now!" Will made his way over to the bar, feeling a whole lot better than when he had come in.

10

Chicago, Illinois. USA

The guy was short, around five-four. Dressed in a sharp, well cut, thousand-dollar suit, he looked a little like a very young Paul Newman. Late twenties, light mousy hair, sunshades, Brodie Metcalf looked every inch the affluent, insurance salesman as he rolled up in his bright red Pontiac Firebird.

The wide, white-wall tyres crunched to a halt on the tarmac drive at the edge of the magnificent estate.

It was an unusually warm day for April; Brodie flicked on the air-con switch for the first time since last October.

The midday sun rose high in the sky; small puffy clouds rolled in on the gentle breeze. Today, the windy city could best be described as toothless.

Metcalf swung open the car door, stepping out to survey the scene in front of him.

Enormous, jet black, fabulously ornate, wrought iron gates spanned the drive, towering to the sky. A giant capital B adorned each gate.

Beyond, the newly laid drive snaked its way into the hillside, twisting and turning past breathtaking examples of oaks, cedars and firs.

Tall, black, old London-style lampposts— dozens of them— led the way up to the major focal point.

Although the mansion was nearly a mile away, the sheer

64

size of the place was still patently obvious.

Brodie gasped. He could picture himself lording it in a place like this.

Brodie Metcalf was doing pretty well for himself, his own house and cars not exactly too shabby. Home was a neat, five-bedroom detached on Chicago's millionaire's row. His other car was a second Pontiac— a light blue Transam.

Brodie's work could only be described as highly specialised. He had shown a natural aptitude for it.

This particular profession could not possibly suit every individual. It required a special set of skills to make it work successfully— attributes like steady nerves, a lack of conscience— to be able to seize the opportunity.

Metcalf was a little younger than most of the men who were good at this type of thing.

Maybe that was why he would never be classed as good.

Maybe his age was the main reason that he was termed, exceptional.

Brodie Metcalf was the best in the business. That was why he had received the call from the shady people representing multimillionaire, Longthorn Baltimore II.

Longthorn wanted somebody dead, and that was what Brodie Metcalf, aka the Viper, did best.

* * *

The young assassin had learnt his craft from the Master, the late, great Jack Feltham.

Feltham was an ex-FBI agent who had decided to branch out on his own, when he realised that a guy of his calibre could make a fortune working on the dark side. The role of the mercenary had suited him well; his burgeoning bank balance testament to the fact.

Four years ago, a cocky kid had appeared on Feltham's

radar in the middle of a job. The youngster had wandered into a hit on a local mobster, taking a bullet in the side for his troubles— a bullet meant for Jack Feltham. The older guy had taken young Metcalf to hospital, paid for his treatment, and even visited him as he recuperated. The two had then become unlikely allies; Feltham inexplicably chose to take the apprentice under his wing, and taught him everything he knew about the art of killing.

A couple of years later the apprentice had become the Master, the Viper hired by the drug-baron father of a slain pusher that Feltham had taken out.

Brodie looked deeply into the eyes of his mentor before he pulled the trigger. The delay almost cost Metcalf his life; the Master somehow managed to spear his ex-student's shoulder with a hunting knife. As a result, Brodie had inherited an unsightly scar— all part of the learning process. To kill quickly, without displaying even a micro-fibre of conscience, was now the unique selling point of the Viper.

*   *   *

A brief introduction via the elaborate intercom system led to the giant gates sweeping across the drive, inviting the Pontiac into the estate.

Brodie was surprised at the apparent lack of security on the grounds. He couldn't help feeling how easy a job it would be, had he been sent to terminate the owner of this house.

Pulling around the final bend towards the main entrance he was flagged down by a tall, dark-suited man, walkie-talkie at his face. The man beckoned to Metcalf to roll down his window.

"Park over by that building. Mister Baltimore is waiting for you in the summer house at the far side," the man said, emotionless.

Brodie nodded, almost running over the guy's feet as he zipped across the large car park at the front of the house. Glancing in his rear view mirror, Brodie was able to easily lip-read the immediate reaction of the man. He laughed loudly, realising that the comments were less than complimentary.

Another couple of sharp-suited security men, alerted by the sudden roar of the engine, sprang out from behind thick, rhododendron bushes at the far side of the house.

"Relax, guys!" Metcalf raised his arms in mock surrender before heading across to the double doors leading into the summer house. He could feel their death stares burning into his brain.

Brodie strolled in, instantly admiring the style and size of the so-called summer house.

The house was set on two levels, expensive, polished mahogany skirtings, soffits and facings in evidence throughout. Canadian, white-maple floors, machine buffed to an incredible shine, luxurious royal blue leather sofas and giant, light cream Persian rugs combined to present a stunning visual effect.

At the far side of the room, a huge feature fireplace, set in the finest marble, literally took the breath away.

Brodie Metcalf stood in the middle of the room, looking up at the complex design of the open rafters. He blew out his cheeks in admiration.

"Up here, Mister Metcalf. Please?" The voice rang out from upstairs.

Brodie glanced up to see a tall, thin, grey-haired man of around sixty, standing at the top of the open-tread stairway. His dress reminded Metcalf of a character that he had recently seen in an early Batman movie.

That's it, Brodie mused. *He looks exactly like Alfred, faithful butler of millionaire, Bruce Wayne.* He chuckled at the comparison before starting up the steps.

"Please take a seat over here, Sir. Mister Baltimore will be here presently." Alfred guided the young man towards a soft, leather easy chair by the window, looking onto huge tennis courts at the back of the estate.

Brodie stifled a smile at the butler-style statement. "Thank you."

The old man walked stiffly down the wooden staircase, leaving by the double doors. The thought of him standing in the utility room, frantically polishing up his master's walking boots, suddenly sprang vividly into Brodie's mind.

"Mister Metcalf. Thank you for coming. Can I get you some tea or something?" A big voice with an obviously well-bred, cultured accent, gave the hit man a bit of a start.

Longthorn Baltimore II strode from the bathroom area of the summer house, a large silk robe covering his ample frame. He had a slight wheeze, a hint of hay fever floating in with early spring, toying with his chest. He was in his mid sixties with receding hair and greying temples. Flat feet and a fifty-inch waistline made up the profile of the man.

"No thanks."

"Would you like something to eat? It *is* nearly lunch time, after all," the man persisted, obviously feeling the need to feed his fat face.

"No. No really. Can we just get down to business?" Brodie asked, feeling a bit like the young upstart, given the circumstances.

"Very well," Baltimore said coolly. "I have a... A situation that I would like you to resolve for me. They tell me you are the best at this sort of thing?"

The young man nodded.

"Well... two days ago, my son was murdered."

"I'm sorry," Metcalf said.

"Thank you. He was a good boy, deep down. Had a bit of a... drug problem." Baltimore found it difficult to admit weakness in the family.

Brodie stayed silent, allowing him to continue.

"A couple of years ago, he left the house— left the country, in fact. We had a bit of a... falling out and he decided to go overseas... to Scotland. To a place called Glasgow. Have you heard of it?"

Brodie had been named after his Scottish grandfather on his mother's side. The family had originally come from Paisley, the place nearest to Glasgow, and, as he had been close to his late grandfather, he had indeed heard countless tales of family visits to 'the town'. Glasgow people were often referred to as 'townies'.

"Yes. I do know of it," Metcalf replied.

"Lonnie... He's... Was... my son. I have some contacts in the police force in Chicago. They made some enquiries for me. Apparently, Lonnie was involved with one of the local drug dealers. We... We got the call yesterday... telling us that he... He had been killed." Baltimore struggled with the words. He quickly composed himself. "Killed in his own flat. The police are investigating, of course. The one thing that worries me is not so much that they won't be able to convict the bastards responsible. No, it's the fact that they don't have the goddam death sentence in place over there!" He began to launch into a tirade.

Metcalf's eyes never left the ranting millionaire.

"I want the bastards to fry! Hear me! No, not only them, but their fucking families, as well! Anybody connected to them— I want them dead!" The big man's words echoed among the high rafters in the summer house. The reference to the killing of families, etcetera, would just not be taken seriously. Even a cold-blooded killer such as Brodie Metcalf would never have considered such actions. The very thought of it went against the code of conduct, if one could imagine such a thing among killers.

Brodie paused for a few seconds, letting the

reverberations peter out completely, before taking his opportunity.

"Half a million dollars in advance, and another half a million when the job's done. For that, I can promise you a show." Brodie sat forward in the chair, waiting for an answer. He did not have to wait long.

"Agreed. When can you go?" Baltimore replied, as if he had just agreed to spend two dollars on a beefburger.

"Give me the money and I'm there!" A hint of a smile crossed the killer's face.

Baltimore liked a man who could make a quick decision. He could not abide dithering assholes.

"Come back tomorrow at ten o'clock. I'll have the money and all the details that you need. First-class flight okay for you, or do you need to travel low key?"

"First class will be just perfect." Brodie Metcalf thought that he might as well get used to some five-star treatment. He stood to shake the hand of the man who had just bankrolled the Viper's new house.

11

"Buzz me when Mister Letterman comes in, please, Irene."

"He's always late, Will. You go ahead and have your lunch now. I brought in some salad sandwiches. They're in your fridge. I'll man the phones for the next fifteen minutes until Cathy gets off her lunch."

"Thanks, Irene. Don't know what I'd do without you." Will Munro replaced the receiver, leaning under his desk to flick open the concealed fridge door and pull out the pack of sandwiches.

In a compartment below, he found a small bottle of diet coke.

Checking his desk diary, he began to plot his movements for the rest of the week. The family were bound for the local cinema on Saturday afternoon, with a visit to the house of his friend, Ben Vieri, planned on the Sunday. The two families had organised a get-together barbecue, depending on the early spring weather, of course.

Taking a mouthful, Will casually leant back in his chair and began to reflect on the events of the last couple of days. He had felt a great sense of relief after the meeting with lawyer, Vieri, in the local pub. Somehow, things hadn't seemed so bad following Ben's advice, and Will became more and more relaxed with every passing minute. He was still a free man and intended to remain that way.

Another reason for Will Munro's cheerful demeanour undoubtedly had something to do with his following

71

another piece of sound advice from his good friend. He had then gone home and immediately come clean to his wife, Mary, about his actual whereabouts on the night that he went to meet his old flame, Penny Richards.

Confused and hurt, Mary had initially, and understandably, not taken the news too well. Will's heartfelt explanation had eventually done the trick, however; the pair ended the evening firmly entrenched in each other's arms.

He had woken up that morning with a huge weight off his mind. Now it was time for him to take the final piece of Ben Vieri's advice and forget about the whole thing. Get on with his life.

The phone buzzer gave him a start. Tossing the small piece of sandwich, which he had left, in the waste bin, he wiped the crumbs from his expensive suit and prepared to greet his tardy client.

"Thank you, Irene. Just show Mister Letterman in, please."

"Will, there are two policemen here to see you. Sh-shall I send them in?"

The words tore like a bullet into Will Munro's mind. His heart began thumping strongly in his chest, causing him to experience a light-headed sensation. Tiny beads of sweat formed on his brow.

"Will? Are you still there?"

"Er... yes, Irene. Please... send them in." He rubbed his damp palms on his trousers and stood to reluctantly greet his unexpected guests.

The door was roughly swung open to the wall and in strode Detectives McMenemy and Watson, the latter gleefully brandishing a set of handcuffs. McMenemy, the orator, began.

"Will Munro, I am arresting you on suspicion of the murder of Longthorn Reeves Baltimore the Third at, or around, the evening of April the tenth. I am compelled to advise you that anything you say may, or may not, be used in evidence against you. You are entitled to legal representation." The detective continued to the bitter end as Watson grasped both of Will's wrists at his back, forcibly clipping the bracelets shut. He nodded a 'job done' gesture towards McMenemy, just as he reached the end of his statement.

"Do you understand the charge?" McMenemy asked.

Will stood there, obviously shell shocked. He peered through the open door into the reception area of his office. Irene Walters and his other assistant, Cathy Taylor, who had just returned from lunch, were joined by the portly figure of his next client, Marcus Letterman.

All three stood, open mouthed, at the unbelievable scene unfolding before them.

"Munro? Do you understand the charge?" the detective asked again, raising the volume slightly.

"What...? Yes!" Will Munro finally decided, his mind racing.

"All right. Let's go." DS Watson held the chain links between the 'cuffs in one hand, giving his prisoner a sharp push towards the open door with his other. Munro stumbled over his feet.

"Steady, Tam. Let's just take it easy, eh?" McMenemy drew his colleague the dirtiest of looks.

"Irene. Phone Ben Vieri. His number's in my notebook, in the top drawer of my desk. Tell him I've been taken to Pitt Street police station, and to get down there as soon as he can. Okay?" Will craned his neck beyond the policemen, desperate to get his message across before they hit the stairs.

"Y-yes, of course, Will." Irene raised her voice to make sure that he got the reply. A minute and a half later, the young lawyer's mobile phone was ringing.

12

Detective Inspector Mason Blackwell pressed the play button on the tiny, hi-tech recording device sitting on the table between them.

Will Munro and Ben Vieri were seated opposite Blackwell and Detective Sergeant Mick McMenemy.

The less than diplomatic, Detective Sergeant Tam Watson, raging at being excluded from the interview, had decided to bail out of the police station and attend to some pressing personal business.

Mason Blackwell had already exchanged some very stern words with Watson regarding his procedures for entering the murder flat the previous evening. The last thing Blackwell wanted was for Watson to throw the interrogation of the main suspect into jeopardy through ignorance and complacency.

"For the purposes of our records, this interview is being recorded. My name is Detective Inspector Mason Blackwell. Also present is Detective Sergeant Michael McMenemy and local Glasgow solicitor, Mr. Benjamin Vieri. I am going to ask the suspect to confirm his name, address and date of birth." Blackwell nodded towards Munro.

"William Munro. 59 Roman Road, Bearsden, Glasgow. January the fourteenth, 1980," Munro replied, a little shakily.

"Mister Munro's solicitor, Mister Vieri, will confirm

his name and the law firm he represents." Vieri was encouraged to respond.

"Benjamin Vieri, junior partner of Martin, Martin and McCreevy, Hope Street, Glasgow," Vieri said, deadpan.

"It is precisely 3:30 p.m. on the thirteenth of April, 2009, and this interview is being held at Strathclyde police headquarters in Pitt Street, Glasgow." Mason picked up a typed script from the file in front of him, holding it at arm's length. "William Munro, you do not have to say anything, but it may harm your defence if you do not mention, when questioned, something that you may later rely on in court. Anything you do say may be given in evidence. Do you understand this caution and what it means?"

"Yes," a grim-faced Munro replied.

"Okay. You have the right to speak to your solicitor in private at any time. The tape can, therefore, be stopped to allow you to do so. Is anything unclear?"

"No."

"Very well, I will commence the interview." The inspector tidied the prompts in the file in front of him, took a deep breath, and continued, "I would like to start by concentrating on the events of the evening of the tenth of April. Please run through an account of your movements that night."

Munro glanced at Vieri, who nodded his approval.

"Well, at around seven o'clock, my wife, Mary, was upstairs getting the kids down. I got a phone call from one of my clients. He needed some information from his file. He has a small business and had handed his accounts in to be finalised for his year end. The Inland Revenue had carried out a spot check at his premises— something to do with a dodgy invoice sent from a haulage contractor that he deals with. Anyway, the following day, I was to be spending the holiday with the kids while Mary hit the shops." Munro sensed a knowing smile from DI Blackwell. "I had to go into the office there and then."

"Couldn't it have waited until the Tuesday? After all, I would have expected most businesses to be closed on the holiday— even the Revenue," Blackwell said.

"Aye, I don't doubt it. Trouble is that this particular client is a panic merchant. He wants everything done yesterday. I'm sure you know the type, Inspector?"

"All right. You went to the office. How long were you gone?"

"Don't know exactly. Around an hour and a half or so?"

"Seems a wee bit excessive, doesn't it?"

"You obviously haven't had to deal with accountants before, Inspector. It took a considerable time for me to track down the plastic bag containing the information, isolate the invoice, scan and email it to the client. Then, take the travelling time there and back, and..."

"Plastic bag?" McMenemy asked.

"Yes, Sergeant. We still get a whole year of accounts in a Tesco bag sometimes."

"Was there anyone else in the office on that night?" Blackwell again took charge.

"No. Never on a Sunday."

"You can supply details of the client and the sending of the email?"

"Of course."

"Did you see or meet anyone while you were out who can confirm the journey?"

"Er... I don't think so. No."

"Okay. What happened when you came back?"

"Nothing. I came home, watched a little television and went to bed. It was around eleven o'clock, give or take."

Mason Blackwell looked down at his notes, flicking over to the next page. Ben and Will exchanged glances. McMenemy's eyes switched between the two of them, the rest of the time fixed on his superior officer, drinking in the moves.

"Mister Munro, do you know a man called Longthorn or Lonnie Baltimore?"

"No. Never heard of him."

"Have you ever been to Mountfield Place, specifically Flat Number 2, on the ground floor?"

"No. Absolutely not. Why?"

"Have you ever used drugs?" Blackwell asked, ignoring the question.

"What? No! Never!" Munro blurted indignantly.

"Really? Never?" Blackwell retorted. He reached into the back of his file, producing a buff-covered folder.

Ben Vieri sat up as the inspector opened the folder, placing it in front of Will Munro.

"July twentieth, 1998," he stated.

Ben Vieri spent the next few seconds tightly clenching his teeth. His eyes flitted between Munro and Blackwell. He really felt like he wanted to strangle his best pal at that point.

The conviction for possession of marijuana was a fairly minor offence, and Will had genuinely not remembered his brief visit to the local sheriff court. Memories of the modest fine and acute embarrassment, however, returned to haunt him as he sat there, uncomfortably unsure of what to say.

Vieri stood up to the plate. "Inspector, I hardly think that a sixty-quid fine and a slap on the wrist make my client out to be a major drug trafficker. Probably half of the student population at that time have similar records. A little grass? So what, eh?"

"No, Mister Vieri. It doesn't prove that your client is a regular drug user. Last time I checked, though, it is against the law and it also means that maybe he's not quite as squeaky clean as you thought he was." The DI studied Vieri's reaction.

It was Ben's turn to squirm. Blackwell had picked up

on the fact that the young lawyer had indeed not been aware of the conviction.

What else remains a secret between the two for the moment, but is about to be unearthed?

"All right. Let's move on, Mister Munro. You say that you have never been to Mountfield Place?"

"That's right. Don't even know where it is," Munro replied tentatively.

Vieri's eyes narrowed. The situation had 'set up' written all over it.

Surely, a policeman the calibre of Mason Blackwell cannot be capable of that? The thought flitted through the young lawyer's mind.

"What clothes were you wearing on the night of the tenth?" Mason Blackwell continued confidently.

"Why? What has that got to do with anything?" Munro asked, a little uneasily.

"Just answer the question, please," Blackwell reiterated.

Ben nodded his approval, somewhat reluctantly.

"Er... I had trainers, jeans and, eh... a white shirt, I think... Yes, a white T-shirt."

"What about a jacket?"

"Yes, I had my navy blue jacket on. Wasn't going to bother, but it's still quite cold when the sun goes down. What is this about, Inspector? I've already said that I had to go out to the office on that night." Munro's heart was now pounding, his voice fluttering with nerves.

Mason Blackwell was once again leafing through the folder, producing a series of slightly grainy, colour photographs. He set them down one at a time in front of the pair. Vieri noted the time etched in white in the top right-hand corner of the images. Four stills, a few seconds apart, detailed what looked like the figure of a man.

Munro's heart nearly arrested; the figure was wearing trainers and jeans with a navy blue, waist-length, jerkin-style jacket. The collar of his shirt was plainly visible from behind— it was white.

"What...? What is this? Who the hell is that?" Munro barked.

"This is CCTV footage taken from the flat— more specifically, the common areas outside Flat 2 in Mountfield Place. As you can see, the times on the stills range from 7:14 p.m. and twenty seconds to 7:14 p.m. and twenty-eight seconds. The date is shown directly under that, as you can also see— April the tenth. Now, Mister Munro. Do you see anything familiar about the individual in these photographs?" Mason paused for the inevitable reaction.

"Inspector, I can assure you. That is not me in these photos, I swear! That could be anybody! This is a set up!" Will Munro was now panicking big time, his voice becoming shrill with nerves.

"Will. Take it easy! Do you need a break?" Ben tried to guide his friend towards a regroup.

"No, Ben. I've done nothing wrong here. I'd rather go on— clear my name." Munro was taking deep breaths, beginning to calm down a little.

"Okay, Mister Munro. Maybe you'd like to explain this?" The inspector produced a fifth still from his file. The state-of-the-art police laboratory at Pitt Street had really earned its corn on this occasion; the latest technology contained within highlighted a blow-up image of the left hand of the alleged protagonist.

Munro felt his lunch coming back up to meet him as he stared at the image. Unconsciously, he lowered his left hand out of sight below the table.

Ben Vieri's face went chalk-white as he realised exactly what they were looking at. In the photograph, the mnemonics, RFC, were arranged in an all too familiar way— just as they would be embroidered onto a replica shirt of Will Munro's favourite football team, Glasgow

Rangers. Unfortunately for him, the letters were also tattooed in the same way— on his left hand; the legacy of a teenage impulse.

"We'd like to take a break, Inspector. I'd like to consult with my client."

This time, Ben Vieri's request would meet little resistance from his friend.

Mason Blackwell switched off the recorder and sat, winking at the silent DS McMenemy. The inspector was obviously pleased with the progress.

13

Glasgow Airport

Brodie Metcalf stood for a few seconds at the top of the portable steps near the forward door of the aircraft. The flight from the States had taken around six hours, and he had spent the last few minutes since landing, gathering together paperwork.

During the haul, Brodie had meticulously studied the documents supplied earlier by Longthorn Baltimore II. He felt confident that, with the final pieces of information nearly to hand, he was almost ready.

Metcalf politely stood aside to allow an elderly gentleman to brush past, making his way unsteadily to the tarmac.

This was Brodie's second visit to the birthplace of his grandparents, and he was pleasantly surprised at the feeling of the warm spring sunshine flushing his face. The hit man reached into his pocket for an elegant pair of Rayban sunglasses, before starting down the steps. At the bottom, Brodie exchanged smiles with the pretty stewardess, who had at times provided welcome breaks from the paperwork. He had been close to asking her for her contact phone number; only the importance of maintaining resolute professionalism on this, his most rewarding mission to date, prevented it.

Little did the stewardess know how close to death she

could have come. People invariably tended to die in the
company of the Viper.

A short, brisk walk to the baggage carousel was
followed by a ten-minute wait for a burgeoning holdall.
Metcalf then easily passed through customs identified
simply as John Mitchell.

Floods of people streamed through international
arrivals, appearing to evaporate into the Scottish sunshine.
Brodie immediately spied the tall, thin man holding a name
board with his alias— John Mitchell— etched across it.
The Viper chose to observe the man and all around him
from afar for the next five minutes or so, eventually
satisfying himself that he was not walking straight into
some kind of set up. Luckily for his well being, Metcalf had
been trained by the best. The Master himself would
undoubtedly have been so proud of the young pretender—
had he not already lost his life to him.

"I'm Mitchell. Have you brought the information?"
Metcalf asked the man tersely.

"It's in the car. Where's the money?" the man replied,
equally rudely. He lowered the name plate, leaving it
propped up on its end, against a wall.

"Let's go, then. I have the money. And I suggest that
you take that board with you." The Viper shook his head at
the big Scot's stupidity.

He couldn't have cared less. A wide smile had flashed
across the face of the man at the mention of money. Brodie
Metcalf shot him a withering look. He had taken an instant
dislike to him.

The pair left the terminal building by the main door;
Metcalf constantly checked for any unwelcome attention.
By the time they reached the blue Toyota sitting in the
short-stay car park, Brodie was as certain as he could be
that his safety was not in question.

The tall man flicked open the boot of the car, throwing

the name plate inside, before reaching into the back seat. He picked up three large brown envelopes, one markedly heavier than the other two, and slammed the boot closed.

Brodie opened the passenger door and sat inside waiting for the man to get in.

"My money?" This guy certainly was impatient.

Brodie pulled out a white envelope stuffed with notes and handed it to him. The envelope was split open in a heartbeat; the man counted out ten thousand pounds in hundred-pound notes in only a matter of minutes.

Metcalf remained silent, preferring to study the man's body language as he openly drooled over the cash. Part of his early training under Jack Feltham had included the study of people and their habits. He should be able to tell exactly what an individual was going to do at any given time. This talent would give Brodie the edge when he required it. How he would love to wipe the smug smile from this man's face.

"The information? Please?" Brodie was forced to ask.

"Eh... Oh aye! Here." The ignorant swine tossed the first of the envelopes at his passenger. It landed at the American's feet.

Metcalf bent over to pick up the package, carefully slitting it open with the edge of his finger. He quickly leafed through the precious contents, returning them inside when he was satisfied that the puzzle was complete. One more thing— Brodie reached out for the other two envelopes, now sitting between the front seats next to the handbrake. He began to open the bulkier envelope.

The man was too busy to notice, intent on quickly transferring his ill-gotten gains to his jacket pocket, buttoning it securely.

"You've a room at the Hilton. I'll drop you off there right now," he said. The big man slotted the key into the ignition.

"That won't be necessary."

Metcalf's reply made the man immediately take notice.

He hardly had time to register panic; a bullet passed through the silencer at the end of a Glock 9mm semi-automatic handgun, ripping into his forehead. Slumping forward, the man's lifeless body was then forcibly wrenched back onto the seat.

Brodie sat there for a moment, staring into his dead eyes.

"Fuck you, you asshole!" he said to the corpse with real contempt.

Retrieving the envelope containing the cash and replacing it in his own jacket, Metcalf then pulled a linen handkerchief from his trouser pocket. The following few minutes were spent painstakingly wiping down fingerprints in the car.

The Viper then got out, remembering to remove the name plate from the boot... He stuffed it in the front of his bag, stealing a final look inside the car at the horrified expression forever cast on the face of Detective Sergeant Tam Watson.

Two minutes later, Brodie Metcalf was on his way by taxi to check in at the Hilton Hotel in Glasgow's city centre.

14

"All right, Will. What the hell is going on here?" Lawyer Ben Vieri wanted answers.

He and Will Munro were in the process of exercising their lawyer–client privilege, before being dug deeper into the shit by wily policeman, Mason Blackwell. They were sitting alone in Interview Room One. Vieri was desperately trying to make some sense of it all.

"What d'you mean, Ben?" Munro had never before seen such a look on the face of his best friend. He was getting the distinct feeling that the lawyer was having trouble believing him.

"I don't know. It doesn't look good, does it?"

"Are you saying that you think I'm guilty, Ben?"

The question was met with a stony silence. Vieri leant back in his chair, rubbed his face vigorously with both hands.

"Ben?" Will again asked, this time more forcefully.

"No. Of course not, Will." The lawyer straightened up, cursing at the uncomfortable chair. "It's just that... I told you about Blackwell. He's clever. He's building a case here."

"Ben, I'm innocent. I swear on the life of my children." Munro was staring into the eyes of his friend.

Vieri felt a little uncomfortable at the sudden baring of the soul. A few seconds later Ben's face broke into a kind of forced smile. He patted Munro reassuringly on the shoulder.

"Okay. Let's see what we can come up with here." Ben was switching again from concerned friend to lawyer mode. "We have the CCTV evidence, pretty damning as it is. However, we know it's an elaborate set up. And, the face can't be seen, although the tattoo on the hand doesn't help. The question is— why? A murder has been committed, and whoever's done it wants you to take the blame for it. Now we know the dead man was a drug user. Simpson and Anderson are definitely involved in drugs. There's no doubt about that. Proving it is another matter."

"So what do we do?"

"All you can do is to give Blackwell your side of the story. As I said before, he's a good cop. One of the best. The evidence that they have isn't enough. They can't possibly make a positive ID on the stills that they showed us. And just how many of these Rangers tattoos do you think there are in the West of Scotland? All these arseholes walking around with poisoned hands!" Ben laughed, signifying his particular allegiance to the green side of the city— and bitter rivals, Glasgow Celtic.

Will found it hard to smile, given the situation.

"Is there anything else I should be aware of before they come back in, Will?" Vieri asked, getting down to business.

Munro slowly shook his head, and tried to clear his mind before they again crossed swords with Mason Blackwell.

15

DI Mason Blackwell and DS Mick McMenemy sat quietly as murder suspect Will Munro delivered his account of the events of the previous Bank Holiday Monday evening. Lawyer, Ben Vieri, took short notes in a little handbook, also preferring to remain silent. Just as Vieri had predicted, Blackwell was taking in everything that Munro was saying. The inspector never took his eyes off Will throughout the interview.

Ben Vieri was certain of one thing. Blackwell always kept an open mind; considered every possibility before trusting the evidence to lead him to a conviction.

"I decided to come here with Penny Richards on Tuesday morning— to give her some moral backing. That's all. You know the rest." Munro sat back in his chair, relieved that he had been able to finally have his say.

Mason Blackwell rubbed the tips of his fingers slowly along his forehead, as if trying to quell the first stirrings of a migraine.

"That's all very interesting, Mister Munro, but it doesn't quite tally with the story we got from Miss Richards. She says that you contacted her— said that you were in trouble and needed her help. She also said that she was frightened of you and felt pressurised into doing what you asked."

"What? That's bullshit, Inspector. I hadn't seen her for five years. Why would I want to contact her out of the blue like that?"

"She said exactly the same thing, Will. She explained that she had made a complaint of violent behaviour against you five years ago, and that that was what caused the breakup of your relationship. She had tried to get on with her life since then. The phone call from you opened up old wounds. She had no choice but to do exactly as you said. She was in fear of her life, apparently." Blackwell fed him a line.

Ben Vieri closed his eyes in anguish. He found it hard to believe what he was hearing. *What next?*

"I don't believe this! The relationship ended because of her screwing around. Bet she didn't tell you that, Inspector. The violence? She came at me with a wine bottle— split my head open! All I did was push her away. She hit her head on a worktop. Knocked her out cold. I told all this to the police at the time. No charges were ever brought and the pair of us went our separate ways— until Monday night." Will tried hard to calm down.

Ben placed a supportive hand on his friend's shoulder.

Blackwell sat quietly for a few seconds, processing the information. DS McMenemy glanced towards his superior officer, wondering where this line was taking them.

"Okay, Mister Munro. I have one thing I need to ask. We need a sample of your DNA— a mouth swab. If you're innocent, it'll help to clear you."

Will Munro glanced at his lawyer for guidance before nodding his approval.

"What about the boyfriend, Martin Anderson, Inspector? And Vic Simpson? I'm sure you must have worked out what's happening here. Baltimore must have been a drug dealer working for them. He's obviously outlived his usefulness and they've had to get rid of him. Will's been the innocent victim in all this. The only crime he's committed is one of caring for someone's well being,"

Ben Vieri said, making the most of his opportunity to deliver his sales pitch.

Blackwell shifted uneasily in his seat. He was already way ahead of Ben's theory. One thing was sure. Mason was not nearly as certain of Munro's conviction as he had been on waking that morning.

"We'll look at the case from every angle, Mister Vieri. I promise you that. For now, we have no option but to detain Mister Munro— I think the evidence that we have at the moment warrants it. He'll be held at least until we get the DNA test results back. Should be sometime tomorrow."

"Ben. Can you go and explain to Mary? Please?" A resigned Will Munro issued a last request before his incarceration.

"Of course, Will. I'll take care of it."

A police doctor arrived at the interview room armed with a little leather bag of tricks, including mouth-swab kits.

16

Brodie Metcalf sank deep into the luxurious spa bath in the millionaire's suite at Glasgow's Hilton Hotel.

"This is the way to live," he whispered to himself, the therapeutic powers of the bubbles popping and fizzing over his body.

The Viper was in excellent physical condition, another prerequisite of the profession learnt from the Master.

Get in the gym. Get fit, stay alive. The motto still burned brightly in the brain of the assassin.

Brodie's 'fairy godmother' had been watching over him since he landed; an expensive bottle of French champagne in the ice bucket awaited him on arrival.

He was clearly enjoying the attention— expensive bath salts, luxury Belgian chocolates, huge plasma TV screens in every room. At that moment he was catching up on some American football scores via the satellite link, displayed on a smaller, inlaid screen above the bath. A pearl-white, chunky, towelling bathrobe, heavily embroidered with the hotel's name, hung loosely over the open door of the vast shower unit in the corner of the spacious bathroom.

Metcalf lifted the crystal glass to his mouth, draining what was left of the champagne. Lately, he had developed a real taste for some of the finer things. A man of his standing could certainly afford them.

Unfortunately, Brodie had just broken the Master's main rule, one which he had incessantly drummed into his pupil— stay alert at all times. No booze. No drugs.

Rule Number Two had been strictly adhered to, however— his 9mm Glock to hand at all times.

The Viper reached over and flicked off the bubbles; the aerated water immediately calmed down. The effects of heat, tiredness and alcohol made him close his eyes for a few minutes. It had been a long day for Metcalf, what with the medium haul flight from Chicago and the business with Tam Watson.

He was going to need all his wits and wiles for the day ahead. It was 9:45 p.m., Scottish time, and Brodie was maybe half an hour from settling down for the night. He tended to get a little jumpy the night before work, so he figured that the cocktail of champagne, salmon sandwiches and hot chocolate should certainly help to relax the nerves. All going well, he would be able to work off the excess pounds after the job; maybe even think about a holiday. It had been so long since he had enjoyed a real break. Contract killing, especially in the States, was a booming business.

Brodie had been a very busy man over the past couple of years, doing a lot of stuff for the Chicago families. Fifty grand a pop was not uncommon among that fraternity, and he found trading there akin to taking candy from a child.

The day that he got the call from Baltimore's people, however, was the day he really hit the spot. Brodie Metcalf, only son of a humble delivery driver, was about to become another of America's millionaires.

The Viper glanced at the ornate carriage clock on the bedside table— almost 10:15 p.m. He had set the alarm on his mobile phone for 6:30 a.m. next morning.

Metcalf had a final check through the holdall that his benefactor had earlier left at reception. His face lit up as he rummaged through its deadly contents. He was already picturing the following day's work in his mind's eye. Confident that he had everything he needed to be going on with, Brodie zipped the bag up, carefully setting it down near an open window. The cool breeze filtered through the apartment. He definitely would not want to take any chances with a bag full of unpredictable explosives. A dodgy heating system at the Hilton could prove disastrous. A problem of this nature would be an incredibly long shot, but Brodie Metcalf was not in the business of taking unnecessary risks.

Two empty brown envelopes lay on the small jewellery tray next to the bedside lamp, the documents from them neatly placed in two piles on the unoccupied side of the king-sized bed. A small white envelope, retrieved from one of the larger ones, lay unopened beside the lamp.

Gathering the information from both piles, Brodie decided to make a head count. He was now in a position to familiarise himself with each and every target.

He was looking at a selection of small individual photographs. Metcalf's face straightened in intense concentration as he studied each one in turn. His complete lack of conscience would allow the hit man to take their lives without blinking.

Metcalf turned over another couple of documents. More photographs fell out into his lap. He raised an eyebrow. He was going to be rather busy over the next few days. Somebody was certainly asking for his money's worth. The Viper had decided to sell his services on a job lot basis. In truth, he would have wiped out half of Glasgow for the kind of cash he was being paid.

Hmmm, wonder just how they're involved in this? Brodie mused, leafing through the mug shots. He smiled. Killing these people may have been daunting for most, even in this line of business. For Brodie Metcalf, this particular section of the contract presented a welcome test of his undoubted abilities.

Satisfied that he had a good handle on his targets, Brodie

reached across, placing the information carefully on the little bedside dresser. He was about to turn in for the night when he remembered about the white envelope he had earlier laid down. *More targets?* he wondered.

Picking up the envelope, he shook the contents like an excited schoolboy. He tore a strip across the top and pulled out the innards— an unsigned, typewritten note and what looked like a banker's cheque or draft, neatly folded across the middle. Deciding to save the best for last, Brodie laid the folded cheque down on his lap. He began to read the letter. A smile flashed across his face when he got to the last sentence: 'Enclosed is a cheque for half the contract amount, the balance payable on completion'.

Good work if you can get it, mused Brodie Metcalf. Word of mouth or reputation? Either way, the assassin was in big demand, having just secured a little side contract.

Metcalf's heart did a triple somersault as he read the typed amount in the payee's box of the cheque. Maybe it wouldn't be quite such a little side contract.

The effects of the alcohol kicked in with a vengeance; Brodie lay back on the soft, welcoming pillow. Literally, within a minute, he was sleeping like a baby.

17

The tall cop stood outside the office block on Hope Street in the heart of Glasgow's city centre. DI Mason Blackwell studied the grubby directory on the wall just outside the entrance.

It was unusually warm for an early spring day, especially at nine o'clock in the morning. Mason, jacket neatly folded over his arm, had worked up a sticky sweat during the five-minute walk from police headquarters in Pitt Street.

Let me see, Entertainment UK Ltd... Typical! Fifth floor, he said inwardly, stepping back on to the pavement to crane his neck. He squinted painfully as the low sun found its way between structures. "Top floor! That's just great," Mason said sarcastically.

Blackwell had a choice: to walk up five flights of stairs reaching the top a greasy mess, or simply stroll into the lift and ride there. Claustrophobia, and the fact that the lifts serving these ancient buildings tended to be around two and a half feet square, meant that Mason would plump for the first option.

The inspector stood waiting for the giddiness to pass, propped up by the banister at the very top of the stairwell. The pace and voracity of his breathing indicated to him that some urgent visits to the gym might be in order. Mason patted his slight beer belly, allowing his heartbeat and blood pressure to return to normal before entering.

"Can I help you?" The pretty, young blonde receptionist immediately stood and burst into life as the door to the dingy office swung open.

As she pushed her chest forward in an obviously rehearsed move, the blonde's ample bust strained under a bra that seemed to be five sizes too small. The shortness of the dress suggested to the policeman that material was at a premium in this business.

The decor in the office had seen better days. It was fair to say that the owners of the business did not much believe in shelling out in the name of image. A battered old desk, on which sat a retro-style, button phone, and a rickety old chair, were the main focal points in the office. Dirty, cloth vertical blinds hiding cobwebs and a bare bulb for a centre light completed the effect.

Everyone knew that the owner used the office merely as a front for his criminal activities. Apart from the fixtures and most of the occupants, everything in it was officially squeaky clean. Arrests and convictions against this lot would be extremely difficult, but not impossible, maintained a determined Mason Blackwell.

"I'm here to see Vic Simpson. My name is Detective Inspector Blackwell." He held up his ID in front of the girl.

She hardly batted an eyelid; Mason assumed that a visit from the police might have been a regular occurrence.

"Of course, Sir. Is he expecting you?"

Probably, thought the policeman.

"No."

"All right, Sir. I'll just let him know you're here."

"Thank you."

The girl teetered on ridiculously high heels towards the door marked 'Manager', closing it softly behind her.

A couple of minutes later a red light flashed up on the phone on the main desk, catching Mason's eye. He smiled, imagining the bastard calling around his contacts for the word on the street.

No doubt some of these contacts will be located at Pitt Street HQ, thought the cop, making a mental note to step up the activity on this front. One thing Mason Blackwell hated was a bent copper.

The red light extinguished.

"Inspector. Nice to see you again. Just come through." Vic Simpson stood at the door of his office, peering at the cop over his glasses.

If Blackwell didn't know Simpson better, he would swear that this fat, scruffy, middle-aged man was someone's favourite uncle or friendly, family doctor. Scuffed black shoes, tired and worn, grey trousers and a grubby, white shirt straining over his belly disguised the evil within.

Mason disliked his host intensely, choosing to merely nod an acknowledgement, and walked over towards the door. He had had a couple of recent interviews with the gangster regarding fairly minor incidents, leaving each time with a real urge to shut him up for good.

Blackwell politely stood aside to let Barbie return to her desk.

"So what can I do for you, Inspector?" Simpson slumped back in his chair, a sneering look on his face which the policeman tried hard to ignore.

Concentrate on the job at hand.

"I need to ask you a few questions, Mister Simpson." Mason tried to remain polite.

"Of course. Fire away."

"On Sunday evening, a man was murdered in his flat in the Mountfield Place area of town. Do you know it?"

"No."

"The man's name was Lonnie Baltimore. He was an American— from Chicago. Do you know him?"

"No. Should I?"

"Some of my sources say that he worked for you— for your organisation."

"Really? Worked for me? You'd think I'd know him then, wouldn't you, Inspector?" Simpson was now sitting, arms crossed, apparently not a care in the world. "And what exactly did this guy— Baltimore, is it? What exactly did he do for me?"

"I hear that he was one of your pushers."

"You mean drugs, Inspector? I'll have nothing to do with drugs. They're illegal."

Blackwell smiled and continued, "On Tuesday, we got a visit down at the station from a Penny Richards. Do you know her?"

"No, never heard of her. Look, Inspector. I'm pretty busy just now. Can we try to hurry this up?"

"We can continue it later down at the station if you'd prefer, Vic?"

"All right, Inspector. Just what did this Penny Richards have to say for herself then?" Simpson was becoming visibly restless, deciding nonetheless to co-operate.

Blackwell's brain was slipping into overdrive.

Like any good cop, he had already worked out the play for this particular session before he even rose for work that morning. Normally, two officers would carry out this type of interview. However, Mason knew that there would be absolutely zero chance of producing anything that could be built on regarding any future conviction of this bastard or any of his cronies. And he may feel a lot less intimidated by the presence of an officer flying solo— maybe let the mask slip a little. No, today's objective would be to create a situation— give Vic Simpson and his main henchman, Martin Anderson, something to really think about.

Blackwell had not been present at the interview with Penny Richards, but had listened to the transcript. During the session, she had, of course, implicated her ex-lover, Will

Munro, in the killing of Lonnie Baltimore. At no point in the tape had there been any mention of a romantic connection between her and Martin Anderson.

Of course, Will Munro's account of the incident produced a completely different set of circumstances. The one thing that had been gnawing away at Mason Blackwell was the fact that, according to Munro, Richards had casually yielded the name of her boyfriend. The inspector had looked at it from every angle. He just could not get his head around it; he couldn't figure out why she had chosen to mention Anderson at all. What had she hoped to gain from it? Could it be possible that Penny Richards had a separate agenda?

Blackwell was by no means a betting man, but he was pretty sure which version of events his money would be on. He was already of the mind that he had been rather hasty in his arrest of Will Munro and, after the DNA evidence cleared him, as it surely must, he would have to be released. A good lawyer like Ben Vieri would punch huge holes in the Procurator Fiscal's case.

Mason Blackwell's eyes narrowed in concentration. It was time to make the play.

"Martin Anderson is an employee of yours, I believe?"

"Yes, Martin looks after my nightclub, The Parthenon. What's he done, Inspector? I keep telling him to stop ogling these young lassies in the club!" Simpson threw his head back, letting out a raspy, throaty laugh.

Blackwell thought about his beloved daughter, almost a teenager. He tried hard to hide his disgust.

"No, but he may have done something a whole lot more serious."

The laughter began to peter out. Simpson's face straightened. He was staring at the cop, almost daring him to go for it.

"That's right, Vic. According to Martin's current

girlfriend, who you claim not to know, she saw him kill Lonnie Baltimore on Sunday night."

"That's impossible, Inspector. He was at The Parthenon with me most of the day and night on Sunday. We were checking the books. And I told you the truth. I don't know this girl. Never heard Martin even speak about her. If I know him, he'd never just see one lassie. He'll be nickin' about with as many as he can get his hands on!"

Mason Blackwell smirked at the speed and construction of the alibi. Simpson had spent years perfecting the skill.

"She obviously must have been mistaken then, Vic. You understand that we'll still need to speak to Martin to verify this? Do you have an address for him?"

"Of course, Inspector. Mandy at the desk will give you the details from the file."

Blackwell stood to leave, catching an ever so slightly concerned look on the face of the gangster.

Mason was confident his mischief making was about to create a little holy hell for all concerned. He would be waiting to pick up the pieces.

* * *

Five minutes later, Blackwell was back on the busy street, thronging through the morning shoppers on the way back to the station. He glanced again at the scribbled information contained on the small piece of paper received from Barbie.

Blackwell swapped the note in his pocket for his mobile phone which had just burst into life.

"Inspector? You need to get down here. I'm at Glasgow Airport, Car Park A." The seemingly under-pressure voice of DS Mick McMenemy split the silence.

18

Driving along the M8 motorway towards Glasgow Airport, Mason Blackwell could hear the faint beginnings of an emergency vehicle closing fast behind him.

As he reached the slip road leading down to the main roundabout at the entrance to the airport, he looked across towards the terminal building and the car parks. In the distance, he could see a plethora of revolving blue lights above a host of cop cars and hundreds of feet of yellow and black, police 'do not cross' tape around the vicinity of car park A.

The ambulance eventually screamed past him on the slip, bound for the scene. Blackwell had a gut feeling that help was arriving far too late in this case.

Rounding the last corner before arriving at the various car park areas, Blackwell was aware of a marked increase in the number of vehicles being diverted around the airport. The terrorist attack on the terminal building around two years before, when a four-wheel-drive motor carrying incendiaries was driven through the front of the building, had resulted in security procedures along the setting-down area being drastically altered. This review had meant that the volume of traffic entering the area would be dispersed through alternative routes, clogging up previously free flowing lanes. This restriction on one of the main car parking areas was the last thing the airport needed.

Mason could see maybe four or five of his officers

standing in the middle of the mayhem, frantically gesturing towards the growing queues. They were very slowly beginning to clear the situation, one of the uniforms noticing the inspector's car languishing about five back. Within the next couple of minutes, the efficient officer had somehow extricated his boss' car from the line, directing him into car park A.

At the far side of the park, approximately fifty yards away, Blackwell could make out the somewhat familiar shape of a blue Toyota Corolla, the immediate area around about it cordoned off by seemingly endless criss-crossing lines of police tape. The ambulance that had earlier passed, sat redundant on the other side of the tapes. The paramedics had already made their diagnosis, almost instantly deciding that they would not be picking up from this scene. The basic rule was that they were not allowed to lift dead bodies. In this case that task would be left to the pathologist's department. The call had already been made.

The inspector drew up alongside the car of DS McMenemy. The sergeant could clearly be seen crouching down near the rear of the Toyota, obviously scanning the area for vital clues.

The driver's door was open. Mason could see the outline of a body lying back in the driver's seat. He had already figured out the identity of the occupant.

"Christ, Mick! What the hell's happening here?" Mason ducked under the tapes, walking briskly over to his officer.

"I don't know, Sir. I haven't been here that long myself. It's Tam Watson." Blackwell nodded in acknowledgement. "Apparently one of the early morning workers found him. They thought at first that he was sleeping."

"Aye, well he certainly is now, anyway," Mason replied, definitely not trying to be funny. He hunkered down at the open door, looking up at the stricken body of his officer.

Watson's head had fallen to the side, facing out of the door. A slight trail of hardened blood had made its way from the bullet hole in his forehead, down over the nose, mouth and chin, producing a very small red spot on his white shirt just under the throat. Tam Watson had remained mean and tight, even at the end, his body seemingly unwilling to bleed as it should.

Mason Blackwell was interested in the haunted expression on the face, deducing right away that the DS had definitely seen it coming. He reached up to his forehead, trying to gently stroke the now almost established migraine away.

Mason inwardly chastised himself for feeling nothing at the sight of one of his officers lying with his brains shot out. Tam Watson had not been well liked, but Blackwell's philosophy was always to give people the benefit of the doubt. He preferred to consider that the sergeant's arrogance and general apathy towards everything and everybody may have been down to a difficult upbringing or whatever.

"Did he have any family, Mick?" Blackwell asked, still facing the victim.

"Don't know, Sir. He wasn't married. Never spoke about his parents or anything," McMenemy replied.

The inspector returned to his car, re-emerging with a box of latex gloves. He selected a couple of pairs.

"Here. Put a pair of these on. I don't want the scene contaminated."

The DS did as he was told.

Mason opened fully the remaining three doors of the car, peering inside, especially in the foot wells. He was searching for the bullet casing. It had to have been shed on the floor.

Nowhere to be seen.

He blew out his cheeks in frustration. Mason was willing to bet that the car had been wiped down for prints. He was almost certain that the CSEs would find nothing.

"Whoever did this, Mick, he's a professional— one shot to the head. The car's probably been wiped clean; looks like he even picked up the bullet casing." Blackwell reached over the passenger seat to lightly touch the head of the corpse. "He's stone cold. I'm thinking that the body has been here since yesterday."

"The pathologist is on his way, Sir. He'll confirm that. But what was he doing here?" McMenemy asked.

The inspector shook his head.

A black Landrover was trundling over towards the scene. In minutes, a number of white jump-suited individuals from the forensics department emerged from it, their first job— to erect a makeshift tent around the scene. In no time they were swarming all over the site.

"Mick, I've an idea. We'll leave these guys to do their jobs. D'you know where the security management suite is at the airport?"

"Aye, Sir. It's over behind the main building. Why?"

The DI pointed towards three or four security cameras in proximity, dotted around the car park.

McMenemy smiled a knowing smile at his boss.

"I'm Detective Inspector Blackwell. This is Detective Sergeant McMenemy." The two men flashed their ID badges at Hughie Masters, head of security at the airport.

"Terrible tragedy, Inspector. I'm so sorry about your officer. If there's anything we can do. Anything at all," Masters said.

"Thank you, Mister Masters. I believe that you may, indeed, be able to help us. Your security cameras? I need to speak to the man in charge of their maintenance and operation," Blackwell said.

"Of course. If you follow me, gentlemen, I'll take you

to the comms room right now," Masters replied.

The three men left the spacious, open-plan office at the newly refurbished management suite, pounding along a narrow corridor towards the communications suite at the far end of the building. Hughie Masters was taller than average— six-three or six-four, the inspector fractionally shorter. DS McMenemy, at around five-four, was having great difficulty keeping up with the enormous strides of the other two. By the time they reached the communications suite he was absolutely knackered; his little legs screamed for mercy.

"This is the 'man' in charge of the CCTV systems, Inspector." Masters smiled ruefully. He was pointing over at the luscious blonde security guard sitting among a dozen or so TV monitors at the far end of the suite.

The two cops glanced briefly at each other in disbelief.

The security chief walked over to her, exchanging a few words before returning to the policemen. "If you can ask Claudia to call me when you're finished, I'll come back over and get you." Hughie slipped out of the door, immediately answering a phone request to attend a situation down at one of the car-hire sales booths.

"How can I help you, Inspector?" Claudia called across the room, flashing a perfect smile at the policemen. Her beautiful golden-blonde hair tumbled down over her petite shoulders.

Never before had Mick seen a sexier looking security guard. McMenemy was convinced that none of this was real, and that she was about to launch into a strip-o-gram routine on cue with the radio music playing quietly in the corner.

Claudia swivelled around in her office chair, standing up to her full fighting height of about five-three. She was wearing a crisp, white, beautifully laundered, short-sleeved shirt and matching red tie with the security company emblem displayed on it. Below, her short, grey, pencil-style skirt and black, patent leather shoes completed the effect. Mick McMenemy's mouth hung open as if he was high on something at the sight of her beautifully sculpted legs below sheer twenty-denier stockings.

"Put your tongue back in, Mick. We have a job to do here," Blackwell, professional as ever, whispered to his officer on the way over to shake hands with the goddess.

The DS, feeling the intense heat from his bright pink face, roughly cleared his throat, embarrassed at being found out.

"Hello, Claudia. Pleased to meet you. I'm DI Mason Blackwell and this is DS Mick McMenemy," Blackwell stated, rather formally.

The DS nodded, doe eyed. "As you probably know by now, a police officer was killed in one of the airport's car parks— Park A. Trouble is that we don't know exactly what happened yet, or indeed, when it happened. I thought that maybe your surveillance technology will be able to help us," Mason continued.

"Of course, Inspector. We'd be glad to help," she responded.

"Thank you. Can you explain to us just how the CCTV system is set up and what we can or can't expect it to provide?"

"Well, there are fifteen screens, as you can see here. Each screen flashes images from five high-definition colour cameras."

"That's a total of seventy-five cameras. Some set up." McMenemy sometimes had a habit of stating the obvious, especially in the company of Mason Blackwell. He sometimes tried a little too hard to impress.

"It should be, Sergeant. It cost us a fortune, apparently," Claudia explained. "We monitor images from all over the site, including booking desks and concourses, shopping areas, arrivals and departure lounges, loading bays, car parks— basically everywhere. Well, maybe except toilet cubicles. Not yet, anyway," she joked.

The two men smiled politely.

"Now, the first three monitors, from left to right along the top, receive footage from all of the car park zones. Car Park A can be seen by different cameras linked to all three monitors. The images switch over by the setting of timers. Let's just see if I can bring up the best angle." Claudia's hand landed on the computer mouse. "If you look at the second screen from the left..."

Seconds later, the three of them were studying the live image of the white tent recently set up around the car by the Crime Scene Examiners. Blackwell instantly recognised a tall gentleman with a leather briefcase arriving at the site as being city pathologist, Frank Tilbury. The door of the tent was held open for him and he disappeared inside. "With this technology, we can zoom in and pan out without compromising the quality of the recording. Watch."

Two seconds later, the trio were up close and personal with a small rodent that Claudia's perfect vision had earlier helped spot.

"That is truly amazing!" the DS blustered. *I really need to get some new material,* he lamented.

"It is impressive, Claudia," the inspector agreed. "Can we run the tape from yesterday now?"

"Er, we don't use tapes anymore, Inspector. They're outmoded. All our CCTV information is stored on hard disk. The files are compressed or zipped to make them easier to store. Our policy is to retain six months' worth, and then automatically overwrite them when file space becomes limited.

"Okay. Is there a way to run back the tape— er, file?"

"Aye. I'll just click back to the same time every hour until we see the car disappear on the monitor. We then narrow the search to individual minutes within that hour."

"Okay, Claudia. Let's do it."

It was now 11:30 a.m. Claudia was again clicking away on the mouse, every few seconds rolling the system back an hour. Their eyes were fixed on the blue Toyota as the time changed— 7 a.m., 6 a.m., 5 a.m., 4 a.m.

Eventually, at 3 p.m. the previous afternoon, the Toyota vanished, in its place a red Ford Mondeo. Claudia stopped the process.

"The Toyota Corolla must have arrived between 3 and 4 p.m., yesterday afternoon. Now all we have to do is advance by the minute from three o'clock," Claudia explained.

"That's him arriving." After a few more seconds, Blackwell was staring at the time displayed on the top right-hand corner of the screen— 3:08 p.m.

Claudia scribbled down the time with a brief reference note next to it. They watched the Toyota pull into the parking space. At 3:10 p.m., DS Watson got out of the car, presumably setting off for the terminal building.

"Is there any way we can find out where he goes next, Claudia?" Mason asked.

"Thought you'd never ask," declared the pretty blonde. "This system has an in-built, semi-automatic tracking device. All we have to do is highlight an object or a subject and the system will monitor where it or he goes within the confines of the site. The computer will switch automatically from camera to camera. Let me demonstrate."

Claudia rolled the images back to where Watson left the car. She then tagged him via the mouse, hit real-time motion, and then enter on her keyboard.

Mason Blackwell bent down towards the computer monitor, watching the camera angle change as DS Watson crossed the car park to the terminal building. The system was indeed working perfectly. Watson would have been completely unaware of its existence.

Blackwell couldn't help noticing the flat package Watson was holding under his arm. Inside the terminal building, Tam Watson stopped at International arrivals. He looked at his watch before ripping the packaging from what looked like some kind of board or plate. He put the board under his arm and sat before laying it across his legs.

"Can you stop it there, please? He's got some kind of information board on his knee. Can you zoom in and maybe see what it says?" Blackwell asked.

"I can try," she replied, immediately attacking the keys once again. "I'm sorry, Inspector. The board must be facing down." Claudia's voice held a trace of disappointment.

"All right. Let's stick with him. See what happens." Mason was always positive in his attitude.

Watson stood and held up the board as people streamed past him. 3:21 p.m.

A flight's just come through arrivals. If we can establish which one it is, Blackwell mused.

"There. Can you read it now, Claudia?"

Literally seconds later, the three of them were staring at the name 'John Mitchell' in high definition.

What the hell have you been up to, Tam? Mason Blackwell was, by this time, in no doubt that DS Watson had been involved in something shady.

A few minutes later, a rather short, well dressed man approached Watson. Unfortunately, the man had his back to the camera. Mason's nose was almost pressed against the screen, such was his concentration.

"Come on, pal. Just turn around for us," he muttered.

Ten seconds later, the man obliged; Blackwell cursed his luck when he caught sight of the Rayban sunglasses.

"Can you tail them back to the car, Claudia?" Mason asked.

"Already done."

The computer system tracked the pair for the next few minutes until they reached Watson's Toyota Corolla. Moments later, both men were seen to be entering the car; the stranger took the passenger seat.

"See if you can zoom in for me, please, Claudia."

She increased the magnification just in time for them to see a micro-flash of light illuminating the car's interior.

"Did you just see that, Mick?" Mason asked.

"Aye, Sir. That must have been the kill shot." Once again, the DS found himself stating the obvious. He dug his fingernails into his palms in annoyance. "What's he doing now, Sir?" he enquired, biting his lip.

"Just as I thought, Mick. He's wiping the vehicle down," a worried Blackwell replied.

The three of them watched the images of Brodie Metcalf coolly leaving the murder scene. Blackwell suddenly got a shiver down his spine. He could have sworn that the killer had flashed a smile at camera one on the way past.

Claudia needed no encouragement to continue trailing the man. Minutes later, he turned up at the taxi rank in front of the terminal building, jumping into the one at the head of the queue.

The blonde security expert was already scribbling down the registration number.

Mason Blackwell smiled as he slipped the note into his pocket.

"Claudia, can you print me a face shot of this guy?"

"I already have, Inspector. Here." She handed the DI a clear still of the killer.

Pity about the sunglasses. Suppose it's better than nothing, Mason decided.

"Mick. You stay here and trawl through the seating lists for planes arriving from, say, 2:20 p.m. until 3 p.m. yesterday. I'd love to know where John Mitchell, or

whatever his name is, came from. Then phone around the
hotels to see if he booked in anywhere. You never know,
we might get lucky. I'll go and see the taxi driver."

"Right, Sir. I'll call you when I have anything. It was
nice to meet you, Claudia." Mick flushed slightly as he
shook hands with the girl. Seconds later, he was on his way
to study the tower log.

"Just one more thing, Claudia. I need a copy of what
we've just seen. On a CD or someth—" Blackwell laughed
as he wheeled around to be handed said copy.

A rather butch-looking woman entered the room,
walking over towards the pair. She brushed past the
inspector, smiling at the pretty blonde beside him.

"It's lunchtime, honey. Are you ready?" the woman
asked.

"Mmm, hmm." Claudia put her arms around the
woman's neck, kissing her full on the lips.

It was Mason Blackwell's turn to stand mouth agape.

*Better not mention this to McMenemy— shatter his
illusion,* the DI mused.

"I'll call Hughie Masters over to take you back to the
terminal building, Inspector," Claudia said.

"Thanks for all your help, love." Mason winked at the
gorgeous blonde.

Seconds later, the lovers left for lunch, holding hands.

Such a waste, Mason Blackwell reflected.

19

"I swear, Martin! I never said a thing! I did it just the way you wanted!" Penny Richards' voice seemed to verge on panic.

DI Mason Blackwell's mischievous information, let slip during the interview at Vic Simpson's office had filtered on from Simpson to Martin Anderson. Penny was now feeling the repercussions.

"Then just how did Munro get my name? I said no fucking names!" Anderson's face was bright red with fury.

The bruises on the girl's body from their last heated discussion were almost healed, faint yellow shadows remaining in their place.

The 'lovers' were in the upstairs living quarters of the Golden Hind public house on Great Western Road near Clydebank on the outskirts of Glasgow. The pub was busy most nights, greatly due to the fact that Vic Simpson had been responsible for the early closures of the rest of the hostelries in the local area.

In true Sicilian Don fashion, Simpson had made all of them an offer they couldn't refuse.

Furthermore, those derisory cash incentives to the owners to 'get out of town' had resulted in the acquisition of half a dozen spacious premises, all with potential for extending.

A few months later, the continuing property boom of the late nineties and early two thousands meant that the tasteful conversions of the ex-drinking dens into penthouse apartments and large detached houses, had quadrupled the mobster's original investment.

Whoever said 'crime doesn't pay' did not know the half of it!

The Country and Western band downstairs were churning out another Johnny Cash number. The Men from Shiloh had been a big hit on their last visit to Clydebank, and had been promptly rebooked by the organisers of the local C & W club. The guys and gals from The Hoe Down Club were holding their monthly get together in the Big Muddy lounge bar of the pub. Buckskins, stetsons and Tammy Wynette wigs were in abundance in deepest Clydebank that night, the sound of fake Colt 45s filling the air during the quick-draw competitions.

Vic Simpson had always been a big Country fan, his huge house across the road from the Golden Hind largely decked out in cowboy memorabilia.

The late Glasgow crime boss Arthur Thompson's house had been named The Ponderosa. Vic's gaffe was called simply, Southfork.

One of the perils of living so close to one's work was that one would tend to nip across the road at the drop of a hat. Two of the regular barmen had called in sick with flu' that morning. Vic's manager was away on holiday and he had not had time to organise cover. He had decided to ride point that evening, much to his wife's annoyance.

Owning the pub across the road did have a number of advantages. Firstly, he could have a drink without running the risk of losing his licence, the victim of some over eager, young policeman out to make a name for himself. Secondly, he could actually enjoy the music for a change; all too often Vic would be stuck at a meeting in the bar, subjected to juke box trash. Thirdly, and most importantly, he could escape the eternal nagging from his good lady. At least for a little while.

Unfortunately, for all concerned in the Golden Hind's lounge bar that night, Vic Simpson had an almighty headache. Instead of feeling the urge to line dance with some of the buxom ladies of the club, he would much rather have preferred to see out the event in stuffy silence. The band had been instructed otherwise, however; the guys ready to *increase* the volume, driving on relentlessly to the finish.

Simpson was also extremely pissed off with the developing situation in the flat above him. He had been incandescent with rage following the earlier visit from DI Blackwell. Vic actually felt, obviously in some kind of delusional way, that he was fast becoming a legitimate businessman, genuinely upset at the audacity of that cop to storm into his office, accusing.

How many parents of kids lost to drugs supplied by this animal would agree?

An angry exchange of words with Martin Anderson over the phone had resulted in his request to get the pair together, where he could keep an eye on them; get everything out in the open; determine the truth.

Vic was not especially fond of Penny Richards. He considered her to be a grade one gold digger, definitely not to be trusted. When Anderson and Richards had come to him with the plan to frame her ex-lover, Simpson had initially vetoed the idea; only time, desperation and the lack of alternatives forced his hand in the end. The manipulation of the CCTV images at Mountfield Place had been a doddle for a local junkie, computer geek, bribed by the promise of extra gear for nothing.

Now the pair— Martin Anderson and Penny Richards— were in Vic's private chamber; the place where he would often enjoy an indiscretion or two, away from his nag of a wife.

Vic Simpson's headache was at last beginning to

subside. It was now gone midnight; the last of the cowboys and cowgirls finally moseyed out of the door. Vic slid the inside bolts top and bottom and turned the key in the lock.

He sat at the bar, downing his first whisky of the night. The whole place had been eerily silent for around five minutes— even upstairs.

Simpson scratched the heavy stubble on his chin. A smile crossed his face. This would be one instance when he might just find it in his heart to condone Anderson for flying off on one.

In Vic's line of business there were plenty of ways and places to dispose of a body. In fact, he had a direct number for such a cleanup service. It would cost, but it would be worth it— quick, easy and no trace.

Simpson refilled his glass, slowly sipping the deluxe whisky. His headache had now gone; the alcohol numbed its dying embers. He rose to walk over to a door marked Staff Only, taking the glass and bottle with him. Might as well be comfortable while they wait for the 'Cleaner'.

Trudging wearily up the staircase, Vic became aware of what sounded like people talking in the living room to the right at the top of the stairs. As he reached the landing he realised that the sounds were coming from a TV, volume set on low.

Cruel bastard! Now he watches telly! Vic Simpson pushed his way into the living room, totally unprepared for what he was about to witness.

The body was face up in the middle of the room, staring glassy eyed, almost accusing. One leg had twisted under the other when it fell, giving a discarded marionette, kind of effect. Dark, crimson blood— lots of it— three feet around, framed the head. The murder weapon was in clear view. A large pair of commercial scissors, speared into the jugular, had given the victim no chance.

Vic Simpson fumbled with his phone. Minutes later, the

'Cleaner' would be gathering his equipment, bound for The Golden Hind.

Simpson picked up a bathrobe, untidily left over the back of a settee, and covered the mutilated body of Martin Anderson.

There was no sign of Penny Richards.

20

Mary Munro and Ben and Leah Vieri were sitting downstairs in the huge lounge of the Munros' house in Bearsden. Both sets of twins were upstairs playing in the specially converted playroom, very useful for such occasions when the grown-ups wanted to talk.

"So, what happens now, Ben?" Mary asked.

"The Procurator Fiscal will decide if the Crown has enough evidence, firstly to formulate a case against Will. Then he has to decide if he prefers to hold him until the trial date," Lawyer Vieri replied.

Mary swallowed hard. "Do you think he has?" she asked bravely.

"Enough evidence? At the moment? I very much doubt it. The CCTV is inconclusive and the only witness obviously bears a grudge." Ben's words prompted a kind of forced smile from Leah.

"See, Mary? He'll be home in no time." Leah put her arm around the shoulder of her best friend.

"What about this DNA evidence? When will we hear about it?" Mary asked, visibly heartened by the positive mood in the room.

"Today. In fact, I'll insist on it. I'm absolutely certain he'll be released after the result. I'm going down to the station this afternoon. Why don't you come down with me, Mary? He'll be desperate to see you."

"I think you should, Mary. He really needs you right

now. I'll take the kids over to ours. When Will is released, come back and stay with us. We can have a celebration— all of us." Leah strengthened the case for staying over.

"You're such a good friend, Leah. Both of you. I don't know what I would have done." Mary's voice started to peter out.

* * *

Will Munro had spent a rather uncomfortable evening in the basement cell at police HQ. Another sleepless night had left his handsome face drawn, his eyes blood red with fatigue. He sat on the edge of the little single bed in the corner of the cell. A couple of burst springs, at strategic places in the brick-hard mattress, had painfully pierced their way into his aching back.

It was fair to say that Will was feeling decidedly sorry for himself at that moment– his darkest to date. He felt tears well up, forcibly blinking them away. Wiping his cheeks with the back of his hand, he closed his eyes tightly. He could hear the rough, intermittent snoring of the occupant in the adjoining cell.

The drunk had been manhandled in there around three-thirty in the morning by a couple of uniforms. The ruckus hadn't exactly disturbed Munro's peaceful slumbers. In fact it had proved to be a welcome distraction from his ever-growing insomnia problem.

Will purposely allowed his mind to wander far from the confines of his cell. He suddenly found himself back reliving his teenage years, listening to more wise words from the ultimate role model— his father.

Lachie Munro had been the shining light during the lad's formative years; his wisdom and vast knowledge guided his son through that confusing and awkward time. The old man would read anything and everything, his thirst for knowledge all consuming.

Will had inherited his father's extra special gene: the one that instilled in him the insatiable need to read. Will's house contained a roomy study, which was literally bursting with countless novels of almost every genre.

It was, however, in the world of accounts that the Munros excelled; the father started up the business from scratch. The present company, now with son, Will, at the helm, was one of the most trusted and respected in the city.

Suddenly, Will Munro found himself back in the confines of his cell, his heart sinking quickly to his feet.

What would he give for some more of that golden advice in his present predicament?

Unfortunately, Lachie Munro would now not be able to provide it, his former razor-sharp mind ironically lost forever to Alzheimer's.

Will Munro leant back against the cold wall of the cell, waiting for the next instalment of the nightmare.

21

"How much is it this time, Penny? Two thousand? Three? I told you the last time— no more!" The housewife held her hands up like a barrier in front of her.

"Please, Karen. Just listen to me. I'm in real trouble this time," Penny Richards replied. She sounded genuine. She always did.

"No, you listen to me. I... don't... care! You suddenly appear again after all these years. I gave you all I had then, Penny. And I needed that money. What did you do with it? Eh? I'll tell you, will I? You snorted it up that fucking nose of yours!" Karen's voice cracked. She turned away as she felt the tears threaten. The last thing she wanted was this woman to think that she actually cared a jot about her. The trouble was— she still did.

The two women were standing in the kitchen of the big house. The sounds of boisterous children playing in the playroom above them could easily be heard. There was an almighty thump. Karen was forever telling the kids not to jump off the climbing bars onto the floor, declaring the practice dangerous. Another heavy bump. Clearly, they had chosen not to listen to their mother— again. Maybe it was because their little friends were around. Peer pressure— the need to show off.

"Stay right here! Don't you move!" Karen commanded her visitor. She tore out of the kitchen, taking the stairs three at a time. A verbal volley ensued with the desired end result— there would be no more mini-acrobatics in the house; at least not for a little while.

Karen was back downstairs in a heartbeat. The break had worked in her favour, strengthened her resolve. She was ready to throw her no-good sister out for the last time. Penny Richards was bad news. Her own mother had even declared so on her deathbed. Although her girls were twins, there was nothing identical about them. Not in looks. Not in personalities. And certainly not in their choice of partners— apart from the nice accountant that Penny had been engaged to some years back.

'A rose among thorns,' the mother was often heard to quote. Even more ironic— ex-boyfriend, Will Munro, had actually adored her. Penny had even managed to screw that one up; the fallout no doubt contributed to the mother's premature death from a stroke at the ridiculously young age of fifty-three.

Earlier still, the family had needed to be strong to survive the untimely death of their adoring father. A building site accident had claimed the life of the young Welsh roofer at just twenty-five.

In her defence, during the next few years, the mother had tried her damnedest to do the right thing by her girls. She could certainly not be held responsible for their teenage needs, or desire to use their looks in a kind of sleazy, casting couch way, operating under the questionable guise of dancing and modelling to further their careers.

Once they were old enough to leave home, they roomed together for a time under the London bright lights. After a rather successful spell of dabbling in the soft porn industry, the twins had actually managed to find themselves a decent agent; a family man; a man who would never dream of exploiting his clients; a man who would make sure that they received everything that was promised to them; a man who was seemingly incorruptible. The same man who had fought long and hard for weeks and months, before finally succumbing to the largely irresistible charms of an evil temptress. Penny Richards had surpassed herself this time; Bob Miller chose to put a gun in his mouth rather than face the rest of his life without his beloved wife and children.

* * *

While Penny continued untroubled on her travels across the world, a sickened Karen Richards decided that enough was enough and landed back in Glasgow, hoping to settle down to a more sedate and honest lifestyle. A change of identity would hopefully erase the memory of her earlier indiscretions, especially those involving the soft porn industry. Only her sister would now refer to her by the name she was born with.

Luckily for Karen, the man of her dreams was just around the corner; the tall, handsome, young professional literally swept her off her feet in a way that she could only imagine. They adored each other and the later addition of two delightful children had made her happiness complete. The last thing she needed was another visit from her sister, threatening to wreck her idyllic existence. Karen had tactfully omitted to mention her chequered past to her husband. Little did she know that pure evil and intense jealousy would later combine to take care of that little matter.

* * *

Karen Richards galvanised herself as she entered the kitchen.

"Right, Penny. I want you to go..." She stopped in mid flow.

Her sister was bent over the sink, dabbing her eyes with

a face flannel. Penny knew exactly how to play people, especially Karen. She had had plenty of practice over the years. Her eyes were red rimmed in no time, creating maximum effect. "Sit. I'll put some tea on." Somewhat reluctantly, Karen felt herself relent. The apparent ploy had been successful.

Penny Richards sat at the family table in the centre of the kitchen, feeling very sorry for herself. Three minutes later, and with no words spoken, the two women were sipping tea. Some things were a tradition. Their mother would cite hot, sweet tea as the giver of all life and the solver of all the world's problems. Penny's current situation certainly felt decidedly less hostile for her than the last two or three days had thrown up.

"Karen. I've done some horrible things recently. Things I've not been proud of," Penny started shakily. "I need to get out. Leave the country for a while."

"So you are here for money, after all. I might have known. What exactly have you done, Pen? Slept with somebody else's husband?" Karen enquired bitterly.

"If only that was it, Karen. I'd be delighted. Unfortunately, it's much worse." Penny's voice was calm, resigned. She spoke in hushed tones, seemed to be in control for the most part. Her demeanour took her sister completely by surprise.

"You're scaring me, Penny. Is there anything I can do to help?" Karen asked, now genuinely concerned.

Penny took a deep breath and began to describe in detail the last two and a half years in her life. She decided not to pull any punches, and when she was finished the two women simply sat in silence. Penny waited for a reaction. Karen was unable to provide an immediate one. This story had the lot— murder, lies, deception, blackmail— and would take a degree of sorting out.

Karen stared, wide eyed, at her sister. She felt vitriol

rise in the back of her throat. She concentrated hard to keep it together. A decision had to be made, and she would have to make it rationally and with a clear head.

The thought had already flashed into Karen's mind to simply distance herself from the problem; deny all knowledge of the information she had just been given; throw this woman out. After all, her sister had treated her disrespectfully; had used her repeatedly all through their teenage years, from stealing Karen's boyfriends to stealing her cash. You name it, she had suffered terrible indignation.

Also, it annoyed her to think that Penny was almost able to assume that Karen would agree to help. Even after all the history that had been racked up between them.

Another one of their dead mother's plethora of sayings would be: 'blood is thicker than water.' This old adage would prove significant in making up the former Karen Richards' mind.

"Okay, Penny. I'll do as you ask. Then, I never want to see you again."

22

"Can I help you, Sir?" Leanne Edwards, solo controller at the Fast Cabs taxi office managed to ask between chomps on her chewing gum. The diminutive, pretty blonde exuded an air of innocence. She was probably about twenty-five, but could easily pass for ten years younger.

"Yes. I rang an hour ago. Asking about Bill Ferguson," DI Mason Blackwell reminded her.

"Oh, aye. I did manage to contact him. He should be in any minute. Take a seat. Would you like a coffee while you're waiting?"

"No thanks."

"Okay. I just have to go somewhere." Leanne took off down the corridor, heading straight for the outside door.

Mason saw her pull out the cigarettes and matches in readiness, the match literally sparking off the box as she crossed the threshold.

Blackwell chuckled to himself. He could not understand such an addiction— one which would take over free will.

Four long pulls on her cigarette later and the girl returned, much calmer.

"Y'sure you dinnae want a coffee? I'm having one anyway."

"Go on, then. Milk and one sugar, please," Mason replied.

She disappeared into the small kitchen area. "So what's Bill done, anyway?" the voice from the kitchen rang out.

"Just need to ask him some questions."

"He's no' the taxi rank rapist, then?" Leanne was referring to a sicko who burst onto the nightclub scene in Glasgow around five years before, raped and sodomised five girls over a five-week period, and vanished as quickly as he had appeared. Police investigations had tenuously concluded that he may be or may have been a taxi driver. Case unsolved.

"I wouldn't think so. Unless you can tell me otherwise?" Mason challenged cheekily.

"Oh, I get it. You cannae tell me because it's an ongoing investigation?" she queried, re-appearing with the coffees.

"Something like that."

"I'd make a great policewoman, y'know that? I'm nosey. You have to be nosey, don't you?" She put the coffees down and sat cross-legged on her chair, like a child, facing the cop.

"It does help." Mason now wanted the door to open and Bill Ferguson to walk in and save him from this hell. At least the coffee was good.

Blackwell heard the door open at the end of the corridor. Heavy footsteps made the ancient floorboards creak and groan. The taxi office in Glasgow's East End hadn't had much spent on it over the last ten years. The walls hadn't been painted for a while and the nicotine-stained colour scheme had been a legacy from the pre-smoking-ban era. No doubt Leanne Edwards had been one of the main protagonists.

"That'll be Billy now, Inspector. I'll go have another fag and leave you to it." She needed no encouragement to shorten her life by another few precious seconds.

Leanne passed a huge guy in the doorway, leaning back against the door to allow him to enter the room. Her neck strained to look up at his face.

"That's the inspector guy I was telling you about,

Billy. You sit. I'll bring you a cuppa in ten minutes, okay?"
"Thanks, doll," boomed the reply.
Leanne was already at the door, a hacking, blood-curdling smoker's cough accompanying her exit.
Mason Blackwell stood to greet the driver. Even he, at six-two, had to lean back to make eye contact.
Bill Ferguson was a giant of a man— at least seven feet, estimated the DI. Mason found himself wondering how much he weighed.
Must be twenty-three stone at least.
No fat. Solid muscle. Bald, apart from a band of dark hair around the back of his head.
Now in his early forties, Bill Ferguson had been a figure of fun for most of his life; a target for the bully boys; the incessant taunts and jibes about his size had unfortunately twisted and distorted his personality. The placid, reticent, gentle giant was a popular character among the other taxi drivers, and the experiences of meeting and serving the general public had proved to be a godsend for him. He very rarely encountered the negativity nowadays, and he reckoned he had found the perfect job— the one that he was most suited to. Also, a monetary bonus for the bosses at Fast Cabs would be that, due to his sheer size and intimidating stature, Bill would never lose a fare to a runner.
The big man sat facing Mason Blackwell. He gently eased himself down onto the chair, as if he were expecting to land in a heap at any time. The chair creaked slightly, but bore up under the pressure.
Mason observed him for a few seconds, both men seemingly waiting for the other to begin. Ferguson found it difficult to maintain eye contact, preferring instead to study his giant feet.
"Mister Ferguson. Thanks for coming in to meet me." Mason kicked it off.
"I'd rather you called me Bill, Sir. I get a wee bit

nervous when I get the Sunday name," the driver replied shyly; a friendly smile flashed across his big round face.

Blackwell smiled back. He found it refreshing to meet a genuinely humble individual in this world of scepticism and antipathy.

"Okay, Bill. I want to ask you about a pick up yesterday, around half past three."

"At the airport?"

"Aye. You remember him?"

"What d'you want to know, Inspector?"

"Eh, can you describe him?" Blackwell asked, a little taken aback at the man's directness, wondering what to expect.

"He was short, about five-four. Trim and fit, ten stone. Kinda mousy brown hair, cut very short. Couldn't see his eyes at first. He was wearing Rayban sunglasses. Bet they cost a packet. He took the glasses off for a second— to rub his eyes. Deep blue eyes— like the sea." Ferguson looked up to see if Metcalf was still paying attention— he was. The big guy continued, "He had a very slight scar on his right cheek, probably from a while back"— Brodie Metcalf had cut his face with a piece of broken glass, aged five. "His suit was sort of shimmery, grey, with a faint stripe through it. White shirt— brand new. Still had the faint box lines down each side of the chest. A kind of powder-blue silk tie with wee motifs on it. Shaped like an 'em'. A bit like the organisation for brainy people."

"Mensa?" Blackwell cut in. The inspector himself was a member, rated in the top half percent of the country.

"Aye, Mensa. That's it."

"Anything else you can tell me, Bill?" Mason asked, a slight smirk on his face at the depth of information he had already heard.

"The guy wore dark socks and sort of dark grey leather shoes— really good ones. Slip-on type."

Blackwell had earlier produced his little notepad and was furiously scribbling the information down. He expected the pencil to burst into flames at any time.

"How did he behave? Did he have an accent, speech impediment or anything?"

"He sounded Scottish, but he wasn't," Ferguson maintained.

"What do you mean?"

"He tried to speak in a Glasgow accent, but I could tell it was fake. Nearly there, though. Would've fooled most people, I think. The vowel sounds were a wee bit short." Ferguson went on to provide an example.

Mason Blackwell stopped writing, shaking the blood back into his fingers. He smiled ruefully at the big guy.

"Where did you take him?"

"To the Hilton. We got there about four o'clock."

"How did he pay?"

"The fare was seven pounds. He gave me a twenty. English bill, I think. I was well chuffed!"

"Don't suppose you have the note?" Mason was only too aware of the wonders of modern forensic science.

The big guy smiled, shaking his head.

"All right, Bill. You've been really helpful. If you ever feel like changing profession, give me a call. We could do with more guys like you. Attention to detail and all that."

Bill Ferguson looked at his feet again, a bit embarrassed at the compliment.

"There's just one more thing. I'd like you to go down to the station and meet our sketch artist. I think you could give us an excellent identikit picture of this guy."

"No problem." Ferguson then swallowed hard as if to summon the courage to continue. "Is this about the murder at the airport yesterday, Inspector? Some of the guys heard the victim was a policeman?"

"You'll understand I can't comment on that."

"Oh no! I know that. It's just that, well, if there's anything else I can do to help, I'd really like to. You know what I mean?"

"You've done more than enough, Bill. Here's my card. If you come up with anything else, call me. I'll just phone the station to arrange the sketch." Blackwell got up, extending his hand towards Bill Ferguson. The big guy shook surprisingly limply.

"Here's your coffee, Billy." Leanne burst into the room, stuffing the cigarettes back into her pocket with her free hand.

Blackwell's mobile phone started ringing, with DS McMenemy's name in the display.

"Mick. I was just about to phone you. Don't bother calling around the hotels. Our guy's staying at the Hilton."

"Right, Sir. I've been checking the flights in. A John Mitchell arrived at 2:50 p.m. on American Airlines from Chicago."

There was a palpable silence.

"From Chicago?" Blackwell eventually offered.

"Aye, Sir. Sir? Are you all right?"

"I'm fine, Mick. Meet me back at the station as soon as you can."

Mason thanked the taxi people and left for Pitt Street police station. His mind was doing cartwheels.

23

"Oh my God, Will! When did you last sleep? You look terrible!" A concerned Ben Vieri was standing outside Will Munro's cell door, waiting for the absent-minded policeman to return with the keys.

"I had a rough night. I think the past few days finally sunk in." Munro dragged himself to his feet, somehow conjuring up a forced smile for his best mate. He slumped forward, head against the bars, staring out.

"I think they must've, pal. Your eyes are bright red!"

"You should see them from my side!" Munro retorted. The pair laughed. "I'll live! How are Mary and the kids?"

"They're just fine, Will. I brought Mary in with me. She's upstairs in the waiting room. Leah's at ours, watching the kids."

Will visibly brightened at the mention of his wife's name.

"Thanks, Ben. What's the latest news, anyway?"

Ben was just about to reply when the policeman returned, examining closely a selection of keys he was holding. After four attempts, he managed to choose correctly, swinging the cell door open for the young lawyer to enter. Vieri waited until the policeman had locked them in and left the area before speaking.

"You know the big copper you met the first time you came in to the station— DS Watson?"

"Aye. What about him?"

"Our office got a call earlier today from one of the other law firms. Tam Watson was killed yesterday. At Glasgow Airport. Shot in the head."

"Christ! Did they catch who did it?"

"Apparently not. He must've lain in his car overnight. Some airport worker found him early this morning. Blackwell and McMenemy are investigating. They're not in the station yet, so I asked another detective to chase up your DNA report. They should have it back any time."

Will nodded in acknowledgement.

"Fuck's sake, Ben. I know Watson wasn't well liked, but..."

"Aye. Well don't feel too sorry for him. The general opinion is that the police think he might have been involved in something dodgy. If he was, it'll come out. Always does," Vieri said, philosophically. "Especially if Blackwell's sniffing around. Talk about a dog getting hold of a burst ball!"

They heard the door at the top of the stairs squeak open; the sound of heavy footwear clattered down the metal treads. The door at the bottom opened to reveal the overweight figure of Detective Constable Brian Wheldon clutching a large, buff coloured envelope and a larger paper bag full of goodies just bought from the local bakers.

"Mister Vieri. I have your client's DNA test results back. If you'll both come upstairs to the interview room, I'll explain the findings." Wheldon was waving the envelope at the pair.

"Much as we'd like to, we can't!" Vieri motioned towards the locked door.

"Ach! Where did that Muppet go? He's supposed to stay down here." The DC turned before bellowing up the staircase.

Seconds later, the 'Muppet' appeared, going through the same jangling selection procedure with the keys as before.

DC Wheldon shot him a withering look, at the same time shaking his head in embarrassment.

* * *

The three of them— Munro, Vieri and Wheldon, had just made their way upstairs and were once again standing outside Interview Room One when a familiar voice stopped them in their tracks.

"We'll be with you in ten minutes, gentlemen!" DI Mason Blackwell and DS Mick McMenemy had returned from their respective assignments.

Vieri noted that they looked hurried, under pressure.

Blackwell snatched the envelope from DC Wheldon before ushering Munro and Vieri into the room. "Thanks, Brian. I'll take it from here."

"Inspector? Will's wife is in the public room. Can she see him while we're waiting?" Ben Vieri asked.

"Aye, of course she can." Blackwell nodded at the constable to sort it out.

* * *

On the way to the station, Mason Blackwell had telephoned the assistant chief constable of Strathclyde police, George Drummond, to arrange a meeting without delay. He had decided that they would not have much time to get organised. Not if he had figured things out correctly.

Mick McMenemy had joined Drummond and Blackwell in the previously unoccupied chief constable's office in the heart of the building. Mick really felt that he had finally arrived in the big league.

The announcement of the successor to the recently retired chief constable was expected any time and it was no great secret that George Drummond was going to get the job.

Might as well try the office out for size first.

"Right, Mason. What's this all about?" Drummond was sitting rather uncomfortably behind the solid mahogany desk. A man of huge stature, he was fiddling with the height control lever at the side of the hydraulically controlled chair on which he sat, eventually arriving at an acceptable position.

"Thank you for arranging the meeting so soon, Sir." Blackwell took out his notebook and opened it, placing it on the desk in front of him. He need not have bothered. The DI's memory capacity was unrivalled.

McMenemy was about to sit in on a master class, waiting to observe the force's two top policemen at work. George Drummond had thirty years' service, all completed at Strathclyde. The big man had become almost a legend in these circles, at the same time earning every commendation and bravery award in the book.

You just don't buy this sort of opportunity, McMenemy decided, notebook at the ready.

"As you know, a few days ago, a local pusher was killed in his flat. Somebody smashed his brains in. Forensics found cocaine, heroin, marijuana— you name it. Our sources say that he worked for Vic Simpson." Blackwell's reference to the crime boss caused Drummond to make a face. Simpson had been Drummond's itch that he could never scratch, for longer than he cared to remember. "You'll not be surprised to know, Sir, that we can't prove a link between the two."

"One day, Mason. One day," Drummond said pensively. His desire to bring this man to book for his crimes still burned brightly.

"Aye, Sir. One day. Anyway, the man was identified as Lonnie Baltimore, an American from Chicago. He had a minor arrest record back there for petty drug offences. We also found out that his father, also Lonnie, is a multimillionaire. Heavily into property, or real estate, as they call it over there. The father tried everything to get the boy off the drugs, but eventually had to give up. I don't know why he ended up here. Obviously got into the wrong crowd and wound up dead for his troubles."

"All very sad, Inspector. But what has the death of another junkie got to do with the reason we're meeting today?"

"Well, Sir. We have an innocent man in custody here right now. I'd bet my life on it. I think Simpson or his sidekick, Martin Anderson, fixed it to try to pin the murder on Will Munro. They used an old girlfriend of Munro's." Mason had a quick glance at his notes to recall her name. "A Penny Richards. She gave evidence against Munro. We've tried to contact her again at the phone number and address given. She's disappeared."

"Munro was charged, Mason. Are you saying that was a mistake?"

Blackwell sighed, waited a few seconds.

"Aye. And I'll explain why, Sir. This morning, Mick and I saw the murder of Tam Watson— on closed circuit TV." Blackwell laid the CCTV still of the assassin in front of Drummond. "This man did it. Mick found out that he landed yesterday under the name of John Mitchell. He flew in from Chicago." Mason paused.

"Where the boy— what's his name— Baltimore, came from?" George Drummond, the old stager, was now on the scent.

"That's right. I think that this man is a contract killer sent by Baltimore Senior or agents acting for him. I spoke to Chicago police about Baltimore. He's definitely not whiter than white."

"Simpson knew that the old man would take

retribution, and tried to pin the murder on Munro. So this guy, Mitchell, or whatever his name is. He's here to kill Munro." The chief constable-elect and his DI were suddenly on the same wavelength. DS Mick McMenemy watched on in admiration.

"I think so, Sir. And we've searched Martin Anderson's apartment in the West End. He also seems to have disappeared; no bags packed; clothes hanging up neatly in his wardrobe; newspapers piling up on the mat. Maybe Simpson had him done for the Baltimore killing."

"Let's hope so, Mason. I've never met Anderson, but, by all accounts, he's a right nasty piece of work."

The men nodded in unison.

"The killer? Have we any idea where he is now?" Drummond asked.

"That's what I wanted to see you about, Sir. A taxi driver dropped him at the Hilton."

"Christ! You could nearly touch it from here. The cheeky bastard!" The luxury hotel was literally a five-minute walk from Strathclyde police headquarters.

"I know, Sir. And this guy worries me. It's as if he's trying to lead us there. He's bound to have known about the cameras at the airport. Surely he'd know we'd track him down."

"Have you passed these details to our friends in Chicago?" Drummond picked up the CCTV image by its corner, already knowing the answer. His policeman's instinct still forced him to ask.

"I have, Sir. Nothing to date, though."

"And what about Tam Watson?"

Blackwell shifted uncomfortably. It was not his way to condemn a fellow police officer, not least a dead one. But all the evidence pointed to dishonesty. Mason had no choice.

"Watson most likely took a payoff for providing information, maybe even the killer's target details."

"Then why would this man kill Watson?"

"Who knows? Maybe he just didn't like him! Or he'd seen his face— could identify him." Mason Blackwell, and especially Watson's work partner, Mick McMenemy, knew that the first option might not be that far from the truth.

"There's another thing to consider, Mason. Who was Watson's link to Chicago? His contact here? Who set it up?"

"I had already thought about that, Sir. And I aim to find out."

A few moments passed. McMenemy's eyes flitted between the two men.

"So what do we do now, Mason?" Drummond asked.

"First thing's first. Call Special Forces, Sir. Give them the details. We need to get this killer off the streets. And, Sir, tell them to move with great care. I have a bad feeling about this man."

"I agree. I'll attend to it now. Then what?"

"I need to see Will Munro. To make sure that he's protected. And to clear up a DNA issue. Then Mick and I will go and visit Vic Simpson. See if he knows anything about the latest whereabouts of Martin Anderson and Penny Richards. It'll be great to see the bastard squirm. And one more thing, Sir?" Blackwell asked tentatively.

"Go on, Mason."

"Well, Sir. I reckon we need to go to Chicago. I think we should speak to the police there in person. I also think we should interview Lonnie Baltimore; do some digging; find out more details about this contract. Maybe we can unearth our mole here."

George Drummond now found himself in uncharted waters— political chief constable mode, considering budgets. After a moment, he was of a mind to concede that Strathclyde police could probably afford to send a couple of officers to Chicago in the USA. For a few days, at least.

"Let's get a grip of this bastard, Mitchell, or whatever his name is, first. Then we'll see where we stand," Drummond said gruffly, lifting the phone to dial his contact at MI6.

24

"I'll leave you to it. I'll be right outside." Ben Vieri slipped the door shut, then stepped out into the street to get some air.

A burly policeman stood just inside the room, pretending not to listen.

Will Munro and his wife embraced, Mary reluctant to let go of her husband. There seemed to be no end to this nightmare for the young family.

"Everything's going to be fine, love. Ben says all the evidence they have is circumstantial. Once they clear me on the DNA evidence, then that'll be that. They'll have to let me go." Will tried so hard to reassure his wife.

She smiled bravely. "I so hope you're right, Will. I... We miss you so much. Molly's always asking when you'll be home. You know what she's like."

Will ran his fingers roughly through his hair, trying hard to hold back the tears— stay strong for the sake of the family.

"So what have you been doing the last few days?" He attempted to change the subject.

"I've kept the twins off nursery. I need them close to me right now. I..." Her voice trailed off. She tried to compose herself. "We went to see Papa in the home. Jack wanted to go. Can you believe that?"

Will's father, Lachie Munro was deep in the final throes of Alzheimer's disease. Although visiting a relative stricken with such an illness could be traumatic for an adult, the experts reckoned children tended to take such visits much more easily in their stride, especially girls. Molly Munro would chatter away happily to her grandfather, blissfully unaware that, more often than not, he wouldn't have an earthly as to who the cute little girl was.

The experts believed the phenomenon could provide excellent therapy for grown-ups facing similar situations; make them feel better about themselves; help them cope more easily.

Little Jack, however, would usually try to make an excuse not to visit. A more timid individual than his over-confident sister, the lad's root problem seemed to be borne out of a genuine fear of his previously gentle, but now unpredictable, grandfather, rather than any great emotional distress caused by the visiting process.

That said, every visit to see the old man had definitely helped the little boy come to terms with it, the latest actually proving to be a pleasant experience for all concerned.

"How was Papa?" Munro asked.

"Fine, actually. It was a good day for him." She nodded.

Will smiled. At least there was some good news today.

There was a knock on the door. It was Ben Vieri with the news that the police were ready to talk again.

The main players were back on their old stomping ground— Interview Room One.

DI Mason Blackwell, DS Mick McMenemy, Ben Vieri and Will Munro sat around the table.

Once again, police protocol was observed, the tape machine set in the middle of the little table dividing the rival factions.

Mason slipped his finger under the flap of the buff coloured envelope, pulled out a number of plain documents. He began to leaf through them. Ben's eyes narrowed. He instantly read the expression on the policeman's face. He had a bad feeling— again.

Blackwell shook his head and, in an unprecedented move, leant over and switched off the tape. McMenemy turned to stare in disbelief at his superior officer.

"Sir? What's wrong?" he asked.

"This is not right, Mick, and I don't want another word on record until I find out what's going on here! It's as if someone's one step ahead of us all the time!" Mason Blackwell slapped the papers down on the table, inviting the lawyer to interpret for himself.

Ben Vieri pounced, speed reading the pages. He stopped when he reached the relevant part.

"It's a match! A fourteen billion to one chance that the DNA markers the lab found on a cup do not belong to Will. I can't believe it!" Ben slumped back in his chair, hands behind his head, staring at the ceiling.

"What? B-but that's impossible! I swear I've never been to that place!" Munro said, horrified.

There was a pause.

"I believe you, Will," Blackwell replied. "Have you any idea where someone could get their hands on a cup with your DNA on it?"

"I don't know. Wait! The café! The Loving Cup! I went there to meet Penny! I drank some coffee!"

"That's it. She must've slipped the cup into her bag. Oh, there's definitely a stitch up here. And I know exactly who the main stitcher upper is!" Mason Blackwell would certainly be mentioning this to Vic Simpson during their next meeting.

"So what do we do now?" Will asked.

Blackwell thought for a few seconds. He glanced at Mick McMenemy, searching for some kind of sign. The DI was trying to gauge whether or not he should tell this man the rest of the story— the part where his life was probably in danger at the hands of an overseas assassin. The sergeant would give nothing away. Blackwell would have to decide alone. Eventually...

"Will. I want you to listen very carefully. And understand why it has to be this way." Blackwell leant forward, at the same time lowering his voice. He had become jumpy, paranoid even, considering the possibility of all conversations being bugged.

Munro did not reply. Blackwell certainly held his attention.

"I want to hold you officially on remand— for your own safety. And the safety of your family," Blackwell whispered.

"H-hold me? But why? What do you mean, the safety of my family?" Munro could hardly believe his ears.

"The man who killed DS Tam Watson— I assume you know of the killing yesterday?"

Vieri and Munro nodded.

"We think he's a hired assassin, sent by the family of Lonnie Baltimore to kill the murderer of his son. We discovered he had flown in from Chicago, Baltimore's home town."

Will Munro was stunned. *An assassin? What is this? The Godfather or something?*

"Let us do our jobs and catch this man. You'll be a hundred times safer in custody. And the further away you are from your family, the safer they'll be." Mason Blackwell sounded reasonable by habit.

"He's right, Will. It'd be just for a little while. Until they catch this man." Lawyer Ben Vieri could also be reasonable.

Munro ran the palms of his hands slowly over his tired face.

"Okay. But what do I tell Mary? She's expecting me home tonight. She'll be so disappointed," Munro reflected.

"Leave it to me, pal. I'll explain," Ben said.

"No. I'll do it, Ben. I owe her that much," Will replied. A strong sense of guilt would drive him.

"I'd appreciate it if you didn't go into detail, for obvious reasons. Ask your wife to take the kids to her mother's or something. For a few days, at least. Just in case," Blackwell requested.

"Unfortunately, her folks are in Australia, Inspector. I'll see how Mary wants to play it. So, eh... where do I stay for now?"

"I'll arrange for the security van to be here in the next couple of days. I'm going to sneak you on board. We'll decide at the very last minute which prison you go to. And I'll make sure you're in isolation and comfortable. How's that?"

"I appreciate your help. Thanks, Inspector."

"Don't worry. This'll be all over soon. You'll have your life back."

Mason Blackwell, ever the optimist, had spoken.

The immediate problem was the sick feeling growing in the pit of his stomach.

25

The sister of Penny Richards would reluctantly leave her house that morning. Her husband had left for work as normal and, as she readied the kids for the trip to nursery, she began to regret her promise to help Penny in her seemingly desperate hour of need.

The former Karen Richards unclipped her purse, before pulling out and unfolding a piece of paper with her instructions clearly marked. Reading the note for the zillionth time, her breathing quickened, keeping pace with her heart.

Come on. Pull yourself together girl. I mean, what could possibly happen? You have one simple task to do.

She clipped the children into their car seats and set off the mile and a half to nursery.

Holding the note in front of her, Karen tapped the address into her car's satellite navigation system. A few seconds later, the display read three point eight miles to the destination with an arrival time of 9:15 a.m., in ten minutes' time. She smiled bravely at her cherubs' faces in the window of the Tweenies room, giving them a final wave, and headed for the East End of Glasgow.

Minutes later, Karen pulled up outside a row of industrial units on Arrol Place, in the shadow of Celtic Park. The last one in the row, Number 7— her destination— seemed to be banged up, its roller-shutter door firmly closed and padlocked. The only sign of life was a gleaming, new, silver Audi, parked by the main office door. The registration number was 8IG T4M— Big Tam. She checked the name at the head of the instructions— Thomas Mulraney.

Satisfied that she had arrived at the correct address, she walked up to the door, quickly pressing the intercom system's buzzer before she changed her mind and chickened out.

"Who's there?" Karen's stomach lurched with nerves at the man's aggressive tone.

"My... My name's Karen Richards. I'm here on behalf of my sister, Penny."

There was a momentary silence.

"Oh aye. She said you'd be here. Have you got it?"

She took in a sharp breath, only relaxing when she felt the package that Penny had left with her in her coat pocket.

"Y-yes. I have the package."

"Okay. You'd better come in."

The entry buzzer gave her a start. Truthfully, at that moment, a fly farting in the hills would have spooked her.

Karen pushed open the metal door into the unit. The strong retainer spring initially resisted, finally allowing the door to slam shut behind her. She was aware of the fresh smell of pine filtering into her nostrils. The déjà vu moment instantly reminded her of primary school and the aroma from the floor gel that every cleaner, bar none, seemed to prefer in those days. A bright yellow 'wet floor' sign sat in the middle of the reception, streaks of dampness from a mop still evident on the vinyl surface.

"Morning!" the cleaner said cheerfully, emerging from a side office. She began to pull on her coat, heading for the exit door and her next job.

"Oh, eh... Morning," Karen replied, almost as pleasantly. She started to feel more at ease. Perhaps this wouldn't turn out as badly as she had first feared.

"Up here!" a voice from upstairs commanded.

She nodded, peering up at the man through a blur caused by the harsh strip lighting in the unit ceiling. Karen carefully climbed the metal staircase to a small office on the first floor of an internal block.

As she reached the top, she couldn't help but look down at the area below. She immediately noticed how neat and tidy the warehouse section of the unit was. Then, she realised that it was only neat and tidy because it was almost empty. Apart from a few workbenches, tables and sets of racking, this works unit had no stock, no warehousemen.

Wonder what it is they do here apart from loan sharking?

The door of the office was wide to the wall and Karen hesitated slightly before entering. Her instincts screamed at her to turn and run, but she had given her sister her word that she would help. She intended to keep her end of the bargain. Penny had got herself into serious money trouble once again and needed help. End of story.

"I... I'm here on behalf of my sister." Karen attempted to open proceedings.

"Sit, over there!" Thomas Mulraney barked, cutting her off. He was standing behind his desk.

Karen's mind flashed back to the Audi registration plate— 8IG T4M— Big Tam. Mulraney, standing tall at around five-four, she deduced that Big Tam must surely relate to something else. Bizarrely, she found herself trying to suppress a smile.

She didn't answer, turned to sit on a small padded chair at the other side of the desk. Sensing a presence at her shoulder, Karen shook with fright as she realised that there was another man in the room, in the corner. She turned around, nodding bravely at him. The man simply stared right through her, expressionless. She felt distinct palpitations in her chest, a little nauseous.

Karen turned back to face Mulraney. Charged full of nervous energy, she burst into a rehearsed spiel.

"As I said, I'm here on behalf of my sister, Penny, who was, in my opinion, too embarrassed to come down and speak to you herself."

A puzzled look flew across the chiselled features of Thomas Mulraney. He exchanged glances with his colleague.

"What?" he replied, his face contorting.

"I've some of the money here. In… In this padded bag," she babbled, producing the bag from her sweaty hand. "She asked if you could count it out and give me a receipt for her. She swears she'll pay the rest off very soon. Those were her exact words. She said you'd get it very soon." Karen repeated the message carefully and concisely.

"What the fuck are you talkin' about? Gimme that bag!" He snatched the little parcel from her outstretched hand.

By this time, Karen's heart was thumping a message throughout her whole body. She suddenly felt faint as he tore open the bag. "What the…?" Mulraney pulled out the contents, laying them down on the desk in front of him.

Karen froze as the other man stood. She felt him slide past, standing at his boss' shoulder as he read a short, typewritten note. Thomas Mulraney reached the end, immediately returning to the beginning in case his eyes were deceiving him. They weren't.

"Fuckin' cow!" Mulraney hissed.

Both men looked up from the note at the same time, as if waiting for an explanation. Karen Richards would not be able to supply one. Tears welled in her eyes. She sat, unable to speak.

"Right, I'm only gonnae ask this once. Where's the heroin?" Mulraney demanded, menacingly.

"What? Heroin? I… I don't know what you mean. I… There should be money. In… In the package. Part of the loan she still owes you?"

"You really dinnae get it, do you? Your sister's got a contract out on her. This man here." He jerked his thumb at his colleague. "He's gonnae take care o' it."

"I... I don't understand. A contract? You mean...?"

"Aye. That's right. She's dead meat. Just a matter o' time."

"But, the money..."

"Money? What money?" Mulraney tossed the package full of pieces of scrap paper into her lap. "Looks like you've been turned over an a'. She was gonnae buy out the contract. Said she knew people. Fifty grand o' heroin to make it go away. That's what you were supposed to be bringin' me."

Karen desperately fumbled with the package, her futile attempts at conjuring up bank notes doomed to failure. She threw the bundle on the floor in frustration.

Karen's mind went sharply back to the last conversation she had had with her sister. She began to think that the story she had been told— murder, lies, deception and blackmail— had been bordering on fantasy. Her whole body started to shake with fear. What had this loving wife and mother got herself into? Why? Her own sister!

Karen slipped automatically into survival mode. "I... I can get the money. I just need a few days. I..." she rambled incoherently.

"It's too late for that. We intend to honour Vic Simpson's contract. Tie up some loose ends. That'll be the end o' it." Mulraney nodded at his killer for hire, Sean Patrick McGlinchy, ex-IRA, hater of all things British.

"Oh no! Please! I won't tell anyone! Please!"

The former Karen Richards' cries reverberated through the cold empty unit. Seconds later, there was an eerie silence.

* * *

"Let's clear up. We've a shipment o' goods booked for later. Open the shutters and bring her motor in, will you?" Thomas Mulraney asked Sean McGlinchy.

The air intake system in the unit pushed Penny Richard's note from the desk onto the floor of the office, face up. It read:

FAO Thomas Mulraney:

We all have to make sacrifices in this life. Please be gentle with my sister.
And be aware, you will be made to pay for your sins. Very, very soon.

A few minutes later, the trussed up body of Leah Vieri, the former Karen Richards, was unceremoniously dumped in the boot of her black Saab 93. During proceedings, McGlinchy spotted her handbag lying in the foot well on the passenger side.

"Tom! I've found a handbag here, so I have!" he said in a heavy Irish brogue.

"Throw it in the boot!" Mulraney commanded.

McGlinchy popped the boot before grasping the bag from the foot well. He hesitated when he felt the bulky contents. He couldn't bring himself to pass up an opportunity to pick up some extra cash. Subconsciously, basic IRA survival training kicked in. Making sure that his boss was otherwise engaged— Mulraney had taken a business call— McGlinchy rifled through the bag, pocketing a black leather purse which he was certain was full of cash. He would check it out when he was alone.

* * *

Later, Sean McGlinchy prepared to jump into the Saab. Unfortunately for the Irishman and unbeknown to him, Leah Vieri's purse also jumped— straight out of his back pocket onto the unit floor.

The car and its contents were then bound for Thomas Mulraney's other business— a scrap metal dealership— and a date with the crusher.

26

"He's on the seventh floor. Room 733. The desk clerk said he checked in late yesterday afternoon. He hasn't been seen since by anyone." The armed agent had scurried in and out of the reception area at the Hilton Hotel near the centre of Glasgow, unwittingly causing mini panic among both staff and guests. He was relaying the message by radio, before darting down to the underground car park of the hotel and joining the rest of the task force.

The people in the hotel lobby had done exactly what they had been asked to do, albeit in a frantic sort of way, shoehorning three at a time out of the fire escape exit at the back of the hotel. Last seen, they were legging it like massed hordes towards the city centre and safety.

It's amazing what the sight of a real gun will do, Special Agent Tim Fullerton pondered.

Satisfied that everyone in the vicinity had cleared, Fullerton led his men up the back stairwell.

The elite squad of six had been mobilised at a moment's notice following the call from Assistant Chief Constable George Drummond of Strathclyde police force.

Dressed all in black, army issue combat gear and armed with Heckler and Koch MP5 Carbine rifles and Remington pump-action shotguns, this team was ready to take on all comers. Fullerton had taken on board the warning passed on by George Drummond requesting the team to exercise special care.

150

"Wait," Fullerton hissed, holding his arm across the next man's chest. He held up his free hand, stopping the rest of the team, and pointed upwards at the next level.

The other five stood stock still, allowing the leader to ghost around the railing leading to the next level. He peered up the stairs, a vision in raw concentration, ready for anything; his finger tightened on the trigger of the MP5.

"D-don't shoot!" a tentative voice from above broke the silence.

Fullerton raised his rifle in readiness, only easing back when he caught sight of the imminent 'threat'.

A short, stooped, bespectacled grey-haired man of around sixty stood right in the line of fire. He wore black trousers and safety boots; his dark blue pullover bore the name 'Initial'. The man was holding a small, yellow socket mop; the accompanying, half-filled bucket of water lay at his feet. The look of terror on his face was plain to see.

Tim Fullerton lowered his gun, instantly recognising the logo as belonging to the huge industrial cleaning company. His mother, widowed at a young age, had worn similar clothing during her lonely struggle to bring up her only son on her own.

Fullerton stayed silent, waving the man down the stairs. He did not need to be asked again, dunking the mop into the water, before lifting the bucket. The team gave way as he thundered down the steps, nodding passively at each one on the way past. A trail of soapy water accompanied his descent.

"Let's go," Fullerton whispered to his soldiers, pointing upwards. "Stay alert."

The squad effortlessly climbed the steps until they reached a slightly faded '7' etched on the wall next to a door leading to the rooms on that floor.

Fullerton stood at the entrance, waving the others past him, one at a time. The team exploded into the communal area, hugging the wall at one side, slipping silently towards Room 733.

A door slowly creaked open along the corridor; the occupant stepped out among the soldiers. A gloved hand swiftly covered the woman's mouth before she could scream; the soldier guided her gently back into her room. He put his forefinger to his lips, only releasing his grip on her mouth, when he was satisfied that she understood his wishes. She nodded, terrified, tears beginning to well up.

"Stay here. Don't leave your room. You'll be fine. Okay?" he whispered, almost as if he cared.

She nodded again. He clicked the door shut behind him, leaving her whimpering in the corner of the room.

Seconds later, the team had arrived at 733, preparing to storm the room. They lined up two at each side, one in front, Number Six wielding the battering ram.

The splintered door was smashed against the wall, the elite team immediately swarming the apartment, to a man screaming at the top of their voices in an attempt to disconcert the enemy. Even for such experienced and highly skilled soldiers, the moment they entered an unsecured room— stepped into the unknown— was the most crucial— the time when they were most at risk.

After about a minute or so, the elite squad had hit every room, every cupboard, under beds— the lot. It was clear that John Mitchell was not at home. The team was empty handed, but secretly relieved. At least everyone was still alive.

Tim Fullerton was immediately on the phone to George Drummond, suggesting that he let the hounds loose. The policeman now had an assassin at large in his town.

Tim took off his skip cap, wiping the gathering sweat from his forehead. He replaced his mobile phone in the little mobile phone pocket in his padded vest and sat on a soft chair, staring out at the beautiful spring sky developing over

Glasgow.

A tiny, flashing red light caught Fullerton's eye. The device was stuck to the wall next to the window. Tim's heart stopped dead. Almost frozen to the spot, he slowly scanned the room, stopping when he spotted the identical twin blinking away on the wall at the other side. Amazingly, the grand entrance of the team had somehow not managed to break the electronic beam coursing between the 'twins'.

"Sir, maybe we can spot him down on the street." The well-meaning soldier lurched towards the picture window.

"*Noooooo!*"

* * *

The blast almost took out the whole of Floor 7, the incendiary device apparently much larger than it needed to be— as if some people required to be taught a deadly lesson.

Hundreds and thousands of glass shards showered the area around the hotel, their trajectory taking most of them all the way onto the adjacent Kingston Bridge, the busiest in Europe.

Cars, trucks and vans slewed across the lanes, shunting and bumping, their tyres tearing to shreds among the razor-sharp glass. Steering wheels were violently ripped from their drivers' grasps, the uncontrollable projectiles playing deadly games of pinball with each other.

A lorry carrying huge concrete pillars began to broadside across the lanes, its air brakes hissing furiously. The hulk finally came to a halt, teetering on the edge of the bridge, the cab nodding ominously at the River Clyde below.

The driver just managed to leap to safety as the juggernaut finally launched over the side and into the water like a giant torpedo, vanishing below the surface in seconds.

Huge billows of smoke spiralled into the sky from Floor 7. Localised fires had already broken out at various positions on the floor, crawling and licking up towards Floor 8; the gentle breeze cruelly exacerbated their intensity.

In the distance, the first stirrings of the fire engines could be heard, as they started their short journey from the station in nearby West Nile Street.

Safely down on the street, the old cleaner from the stairwell was calmly depositing stuff in the hotel wheelie bin— a grey wig, glasses, latex wrinkles, blue 'Initial' pullover— etcetera, etcetera.

Brodie Metcalf smiled broadly as he picked up his bag of tricks, planted earlier inside a wicker basket in the surprisingly unsupervised laundry room at the Hilton.

I think I'm going to like it here, he mused, merging into the gathering crowd.

27

"Who's at the door, Vic?" Rena Simpson had earlier heard the door chimes grinding out a tacky, annoying version of the Dallas signature tune.

Blackwell and McMenemy stood outside the gates at Southfork, near Clydebank, smirking at each other when they heard the rousing strains filtering through the intercom system.

"Fucking answer it and you'll see, Rena!" Vic Simpson shouted to his 'beloved' wife from the upstairs room, which he had recently had converted into a sauna.

Simpson had read somewhere about the adverse effects of obesity on the Scottish population. The article had highlighted his overweight age group as being five times more likely to suffer heart disease. Given his appalling health record to date, Vic allowed himself a less than even chance of surviving another ten years on his present heading. Lately, fish and chips and greasy lunchtime pies had given way to salads and pasta dishes. Beers and spirits had been replaced almost exclusively by fruit juices and diet drinks.

The only downside of the exercise was the increasingly paranoid suspicions of Rena Simpson when it came to her husband's extramarital activities. She had convinced herself that the only reason for his change of health regime was because of his insatiable need to still be fancied by the ladies. This contributed greatly to Rena becoming even

155

more of a miserable cow than normal. Vic Simpson, serial cheater, had already weighed up the pros and cons of the exercise. If this was a parliamentary vote, the pros would have it.

Obviously, still a bit to go on the diet, Simpson had thrown on a tacky, gold-coloured bathrobe, recently purchased to form part of his new look. The garment looked ridiculous, stretched across his bloated body. Sweating and blustering, Vic waddled past his dear wife who was lying like a beached whale on the lounge sofa, munching chocolates. He muttered something about fat lazy cow, carefully out of earshot.

The CCTV monitor just inside the door displayed images of the two policemen to piss him off even further.

"Fucking hell! What do they want?" he moaned.

"Who?" Rena asked again. "Who's there, Vic?"

"Just eat your fuckin' chocolates, Rena!" Simpson was already halfway down the drive, heading for the front gates.

The slight breeze managed to blow up the front of the gold robe, giving the cops an unwanted eyeful of the gangster's sweaty body.

"Jesus, Mick. Glad we haven't had our dinner yet. I'd have struggled to keep it down!" Mason Blackwell whispered in his colleague's ear.

McMenemy had to turn away, unable to keep a straight face.

"And what can I do for you this fine day, Inspector?" the crook asked in his most pleasant voice. He was, by now, standing at the other side of the gate.

"This is Detective Sergeant McMenemy, Mister Simpson. We'd like to come in and ask you a few questions."

"I've already told you all I know, Inspector. I don't see how I can help you."

"There have been some developments since we last

spoke. Maybe you can fill in some of the blanks?" Mason was not about to give up easily.

The pleasant smile left Simpson's face, replaced by what seemed to be a look of growing hatred. The crafty policeman tended to get that a lot from the criminal fraternity.

Vic opened a little security flap on the stone pillar supporting one of the heavy iron gates. He made sure to stand between the device and the two cops when he punched a four-digit code into the keypad. He certainly did not want that information bandied about. All cops were bent cops as far as he was concerned, and he reckoned his rivals in the crime world might just pay a right few quid for that code. Maybe he should change it again, just in case.

The gates opened up, allowing the pair to enter.

"Er, not the house. Let's go in here." Simpson led them to a small, secluded summer house at the bottom of the garden, some fifty yards from the main house. He pushed the door open, clawing away a couple of cobwebs from the standard, and invited them to sit on some cane furniture— the sort you might find in conservatories belonging to the world and it's wife.

Mason Blackwell smiled. He had recently had a conservatory built, resisting the temptation to order the obligatory cane furniture. He congratulated himself on his wise choice, at the same time squirming uncomfortably in the bamboo chair.

"Right, gentlemen. Can we make this quick? I really have a lot to do today," Simpson said, rather impatiently.

McMenemy glanced at his boss. That sort of statement delivered to DI Mason Blackwell would usually be treated as per the proverbial red rag to a bull.

Expect steam from the nostrils any minute. Mason's eyes narrowed.

"I'm sorry, Vic. I should have realised that your daily

shenanigans were much more important than people's lives." Blackwell could barely bring himself to look at the fat bastard.

"I suppose I could spare a few minutes," Simpson conceded, quickly realising that he had riled the cop.

"That's very big of you, Vic. Appreciate it," Mason said dryly.

Mick McMenemy somehow suppressed his laughter. "You'll remember at our last meeting that I was investigating the killing of a Lonnie Baltimore?"

"Aye. And I told you I'd never heard of him."

"That's right. So you did. And that's what I think is strange because, since I last spoke to you, everyone else involved in this case has bailed out. I can't seem to get a hold of Martin Anderson. It's like he's vanished. The girl, too— Penny Richards. She's disappeared as well." The cops watched for the reaction.

Simpson stared them out, as if thinking through his answer.

"Martin no longer works for me, Inspector. I paid him off. Didn't really need him anymore. Y'know, the credit crunch and all that."

"Really, Vic? After all these years' faithful service? Bet he didn't see that one coming."

"We parted on good terms. I made sure he got a good severance package. It was the least I could do. Felt terrible, you know. He said he was going to take a break before he figured out what he wanted to do next."

"How convenient. Don't suppose he told you where he was going?"

"No. Sorry, Inspector. And I didn't even think to ask."

"And why would you, Vic?" Mason asked with more than a hint of sarcasm.

"Oh, I did tell him you wanted to speak to him but, eh... Well, he's a big boy. He can make his own decisions."

The mobster sneered.

"He didn't mention Penny, did he?"

"Who?"

"Penny Richards. The girl who says she saw Anderson kill Baltimore. The one who's mysteriously vanished like a seal in a shark pool."

"Don't know this girl, Inspector. Never heard of her. She does sound as if she's out to make a name for herself, though," Vic stated, completely off the cuff.

"What do you mean?"

"Well, it seems to me as if maybe she was an ex-girlfriend. Or maybe one of those neurotic groupies from the nightclub who he's shagged and discarded. He was... He is a good-looking boy, Inspector." Simpson shrugged.

Blackwell and McMenemy had both picked up on the reference to the past tense.

"You know, Vic? When something doesn't quite fit with me, I get a sort of funny feeling right about here." Mason tapped in the region of his solar plexus. "Right now, I have raging heartburn. Now, I don't know if we'd have to hire a medium to talk to this pair, but I'll tell you one thing— if they're out there, you'd better hope that I don't find them. If I discover that you've been telling me a bunch of porkies, I'll make sure that your flabby arse gets put away for a long, long time. We'll see you soon, no doubt." Mason Blackwell stood to leave.

Vic Simpson just sat there, mouth firmly shut. Clearly, this was not the time for backchat.

Blackwell had laid it on a bit thicker than he would have preferred due to his deep dislike of this man and all that he stood for. But he knew one thing— he certainly felt a whole lot better.

The two policemen left without another word. Climbing into their car, Mason Blackwell eventually piped up.

"I've a good mind to organise search warrants for all of

that bastard's operations. I'm certain we'd find something linking him to the killing."

"I agree, Sir, but we tried that before. Remember? Never even got past first base. No evidence to support such an action, they said," McMenemy reflected.

"Aye. You're right, Mick," Mason conceded. "So here's what we'll do instead. I want you to organise forty-eight-hour surveillance on Simpson. Split the shifts with another couple of officers. If either Anderson or Richards is still alive, he'll be desperate to find them before we do— shut them up. I reckon he'll be panicked into making a mistake, and, when he does— we'll have 'im."

"Aye, Sir. I'll get on it right away. And, Sir? What about Will Munro?"

"I know. I hadn't forgotten. Think we'll leave him where he is right now. If he's not safe in a police station, what chance has any of us got?"

McMenemy agreed.

Blackwell's mobile phone kicked off, signifying the acceptance of a new voice message to his phone memory.

It was Assistant Chief Constable George Drummond reporting the events surrounding the Special Forces team's storming of the Hilton Hotel:

Six Special Forces operatives: four killed; two missing— presumed dead.
Fourteen hotel guests and three staff— killed.
Six drivers— injured: five minor; one suffering a serious heart attack.

And, just for good measure, MI6 agents had arrived on the doorstep at HQ. It was to be double shifts for all that day.

Mason gently rubbed his temples. He had a feeling that the migraine was about to return with a vengeance.

28

"Can I help you, Sir?" the desk sergeant called across the large reception area at HQ.

A tall, dark-haired man was standing at the main window, his back to the desk, staring out into the street. He looked kind of stooped over, hands in his pockets. "Sir, can I help you?" the policeman tried again, raising his voice slightly.

"I hope so," was the reply. The man turned around to face the desk.

Sergeant Evan Walker immediately recognised him, having had to sign him in on his last three or four visits to HQ.

"Mister Vieri? Are you all right, Sir? What brings you in today?" Walker's voice held a trace of concern. He had detected a real sense of despondency in the face of the young lawyer. In truth, Ben Vieri looked as if he hadn't slept for a week. Pasty faced, eyes sunken and unshaven, he had definitely seen better days.

"Could be better. Is Inspector Blackwell in?" he asked, trying desperately to brighten a little.

"No, Sir. He's out on a case. Can anyone else help?"

"DS McMenemy?"

"Sorry, Sir. He hasn't checked in yet, either. Maybe one of the other detectives can help you?"

Ben thought for a couple of seconds, then nodded.

161

*   *   *

Sergeant Walker appeared at the side door leading to the interview rooms and led Ben Vieri into seclusion in a room at the end.

Two minutes later, a young, fresh-faced cop breezed in beside him, notebook in hand.

"I'm Detective Constable O'Reilly, Sir. Can I take your name?"

"Benjamin Vieri." He spelt out each letter of the surname, a common procedure for an Italian-slash-Scotsman living in Scotland.

"And how can we help you, Mister Vieri?" O'Reilly, fresh out of Interview Training Techniques and Procedures, had a huge grin planted on his face.

"I've come in to report a missing person," Ben replied sadly.

The young constable tried, but failed, to disguise his excitement.

My first case— a missing person. What are the odds?

Eagerly, he proceeded. He tried to remember the relevant sections of the manual. 'Establish facts. Gather information. Empathise'.

"I'm sorry to hear that, Mister Vieri. What's the full name of the missing person?" the constable responded rather clumsily.

"Leah Vieri. She's my wife."

Ben Vieri continued to provide the mundane details. O'Reilly filled in the boxes until it came to the 'notes' section. This was the part where, on the courses, the trainers would encourage the candidates to really develop their interviewing techniques; to gather as much relevant information as they could.

'It would make the investigative process much easier and a whole lot more potent', they would bleat.

"What state of mind was Mrs. Vieri in prior to her disappearance? Did you notice if she was depressed or anxious about anything?"

"Leah was fine. Same as always."

"Okay. Had she been acting strangely or out of character in the days or weeks before?"

"No. Not that I could see."

"Had she had any... er... disagreements or arguments with anybody? Was she short with anyone? The children, for example?"

"No. Where the hell is this going, anyway?" Ben demanded. The young policeman was now clearly annoying him.

"Did the two of you have a fight recently?" O'Reilly carried on, undeterred.

"Absolutely not!"

"A slight difference of opinion, maybe? Anything that may cause her to run away?"

"No."

"Have you ever been violent towards your wife, Mister Vieri?"

"I have never laid a finger on my wife, Constable. We have a normal, loving relationship. End of story," Ben Vieri hissed through clenched teeth.

"I'm sorry, Sir, but you must understand that I need to establish as many valid facts about your wife as I can. That includes her relationship with you." O'Reilly quoted the manual.

Vieri preferred to nod instead of responding verbally. The policeman smiled again and continued. Ben looked as if he wanted to punch the smile from his face.

"How long have you known your wife, Sir?"

"Four and a half years."

"What's her relationship with her parents, siblings?"

"Her father was killed in an accident when she was

really small. Her mother died a couple of years before I met her. She has no brothers or sisters."

"Then she has no immediate family close by?" O'Reilly, running out of space, flipped the form and began to scribble on the other side.

"That would be right," Ben replied, bordering on the sarcastic.

"Does she have any close friends, girlfriends, anyone she might just take off and visit? Y'know, spur of the moment type of thing?"

"She has a few friends. Only one particularly close, though."

"What's the name of this friend, Sir?"

"Mary Munro."

"And how long has she known Mary?"

"A couple of years. Our kids are the same age, go to the same nursery school. Will, her husband, is also my best friend."

DC O'Reilly continued to log the details. He paused to shake the feeling back into his hand, flashing the lawyer another forced smile. Vieri felt the hackles rise.

"Okay, Sir. Could she have gone to stay the night at Mary's? Maybe something bothering her? Anything? Maybe even something she's done that she thinks may upset you or make you angry with her?"

"Constable O'Reilly. My wife dropped my kids at nursery school at nine o'clock yesterday morning. She was supposed to pick them up again at eleven-thirty. She didn't turn up. The school then contacted me. I went down to pick up the kids. Took them home. Since then, I've called her mobile phone a million times. I've called all of her friends, asked them to phone me right away if they hear from her. Nothing. This just isn't her. There's something far wrong."

Ben's voice began to crack.

"All right, Sir. I'll have to process this information." O'Reilly closed his notebook before continuing, "To let you understand, we get so many of these cases... er... incidences of people seemingly disappearing out of the blue. In the vast majority of circumstances they return home very soon, especially in the first two or three days. Now Mrs. Vieri has only been gone twenty-four hours. It's still very early days. The chances are she'll turn up safe and well before you know it." He was obviously getting the hang of the concept of 'tact and diplomacy'. "Is there anything else you can tell me before I put this through the system, Sir?"

"Well, there is one thing, Constable. Over the last few days, I've been representing Will Munro in a recent case. In fact, the enquiries are being carried out right here. Briefly, he's been wrongly accused of murder. As you can imagine, the strain on his wife has been huge. She seems to be bearing up pretty well, though."

"Will Munro's wife being Mary, your wife's best friend?" O'Reilly confirmed.

"That's right."

"That could be your answer, Mister Vieri." The young cop believed that he was onto something. "Your wife could be taking a lot of the strain on her shoulders. Especially if she and Mary are as close as you say. She probably just felt that she had to get away for a little while. Take the pressure off. The human mind works in curious ways, y'know, Sir?"

Ben Vieri's handsome face twisted at the last statement. After all, his particular profession was all about mind games and the pantomime of the trial process.

"Maybe you're right, Constable. If you need any more information about Will Munro, the policemen in charge of the case are DI Blackwell and DS McMenemy." Ben Vieri stood to shake the young cop's hand. "You will let me know if you hear anything?"

"Don't worry, Sir. I'm sure your wife will be home soon." DC O'Reilly escorted Vieri to the front door, uttering the immortal line, "We'll be in touch."

Then, he was off to share the news with his peers about his first case as detective constable.

'This is not a straightforward case', he would proudly tell them. 'This is a case with side issues'.

Never a truer word, some might say.

29

"What are you doing, Vic?" Rena Simpson sensed a movement in the hall of the house.

The longsuffering gangster's wife had progressed past the chocolate stage, and was now eyeing a packet of marshmallows, purchased earlier from the local corner shop. The marshmallows hadn't yet seen the inside of a cupboard. It looked increasingly likely that they never would. Willpower was a thing of the past for this woman as she hastily tore open the bag.

Rena and Vic had been married for close on forty years; the first ten or so the happiest, the middle twenty, so-so. The last ten had been a living hell for Rena, her increasing weight brought on mostly by comfort eating, caused by the many illicit affairs of her rat-bag of a husband. She had not been able to go out regularly in the community for many years, deeply ashamed of the way she looked; mortified at the manner in which Vic would speak to her if they did happen to venture anywhere.

Yes, Victor Simpson had contaminated the life of this woman in much the same way as he had wrecked the lives of so many young drug addicts and their families over the years.

"I'm looking out of the window, Rena. Is that a fuckin' crime?" Simpson snapped. He had spotted a blue Ford Mondeo parked across the road. Vic could clock a cop car a mile away. He had seen enough of them during his many years on the dark side. He afforded himself a wry smile.

Who are they kidding? They can't catch me; I'm the gingerbread man.

Simpson chuckled under his breath. His smile faded somewhat as he began to consider the possibility that the filth would soon catch up with that bitch, Penny Richards. *Especially if that bastard copper, Blackwell, has anything to do with it,* he mused.

Simpson was genuinely worried about the potentially calamitous effect that Penny might have on his business. He was not exactly sure how much Martin Anderson had let slip to her during their short time together— a question to which he would never find out the answer. Unless, of course, he happened to come across the girl before the police caught up with her. Then again, he hadn't exactly planned to engage her in any kind of deep, meaningful conversation.

Vic Simpson had spent the last few days calling in favours from some of his underworld cronies. Deep down, he was confident that they would soon put the matter to bed. Penny Richards would be dead and he could again relax into his life of crime.

"I'm just going out for a wee while— check on the pub. I'll see you in a bit." Vic actually spoke pleasantly to his wife for a change.

Maybe she was in shock or something, but she decided not to reply. Simpson checked his new shirt and slacks in the full-length mirror in the hall— maybe he would get lucky tonight— and slipped out of the back door, glancing around the corner at his guardian angels. Two rather fed-up looking cops sat slumped in their seats.

"Fuck!" Vic hissed. The infrared sensor light should have illuminated by the time he hit the small footpath at the back of the house. It hadn't. "That's the fucking third time this month. They don't make these bulbs the way they used to." He made a mental note to give the spark who had advised him to get the thing installed a right rollicking in the morning. He stumbled along the path, appearing to catch every raised slab with the soles of his shoes.

Simpson was winding up for a major rant when he realised that he had to keep it down for fear of alerting his stakeout buddies.

Another couple of steps later and down he went— right on to the knees of the brand new ivory trousers.

"In the name of Christ!" He didn't care now. He was about to let rip when he became aware of a ghostly shadow standing a few yards in front of him. "Who's there?" Vic was peering into the gloom, hands shielding his eyes from the glare of a solitary lamp out in the street. He was unable to identify the stranger.

The figure took a couple of tentative steps towards the still-kneeling Simpson. Vic's eyes widened when he realised that a random ray of moonlight was glancing off the wide blade of a machete.

* 	* 	*

The back door of the house opened slowly, deliberately.

"Vic? Is that you?" The light was off in the hall. Rena Simpson opened the lounge door, fumbling to find the switch to turn on the hall light. "Vic? Are you there?"

The hundred watt bulb lit up the hall and part of the way into the spacious lounge towards the front of the house. It also highlighted the shadowy presence of a visitor— a visitor whom Rena did not recognise. Blood— lots of it— dripped from the end of the machete.

Rena Simpson closed her eyes in simple resignation.

30

"I saw the report on the news— about the woman who disappeared?" The little silver-haired lady stood at the desk at police HQ reception, trying her utmost to muster her best posh voice.

Maisie Rodgers, coat buttoned to the neck, clutched her handbag to her chest. She came from a part of Glasgow, where a popular saying about the locals was that 'they would take the sugar oot yer tea'.

Anything she had, she certainly was going to make sure she was hanging onto. That said, Maisie had found a purse full of credit cards, childrens' photographs, and probably more cash than she could earn in six months.

The woman was old school, brought up firmly believing that if one chose to yield to temptation, one would endure a lifetime of bad luck. In this case, there would be no question of Maisie Rodgers pocketing this lady's purse.

Sergeant Evan Walker was new on the dayshift desk, but immediately realised to which case this woman was referring.

"Please, follow me, love." He gently took Maisie by the arm and led her into the same private room that Ben Vieri had occupied the previous day. "Have a seat there, love. Can I get you a cup of tea or something?"

"That would be lovely. Thank you, son. It's milk and four sugars, please," Maisie replied.

The sergeant raised an eyebrow. A lifetime spent

scratching and fighting for scraps would always result in the old woman seizing every opportunity that might come her way. Similarly, the offer of a chocolate biscuit from a barrel might see her clutch a handful, at the same time filling pockets with her other hand. If anyone happened to be giving away a pair of ladies' shoes, Maisie would excitedly list her shoe size as four, five, six and seven, keeping most of her options open.

Sergeant Walker returned with the tea. Maisie relaxed her grip on the bag long enough to start drinking it. Five minutes later, DC Jock O'Reilly entered the room, notebook in hand, seemingly now complete with an eternally forced smile.

"Hello there. I'm Detective Constable John O'Reilly," he said warmly, extending a hand.

The woman quickly shook it, her hand snapping back to the bag.

"Sergeant Walker told me you may have some information for us on the missing woman?" He nodded at her as if she were a child, before continuing, still smiling, "What I'm going to do is ask you a few questions. I'll just jot down some notes at the same time, if that's all right?" O'Reilly asked. He was getting the hang of this business.

Maisie Rodgers nodded.

"Right. We might as well start with your full name."

"Maybelline Euphemia Rodgers." She accentuated every syllable. "People call me Maisie," she said pleasantly.

O'Reilly was still smiling. "Date of birth... er... Maisie?"

"Fourteenth of January, 1941."

"Okay, that would make you... sixty-eight? Is that right?"

She nodded, frowning at his obvious lack of sensitivity.

O'Reilly roughly cleared his throat, quickly moving on.

He made a mental note never to state the obvious when it came to asking a lady her age. "Address?"

"194 Old Shettleston Road. It's Flat 1."

"Married?"

"Yes."

"Husband's name?"

"Jimmy. They call him Jolly... Jolly Rodgers." She giggled.

"Occupation?" O'Reilly continued, still smiling.

"Cleaner."

"Place of work?"

"I have three jobs. For three different companies."

"All right. I should've just enough room in the box to list them. Please?" He encouraged her to continue.

"Well. There's the accountants at West George Street. Number 197, I think. That's for a cleaning company called Blitz Group. They're based in Muirhead, near Glasgow. Then, there's a little hairdresser's shop I do for cash in han... I mean for the owner." Maisie cringed when she realised where she was. Her heart quickened at the thought of the Serious Fraud Squad hammering down the door of the shop. She needn't have worried. Jock O'Reilly had bigger fish to fry. "The shop's in Pollokshaws Road, Number 51."

"Okay Maisie. And the third premises?"

"It's a works unit at Arrol Place, near Parkhead. D'you know where I mean?" she asked.

"Aye, I do. It's more or less across the road from the football ground. Celtic, is it?"

"Aye, or 'Hell on Earth', as Jolly calls it!" She chuckled before breaking into a raspy, smoking-fuelled cough.

He tried to force a smile. Jock O'Reilly hated football and most references to it.

"What's the address of the unit?"

"It's Unit 7, at the end. Tom Mulraney's place."

The young policeman stopped writing at the mention of

the name. Involuntarily, his hand began to shake with nerves.

"How...? How long have you been working there?" Despite a sudden attack of the shakes, O'Reilly managed to force the question out.

"Three years and a bit. He's a good payer."

O'Reilly had more or less just arrived on the team at Strathclyde, but already in his short time, had heard of some of the shenanigans of this particular villain.

He knew that Mulraney was suspected of being involved in resetting stolen goods— on a grand scale. The Fraud Squad were eternally on his tail, so far unsuccessfully.

There had also been rumours of a contract-killing service. A handful of hits had already taken place among the underworld fraternity. The general consensus was that this was not necessarily a bad thing— as long as they kept the service 'in house'.

There had been the establishment of new turfs around the suburbs of Glasgow providing all classes of drugs: heroin, cocaine, cannabis, ecstasy, amphetamines.

And there had been talk of a high class prostitution service; the girls commanded fees as high as five thousand pounds for an evening's work, Mulraney's company snaffling half of that in royalties. No doubt, solid, upstanding pillars of the community, from sections of the justiciary and legal departments, would have their grubby fingers in that particular pie.

DC O'Reilly somehow steadied the nerves sufficiently long enough to continue.

"Right, Maisie. I've nearly completed the form. All I need now is the information you have." A horrible thought flashed through his mind just as he reached the end of the sentence. *What if this nice old lady is one of those perennial wasters of valuable police time?* Her general demeanour did not exactly fill him with great confidence as she sat in front of him, white-knuckled hands still gripping her handbag close to her. He sat back in his chair, praying for a break.

Maisie Rodgers unzipped her bag, producing from it a black purse, the contents still intact. Jock O'Reilly, hands steady, accepted the gift and unclipped it, efficiently sifting through the compartments. His eyes lit up as he slid out a driving licence belonging to Mrs. Leah Vieri.

"Where did you find this, Maisie?" Surely it couldn't get any better. It could.

"At Mister Mulraney's place. I went in to work around half past seven this morning. The purse was lying on the unit floor, near one of the shutter doors,' she said, matter-of-factly.

"Listen to me carefully, Maisie. Does Mulraney know you found this purse?" O'Reilly held his breath.

"No. I'd finished my work before he or Sean got in. I…"

"Sean? Who's that?" he cut in.

"He works for Mister Mulraney. I don't know his second name. He's always been nice to me. Cruel face, though. Y'know, for an Irishman. They're usually kind of jovial, don't you think?"

He nodded in agreement without registering any of her last statement.

"Son, do you have a photo of the lady? A recent one?" Maisie asked.

O'Reilly fumbled with his notebook, at a little pouch in the back. Ben Vieri had given the policeman a small snap of his wife hoping that someone would get the chance to see it. He held the image up in front of Maisie Rodgers.

"That's her. I saw this lady yesterday morning— at the unit. She came in just as I was leaving. Looked very nervous. I didn't think any more of it until I found that purse this morning. Then I heard the news."

DC O'Reilly slipped the photo back into the pouch and looked to the skies, trying to work out in his mind exactly how he would put this information into practice.

"Does this mean that I'm goin' to lose my job, son?" a concerned Maisie Rodgers asked.

31

"Mason, I want you to meet Special Agents Doug Mailer and Andy Wells." Assistant Chief Constable George Drummond was again trying the chief constable's chair for size.

It was now gone 10 p.m., and Blackwell had decided to grab a coffee and sandwich from a nearby Starbucks, after being dropped there by Mick McMenemy. The DI had felt a little light headed after his and McMenemy's meeting with Vic Simpson. He had put it down to a little nausea, compliments of having to deal with the scumbag at close quarters. The real reason was probably closer to not having eaten since breakfast. In either case, Mason had felt revived enough to plough on with this seemingly never-ending shift.

His face broke into a smile as wide as the nearby River Clyde, as he and Special Agent Mailer grappled together in a huge bear hug. Drummond and Wells stood back, embarrassed at the unabashed show of masculine emotions. The pair had remembered too late that they were in company— male company— and broke off, slightly pink faced.

"I take it you two know each other, then?" Drummond asked tersely.

"Er, yes, Sir. Doug and I went through our initial training together at Tulliallan," Mason replied.

Tulliallan Police College near Kincardine, on the banks of the River Forth, was where the Scottish recruits went to complete their basic induction training. The six-week long, highly intensive course would often sort out the order of things— bring down the arrogant types and encourage the timid trainee.

Doug and Mason had hit it off from the start, both around the same age, similar backgrounds, from the same part of the world. Mailer hailed from Arbroath, literally a stone's throw from Dundee, Blackwell's home town.

Although they did not manage to attend many games nowadays, both men were avid supporters of Dundee Football Club. Many an enjoyable day had been spent watching their heroes play at Dens Park. Recent seasons had been disappointing, however, the club falling out of the top flight, desperate for a sugar daddy to take over and guide them back to where they belonged.

Doug Mailer had done a stint down south, after brief appointments at Paisley and at Aberdeen with a certain Mason Blackwell. One day, out of the blue, Detective Sergeant Douglas Mailer found himself drawn to an internal advertisement for 'trainee agents in a government agency'.

'In the first instance, interested parties should apply to MI6 HQ, Cheltenham for an application form.'

Mailer had done just that, receiving an invitation to interview. The rest, they say, is history.

Mailer and Blackwell had naturally drifted apart over the last five years, hardly speaking at all for over eighteen months— no fall out, just plain busy lifestyles.

Tall, dark and considered by some to be good-looking, eternal bachelor, Doug Mailer, had done very well for himself at MI6. Already a number of operations in various trouble spots across the globe under his belt, the big Scot had been handed the task of helping to sort out the problem that was Brodie Metcalf. The power brokers at MI6 had hastily mobilised the agents following the earlier aberration at the Hilton. Because of the circumstances and number of fatalities involved, the incident had already been listed under the heading 'terrorist activities'.

"Please sit down, gentlemen." Drummond was keen to start the process of collating any information that either party had at its disposal. The dramatic events of earlier in the day would not look good on the résumé of a prospective chief constable, and Drummond's main priority was to catch or kill this menace, before he had a chance to repeat his actions. Also, it would not be good for his career— professional or political— to be seen sitting passively— waiting for things to sort themselves out.

The four men in that room knew that they were dealing with an extremely dangerous opponent— resourceful and elusive; just how resourceful and elusive they were still to discover. Mason Blackwell still had that gut-churning feeling in his stomach.

"Mason. I've already briefed the agents on the current situation, as far as we know it. Agent Mailer was just about to update me with some information they'd received when you came in. In the nick of time, as usual." George Drummond often addressed people like a school headmaster, erring slightly on the strict side.

Blackwell smiled politely, as you would expect from a model pupil, before asking the question he had been just burning to ask since he had first walked through the door.

"Sir, before Doug begins, just exactly what is MI6's role in this investigation?"

The question brought a wry smile from Doug Mailer. It was typical of his good friend. Mason Blackwell would always determine to establish the pecking order in any ongoing investigation.

"I was going to cover that later, Mason. I..." Drummond was interrupted.

"That's all right, Sir. There's really not much to say on the matter, anyway. Agent Wells and I are here merely to assist the investigation— to be the link to MI6 HQ. Of course, the upside is that we have access to a network of criminal databases throughout the world— can dovetail with other agencies like Interpol, the FBI, even the KGB nowadays." Mailer nodded at his friend, almost as if requesting his approval.

"And which handbook did you just pluck that from, Doug?" Mason asked, with a trace of cynicism.

"I might have known I'd never be able to fool you, Mason. Okay, maybe there was a little banging of the company drum," Mailer conceded. "However, everything was true. We are here to help. This case is still your baby. All right?"

"If you're both quite finished, gentlemen? I'd like to crack on. It is nearly eleven and everybody's a little tired." The headmaster had spoken.

"Sorry, Sir. Please, go on, Agent Mailer," Blackwell said, purposely a little heavy on the formal.

Doug smiled at another example of the inspector's notorious mischief making. He already realised that Blackwell had known the answer to his question before it was even asked. It was all part of the game. Mailer felt a compulsion to play along with the pretence.

Doug stole a quick glance at his colleague. Andy Wells' face was a picture. He appeared a little unsettled by what he had witnessed over the past few minutes. Wells was a company man— everything had to be done exactly by the book or not done at all. The product of a broken home, Andy had spent some time off and on in America with his second family. Doug Mailer was forever ribbing his colleague about his transatlantic accent, which would invade his vocabulary at the drop of a hat.

In his late twenties, Andy Wells was undoubtedly one of the good guys, if slightly lacking in humour. He was the kind of man who always liked to know where he stood in any given situation. The mind games of people like Mason Blackwell upset him. Deep down, Wells felt genuine concern at the thought of having to work with this troublesome policeman. Worse still, his colleague just happened to be one of this man's best friends. What was he to do? A deep frown set on Andy Wells' face.

Doug Mailer certainly had a lot of time for his younger colleague. On a recent mission to the Middle East, Andy Wells had placed himself in grave danger, his unselfish bravery saving his fellow agent from enemy capture and guaranteed death. Doug had not been entirely sure of Wells until that point. He initially felt that there was something not quite right about the young Scotsman. Now, Doug Mailer would trust him with his life.

Mailer flashed his colleague a comforting smile, the gesture immediately settling Wells down a little.

Doug reached down to the floor, lifting up a little leather document case— the type with a zipped top. From it, he produced a small folder. Mailer carefully took out the contents of the folder— a few typed documents and some photographs. Blackwell recognised the CCTV still of the assassin known to them as John Mitchell. He had taken the liberty of having the image sent directly to MI6. He already knew the procedures that they would carry out, as Doug Mailer had earlier explained. Blackwell reckoned that this photograph would find its way onto every system in the world— most importantly, onto the FBI's system.

"This still photograph was emailed to our headquarters yesterday. We immediately relayed it to the FBI offices in Washington. Earlier this afternoon, I got a call from a Richard Belzer, one of their federal officers. He didn't even have to run the still— identified the villain right away. Gentlemen, let me present Brodie Metcalf, aka John Mitchell, aka Thomas Tremayne, aka the Viper."

"The Viper?" Blackwell screwed up his nose.

"Aye, the Viper. Don't have a clue," Mailer said, anticipating the next question. "Belzer's been tracking this one for a couple of years. Never been able to pin a thing on him." Doug paused to take a sip from a glass of water, allowing the others to catch up. He picked up the next photograph in the set. "This is ex-FBI agent, Jack Feltham. He retired from active duty around twenty years ago. It was said that he was disillusioned with the bureau. Feltham disappeared off the radar soon after. He'd sold his house, his car, and emptied his bank accounts. It was as if he'd vanished off the face of the Earth."

"What does Feltham have to do with this other guy, Metcalf?" Mason asked.

"I was getting to that part, Mason. Around two years ago, a man's body was found on some waste ground just outside Chicago. He'd been shot in the chest, point blank. The killer used a semi-automatic, 9mm Glock handgun. The body was identified as being that of Jack Feltham. He had been living in Chicago as Jack Kilgour, a part-time film and TV makeup artist."

"Not so much a change of profession as a complete change of everything! But why go to the bother of changing his identity? Okay, he left the service. So what?" Blackwell was confused.

"Apparently, he worked as a freelancer for only about three months of the year. The rest of the time, he freelanced in something completely different— Jack Feltham killed people for a living."

There was a stunned silence.

"He was an assassin?" Blackwell asked.

"Aye. After his death, leaked reports flooded into FBI headquarters from mob connections, detailing some of the hits Feltham had been responsible for over a good number of years. It was as if the crooks got off on getting one over on the seemingly untouchable FBI. You know— how one of their own had turned bad and all that?"

"And this... Brodie Metcalf? I'm guessing he must have set up in competition with Feltham?" Mason was beginning to figure it out.

"That's the way it turned out— sadly, for Jack Feltham. Belzer unearthed sketchy reports of an assassin known to the underworld as the Master— almost certainly Feltham— taking a youngster under his wing, training him. He thinks this youngster might have been Metcalf. In fact, he's convinced of it. Eventually, Metcalf, hired by a mobster to gain revenge on Feltham, came calling on his mentor. He must've caught up with him in Chicago. Belzer reported that forensics discovered three different blood samples at the crime scene where Feltham died. One was obviously Feltham's. They think that the second sample belonged to Brodie Metcalf."

"So Feltham managed to put up a fight?" Blackwell deduced.

"Looks like it. Forensics tagged the details on the FBI database, but, as no one has managed to pin a thing on Metcalf, they don't have his DNA to compare it with. The third sample is of unknown origin— tests showed the blood was definitely human. Female, in fact. And, only one body— Feltham's— was found at the scene."

"So now that we know the identity of this killer, it must get easier. We can squeeze every last man hour into this to bring him down quickly." Blackwell was beginning to formulate a plan. These notions were soon to be dispelled.

"Aye, well, if only life were as simple," Mailer reflected.

"Why? What do you mean, Doug?" Blackwell asked. Judging by Mailer's tone, he had a feeling that he shouldn't have.

"Jack Feltham's parents were circus people, travellers;

moving from town to town, living in caravans, motor homes, anywhere they could find. The family name was Costello. Esther Costello, Feltham's mother, had earlier worked in Hollywood as a makeup artist to the stars. She was supposed to be good, the best. Esther eventually hooked up with Walter Costello, an old-fashioned lion tamer; she gave up her job and joined the circus. The couple travelled across America for years; their only son, Jack, developed into a more than useful acrobat. These skills, and the legacy of his mother's artistic attributes, would eventually combine to create the perfect killer. Virtually no place would prove impossible to enter. And, after the kill, Feltham would escape disguised as more or less anything or anyone. Belzer detailed reports of an old man, a priest, a pizza delivery guy, and even a woman. All reported by eye witnesses to have been sighted at the aftermath of some of Feltham's jobs."

Doug Mailer paused for a moment. "I know you don't particularly want to hear this, but the FBI, or, more specifically, Richard Belzer, is certain that part of Brodie Metcalf's training under Feltham involved the use of disguises for every occasion."

"So we could be looking for anybody?" George Drummond asked, feeling more than a little concerned about his political and professional future. This was all he needed right now, just before the announcement of the new chief constable of Strathclyde Police Force. A loose cannon running amok in Glasgow.

"Frankly, yes, Sir," Mailer conceded.

"Well, that's just great! What do we do now?" Drummond asked, the frustration threatening to boil over.

"We still have an edge, Sir," Blackwell cut in.

"I'm all ears, Mason." The chief constable-elect was willing to listen to any suggestion.

"Let's remember why we assume Metcalf was sent

here."

"To kill Baltimore's murderer."

"That's right. The killings at the Hilton— they were just for show— to flex his muscles. As far as he's concerned, he still has to complete the main event."

"What's that, Mason?" Doug Mailer asked. He had still to be briefed on the rest of the puzzle from the Strathclyde angle.

Blackwell stayed silent. He had spotted the top section of a Reliance security vehicle outside the office window as it slowed down, preparing to take the turn and head for the station's tradesman's entrance at the rear.

"If you'll excuse me for a moment, gentlemen? I'll be right back."

With that, DI Blackwell slipped out of the door, leaving behind a host of puzzled looks.

32

Mick McMenemy looked at his watch— 11:15 p.m. The lights in the house had gone out around thirty minutes ago.

The DS and his assistant, Detective Constable Fred Boyle— the 'Strathclyde Stud'— were sitting in an unmarked vehicle about thirty yards down the road on the opposite side from the entrance to Southfork, Vic Simpson's luxury pad.

Mason Blackwell's idea to place Simpson under forty-eight-hour surveillance was sound in principle— past experience would indicate that anything can happen at almost any time in the lives of these underworld figures. It didn't, however, make it any easier for the chosen ones to carry out the donkey work— the suffering of hours and hours of endless, mind-numbing inactivity.

McMenemy had only just managed to press-gang a rather reluctant conscript in DC Boyle. After dropping Mason Blackwell in the city, Mick had made three phone calls to the rank and file, requesting a partner for the first leg of the surveillance operation.

Call number one was eventually answered by Detective Constable Trevor Fields after a number of rings, the DC no doubt utilising the time to get his excuse for being unable to attend at short notice just right.

Detective Constable Juliet Baxter— or Juliet Bravo as the boys in the station would often refer to her— was at the cinema with a friend. At least that was what her husband had been instructed to say.

McMenemy hit pay dirt with his third call, catching Fred Boyle completely off guard. The DC had bravely tried to furnish an excuse, Mick McMenemy having none of it. Result: DC Boyle's next few hours would be spent among male company instead of his original plan— to pay a late night visit to his new girlfriend. Tonight was the night the Strathclyde Stud had set aside for some serious moves in the bedroom department. After all, this would have been their third date. He had already received serious ribbing from the other guys at HQ; the general consensus throughout the department was that the Stud was slipping in his old age— all of twenty-six years. At least, tonight, he would have a valid excuse.

Boyle glanced across at McMenemy and smiled. He was checking out his boss' profile against the moonlight. Not exactly George Clooney— short, fat and hairy.

Got the Good and the Ugly; just need the Bad. Wait, Vic Simpson is obviously the bad, Fred chuckled silently to himself.

The endless working day was beginning to take its toll, causing McMenemy's head to loll backwards and forwards with fatigue; he would jerk himself awake, cracking his neck every few seconds. Mick simply muttered 'fuck' with each whiplash, his chubby fingers clutching the back of his neck. It was all Fred Boyle could do to contain himself.

"What the fuck are you laughing at? Just remember where you were supposed to be tonight," McMenemy said almost triumphantly, catching his colleague in the act.

"That's a bit below the belt, Sergeant. You know I'd rather be out here helping you. Anyway, I think sex is overrated. Believe me."

"Is that right? From what I've heard, you're that desperate you'd have a go at a hole in the barber's floor."

The two of them laughed heartily.

Fred Boyle secretly aspired to be a policeman in the same mould as Mick McMenemy. He had enormous respect for the man and everything he stood for. Courage, integrity, loyalty, compassion— Mick had the lot in abundance. He was a man's man, no doubt about it— willing to put himself in where it hurt for the common good; to muck in with the boys. Boyle respected that; one day, he hoped to be there.

On this particular evening, however, both men were just looking forward to 5 a.m. and the arrival of the relief squad of Juliet Baxter and Trevor Fields— the pair had not escaped entirely scot free.

Fred Boyle sighed, leant back, trying to make himself more comfortable; both hands were clasped firmly behind his head.

A flickering shadow caught the corner of Boyle's eye. As he turned to investigate, he drew in a sharp breath; Fred's heart stopped.

The passenger window next to him suddenly shattered into a thousand pieces, raining tiny blocks of safety glass across the side of Fred's face and into his lap. Boyle's hand instinctively went to reach out for the door handle, tightening on it in shock as the bullet thundered into his brain.

Fred Boyle fell heavily to the side with the impact, his warm blood spraying liberally over the face of his passenger. This left the way clear for the killer's next shot.

DS Mick McMenemy had little time to even move a muscle.

33

The unmarked police car pulled off the main drag into Arrol Place in Glasgow's East End.

Rookie plain-clothed officer, DC Jock O'Reilly and his slightly more experienced colleague, DC Aileen McAteer, were following up on the information received earlier at the station from cleaner, Maisie Rodgers. It was not common policy for a police force to let such inexperienced staff handle a potentially difficult meeting. However, due to recent events, there were no alternatives. The facility was stretched to the limit. There would be no holding of hands for the foreseeable future; everyone was told that they would just have to get on with it as best they could.

O'Reilly's heart lurched when he saw the two cars parked directly in front of the unit. Someone was home.

Driver McAteer silently steered the blue Honda safely to rest beside the other cars.

"If I was a betting man, I'd bet that was Thomas Mulraney's car," Jock O'Reilly proudly stated, clocking the number plate— 8IG T4M; a similar conclusion to the one recently reached by the unfortunate Leah Vieri. "Maisie mentioned another man— an Irish guy called Sean; that must be his car." He motioned towards a silver Jaguar in the next bay.

"Let's do it," McAteer said, keen as mustard, which was worrying for the ultra-cautious O'Reilly.

The roller-shutter door at the front was padlocked.

188

Given the nature of the business, it would only be raised for special deliveries, for instance, the recent hijacking of a juggernaut full of flat-screen TVs.

The two cops were standing outside the door marked Reception. In character, DC O'Reilly would allow the woman to press the buzzer.

Twenty or thirty seconds passed without reply.

"Maybe the intercom's not working." McAteer leant over to try the door. She smiled at her partner as it swung open.

He tried his best to smile back, swallowed hard and followed her in.

"Mister Mulraney! Mister Thomas Mulraney!"

O'Reilly visibly jumped as Aileen's voice echoed through the unit. No reply.

The shrill tone of a telephone split the silence. After six rings, the system's answering machine kicked in, the generic BT message reverberating around the metal building. The caller hung up before the message finished, leaving a ghostly hush floating through the building.

"Mister Mulraney!" McAteer persisted.

The door from the reception area into the workshop was wide to the wall and McAteer spied the beginnings of an open-tread, metal staircase, which she assumed led to offices up in the Gods.

She immediately thought of her father, a successful haulier, who traded out of a unit very similar to this one. Almost like some kind of bird of prey, such an animal tended to nest in high places, hovering over his kingdom, looking out for any nasty predators that may happen along. At least that was her theory.

"Come on. Follow me." She headed for the stairs.

"Wait a minute, Aileen. We can't just barge in here. We need to get a search warrant." O'Reilly, fresh out of college, tended to spout the law, and probably had more of a regard for it. Especially when charged by healthy dollops of fear.

O'Reilly especially, was well aware that they were slap bang within the belly of the beast. Both were unarmed, but only one seemed prepared to take it to the next level.

"Aye right. And how long is that gonnae take? Come on, O'Reilly, we'll have a quick look around. It's obvious that there's nobody here. Maybe they've been called out to a job or something."

It was hard to argue. In any case, she was already halfway up the metal staircase. O'Reilly's nose was pressed hard against the window at reception, peering along the length of Arrol Place for any signs of life. It was almost as if his pessimistic demeanour insisted that these premises, and their dark secrets, be granted some kind of protection from prosecution. As if he expected, even wanted to be caught in the act.

O'Reilly's heart seemed to quicken by ten beats a minute for every clattering footstep she took.

"Jesus! Oh my God! O'Reilly!" DC McAteer shouted. She had reached the top of the stairs and was now staring through the office door in disbelief at the scene in front of her. She could feel the contents of her stomach rise deep into her throat. She worked to swallow it back down. *Where the fuck is he?* "O'Reilly! Get up here!" Her voice became shrill as she battled to control it. She backed up against the top rail of the staircase for needed support. Glancing to her right, she was aware of her partner on the staircase. O'Reilly was grasping both rails as if he were Indiana Jones on a rickety rope bridge across a gaping chasm a thousand feet off the ground.

"Wh-what is it?" His voice quivered.

"We need to call in," his partner replied, calmer, beginning to put a lid on her emotions.

Jock O'Reilly finally made the top of the stairs. McAteer, ashen faced, nodded into the room as he passed her. Reluctantly, he turned to face his demons.

There were a few patches of the walls inside the office that were still white, their original colour.

It is a fact that the colour of blood markedly changes as it leaves the body. Instead of a bright, almost cherry shade of red, blood becomes dark, crimson; some say the colour of night.

The clear, sunny April morning had, in the last few minutes, given way to a murky, gloomy atmosphere, courtesy of a giant rain cloud spreading over from the West.

In the office, arterial spray from the two men had combined with the general darkness to present an almost surreal, gothic style canvas. One of the victims was spread over a desk on the far side. Face up, eyes staring accusingly, arms outstretched, this man had endured a violent end, as befitted his chosen way of life.

O'Reilly physically baulked as he realised that the man's head was lying at an extremely unusual angle. It had been cut almost clean through, only remaining joined to the rest of his body by strips of mottled skin and a few nerves and tendons.

The second body lay face down in the middle of the floor, vicious hacks all over it. Gaping wounds, exposing muscle and bone, still seeped blood out over the floor. This body had provided most of the artistic spray patterns over the walls, clear evidence of severed arteries on the neck, hands and feet, there for all to see. The frenzied attack had not long taken place, and the detectives' blood ran cold at the very thought of it. Experienced officers had often explained about sensing the smell of death at a crime scene. This particular scene was even too recent for that sensation. The souls had just departed.

Their extensive training, and time spent in the local morgue looking at and studying dead bodies, could not prepare them for this. That said, Aileen McAteer had survived her ordeal relatively unscathed, apart from maybe the possibility of a nightmare or two.

On the debit side, she found herself bending over the prostrate form of her colleague, out cold in the line of duty.

Satisfied that he was still in the land of the living, she called in her first murders efficiently and professionally. She had passed her initial test with the proverbial flying colours.

Later that day, Detective Constable Jock O'Reilly would knock on his boss' door and hand in a letter of resignation.

An already depleted police force had lost yet another potential talent.

34

One hour previously

Mason Blackwell rattled the side of the Reliance security van with the flat of his hand before it sped away from police HQ. Raw instincts forced him to peer up and down the length of Pitt Street, check every window in every building in the vicinity.

He stood quietly, hands on hips, at the top of the steps leading into the station. Mason tenderly rubbed the palm of his hand against his belly. The knotted feeling in his gut had returned with a vengeance.

Is he watching right now? Does he know every move we are going to make? Have I just done the right thing?

The mere thought of this American assassin spooked Blackwell. The recently added information about his probable changeling qualities only served to heighten the mystique.

The Master. The Viper. Dead cops. Murdered villains. Civilian casualties. Blackmail. What the hell is happening here? Who is going to be next?

Mason felt a distinct shiver, pulled the collar of his jacket up to protect the back of his neck from the advancing frost on a typical April evening in Scotland. Final, searching looks all around the area next to the station were duly carried out before he went back inside. HQ was probably the only place where he felt really safe at that moment.

Blackwell was heading back to the chief constable-elect's room to continue the exchange of information with Assistant Chief Constable Drummond and MI6 agents Mailer and Wells.

Mason was both satisfied and confident that he had done the right thing by Will Munro and his family. Rounding the corner to arrive outside the meeting room, he nibbled nervously on a digestive biscuit, lifted from a tray outside the door; he took a small sip from a mug of coffee earlier laid out for him.

Blackwell entered the room, sat down, and made himself as comfortable as he could; he apologised to the three men for his earlier hasty exit.

* * *

The Reliance van had taken a right onto Sauchiehall Street, carrying on east as far as it could towards the pedestrian area at the end. Normally one of the busiest streets in Scotland during peak times, this particular evening— probably courtesy of the descending ground frost— was proving to be less profitable than normal for the local pubs in the city centre area. A small deputation of young party goers could be seen heading for Victoria's nightclub, which was slap bang in the middle of the pedestrian precinct.

The van rolled up towards the red light, preparing to turn left. The M8 motorway was only a few minutes away.

"Jesus, Tam! Would ye look at these girls? It must be two below out there!" Driver Ronnie Wilson was staring in disbelief at the females in the group— everyone wearing a flimsy top that you could spit peas through and skirts almost disappearing up their arses.

Arms folded across their chests, they walked briskly, as well as their high heels would allow; their bodies visibly shuddered in the freezing atmosphere. Small, icy puffs of fog quickly dispersed from their heavily lip-glossed mouths as they chattered away, no doubt looking forward to hitting the dance floor, if only to get some much needed heat into their bodies.

"Damn sure it wouldnae be my lassie going out like that! No fuckin' way!" Passenger Tam Smith furrowed his brow, his mind wandering.

His daughter had just turned seventeen. Smith's job, by its nature, always meant that he would have to work all manner of unsocial hours. There would be plenty of opportunity for the right-minded teenage female. Tam's wife was not exactly a firm disciplinarian, the girl more than able for her. All of these thoughts flashed through the guard's mind in seconds. This particular shift would soon be coming to an end. He made a mental note to investigate the situation when he got home.

"Hey, Tam! Check this guy!" Ronnie pointed towards a figure coming out of the shadows, the green man indicating for him to cross.

The guards watched, smirking as the man came into full view; three steps forward, two back, he lurched into the middle of the road. The drunk then stood before them, his arms raised in defiance, squinting into the van's powerful headlights. In his coat pocket, the nozzle of half a bottle of spirits— probably whisky— could be seen sticking out.

"Heh heh! Go yersel', pal!" Tam's attention had now deflected from his daughter. He shook his head at the sorry sight in front of them.

The traffic lights were changing to green.

"Come on, let's get movin', then!" Ronnie's mood was changing. One of those impatient driver types, he was now leaning on the horn in an effort to blast this useless bastard out of his way. "Come on! The fuckin' lights'll be back to red any time!"

The drunk appeared to fumble about in his pocket for

something.

"What the fuck's he doin' now?"

"Christ knows! I've had enough of this anyway!" Ronnie reached for the door handle, taking his eyes off the man for a second— long enough for Tam Smith to bark a futile warning.

A hail of bullets rained relentlessly into the cabin, tearing both men to pieces. Smith slumped forward, his bloodied head smashing against what was left of the huge windscreen of the van. A trail of blood snaked down the glass towards the dashboard. Wilson, already dead, sat bolt upright against the back of his seat, eyes staring into the face of Brodie Metcalf.

Metcalf, semi-automatic in one hand, incendiary device in the other, calmly strolled to the back of the van. Bending down, he swiftly clipped the device to the underside— at the axle— before smartly disappearing into the night.

Ten seconds later, holy hell broke loose. The van violently somersaulted with the blast, landing heavily on its roof across the precinct. All shops and offices within fifty yards suddenly lost their windows and doors; flying glass speared like daggers through the darkness. To say that it was a miracle that nobody on the street lost their life would be a gross understatement.

The young kids had long since bolted for safety and the only slight noise that could now be heard was the gentle drip of fuel from the punctured tank of the van. The beginnings of a small fire inside the cabin then became evident.

*   *   *

Boom!

Half a mile away, at police HQ, the commotion caused four men in a meeting room to stop what they were doing and stare at each other in silence. One of them was then heard to ask the blindingly obvious.

"Did you just hear that?"

Mason Blackwell gently rubbed his belly.

35

The tall blonde had entered the city centre beauty salon, Laisser Faire, over three hours ago. She had decided on the spur to go to town; hair, nails— including toenails— face pack, waxing in all manner of places. The process had also included a change of hair colour— back to brunette.

Michelle Wellbeck had just enjoyed the finishing touches to her makeup; nothing too severe. Gina, her personal chaperone throughout the experience, had decided that Michelle was so naturally beautiful that she would have no need for excessive war paint. Gina had held her breath as she watched her assistant apply some faintly flesh-coloured lip gloss. Her face broke into a warm smile.

"Purrfect! Dahling, you look absolutely heavenly! Your lunch date must be the luckiest man alive!" Gina, who also just happened to be the owner of the salon, had perfected the art of mixing it with the rich and famous; celebrities and supermodels stored her number on their mobiles. Not bad for a wee lassie from Govan with no qualifications, and who used to slog in sleazy dives, perming the hair of old wrinklies for fifteen quid a week and tips.

Now she could charge in excess of four hundred pounds for a full treatment, seven hundred for what she described as her diamond service.

Gina's latest client had strolled in off the street, plumping for the diamond without batting an eyelid at the cost. Aside from the cash, such a client was a godsend for any reputable salon. Who wouldn't want a beautiful woman such as Michelle Wellbeck to walk out of their establishment into a busy street? Especially after such an intensive makeover? One couldn't possibly put a price on advertising on that scale.

Whilst annoying for Gina at the time, the earlier last minute cancellation of a boring, low-cost regular— a mere hundred quid shot— had ended up putting a huge grin on her face.

The two women did the old, fake cheek kissing bit before Michelle peeled off seven new, crisp hundred-pound notes, part of the proceeds of her latest job. Little did the salon queen know exactly how Ms. Wellbeck had earned the money.

*   *   *

"Wow! You look absolutely stunning, blonde or brunette!" the tall man exclaimed as he rose to kiss Michelle on the cheek.

"Thanks, love. All for you, you know," she replied, literally feeling like a million dollars.

Michelle had not felt as good for a long time. Her job had taken her to many places, into numerous tough situations. How she had looked or what she had worn had been unimportant to her during those times. She had worked hard for the past three years, especially in more recent times. Another couple of vital pieces of the jigsaw to complete and that would be it. All Michelle would then have to consider would be: where, and with whom? She felt that those days were definitely now within touching distance. The many months of hard work and planning were about to pay off.

The beautiful couple was having lunch in the salubrious surroundings of the Salle a Manger in the West End. It was a relatively low-lit type of establishment and, although they were so obviously taking a risk by meeting in public, they felt safer in the far corner amongst the candles and long shadows.

The lovers embraced. "So, you like the change?" she whispered softly into the man's ear before they broke apart.

He slipped the chair back as she sat. He gazed into the eyes of the dark beauty as she leant back allowing her split skirt to fall across her thighs. Beautiful, toned, slender legs reeled him in closer, closer.

"Oh, I like. I like very much," he replied, almost under a spell. He brushed his hand provocatively against her knee under the table.

She grinned. The magic of this sorceress was powerful and dangerous.

"It won't be long now, my love. Then we can be together, forever." She lowered her voice as the waiter came into earshot.

Besotted, her lover could hardly take his eyes off her, as she ordered for both of them.

Halfway through the order, Michelle leant forward, gently tugging her skirt back across to re-cover her legs. The waiter, pen and notepad in hand, caught the move. What red-blooded guy wouldn't have? He found himself staring into the eyes of this beautiful woman in the same way that his unfortunate predecessors had done. She had an uncanny, almost telepathic knack of sending the right signals to her prey at exactly the right time. Michelle could work a room, play a dozen guys, each one unaware that he was in competition with the other.

The smitten waiter, eager to please, scurried back with two glasses of house wine for the table. As if becoming bored by it all, the temptress destroyed him with an icy stare. Crestfallen, he sloped back into the shadows.

Lawyer, Ben Vieri, was sure that he was in heaven. He reached across the table, tenderly stroking his lover's hand. Then, as if by the flick of a switch, he snapped back to reality mode, a worried frown crossing his handsome face.

"You're sure Leah's all right, Michelle? I mean, they won't hurt her, will they?" Vieri asked with a mixture of guilt and concern.

"Ben. Leah's my sister. Do you think that I would let anything happen to her?" Michelle Wellbeck aka Penny Richards asked curtly.

"No, of course not. It's just that... Well... maybe it wasn't exactly the brightest thing to do."

"Would you listen to yourself? You're unbelievable! Don't you remember how she lied to you? She wouldn't even tell you her real name, for God's sake! She's fine. We just want to teach her a lesson. Okay?" Penny was getting visibly agitated at the lawyer's lack of strength.

After all, Ben had been full systems ahead for making Leah suffer for the lies and deceit that he'd been unaware of for the past four years. How his wife had been a soft-porn actress, a stripper, a good-time girl. The shame of it all. Did she think she could just change her name and start over again? How many other things had she lied to him about? The twins were at nursery every day. How many men had she slept with in their bed while he was slogging away, making a better life for all of them? *The fucking lying cow!*

All manner of thoughts were racing through his head. For all that, he knew one thing. If it hadn't been for a chance meeting with this wonderful lady— his sister-in-law— whom he didn't even know existed, Ben would have carried on blissfully unaware. Unaware of how his wife had deceived him; of how she was still cheating on him; of how she was stealing his money. And of how she had disowned her own flesh and blood in her desperate time of need.

He was now deeply in love with this angel of mercy.

She had reluctantly agreed to organise the kidnap of his wife. Nothing serious. Vieri merely wished to teach her a lesson, before he would leave her for good, taking the twins with him. He would start a new life with Michelle without this liar and cheat.

Ben reckoned that his wife's chequered past would present little problem when it came to custody of the twins. Christ, he was a lawyer. And a damned good one. She would not stand an earthly.

Cleverly, Penny Richards had nudged the conversation in the desired direction. Her lover was now back firmly in wife-hating mode once again.

"I have to go to the wee boy's room. Don't go away now!" Ben Vieri said, flashing a cheeky grin.

Two or three minutes later, he re-appeared, still grinning as if he could not believe his luck— like the cat with the cream. He leant over to kiss her.

"What's the house wine like, anyway?" Ben asked, sitting again.

"It's one of the better ones,' she replied, her face becoming more serious. She watched him take a sip, then a mouthful.

"Mmmm. It is good. Better get used to this," he announced. "We're going to be doing a lot more of it very soon. I fancy a holiday in Hawaii.— on me. What do you think?"

Vieri smiled. Blinking with sudden weariness, Ben suddenly felt very warm. Large globules of sweat formed across his brow. He began to loosen his tie, undo the top two buttons on his shirt. "Phew! It's really warm in here all of a sudden!"

Penny Richards quickly checked around the room. This gloomy corner was perfect. Nobody would suspect anything. She turned back to face her lover.

The lawyer's eyes were bulging out of their sockets.

His brain was telling him what was happening, but he was unable to get his mouth, his speech to function. The powerful poison began to invade his senses, like hot pokers searing deep into his head.

"M-M-Michelle. Wh-what's wrong with me?" Ben hissed. He wanted to shout at the people all around, only feet away. He tried desperately to move his legs, his arms. He was paralysed.

Penny reached over, gently pushing against his forehead, guiding him back into his seat. He was completely powerless to prevent it.

"The name's Penny. Penny Richards," she said with a faint smile.

Vieri's eyes widened as the truth hit him hard. His dying image was the almost curious expression on his lover's face as he slipped into the dark void.

36

"Mason, it's five o'clock. You look absolutely done in. Go home, now! Get some rest. You're no use to anyone in this state. Just fill me in first. Okay?" The pretty policewoman sat beside Blackwell on the concrete steps outside one of the large department stores, just off the Sauchiehall Street pedestrian precinct. She patted him on the knee.

Old friend, Detective Inspector Theresa Bremner, from Central Scotland police force HQ in Stirling, had just arrived at the murder scene. Blackwell had called her requesting backup following the events that had taken place the previous evening.

Assassin, Brodie Metcalf, had done his utmost to ensure that Strathclyde police were stretched to the limit. Mason figured that there was no one more qualified than his glamorous ex-partner to take charge of things, when he eventually succumbed to the need for sleep. That time would have to be soon. Mason knew Bremner was right. He was no good to anyone in such a state.

Theresa Bremner had received the call whilst still very much in holiday mode. The confirmed lesbian had taken a few days off to celebrate a two-year association with her faithful partner, Lindsey Wallace, another pretty cop attached to the same force. Theresa had met the young American whilst on holiday in California. Within the space of two weeks, the pair had fallen deeply in love; Theresa convinced Lindsey that she should leave her dead-end, shop

204

assistant job and come back to Scotland with her. The police force in Stirling was looking for promising young people. The bright, bubbly Californian certainly fitted the bill.

* * *

Theresa agreed right away to help Mason Blackwell, because that was the kind of person she was. And, she just happened to be very fond of him. Also a university graduate— also with honours— she and Mason once served together within the ordinary rank and file at Dundee. It was clear to him, even then, that she was going to be a star.

The only fly in her particular ointment was the question of her sexuality. Although the force's attitudes to such things had moved on a million miles in the last few years, certain old Draconian sympathisers might prove to be obstinate in their future decisions, when it came to evaluating promising promotion candidates.

At thirty-four, shapely, brunette, average height and build, the DI was used to turning the heads of males everywhere— cops and villains alike. During a boozy police internal graduation ceremony, Theresa had felt the need to confide in her closest pal her deepest feelings and innermost secrets. Blackwell advised her there and then to admit most of those feelings to top brass, stating that, if they were to find out from another source, they might tend to be unsympathetic towards any case that she may have for promotion. Bremner took his advice, undoubtedly her finest career decision to date. Unless she was to confront a morbidly homophobic superior officer, Theresa Bremner, like Mason Blackwell, was destined for big stuff.

That would be a subject for later. There were more pressing issues to deal with at present.

"My God! What the hell's happened here, Mason?"

Bremner surveyed the destruction in front of her. Daylight had taken a little longer than normal, due to a sudden change in the weather conditions. The cold, biting frost of the night before had given way to heavy rain. Dark, angry clouds did their best to blot out the sunlight, as if they wished to conceal these atrocious post-apocalyptic scenes from the good citizens of Glasgow for as long as they could.

Mason Blackwell could only shake his head in reply to her question.

He leant back against the metal frame of the store window, taking care not to fall straight in— the glass there had been shattered, as had most of it within the epicentre of the blast. The exhausted policeman felt himself begin to drift away on a cloud.

"Mason! Come on, you can't sleep here," Theresa scolded. "Here. Take this." His guardian angel produced a small, tartan flask from her handbag, unscrewing the top and pouring out the milky sweet, golden elixir.

The seductive smell of the instant coffee stimulated Blackwell's senses. He smiled. She had remembered exactly how he loved his coffee. And, by God, he needed a brimming cupful right there, right then.

"Ahhhhh! That is just fantastic! Are you quite sure you wouldn't consider becoming my wife?" He took a huge gulp, rubbing his eyes firmly with his free hand.

"Sorry, love. You're just not made up in the right way for me, I'm afraid. Now, if I should suddenly get different impulses, I'd let you know!" Bremner put her arm across the back of his neck, tenderly kissing him on the cheek.

Mason rested the side of his head against hers.

"How've you been, Theresa? It's great to see you again. Thanks so much for coming to the rescue."

The temperature of Theresa's coffee was always precisely right— just off the hot— and cool enough to drink in two or three gulps. Mason drained the lot, flicking the plastic cup dry before screwing it back home.

"Been okay, Mason." She paused.

Blackwell saw the expression on her face change slightly. He would bet money that she hadn't been okay.

"Well..."

Here it comes.

"My... My dad died. Nearly three months. It was his heart, apparently." She sniffed. "How's that for irony?" Theresa tried hard to fashion a smile. Her father had been a leading heart surgeon over a number of years. Only the year before, Mason had attended William Bremner's retirement party.

He immediately recalled speaking at length with the old man about his plans to while away the hours. Golf, bowling, fishing. Mason found himself hoping that he had indulged fully in all hobbies during his final months. He then recalled how William had opened his heart to him, detailing his greatest regret that his only child would never produce a grandson or granddaughter for him. How he would have loved them as much as he loved his wonderful Theresa. Blackwell felt a tinge of embarrassment as he replayed in his mind the old man's final words to him that evening:

'I'd have been so proud to have had you as a son-in-law, Mason. I can think of no finer man.'

Blackwell had made the decision not to mention this to his friend. The last thing he would want would be to drive an embarrassing wedge between them. In any case, any such revelation would be of no use to either of them. He was happily married with a family and she was a confirmed lesbian.

"I'm sorry, kid. I didn't know. I would've come."

"I know. I just couldn't face anybody. We had a very small service— only family."

"I understand, love. No need to explain." He pulled her

tightly to him.

Emotions still bubbled just below the surface. Tears began to roll down her pretty face. She stood, wiping them away. Her face flushed bright pink. *Time to discuss business.*

"So, are you going to fill me in here or not?" Theresa tried to replace the barriers that she had inadvertently let slip.

Mason's heart sank when he was asked to outline the case. He secretly welcomed any distraction from the carnage that lay in front of them.

Masses of yellow and black, 'Police: Do Not Cross' tapes adorned the precinct and much of Sauchiehall Street from as far away as the junction with West Nile Street at the east, almost reaching Blythswood Street at the other side. The charred remains of the Reliance security van were discreetly covered by a large, white protective tent, thrown up by the CSEs on the scene. It had been imperative that they secure the scene quickly, limiting the erosion of vital evidence by nature's elements. The bodies had been taken away by the pathologist's department within the last hour and a half, still under cover of darkness.

Fifty yards or so, up and down each side of the explosion, hardly a piece of glass larger than one foot square could be seen. The street was littered with hundreds of thousands of shards; the forensic team sifted painfully through the debris— all of it— tagging and bagging as though their lives depended on it.

The coffee had definitely revived Blackwell, and he spent the next few minutes bringing Theresa Bremner right up to date with what was happening in Strathclyde.

He gave it to her straight; no sugar coating; no omitting important details; the works. Well, maybe he felt justified in leaving out one small detail. Time would tell.

The look on her face as he neared the end was

unforgettable.

"Sorry, kiddo!" Mason read the signals.

"For what?"

"For getting you into this mess."

"I must admit. It does make Stirling seem like a succession of WRVS meetings!" she conceded. "Gimme your phone."

"No, it's okay. I..."

"Gimme the phone, Mason. If you take it home you know you'll never get peace. I can field the calls for you. Don't worry, I've your landline number on my phone. If it's really urgent, I'll call you on that." Theresa held out her hand. She was right. She was always right.

Sheepishly, he handed over the phone.

"Okay, then. I'll only be a couple of hours. Promise. I've briefed Drummond. He knows that you'll be..."

"Just go, Mason. I'll take care of it." She turned him around like a naughty schoolboy, giving him a gentle nudge to be on his way.

He waved over his shoulder, trudging wearily towards his car, which was parked on the pavement just inside the tapes.

Theresa Bremner stood there, arms folded, until the car disappeared from view. "Right. First thing's first." She made her way over to the senior CSE, Kenny Tilton—earlier pointed out to her by Blackwell— to get an update on the operation.

On the way, she heard a jingle in the background. At first she did not realise that it was Blackwell's phone, her own set to an old-fashioned ringtone mode.

"Fuck!" Bremner wrestled in her pocket, answering the call just before the message options cut in.

"Er... Sir. Is that you?" The voice, hearing the female tones at the other end, sounded hesitant.

"This is Detective Inspector Theresa Bremner. DI

Blackwell has just gone off duty. I'll be in charge of things
for the next few hours. Who am I speaking to?"

"Ma'am, this is DC Trevor Fields. I'm on surveillance
with DC Juliet Baxter. We were supposed to be relieving at
five. I... er." His voice was trembling, barely audible.

"Yes, Fields. DI Blackwell has briefed me on this
operation. Is there a problem?" Her heart quickened,
somehow sensing the worst.

"Aye, Ma'am. They're both dead. There... There's
blood everywhere!" Fields was a decent policeman,
although better at the administrative side. He had never
before confronted this type of situation.

Bremner picked up on this right away. She had to act
fast.

"Okay, Fields. Tell me, who's dead? Where are you
right now?"

"I... I... We're at the car. McMenemy and Boyle...
They... They've been shot! The blood... it's everywhere!"
His voice became shrill just before he threw up.

Bremner rolled her eyes when she identified the sounds
coming over the airwaves.

"Christ! Fields! Put Baxter on the phone, will you?"
Bremner commanded, in exasperation. She heard
murmurings in the background before a female voice cut
in— a mercifully rational female voice.

"Ma'am. This is DC Baxter."

"Baxter. My name is DI Theresa Bremner. What is
your location?"

"We've just pulled up behind DS McMenemy's car on
Great Western Road, near the junction with Kilbowie Road.
We arrived at five to relieve them. They're dead— DS
McMenemy and DC Boyle— they've been shot, Ma'am.
At close range. Must've been a few hours ago."

"How do you know, Baxter?"

"They're cold, Ma'am. I only lightly touched their skin.

Don't know if they're in early rigor or not. Can't be far away, though."

"Okay, Baxter. What have you done, so far?"

"I've called it in. Back up's on its way. We've secured the site. Luckily enough, there's hardly any motors on the road at this time. Traffic's pulling up just now, Ma'am. I'd better go and brief them."

"Good work, Baxter. What about the surveillance target? Has there been any sign of him?"

"No, Ma'am. I was going to wait for backup to arrive before we investigated."

"Fair enough. Don't let anyone touch anything at the scene until the CSEs get there. Let me know the minute you find out anything else. I'll call you back in a few minutes. Got that?"

"Yes, Ma'am."

She rang off.

Bremner sensed a strength in DC Baxter. Reminded her of herself, ten years ago.

She now had a decision to make. Does she disturb Mason Blackwell at home and report the bad news? He would surely be just in the door, minutes in bed at most.

Theresa had, many times in the past, heard Mason talk fondly about Detective Sergeant Michael McMenemy. He had told her of his high hopes for the DS' career. He would surely want to know about something as serious as this. She pulled her phone from her pocket, quickly locating Blackwell's number. Her thumb hovered over the key.

What am I doing? What could he possibly be able to do right now? After all, they are dead. Nothing can be gained from this.

She hit cancel and replaced the mobile in her pocket.

37

The rain was at last beginning to subside at the Sauchiehall Street crime scene.

"Kenny? Kenny Tilton?" DI Bremner placed her hand gently on the shoulder of the senior CSE.

He was hunkering down, lifting minute pieces of evidence with a tiny pair of tweezers. In his other hand, he was holding open a small, plastic resealable bag, into which he was carefully dropping the items.

"Yes?"

"DI Bremner. I've been drafted in to assist Mason Blackwell." She extended her hand to Tilton.

Kenny straightened up to his full fighting height of six-two, holding his aching back as he rose.

In his early forties, the forensics expert had encountered chronic back trouble over the last couple of years or so, blaming it on the onset of hereditary osteo-arthritis. He shook her hand warmly, grinning as cheerfully as he could through the pain.

"Nice to meet you, Inspector. Getting too old for this, I think!" he said ruefully, continuing to rub away at the painful area in the small of his back. Bremner smiled.

"Not according to Blackwell. He says you're the best in the business."

"Really? He said that?" Kenny enquired. Shaking his head thoughtfully, he began to unzip the front of his white coveralls. He slipped the elasticated hood back, his hair stuck to his head with sweat. The general consensus among the CSEs was that, although the suits were practical and feather light, their protection tended to heat the body up at times to a point that was more than a little uncomfortable.

"Yes. He did."

Tilton scratched his head, a lop-sided smile crossing his face. Inside, he felt really chuffed. Any compliment from the cops was always welcome. A pat on the back from a policeman of the calibre of Mason Blackwell was really something to treasure.

"So, what have you found so far, Kenny?" Now that the pleasantries had been observed, it was down to business for this career woman. She was looking forward to getting her teeth into some real police work. Central Scotland had the odd murder or rape, but if you wanted to experience real edge of the seat crime, you came to Strathclyde.

"The van was destroyed by an incendiary device." Tilton lifted the edge of the canvas tent around the vehicle, ushering the inspector inside. Battery-powered halogen lamps illuminated the scene. "This is the area around the blast." Tilton pointed to the smashed axle. "It was probably set on a timer. Because the device was clipped to one side, when it went off, it had the effect of spinning the vehicle around, eventually ending up like this." He made a motion, rolling his hands in the same way a substituted player might be summoned from the pitch in a football match. "The two security guards inside the cabin area were probably already dead when the bomb went off. There was strong evidence of bullet holes all around the cabin. Probably a close-range shooting. "

"What about the prisoner in the back?" Bremner asked.

"Er… what?" Tilton tried to fashion a reply, buy a little time by asking for clarification.

"The other body? Has it been taken to the morgue?" she asked once more.

"Em… you'd have to ask DI Blackwell about that, Inspector. I've been instructed not to comment," he replied, cryptically.

Bremner decided not to press the issue. Obviously she was not in possession of the full facts after all.

Cursing Mason Blackwell under her breath, she thanked Kenny Tilton for his time and left the scene.

*   *   *

DI Bremner hooked her Bluetooth earpiece onto her ear, set the device up on Blackwell's phone, and dialled the last number received.

"Hello. DC Baxter."

"Baxter. DI Bremner. What's the situation down there?"

"Backup's just arrived, Ma'am. The guys are setting up makeshift screens right now. The traffic police have closed the road a hundred yards both ways. They're diverting the vehicles down onto Glasgow Road. That'll solve any problems with rubberneckers. We'll still need more officers to handle the ghouls, though," Baxter said.

No matter when or where, these somewhat sad and obviously lonely individuals would appear, as if attracted by the smell of death. Even though it was very early in the day, a small band had already gathered behind the police tapes. Unbelievably, a few had brought flasks of tea and sandwiches, were sitting on fold-away chairs preparing for a long session.

"Okay, I'll call for extra backup. Have you approached the surveillance target yet?"

"No, Ma'am. We were just about to."

"Hang fire. I want you to wait for me. Okay?"

"Yes, Ma'am."

"Give me your postcode and I'll be there in minutes."

DC Baxter checked her paperwork before relaying the address and postcode to DI Bremner.

"Thanks. See you soon. Oh, and eh, Baxter?"

"Yes, Ma'am?"

"Good work!"

"Thank you, Ma'am."

Theresa Bremner had rung off. She was already tapping the details into her satellite navigation system.

* * *

Bremner flashed her badge at the traffic cop on the eastern perimeter of the crime scene. He duly shifted some cones, allowing her car inside. As she trundled slowly up to the scene, she was aware of another car entering just behind. Drawing to a halt within the tapes, Theresa stared into the rear view mirror. She could identify the outline of two occupants inside the sleek, black Saab 93. To her, the car reeked of Secret Service.

Bremner's car had pulled up about twenty yards behind the masked vehicle of the late DS Mick McMenemy. A uniformed officer was standing guard at the entrance to the makeshift boundary around the car. Another two cops were positioned near the gathering of ghouls, poised to confiscate any equipment that could be used to record details of the crime scene. That would include mobile phones used to take pictures or videos.

On the other side of the road, outside the gates of Vic Simpson's mansion, stood a couple of plain clothes— Bremner assumed they were Trevor Fields and Juliet Baxter.

In the distance, she could see the coned off area at the west side perimeter; the flashing blue lights of the brightly marked traffic car barred the way.

Just then, Bremner caught sight of another vehicle being

allowed to enter from that side, no doubt the backup she had called in, requested earlier by Juliet Baxter.

The police car killed lights and siren before making its way steadily down the hill towards the scene. The two uniforms got out and prepared to take up position in front of the growing crowd. Word was obviously getting around, stories growing arms and legs by the minute.

Bremner sat in her car until the driver and passenger of the Saab, which had stopped behind her, got out. She smiled.

Dark suits and sunglasses. Definitely MI6.

DI Bremner had only once before encountered this particular branch of law enforcement; the identification and apprehension of a known IRA terrorist in Alloa, Clackmannanshire, and the subsequent arrest of three other sympathisers in the same area, brightened the otherwise dull, humdrum existence in her own constabulary.

The two men stood aside, allowing another two vehicles to pass them, both coming to rest next to the scene.

A team of Crime Scene Examiners, in a minibus and an unmarked meat wagon, had arrived, completing the set. The driver of the wagon climbed out, shaking his head in frustration. Past experience would mean that it would be some time before he could get near the bodies to remove them from the scene. By order of seniority and importance, the CSEs would have the opportunity to strut their stuff first.

"I'm Agent Mailer. This is Agent Wells. We're with MI6. And you are?" One of the men took the initiative.

"DI Theresa Bremner, Central Scotland Police Force. I've been drafted in. Short staffed."

She received a knowing nod from Mailer.

"DI Bremner. Heard a lot about you," Mailer said, removing his shades and shaking her hand.

Wells repeated the gesture, flashing a toothy smile at

the good-looking female cop. He couldn't know that his moves would be lost on the confirmed lesbian.

"All good, I hope!" Theresa recalled Mason Blackwell speak about some friend in the Secret Service.

"Of course," Mailer replied, ever the diplomat.

They strolled across the road to join Fields and Baxter outside Vic Simpson's house.

The quintet managed to successfully swap introductions before DC Fields hit the call button on the elaborate intercom system between the gate and the house. No response.

A moment later, he tried again. Still there was no response. Baxter and Fields turned to DI Bremner for guidance. Bremner, in turn, glanced between Agents Mailer and Wells, her expression suggesting that she was not exactly sure who had jurisdiction. Mailer, instantly picking up on the signal, held his hands up in front of him.

"It's your bag, Inspector. I've already told Mason Blackwell that we're only here to assist the investigation in any way we can."

Aye, right! For now, Theresa Bremner mused. "Fine. Then let's see if we can find a way in here. Fields, nip in to the next-door neighbours and borrow a ladder. He's got tall conifers up the driveway in there. They certainly won't prune themselves."

"Right, Ma'am," he replied, heading for the open driveway leading to the house.

Andy Wells spent the next few minutes giving Theresa Bremner the eye, jabbering some uninteresting small talk. To her credit, she responded politely, only rolling her eyes at Juliet Baxter when he returned to his car to retrieve his mobile phone which he had left in the glove compartment.

"It's okay. I'll call him off," Mailer said to Bremner, picking up the vibes, deliberately out of earshot of the other woman.

"Thanks. I didn't want to hurt his feelings. He seems like a nice lad."

"Don't worry. He'll live!"

Trevor Fields came into view, lugging a set of aluminium stepladders. He set them up against the sandstone wall making up Vic Simpson's perimeter boundary. Trevor liked to think he was a sporty type. Leaping over the top of the ladder, he almost broke his neck dropping down the other side.

A little embarrassed, Fields dusted himself down before quickly locating a rather poorly concealed emergency entry button; the security gates finally creaked open.

The love-struck Andy Wells returned just as they entered the property.

Bremner took a deep breath and led the way. She had an uneasy feeling.

"Baxter. You and Fields sweep the garden area. And remember, don't touch anything. The CSEs would have our guts for garters," Bremner warned.

"Understood. Let's go, Trevor." DC Baxter took charge, not unusual when the two were teamed up.

Bremner fashioned a wry smile, turning to address the MI6 agents.

"Gentlemen. Shall we?" She invited the pair to lead the way up the path to the front door of the house.

Doug Mailer made a strong fist and hammered loudly against the front door. Net curtains, hung on the inside, made it difficult for him to make out anything but fuzzy shapes along the hallway. He thought it was odd that there was a light on at the end, possibly coming from a sitting room? It was now broad daylight and the sun was strong in the sky, as if apologising for the earlier miserable conditions.

Mailer tried the handle. Locked. They were just about to move around to try the side door when panic merchant,

Trevor Fields, appeared in front of them, ashen faced. He muttered something about following him around the back. When they rounded the corner towards the back entrance, they could hardly be prepared for the horror scene that met them.

A body was lying across the pathway, right leg twisted under left, the brand new ivory trousers now soiled with mud, grass, blood and urine. The heavy rain through the night had diluted and spread the blood pool like a large oil slick, down the path almost to the end. Theresa Bremner did a double take; a football-sized object lying on the grass next to the path caught the corner of her eye. The second take told her that the object was, in fact, a man's head.

"Oh, God!" She put her hand to her mouth. *Please! Please, don't throw up, Theresa!* She took a deep breath, somehow managing to hold down her stomach contents. Thank God she hadn't had breakfast yet.

"It's Vic Simpson, Ma'am. I've seen him before. Interviewed him last year with DI Blackwell," DC Juliet Baxter stated matter-of-factly.

Bremner nodded a reply, by now tight lipped; waves of nausea finally subsided.

DC Trevor Fields was crouching in the corner of the garden, violently throwing up. At least he was far enough out of the way that he wouldn't be contaminating the crime scene.

Doug Mailer and Andy Wells were standing over the severed head; the younger man displayed a greater degree of uneasiness. Mailer knelt to study the head. He had already seen such a sight on a couple of occasions. The only difference this time was that the injury had not been caused by an explosion. Instead of a heavily charred, horror-movie-type, made-up head, this one was as real as it could get. Tousled, grey hair, matted with blood on one side; blue eyes staring in shock; trails of skin, muscle and bone at the neck. The gruesome discovery almost resembled an extremely lifelike, prosthetic type head.

Mailer calmly studied the scene.

"He was killed by some kind of large knife, like a machete or similar. Look here, Andy. The killer's had three or four swipes to take the head off. See the deep cuts?" Doug carefully pointed out the area.

"They always get what's coming to them, don't they?" Wells commented philosophically.

From the little he had heard about Vic Simpson, he still managed to draw the conclusion that the world, more specifically vulnerable young people, were infinitely better off without him. These thoughts certainly made it much easier to stomach the scene.

"Aye, true. Very true," Mailer conceded. He straightened up.

Wells recognised a strange look coming over him.

"Doug? What is it?" Andy asked.

"Simpson's married."

The two men turned to see the door at the back lying slightly ajar. Andy nodded slowly, both men breaking off.

Theresa Bremner watched in admiration as the special agents used their best moves to enter the house, guns in readiness, backing each other up.

They were standing in the long hall. At the end, lying against the living room door, was the crumpled body of Rena Simpson. Thankfully, at least she had managed to hang on to her head, the cause of death attributed to a slash across her back, probably sustained when she was trying to run away. Her nightdress was heavily bloodstained, and the hardwood floor looked as if it had soaked the very life out of her. Mailer's training compelled him to go through the routine anyway. He put his fingers lightly against Rena's neck. No pulse.

"Better call this lot in. The forensic guys are going to

love us; that's for sure!" Theresa Bremner said, ruefully.

Undoubtedly, more white-coated staff would have to be brought in.

She felt that she had seen more action in the last few hours than in all her time at Stirling.

38

Mason Blackwell sat bolt upright in his bed. The digital clock on the bedside table displayed 2:57 p.m. He had been asleep for nearly eight hours, vaguely recalled kissing his wife just before crawling under the duvet at 7 a.m.

The rumbustious, early morning carnival known as 'getting ready for school' had come and gone as normal; the devoted husband and father, so tired that he hadn't heard a thing, could barely move a muscle. The house had finally fallen silent at 8:45 a.m.

A priceless arrangement by Strathclyde police to supply the Blackwell family with an ex-directory landline telephone number had prevented an endless procession of direct sales companies from relentlessly pestering him, depriving him of some much needed rest.

A creature of habit, Mason always made sure that his mobile phone sat next to the clock on that same bedside table. He reached over towards the spot, his heart sinking in his chest when he found it vacant— until he remembered leaving the damn thing with DI Theresa Bremner.

Dragging himself out of bed, he wearily made his way downstairs to check the answering machine. Mason recalled Bremner assuring him that she would call his landline number if there was anything really urgent to report. He had been in such a deep sleep that he considered the possibility that he may have slept through such a call.

He hit the play button: no new messages. Mason felt

relieved.

He made himself a coffee and sat at the breakfast bar. The BBC News channel was duly selected on the small portable at the end of the worktop. As luck would have it, the regional news programme had just begun. Blackwell listened carefully as the newsreader described sketchy details of the Sauchiehall Street bomb blast. Mason managed a slight smile despite the severity of the incident. *At least no one in the department's let anything slip.* Mason had always been a great believer in the adage: 'only tell them what they need to know, nothing more'.

At the moment, the media were not linking this incident with the blast at the Hilton. However, that could all change. All that it would take would be an off the cuff remark to the wrong person. The department was closing ranks— for the moment.

Blackwell drained the last of the coffee and stood, ready to hit the shower. As the newsreader moved on to the second item, the policeman almost dropped his mug.

"After a separate incident early this morning, police have cordoned off, in both directions, a hundred-yard section of the A82 Great Western Road, near Clydebank. As you can see from our live pictures, forensics officers are attending the scene and have been for a number of hours now. It's thought that a motor vehicle, believed to be hidden behind screens here, is involved in the investigation. Unconfirmed eye witness reports indicate that a shooting may have taken place. I must stress, however, that these are unconfirmed reports. Officers are also believed to be in the process of interviewing the owners of nearby homes in an attempt to piece together exactly what has taken place. Police say that the road will be closed off for the rest of the day while their investigations are continuing. They are unwilling to elaborate further..."

"Bloody hell! This is unbelievable!" Blackwell barked.

He was already dialling his own mobile.

"Hello?" came the reply.

"Theresa? Is that you?"

"Oh, hello, Mason. I was just about to call you."

"Really? Is it not a bit late for that, Theresa?" he asked tersely.

"I take it you saw the news report, then?"

"Aye. Damn right I did!"

"Mason. I got the call just after you left. You were absolutely done in. What good would…?"

"I think that you should let me be the judge of that, Theresa. You should have called me straight away. What bloody right do you think you have to make a decision like that?"

"Look, I'm sorry. But this isn't helping. Tell you what, I'll see you when you get in." DI Bremner, not exactly a shrinking violet, hung up the phone.

Blackwell felt the rage rise. In his moment lost to the red mist, he had left out the most important reason for calling his friend. To simply ask, what happened? Deep down, he already knew. He tried to redial. The mobile had been switched off. Clenching his teeth tightly, he launched the hands-free phone into the corner of the room; the plastic casing split open on impact, spilling the innards all over the new laminate flooring.

"Fuck!" He berated himself for his own stupidity. It was totally out of character for him to go off like that. The normally super-cool policeman was now feeling under intense pressure; an out of the ordinary chain of events had spiralled things way out of control.

Mason sat again, drawing in some deep breaths, and did what he would always advise others to do in these circumstances— put themselves in the other person's shoes.

"Fuck!" he hissed again through clenched teeth.

Blackwell confirmed one thing in his mind— Theresa Bremner was due an apology.

"Fuck!" Strike three! Mason had just remembered the funeral of Tam Watson, due to take place at Daldowie crematorium at 4 p.m. He was immediately back on the phone— the, so far, undamaged unit in the hall— to DI Bremner. Blackwell firstly apologised, then invited the pretty cop to a Strathclyde police force funeral. Thirdly, he tentatively asked her the reasons for the full day closure of the A82 near Clydebank. The answers he received confirmed his worst fears.

39

George Drummond's appointment to chief constable of Strathclyde police force was finally confirmed in a rush job. The big guy had got the call from the suits late on the night before, no doubt in an attempt to deflect some of the recent heat. The press had been summoned to a hastily arranged conference the next morning; the simple ceremony took little longer than fifteen minutes.

Drummond was a wily old fox— there was no getting away from that. He had finally arrived in his ultimate post; the one he had dreamt of ever since he stepped out on the beat in his native Dennistoun more than thirty years before.

Drummond was under no illusions. He knew that top brass were either going to hang him out to dry or hail him as a hero. The next few days were going to determine which way it would go: accolades or oblivion.

For sure, he had plenty to sort out. There was a maniacal, American assassin on the loose in the city. People were getting blown up, shot, sliced and diced everywhere. There was corruption by the bucket load in the force. His officers were losing their lives, two at a time. And MI6 were waiting in the wings, poised to take over the investigation. This wouldn't necessarily be a bad thing for George Drummond. His short tenure to date would surely absolve him of any blame. Drummond was no quitter, however, and his preferred option was always to solve the problems using tried and trusted, old-fashioned police methods.

Drummond's first decision in his new post was to gather his best people together, or what was left of them, for a meeting at HQ that night. The funeral of Tam Watson would have to be put to bed first. The force would, of course, stand firm in its finery for that one. George Drummond had accepted compelling evidence, and Mason Blackwell's learned analysis, that Watson had played an integral part in Brodie Metcalf's mission, possibly out of sheer badness, probably for money. Either way, some of the darker details would be omitted from the official records. That was the Strathclyde way.

Mick McMenemy, in both George Drummond's and Mason Blackwell's considered opinions, had been a policeman destined for great things. Fred Boyle had looked a promising prospect, no more.

On the credit side, two malignant tumours in the shape of Vic Simpson and Martin Anderson had been removed from this Earth. At least the lives of some of Glasgow's most vulnerable kids had been made that much safer.

Regrettably, a number of innocent people, including Vic Simpson's long-suffering wife, Rena, had lost their lives.

George Drummond checked his immaculate uniform for the final time in the toilet mirror at HQ, quickly looked at his watch— he hated being late— and left for the crematorium.

Just as he reached his car, Drummond's mobile rang. It was Mason Blackwell. Within the last five minutes, Blackwell had been informed about the untimely death in a restaurant of lawyer, Ben Vieri.

Juliet Baxter and Trevor Fields were now at the scene. Drummond wearily replaced the phone in his pocket. As he started his car, he stole a quick look in the rear-view mirror. Staring back at him was the face of a man visibly ageing, almost by the minute. Drummond took a deep breath, reached back into his pocket. He flicked off the phone and continued on his way.

The weather that day had gone from heavy rain to overcast to bright sunshine. Most of Strathclyde police force was in attendance at Tam Watson's funeral, following an unofficial request by the new chief constable.

Today, only a skeleton staff was actually on duty in the region along with a battalion of Specials, drafted in for the day.

Detective Inspectors Blackwell and Bremner sat side by side, seven rows from the front. Blackwell had again apologised to her for his earlier behaviour, in turn receiving absolution and a full briefing on the morning's events. As Bremner meticulously detailed the happenings at Vic Simpson's house, Blackwell had hung on her every word. At the end, the two officers were in agreement on one seriously worrying fact— they were looking for two killers. McMenemy and Boyle had both been shot in the head. That was clear.

Senior CSE, Kenny Tilton, attending the scene later in the day, had confirmed the cause of death for both Vic and Rena Simpson as by blade— sword— or, most probably, machete. It was considered highly unlikely that a killer would change murder weapons between sessions.

Mason found himself hoping that a rival underworld villain of Simpson's had decided to even up an old score. He also hoped that the perpetrator would then simply vanish into obscurity— or at least stay low until they could sort out the rest of the mayhem. His gut feeling again told him that he was probably way off the mark.

The Ben and Leah Vieri situation was mystifying. *How are they linked to the rest of this?*

Mason was considering a face to face with Will and Mary Munro, when his next problem presented itself.

"Why did you lie to me, Mason?" Recalling an incident

during her first meeting with Kenny Tilton, Theresa Bremner leant over and whispered into her colleague's ear.

He felt her breath against his cheek, smelt the sweet smell of expensive perfume.

"'Bout what?" Mason asked, fearing his game was up.

"You said that Will Munro was being taken to prison in the van that was blown up."

"Oh, yes. I did, didn't I?" He realised it was time to come clean. He smiled ruefully and continued, ensuring that he kept his voice down, "I had to make the killer think that Munro was being taken to prison. I thought that there would be no way he could get to him inside. The security van turned up and I was just about to send Munro." He paused.

"Mason?" Theresa prompted.

Blackwell lowered his voice to a barely audible whisper. He shrugged. "I just had a feeling; no, a gut instinct. I talked him out of going, sent the van away. Never thought for a minute that the killer would do what he did. After what happened, I had to act fast. I checked Will Munro into a local safe house. He's being guarded there by two of my most trusted officers. Sorry I didn't tell you, Theresa. I thought that the fewer people who knew, the…"

"The less chance of any slip ups. I do understand, Mason." She nodded in agreement. Theresa Bremner concluded that she might well have done the same, given a similar set of circumstances.

"Even the officers in the safe house don't know who Munro is, or why he's there. I advised him not to crack a light to them. The only person who knows exactly how things have gone down, except me and you, is Kenny Tilton, and I couldn't exactly fool him, could I?"

"Very true. But… But the news reports. They say a man's body was pulled from the back of the van. Surely Munro's wife has to know? What must she be thinking?"

"I called Mary Munro just after it happened. Asked her to trust me. I assured her that her husband was safe and well, and that I couldn't explain the finer details just yet. She kind of freaked out, but eventually accepted the explanation. I'm going to see her after the funeral. I'd like you to come with me. I need you to be there when I have to tell her about Ben Vieri."

"Of course." Theresa loved to feel needed, to make a difference.

* * *

Mason Blackwell craned his neck to take a look at the people sitting in the first row on the left-hand side, the normal arrangement for close family at this particular crematorium.

At the end of the row sat an elderly couple. Both silver-haired, the woman seemed to be stooped over, appearing a lot shorter than she probably was. *No doubt, the legacy of a life spent fussing over her beloved son,* thought Blackwell. The man was obviously taller, by at least a foot. Mason studied them for the next few minutes. They sat shoulder to shoulder, propped against each other, as if there was a warmth, a closeness between them.

The man looked over his shoulder at the massed congregation behind them. His eyes flitted from face to face. Blackwell got the feeling that he was searching for a friendly face among the strangers. He immediately recognised features similar to Tam Watson. Similar, but most definitely friendlier. *That's the father— has to be*, Blackwell thought. *The old lady must be Tam's mother*. He frowned when he recalled some of the derogatory jokes told about Watson's mother by the lads at the station: of how she was said to have 'jackboot rash'; or how she would have to be forcibly removed from the beach when on holiday— to allow the tide to come in. In truth, Nell Watson was a sad, frail-looking old lady who had just lost her only son in the most horrific fashion.

Donald Watson, his eyes moist with the occasion, managed a warm smile in the way that his son could never have, except maybe at the misfortune of others. Mason Blackwell, making eye contact with the old man, smiled back at him, nodding an acknowledgement.

Mr. Watson turned around to face the front, making a little comment in the ear of his wife. She leant across, kissing him tenderly on the cheek. Who would have thought it? How could this loving and seemingly gentle couple spawn a nasty, insensitive and criminally corrupt creature like Tam Watson?

Blackwell made a mental note to introduce himself to the couple at the end of the service; to find something complimentary to say about Watson to his parents. It would be difficult, but he was sure he could come up with something; maybe he'd have to bend the truth a little.

The service was due to start in around five minutes. Mason scanned the little chapel within the crematorium. He reckoned that it could hold around one hundred and fifty with ease.

There must be at least one-seventy here, maybe even one-eighty, he thought. The overspill stood, to a man, against one of the perimeter walls of the chapel.

Blackwell recognised the majority of the congregation as being police connected. They could always be relied upon to attend such occasions; look after one of their own; give them a decent send off. Even a generally disliked figure such as Tam Watson.

Mason also noted that there were a few strange faces dotted around. He knew that Watson, in life, had not exactly sported a black book bursting with the names of close friends.

"Hmmm. I wonder." Blackwell fed Theresa Bremner a line.

"Wonder what?" She bit.

"I wonder if he's here."

"Who? The killer?" She immediately caught the scent. "That would really be pushing it, wouldn't it, Mason? I mean, nearly every policeman and woman in the district is here."

"I know. That could be the attraction, though. You think?"

Theresa began to feel markedly uncomfortable, undoubtedly wondering if she was about to be blown to smithereens by this nutcase. Shivers flew up and down her spine. Nervously, she felt the inside of her collar. At that precise moment, Theresa Bremner found herself just longing to be back in the comparative safety of her provincial force in the leafy suburbs of Stirling.

There was a loud bang at the back of the chapel; the reverberations bounced around the panelled walls and wooden floors; a toilet door with an over eager door closer was the culprit. Audible gasps followed from most of the congregation. Theresa Bremner felt her chest, inhaling sharply. She then rolled her eyes, cursing the timing.

She turned to share the joke with her colleague. Blackwell's expression was a vision in concentration; a look of steely determination engulfed his face. The CCTV image of the smiling Brodie Metcalf at the airport was firmly emblazoned in his mind.

"Stay here, Theresa. I'm goin' to have a wee look around." He was on his feet before she could reply, excusing himself as he shuffled along the row. At the end, Blackwell made for the exit door at the side about halfway up the room, spotting a member of the crematorium staff standing just inside. The man looked immaculate as you would expect, in a black suit, shoes and tie, with a crisp, starched, white shirt stretched across his rather overweight frame.

Theresa watched from her seat as Mason had a quick word with the man; the pair then vanished out of the door. *What the hell is he up to?* She wondered.

The faint murmurings of the congregation then gave way to the resonating sounds of the piped organ music. The well worn hymn, 'Abide With Me', was suddenly everywhere in the building. Everyone turned to see the coffin carrying Tam Watson's body appear at the start of the aisle, flanked by four pallbearers. The small trolley, upon which the coffin was laid, was carefully draped in a crimson, velvet curtain. The deputation began the slow, deliberate walk towards the platform that would eventually take the body down into the furnace. Most of the congregation would probably be considering the parodies and how apt that type of final journey was for this particular individual.

Theresa Bremner's eyes were everywhere: on the coffin; on Watson's parents; on the congregation; on the door through which Blackwell had just disappeared; on the minister, perched on his pulpit, ready to deliver some carefully prepared untruths— surely a man of God could never lie— to these fine people. And, on the green velvet curtains directly above the pulpit; a slight twitch at the edge of one, caught her eye.

Theresa's heart almost ground to a halt, until she realised that the half-concealed face at the edge of the curtain was familiar.

She winked. Mason gave her the thumbs up. She had a quick look around the chapel, checking if anybody else displayed signs of interest in anything other than the service. Although, of course, she couldn't be sure, Theresa didn't think so.

The coffin was rolled up to the edge of the platform; the pallbearers eased it onto the small, built-in metal rollers, through a pair of tiny curtains and out of sight.

The minister, resplendent in fine, white robes began his eulogy. His booming voice tore through the chapel, needlessly amplified through a small, clip-on TV microphone.

The man who had shown Mason Blackwell upstairs to the tiny room above the pulpit— the room contained all the equipment necessary to provide a funeral service, including amplification and music midi-files— calmly walked over to adjust the volume on the microphone. The congregation, as a whole, sighed with relief as the level decreased.

"Is there anything else I can do for you, Sir?" the man asked.

"No. Thank you."

"Are you absolutely certain of that, Detective Inspector Blackwell?"

Mason Blackwell froze on the spot.

"Now just move back from the curtains and keep your hands high where I can see them," the man ordered.

The accent had changed mid sentence, from authentic sounding Scots, to east coast American.

Mason took two or three deep breaths. He could feel his heart quickening in response to his anxiety. He would have to think, and fast.

Blackwell, still facing towards the window, quickly flashed a concealed, thumbs down sign at Theresa Bremner before turning to face the assassin. She caught the gesture, at first looking slightly puzzled. Seconds later, she was shuffling quickly along the row, stamping on a few toes along the way. Angry rumblings of discontent accompanied her in her wake. The minister, obviously spooked as much as the rest of his audience, stopped in mid flow, his jaw dropping as the events unfolded in front of him.

Theresa hit the aisle, racing for the side door through which Blackwell had earlier vanished.

Next to react, new chief constable George Drummond, two rows behind, was hot on her heels.

"Inspector! Theresa! What's going on?" he called to her as he reached the door. Bremner stopped in the middle of the stairs up ahead.

"Something's wrong, Sir. Mason Blackwell's upstairs. He was watching... in... In case the killer turned up. I..."

Her sentence was interrupted by a dull thud from upstairs. Drummond and Bremner looked at each other, a sickly, gut-wrenching feeling creeping into their systems.

Both suspected that the sound was like the pump of a gun wearing a silencer.

"Oh God!" Theresa cried as another bullet seemed to confirm their worst fears.

Seconds later, a heavy thump on the floor did not make their day seem any brighter.

George Drummond grappled in his inside pocket, pulling out a small handgun— a Beretta.

Bremner watched, wide eyed, as he ran past her on the stairs; his many years of experience in the field instantly kicked in. Unfazed, she followed him to the top of the stairs, reached into her pocket for her pepper spray— it would have to do for now.

Nearing the top, Theresa traded the spray for a small fire extinguisher hanging on a hook on the wall. She pulled in a breath, brandishing the weapon in front of her.

The door into the only room at the very top lay open, about two feet ajar.

George Drummond signalled to Bremner with his free hand, encouraging her to stand next to him, shoulder to shoulder, her back against the wall.

Bremner noted the tremors in George Drummond's gun hand. Even with his numerous bravery awards in the field; even after his sterling work in cutting Glasgow's gun and knife crime by twenty-five per cent in the first two years of his ex-boss' command; even with his unfaltering determination in putting countless drug dealers behind bars; even this great man among men had a healthy fear for the unknown.

Backs still firmly against the wall, they slipped to the top; George Drummond stared through the gap in the door. His heart began to slowly sink, the unbearable silence from within not exactly promoting great hope.

He reached across, quietly placing his hand on the door. Drummond turned to give Theresa Bremner the nod; both officers roughly crashed the door against the wall. The pair lurched into the middle of the room.

"Oh my God!" Theresa Bremner cried.

40

The barman at The Watering Hole looked every inch like an extra from the film, *On the Waterfront*. There was definitely a hint of Terry Malloy about him. Marlon Brando's mean, dumb, brooding character shone out like a beacon.

Tall, about six-three, his slicked-back hair was held firmly in place with a gallon of gel. A washed-out, white, crew-necked T-shirt stretched across his muscular frame, the 'punk' was drying glasses with a bar towel when the pretty brunette entered the pub.

Still in character, Terry expertly flicked the glass onto a shelf, before folding the towel neatly, throwing it over his left shoulder.

The East End pub was busier than normal, probably due to the half-priced drinks happy hour that had just started. In normal practice, and especially on notoriously quiet nights, the owners would often extend the discounts for the entire evening. The locals soon cottoned on to this procedure, making The Watering Hole one of the most popular drinking dens in the area.

Of course, everyone, including the police, knew that the pub was merely a cash laundering front for the much more profitable drug-running business that operated from under its roof.

Majority shareholder and seasoned gangster, Billy 'Bananas' Buchanan, had spent most of his adolescent and adult life taking a rise out of the local plods. In recent years, however, the noose had gradually tightened around the criminal's neck; determined and incorruptible policemen like George Drummond, Mason Blackwell and Michael McMenemy played their part in closing down dozens of his dealers and outlets.

Buchanan was not the only gangster to suffer; the newly deceased pair of Vic Simpson and Thomas Mulraney felt the chill winds of justice in modern times.

Like an expert in the field of cancer research, all that was left for the police to do was find a cure for the cancer— or, in police terms, find a way to put these bastards behind bars for the rest of their lives. Not just the sergeants or the captains, but the generals.

Every eye in the place, male and female, was firmly on the stunning brunette as she elegantly strolled up to the bar.

Terry Malloy was chewing gum, flexing his muscles— yes, he could just about manage the two tasks at the same time. A third would probably have resulted in meltdown.

"What can I get ye?" he barked as if he'd been rehearsing the line all day.

"I'm here to see Billy Buchanan," Penny Richards replied. She didn't even try to weave a spell to entrance this gorilla, already declaring him a lost cause.

"He's no' in," came the cultured reply.

"Are you sure? He's expecting me."

"You need an appointment. Ah cannae let ye in without it." Malloy looked pleased with himself. *What's this posh bitch a' about?* He was only following the boss' instructions.

"Er… I have an appointment," Penny countered.

"Oh, what time for?"

"Duh… Now. And I'm never late."

Terry slunk off, tail between his legs, no doubt trying to work out whether or not he had just had the urine extracted from him.

Penny took the chance to have a good look around. She screwed up her nose at the peeling decor, the tired furniture, the drink-sodden carpet below her feet. In the corner, two worthies were playing pool and insisted on engaging in a deep, meaningful discussion about the rights and wrongs of the smoking ban. Unfortunately for everyone else in the pub, it was not a quiet, deep, meaningful discussion.

"Ah'll tell ye! The pubs'll die! People'll no' go oot any more!" one said.

The other nodded.

Then what the hell are you two doing in here? Penny felt the words on the tip of her tongue.

"Hey, you! Over here!" Terry Malloy waved across at the girl from the door in the corner.

Penny delivered a 'who me' kind of look, eventually throwing her bag on her shoulder and walking over. Malloy let the door go behind him, just as she reached it.

"Just go through," he spat at the girl over his shoulder, heading back to familiar territory.

Penny muttered something caustic.

She pushed open the door into a hall area with three doors, one at each side and one directly in front. *Take the one straight ahead unless otherwise instructed.* Penny recalled an edition of *Reader's Digest*, where the writer had listed his top ten tips of all time. Tip number five might just prove accurate in this case, although the knuckle-headed barman's stupidity factor was not in question.

Penny made a fist and banged loudly before pushing the door into the office of hoodlum, Billy 'Bananas' Buchanan.

"You don't mind if I sit?" Penny Richards asked politely.

The man nodded.

She couldn't help thinking that it was like a scene from a movie. Little boss guy behind a big desk, flanked by a shaven-headed, brick shithouse.

The main man looked as if he couldn't possibly have an unpleasant bone in his body.

Buchanan appeared every inch the nerdy bookworm. Lank, floppy hair and Harry Potter glasses, he was around five-eight and nine stone, dripping wet. He was wearing a cream-coloured T-shirt with a collar buttoned to the neck, unfashionable, drainpipe jeans and an extremely inoffensive smile. He looked about seventeen, first year at university, but was probably nearer twenty-five, thought Penny.

The big guy sported the obligatory tight suit, stretched over his giant frame. He was like the alter ego of Billy Buchanan, hands like shovels, twice the height and size. Arms folded, he sat on a little bar stool at his boss' side, stealing menacing glances at their visitor.

Penny Richards had, as always, done her homework. She quickly discovered that Bananas had been a rather cruel nickname that he had not inherited lightly.

Billy Buchanan had been both ruthless and single-minded during his teenage years, as he looked to expand his business. Realising that there were absolute shed loads of cash to be made in the drugs market, Billy had started operating out of a small, previously unoccupied patch, reinvesting his profits, broadening his horizons. By the time he was fifteen, he had a dozen foot soldiers covering large sections of the city. He was clearing ten grand a week.

Already, at that tender age, Billy had formulated a set of rules that would continue to be his tablets of stone to this day.

He always paid his suppliers on time. He treated his workers well. He would always employ the right people. His gear would be above average at all times. Finally, and probably most importantly, Buchanan's prices were always reasonable.

However, if anyone came close to upsetting his business model, for example, a substandard batch or a rogue dealer, his personal brand of justice would be swift and merciless.

Ronnie Masters had been a great friend of Buchanan's since the pair were toddlers. Their mothers were also the best of friends, and the families had often holidayed together in Scottish hotspots such as Largs and Saltcoats, or as far as their meagre budgets would allow. Billy liked Ronnie and Ronnie worshipped Billy.

Unlike his close friend, Ronnie had not been blessed with great intelligence. He had floated in and out of a succession of dead-end jobs— labouring, cleaning, bar work. Ronnie could never hold down a job for longer than he could hold his breath, and when Billy's mother pleaded with her son to give his pal a break, he relented; he broke one of his golden rules. For the first and last time, Billy allowed sentiment and emotion to cloud his judgement. Mind you, pal or no pal, Ronnie Masters was left in no doubt as to what was expected of him, and the severe consequences of any deviation from that path.

Within three months, Bananas would be telling his mother of how his great friend had fucked up again; of how he had ducked his responsibilities, this time taking off to the continent. 'Don't worry Ma. He'll be back. You know Ronnie.'

Ronnie Masters' body, throat slit from ear to ear, was lying heavy in the Clyde.

Billy had now lied twice to his mother, the first when describing the nature of his work. He adored the old lady, hated deceiving her.

* * *

"So, eh… Miss…?" Buchanan prompted.

"Come on, Mister Buchanan. You don't expect me to answer that?" Penny countered.

"I always like to know who I'm dealing with. Especially one as beautiful as you," he replied eloquently, taking her a little by surprise.

"Sorry, no can do. And that crap won't work with me!" she replied, deadpan.

Billy produced a wide smile. He liked this girl. She had style.

"Okay, you called me. So gimme your pitch. And, call me Billy." He sat back, folding his arms, still smiling.

Penny uncrossed and crossed her long, slender legs. Both men stole a look as if it was their duty.

"Well, Billy, I believe that each and every one of us is put on this Earth to serve a function. Your function is to provide a service to the community," Penny Richards stated like a seasoned politician.

Buchanan's face straightened at the reference to his business. He was like a protective parent.

"And my function is to help people such as you realise their goals by eliminating the competition." Penny paused for a reaction.

Buchanan stared at the beauty for a few seconds. His smile had long since evaporated, replaced by a look of mild interest. "Keep talking," he prompted.

"Okay. By competition, I mean the one remaining organisation in West Central Scotland that could give you a run for your money."

Buchanan looked deeply into her eyes.

"How do I know you're not filth?" Buchanan asked, testing the water.

"You could take my word for it," she replied.

Billy eyeballed her for two or three seconds before breaking into a hearty laugh. Penny Richards joined in. Just for good measure, the heavy's face cracked into the merest hint of a smile.

"You've got guts. I'll give you that. Now take off your

top." He was in serious mode once again.

"I beg your pardon?" Penny asked with some indignation.

"We need to check you for a wire. Then I'll feel a bit more comfortable." Buchanan nodded at his man, who was already on his feet.

"What? Okay! Okay!" She had suddenly realised that she was about to be frisked by the gorilla. No way!

The two men watched, spellbound; Richards slowly unbuttoned her blouse. Seconds later, she was exposing a crisp, white bra. The smooth, perfect curve of her breasts raised the temperature in the room. "Well? Are we done?" she asked, the temper rising within.

"Er… aye. Okay." Billy Buchanan cleared his throat a little uneasily. "All right. We've established the fact that you're probably not a copper. That means you're either a public-spirited defender of the faith. Or you're right into free enterprise, looking to land yourself a few quid?"

At last, they were arriving at the business end of the deal. Penny finished buttoning her blouse before threatening to reach into her handbag. "Uh-uh."

Billy checked the movement, holding out his hand. She passed the bag over to him.

"If you take out the white envelope— it's in the zipped pocket of the bag," Penny instructed, calming a little.

Buchanan had a quick rummage through the contents. He was relieved to find nothing dangerous or earth shattering. He did as he was told, producing the envelope, holding it up for confirmation. Penny nodded.

Billy passed the bag back and opened the envelope. A folded note inside was neatly typed, displaying two lots of numbers. Buchanan knew instantly that they were bank account details.

"Okay, how much? And what exactly will I get for my money?" He saw no point in prolonging the agony.

Richards paused for a second. This was the important part. She would need to get it just right. No room for ambiguity. The words bounced around her head— *Ask for what you want and how you want it, clearly and concisely; nothing more, nothing less.*

"One hundred thousand pounds paid directly into the account, the details of which you have in front of you. Fifty thousand up front; same-day transaction; fifty thousand on completion." *Now shut up*, the words commanded.

Buchanan's face remained deadpan. Penny Richards never flinched.

"And what do I get for that?" He held out his hands.

"Frank Milligan is sent to meet his maker in the same way Vic Simpson and Thomas Mulraney were." *Shut up.*

It was no secret that Milligan and Buchanan hated each other. The two men had crossed swords on a number of occasions— sectarian issues associated with Republican Milligan and Loyalist Buchanan, always high on their agendas. That said, a grudged respect for each other's operations could be assumed, although neither would admit it.

Ironically, Billy Buchanan had tolerated both Simpson and Mulraney. He could quite comfortably have coexisted with both or either of them. However, any fondness felt for the pair would not stop him muscling in on their operations. He definitely saw this as a massive business opportunity; especially now, with this cold-blooded assassin sitting in front of him. He was aware of her capabilities; his inside information described her recent work in graphic detail.

This arrangement seemed perfect. It would make up for the recent squeezes on his turf by Strathclyde's drugs units and their officers.

Yes, in a few short hours, he would be the main man.

"How do I know you've no' offered Milligan the same deal?" Billy asked.

"You don't. But if I had, you'd be dead by now," Richards retorted.

Their broad smiles returned in tandem.

"Drink?" Buchanan asked, reaching into his drawer for a bottle of his finest Scotch.

"Love one."

41

The blue Vauxhall Corsa swung into the hotel car park: inconspicuous hotel; inconspicuous car.

Brodie Metcalf was now in casual gear, his undertaker's dark suit, shirt and tie traded in for a football top, jeans and trainers. He had decided to retain his chubby appearance, courtesy of a specially made fat suit. At that moment, Brodie could not have looked less like a dangerous assassin than if he had worn a twinset and pearls.

As he sat waiting in the car, he reflected on another job almost perfectly handled— one which had seen Metcalf carve the name of Mason Blackwell into the handle of his gun. And one which should have seen him able to cross the policeman's name off his list.

The only problem was— Metcalf had lost the list.

Although the American had been blessed with a photographic memory, he had been trained never to leave anything to chance. 'Mistakes can prove costly' was another of Jack Feltham's well worn sayings. Metcalf had, of course, taken copies of his work schedule. That was not the issue; the issue was the possibility of the document falling into the wrong hands.

Fuck!

He had almost turned the car upside down, searching, retracing his movements. No sign of the list. Brodie tried to put it out of his mind. There was nothing he could do about it. If the police had it, they had it. He felt as if it would be nothing more than an inconvenience at worst; he felt as if nothing could stop him; he felt invincible.

Brodie Metcalf's arrogance could see him move a step closer to breaching another of the Master's golden rules: 'never, never, never underestimate the enemy'.

He checked his watch. A sudden movement behind the car had Brodie reaching. By the time the man's knuckle had tapped the driver's window there was a Glock pointing directly between his eyes. Metcalf's finger tightened on the trigger.

"Bang! You're dead!" the hit man announced, a huge grin on his face.

"Don't shoot, Kemo Sabay!" came the reply. The man straightened up, his hands in the air.

Metcalf dropped the gun on the passenger seat, got out. The two men hugged each other, slapping backs.

"How'd you get so grown up, little bro'?" the visitor asked, breaking away. "Let me look at you." There was genuine affection in his voice.

"It's good to see you again, Wyatt. I've missed you."

"And I you, Virgil."

The man smiled at Metcalf's reference to the famous lawman, Wyatt Earp. Half-brothers, sharing the same mother, the pair had spent many an hour together as kids. One of their favourite capers was to re-enact the famous OK Corral scene in which the Earps and the Clantons clashed. Brodie, the younger of the brothers had played Wyatt Earp's younger sibling, Virgil. The youngsters from the next block were the Clantons. The Clantons always got their arses kicked, the two brothers no mean exponents of the art of catapult firing. On reflection, both had spent some time since, wondering how nobody had lost an eye during the shoot outs.

"Let's go and grab a coffee. Oh, and by the way. Love the disguise. Very classy!" Big brother laughed at the

Glasgow Rangers casual standing in front of him.

Metcalf shrugged it off.

The two men jumped into Wyatt's car, heading for the nearest Starbucks. They had much to talk about; both men now able to relax away from the extreme stresses and strains of their day jobs. At least for the time being, they were enjoying each other's company once again.

The pair failed to spot the man sitting in the hired car at the end of the street. He watched intently as they passed close by on their way to the city centre.

"Contact made, Sir. Vehicle on the move. Will keep you informed of developments," the man whispered over the secure line. Lowering the phone, he swung out in pursuit of the Earps.

* * *

"I have to tell you, Brodie, Delgado's delighted with the progress." Wyatt put a proud hand on the shoulder of his only brother.

"Tell him I'll be looking for the rest of the cash tomorrow night. All going well, I'll be on my way home the following morning." Metcalf's general attitude tended to change to sullen and standoffish when he slipped into business mode.

"I understand that you can't hang about. If things were different, we could spend a little time together. Play some golf, maybe?" Wyatt sighed, sipping his coffee.

"Business first, Wyatt. I got some big bucks to pick up from a billionaire in Chicago. But why don't you come over in a couple of months? My treat. We got some great courses back home. I intend to play a lot of golf over the next fifty years or so," he joked, lightening up.

Metcalf sounded more than a little excited. He was genuinely looking forward to once again forging a close bond

with the man who had been his role model until a certain
Jack Feltham moseyed on in to take over that particular
mantle.

"Aye, Let's do that." Wyatt then leant across to make
sure that the people in the immediate vicinity could not
overhear. "Listen, Brodie. The cartel needs you to take care
of some more business back in the States. They want to set
up a meeting. Delgado will call me with the details. I just
need to let him know if you're up for it?" Wyatt paused for
a reaction.

The hit man took his time before replying.

"Why not? I suppose the golf can wait for a little while.
Tell Delgado it's a goer—.but it'll cost plenty. Especially if
cops are among the marks." Metcalf felt that he deserved
the right to pave the way to a big payday.

"Between you and me, Brodie, the cartel will pay any
money. They're losing millions every week— shipments
getting hijacked all over the country. Last week, they lost
twenty million dollars' worth of heroin to the NYPD. The
narcotics department there seems to know every move the
Colombians make. They're always a step ahead."

"Twenty million on one shipment? Wonder how much
of that made cold storage?" Brodie reflected. He was always
cynical when it came to cops. At least he was up front
about what *he did for a living*.

"The news report mentioned fifteen million." Wyatt
shrugged, confirming his brother's reflections. "Delgado has
a list. He's got guys on the inside in almost every police
department. The drug barons are stockpiling right now,
even as we speak. They need the do-gooders, the pilferers,
taken out. Just a few select names here and there— in high
places. Then they can release the shipments all over.
Brodie, it's costing these guys millions every day that the
drugs are in dry dock. They're desperate to move them on;
restart the process. You can make a fortune here. You're the

key!" He tried hard to keep his voice down; his enthusiasm threatened to bubble over.

"Why me?"

"What d'you mean?"

"There are a dozen guys back home who could do the job. Why me?"

Wyatt looked around the punters in the coffee house, mostly student types at that time of the day. He drew closer, his voice barely a whisper.

"As you know, Manuel Delgado's the official head of the cartel. In the early years, he would only use Jack Feltham to take care of any business."

Brodie Metcalf's mind delved into the past. Feltham had vanished for weeks at a time on a number of occasions during their time together. He had never fully explained exactly who he was working for, never mentioned the name of Manual Delgado. Brodie felt sharp pangs of jealousy thinking of the money the Master must have salted away. Until, of course, he remembered that Jack was not exactly in a position to spend it. However, it did irk Metcalf when he recalled the Master's money eventually going to a useless, good-for-nothing, son of a bitch, layabout cousin, his only relative in the world. He had vowed to pay the guy a visit, once the business in Scotland was concluded.

"Of course, Feltham's no longer with us," Wyatt continued, glancing at the expressionless Metcalf. "Delgado was really hacked off when Feltham was killed. Ready to unleash the power of God and all that. Anyway, he got to thinking. Who better to take over the contracts than a student of the Master? Especially the man who was able to take him out. Step forward the Viper," Wyatt announced, looking pleased with himself.

Metcalf shook his head in annoyance. He despised any reference to the Viper; he had vowed to kill whoever had come up with the name.

"And just what do you get out of this, big brother?" Brodie asked, obviously still annoyed. He was of the general view that people just didn't do things for nothing, especially people linked to his line of work.

He was right. Wyatt Earp paused, checked the room again.

"I want in on the action," he whispered.

Brodie shot him a puzzled look, inviting him to clarify.

"I want you to help me."

"I'm not with you. Help you with what?"

"I want you to teach me."

Metcalf sat back in his chair. He knew exactly what his brother was saying. He had said the same thing to Jack Feltham a few years back.

"But, you're a cop, for Christ's sake!" Brodie hissed.

"I know that. Jack Feltham was an FBI agent, remember? Bro', let's think about it. I already have most of the training. I'm ninety percent there. And this pays much better as well. You said so yourself."

"Nah, look, this is a different ball game, Wyatt. You have to be prepared to kill. Not everybody is able to do it. Without question, conscience or remorse." The words of the Master were flowing freely from Brodie's lips. Unwittingly, he was paving the way, already starting the process.

"I can do it. I promise. What d'you say?"

"I don't know!" Metcalf lowered his head, gently rubbing the gnawing pain away. He could feel the eyes burning into him, desperate for him to say yes.

Big brother held out his hand. Brodie hesitated, shook his head. Eventually, a smile broke out. The brothers clasped hands, hugged.

Across the street, a concealed camera was capturing the scene.

42

Royal Infirmary, Glasgow.

"Time of death was confirmed as sixteen-thirty hours?"

"Yes, that's right."

The big man was nearing the end of his address to a gaggle of eager journalists at a press gathering. The small waiting room at Glasgow Royal Infirmary was full to bursting with representatives from the media. Cameras, microphones and voice recorders at the ready, the pack smelled blood.

Chief Constable George Drummond, still visibly shaken by the earlier incident at Daldowie crematorium, was heading the police deputation. At his side, for moral support more than anything else, stood DI Theresa Bremner. Her pretty face was white, drawn, eyes red rimmed.

Only twenty-four hours ago, Theresa had been on holiday looking forward on her return to fighting her way through piled-up reports on her desk of petty thefts and minor assaults. Now, it seemed she had walked right into the middle of World War Three. She grimaced when she thought of how her own boss at Central Scotland HQ would react when he saw this report run later on one of the brand new, flat-screen, LCD TVs just installed at Randolphfield.

"Sir, is it true that the police are looking at a link

252

between this shooting and the three recent incidents at the Hilton, on Sauchiehall Street and on the Great Western Road near Clydebank?" The question was inevitable.

"We are still actively investigating all of these incidents. As you will appreciate, it would be remiss of me to go through the fine details of each one at such a delicate time. Now, if you ladies and gentlemen will excuse us, we have some work to do."

The politician type retort was typical of George Drummond. He continued, "I'd just like to reiterate that the thoughts and sympathies of everyone in the police department are with Inspector Blackwell's family at this sad time. He was a fine officer, one of the best I've worked with, and he'll be sorely missed. Thank you."

The massed ranks murmured, started to dissipate.

Drummond smiled ruefully. He had just had a relatively easy ride due to the circumstances. The next press gathering would not be quite as forgiving if things weren't resolved; if big steps weren't taken— and quickly.

* * *

George Drummond and Theresa Bremner waited in the room until the media circus had left, giving the hacks another few minutes to say their goodbyes to each other. Outside the door, many voices became few, eventually giving way to the familiar sounds of a regular hospital ward.

Drummond nodded at Bremner; the pair exited, striding towards a small, private room at the end of the ward.

The uniform on the door stood aside to let them pass; Drummond politely tapped before entering.

"Nobody gets in here unless it's first okayed by the chief constable or myself. Is that clear?" Bremner re-enacted her earlier conversation with the constable.

"Aye, Ma'am."

Theresa glanced up the ward. So far so good.

Inside, Alison Blackwell was hugging her husband as if all mankind was about to be wiped out. The petite blonde looked as if she had just had the fright of her life, her little china doll face, chalk-white. Respectfully, Theresa lowered her eyes when she saw heavy tears flood down both cheeks. She did not know Mason Blackwell's wife that well, having only met her on two or three occasions. Despite that, Theresa held nothing but respect for the English teacher, finding her extremely pleasant, with a good heart. Also, she knew that her great friend loved his wife like nothing on Earth, and that was good enough for her.

"Oh, Theresa. I can't thank you enough, both of you, for being there for him." She threw her arms around a startled Bremner, hugging her closely.

"It's good to see you again, Alison." Theresa patted her on the back, smiling embarrassingly at George Drummond.

In the background, Mason Blackwell lay grimacing in pain, just about managing a smile.

On the floor next to the bed sat a bulletproof vest, neatly folded. The remnants of two bent and contorted shells were buried deep into it. Whilst the average vest will certainly prevent penetration of a bullet, it could not stop the sensation of being kicked by a mule. Nothing would. Depending on the type of gun used, many a wearer had suffered a broken sternum following an attack. Thankfully, in this case, severe bruising had been the confident diagnosis.

The guard on the door announced that the doctor dealing with the case wished to come in. Bremner nodded her approval. He knocked and entered wielding copies of a series of x-rays.

"What's the diagnosis, Doctor? Is he going to be with us for a while yet then?" George Drummond joked.

Alison Blackwell failed to see the funny side, much to

the amusement of her husband. Mason chuckled, then winced, holding his chest. Flushed with embarrassment, Drummond roughly cleared his throat, folding his arms.

"You're a very lucky man, Inspector. As I thought, just severe bruising." The medic held up the x-rays, selecting two of the clearest. He pointed at the area in question. "Everything looks fine; no fractures. Not much we can do with the pain, I'm afraid. Rest and painkillers. That's it. Sorry." The doctor had been well trained. Young, and in his late twenties, he had 'a way about him', as Mason Blackwell's late grandmother was often heard to say.

"Thanks, Doctor. Believe it or not, I'd take that diagnosis any day of the week. It's miles better than the alternative!" Mason joked.

The doctor smiled, breezing out of the door almost as quickly as he had come in.

Blackwell turned his attention to his loving wife.

"Ali, honey? I'd love a cup of tea— if it's not too much trouble, could you?" He flashed the big doe eyes.

Theresa Bremner stifled a laugh.

"Of course, love. I'll go to the WRVS. Make my donation to a good cause. Would anybody else like a tea or coffee?" the dutiful wife asked.

Bremner and Drummond politely accepted the offer. Alison kissed her man softly on the forehead, slipped out of the door in search of the café.

"What're you all about, Blackwell? I hope you won't take advantage of that poor woman. She's just had a terrible shock," Theresa Bremner said, half seriously, half in jest.

"Did you do as I asked?" Blackwell, now addressing George Drummond, completely ignored his colleague's remarks. He wouldn't have a lot of time before the dutiful wife returned.

"Been done, Mason. As far as Metcalf is concerned, you're dead," George Drummond replied. "I hope you know what you're doing, though."

"Sir, to be perfectly selfish about it, I'm looking after number one here. If he thinks he's got me, I'm no longer a target. He moves on to the next one."

They nodded in agreement.

"And, it gives us an edge. I've seen his face, heard his voice up close and personal. Even with the disguise, I reckon I can identify him. I have an idea. It's risky, but it just might work."

"Obviously you haven't told Alison about the arrangements yet?" Theresa deduced.

"Don't worry about Ali. I'll take care of her. She and the kids need a holiday anyway. Now'd be a perfect time."

"You said you had an idea, Mason?" George Drummond enquired.

Blackwell stared at the old man for a few seconds.

"Mason?" he again prompted.

"Aye, Sir," Mason began. "It was when I was lying in that room at the crematorium, waiting for the ambulance. Not my choice of situations, for sure. But, lying there, I actually had a chance to think. I began to see things a little more clearly. Theresa and I had already discussed the possibility that we were dealing with two killers. I think that there's absolutely no doubt about that now."

"How could you be so sure?" Drummond asked.

"Well, Sir. Going as far back as the killing of young Baltimore, we know that Metcalf wasn't even in the country at that point. I'm sure that either Vic Simpson or Martin Anderson or one of their skivvies took care of that one. Anderson's vanished and Simpson's dead, killed by a blade. Meanwhile, at almost the same time that Simpson died, Mick McMenemy and the lad, Fred Boyle, were shot, execution style, point blank, the same as Tam Watson. We know that it was definitely Metcalf at the airport and the Hilton. It's safe to assume that he was also behind the

Sauchiehall Street attack on the security van. Now I hear that Will Munro's lawyer, Ben Vieri, has been poisoned, and Vieri's wife, Leah, has disappeared. If you recall, from what FBI man, Richard Belzer, said of Brodie Metcalf, poisoning doesn't sound like his type of gig. Maybe I'm mistaken. It is just a gut feeling. But, if I'm right, then who exactly is this other killer? Then there's the missing girl— Penny Richards? I think she has something to do with all this. We have to try to find her— and fast. She may be in grave danger." He paused. "And there's another piece of evidence to consider. Sir. If you reach into the inside pocket of my jacket. It's hanging up on the peg over in the corner. And, Sir, I have a pair of rubber gloves in the other pocket. Please put these on first."

The chief constable did as he was asked, snapping on the latex gloves and reaching into Blackwell's other pocket. With two fingers, he carefully pulled out what looked like a folded piece of paper— contained within a plastic food bag, sealed at the top. Drummond smiled. He was well aware of his inspector's habit for carrying such useful items in his pocket.

"Please take out the document, Sir. Be careful with it. Try to handle the very edges only. Oh, and, Sir? I'll get you to pass it on to Kenny Tilton at the lab if you don't mind? He'll understand why I chose to remove it from the scene, I hope."

Drummond carefully unfolded a single piece of paper, laying it on the bed beside Blackwell. The inspector said nothing as Drummond and Theresa Bremner began to study the typewritten text.

George Drummond squinted at it uncomfortably at first, his failing eyesight becoming clearer from a little further away. He pulled his head back a little, the paper eventually coming into focus. Theresa Bremner of the twenty-twenty vision brigade had already finished reading the document.

She glanced over at Mason Blackwell. The look told him
that she understood the situation.

"What's this? Michael McMenemy— Detective
Sergeant; Thomas Watson— Detective Sergeant; Mason
Blackwell— Detective Inspector..." Drummond stopped as
he came to the last name on the list. "Christ!" he barked.

"Aye, Sir. It's your name. You're the next target."

Blackwell saw the colour literally drain from the chief
constable's face.

"And you want me to be the bait, Mason?" Drummond
just about managed to say the words. Even after learning
the news that his life would be in danger, this top
policeman's resolve was as sure and steadfast as ever— or
so it seemed. In truth, George Drummond's tongue was
now almost welded to the roof of his parched mouth.

"Something like that, Sir. And don't worry; there are
ways to make sure that the odds are on our side." Mason
pointed at the bulletproof vest on the floor.

"Just what made you consider wearing the vest
anyway, Inspector?" Drummond boomed.

"Intuition, Sir. Raw intuition. And a slice of good
fortune," Blackwell replied.

"Mason?" Theresa Bremner looked puzzled.

"Yes, Theresa?" Blackwell asked.

"Just running through a few things. We think that
Metcalf was originally sent by Baltimore Senior to take
revenge for the killing of his son. And we also know that
Will Munro was set up to take the blame for it. Right?"

"Right."

"Okay. Then why isn't Munro's name on that list? Not
only that, why are the four names on the list all policemen?
What have any of you got to do with the killing of that lad?
It just doesn't seem to make any sense."

Blackwell looked at George Drummond, inviting him to
air his take on things. He didn't. Mason turned back

towards Theresa.

"You're right, Theresa. I agree. I think this thing has gone way beyond the killing of Lonnie Baltimore. That would have been a fabulously paid appetiser, before the main event. There are other forces at work here. The killer, Metcalf— I'm sure he's working for someone else as well as Baltimore."

"You mean he's doing a 'homer' while he's here?" Drummond asked, slightly tongue in cheek. He meant a little job on the side.

"Aye, Sir. With your permission, I'd like to have Fields and Baxter have a look at recent cases; maybe up to twelve, fifteen months old— cases where we've taken an active role. You, me, Mick McMenemy and Tam Watson. Let's see if it throws up a common link."

"Of course, Mason. Do it."

"Thanks, Sir." Blackwell then hesitated. "Sir? I wonder if you could arrange for us to retain DI Bremner's services, at least for a while." He glanced over at Theresa, and continued, "As I said before, I've a plan to catch this guy, and we will need good people to carry it off. Er, that is, if she is in agreement?"

"I'd love to help, Sir." Bremner decided without hesitation. "I'll make a call to the chief constable at Randolphfield."

"I'll do that, Theresa. I know Clive Castle very well. I'm sure he'll be in agreement," Drummond cut in.

"Thank you, Sir," she replied. Theresa Bremner looked pleased that the men rated her as a police officer. She had, at times, considered it unfair that she would often have to shine twice as brightly as any man in a similar job, just to get noticed. At least, here, she was surrounded by appreciative colleagues.

"One more thing, Sir."

Mason painfully dragged himself up to a sitting

position.

"The MI6 agents, Mailer and Wells? Are they still around?" Like any good policeman, Blackwell was trying to maximise resources; use everything and everybody to get the job done. And, he had worked with Doug Mailer previously. He considered Mailer to be a top man, bursting with ideas and solutions.

"As far as I know they were recalled for briefing early this morning. Y'know what it's like with these fellas—cloak and dagger."

Mason screwed up his face, disappointment in evidence across his handsome features.

"Of course, MI6 are in on this, too." Bremner had almost forgotten about them. This was getting more and more interesting by the minute for her.

The two men smiled.

"We'd better go over this plan of yours, then," Drummond mused.

*   *   *

Alison Blackwell returned carrying a tray of teas for everyone. They all looked as if they could now use one, for sure.

The tension felt in the room seemed heightened, stressed.

"What?" Mrs. Blackwell realised immediately that something was in the air.

43

DI Theresa Bremner took a deep breath and reached for the doorbell. She hesitated, almost chickened out. She wanted to be somewhere else at that moment. Anywhere.

Theresa could hear the sound of laughter— children's laughter— coming from around the back of the house at Roman Road in the Bearsden area of Glasgow. The inspector slipped down the front steps and followed the sounds, taking the garden path leading to the back yard.

Rounding the far corner of the big house, Theresa realised that the Munro kids had company over— the Vieri clan. She paused for a moment, smiling at the boisterous antics of the quartet, two boys and two girls. She was already aware of the closeness between both sets of twins and their parents; Mason Blackwell had briefed her before she left the hospital.

Theresa allowed her mind to drift. She became aware that her smile was forced, tinged with sadness. Confirmed lesbian, Theresa Bremner absolutely adored kids, couldn't get enough of them. And they liked her.

Theresa's lover just happened to have three brothers and nine nieces and nephews. Not one of them had a bad word to say about their favourite aunt, Auntie Tress. So, wanting to have kids of her own, Theresa had considered artificial insemination, and even getting it on with one of her handsome police colleagues at HQ. Naturally, the guy was keen on the proposed no strings arrangement. Who wouldn't want to have regular sex with this voluptuous woman until she became pregnant? Cold feet and sharp pangs of guilt combined to prevent it; the women finally decided that they were satisfied, sufficiently fulfilled to grow old together, childless.

* * *

"Can I help you?"

The female voice behind her gave her a start. She turned around quickly. A short, dark-haired woman, mid to late twenties, stood on the path facing her. Her hair was scraped back into an old-fashioned pony tail. She had on no make-up, exacerbating the fact that she looked as if she hadn't slept for a week. A washed-out tracksuit and pair of tired trainers completed the effect.

"Mary. Mary Munro?" Theresa confirmed.

"Yes. Who…? Who are you?" Mary queried, displaying slight annoyance.

"I'm Detective Inspector Theresa Bremner." She extended her hand towards the smaller woman.

Mary warmed a little at hearing the name, then accepted the handshake.

"DI Blackwell obviously couldn't make it, so I've been asked to bring you up to date with what's happening with your husband." Theresa thought that it would be best if she did not involve Mary Munro in the finer details of the 'death' of DI Mason Blackwell.

"Please come in, Inspector. Eh… this way. I like to try to keep my eye on them at all times." Mary indicated towards the back door into the dining kitchen, which overlooked the play area. "Sit down, please, Inspector. I'll make us some tea. Terrible thing about Inspector Blackwell, wasn't it?" she asked sympathetically.

"It was a shock to us all, and please call me Theresa,"

Theresa replied, getting off the subject as quickly as she could. She sat at the breakfast bar, looking out at the children. She laughed. "They're really sweet. Which are yours?"

"They have their moments. Red shirt and jeans, him. Pink top and black leggings, her." Mary clicked on the kettle, turning to face the inspector. Her expression had changed.

Theresa instinctively knew that Mary Munro was ready for the news, any news. *Might as well just go for it then.*

"DI Blackwell saved your husband's life, Mary. The car bomb at Sauchiehall Street? Will would have been in that van if Blackwell hadn't withdrawn him at the last moment. He's been moved to a safe house somewhere on the outskirts of the city. Only a select few know exactly where." Theresa paused for any questions.

Mary Munro kept silent. She put her right hand on top of her left, struggling to stop them shaking. Mary was obviously battling to hold it together.

"Your husband's fine, Mary. We let out a report that an unidentified male was killed in the back of the van. We think... We hope that the killer assumes that he has done his job."

"When...? When can I see him, Theresa?" Mary Munro blurted, along with the inevitable tears. She was sick and tired of keeping things bottled up for everybody. It was time to unload.

"Mary, I understand that you're desperate to see your husband, but just think about it. If this killer gets any inkling that he has unfinished business, he will return. And, if you and the kids are with Will at the time, who knows what might happen?" Theresa put her hand on Mary's arm.

"I know you're right. It... It's just so hard." Mary struggled to compose herself once again.

"Mary, he's still alive. You and these beautiful children are here waiting for him. It'll soon be over. Just a little longer, I promise."

"I hope you're right." Mary smiled at the kindness of the policewoman.

The two women had instantly taken a liking to each other. They could easily be friends under different circumstances.

Feeling all the better for having a sympathetic ear to talk to, Mary began to relax, sipped her tea. She turned to gaze out of the window at the children, still playing happily. She drew in a sharp breath.

"Leah. Leah Vieri. She's missing. She's my best friend. Is there any news?" Mary's eyes widened, though unable to make eye contact with her visitor.

Theresa had seen similar examples of such body language a few years previously, while on a New Age psychology course, which she had been talked into taking on her own time. She initially resisted, but then figured that the knowledge may be a tool that could help her in the field.

This particular subject was displaying the classic 'guilt for a forgotten friend's welfare' symptoms. "Leah's husband, Ben, reported her missing at the station this morning. Do you have any news?" Mary asked again, almost frantic by this time.

Theresa paused for a few seconds, anxious to get her story just right. She did not know any of the people involved, and hoped that this would help her to remain detached, to deliver the news professionally and concisely. *Here goes.*

"I was just about to cover all that, Mary." Theresa took a deep breath. *Maintain eye contact at all times.* "There was a killing at a Glasgow restaurant this afternoon. It's early days, but the signs point to a poisoning. Mary, the victim was Ben Vieri. The staff reported him having lunch with a woman, definitely not his wife, judging by the description they gave." Theresa paused.

"Ben. Ben's dead. But... But why? I don't believe it. I... I saw him this morning. He... He came around to see the kids, told me he was going to the police. Oh God!" Mary lurched forward, throwing herself into the arms of the policewoman.

Theresa Bremner held her close, gently patting her on the back.

"I'm so sorry, Mary. I know this must be hard." Bremner paused again, putting her hands on the other woman's shoulders and straightening her up. They were now eyeball to eyeball. "I have to ask this. Was Ben Vieri seeing someone else? Was he having an affair?"

Theresa stared into her eyes, trying to read a sign, any sign that could help the police shed some light on Leah Vieri's disappearance. Nobody could help her husband now, but, while there remained hope that Leah was still alive, maybe they could catch a break, find something that may lead to her whereabouts.

Mary lowered her eyes, which immediately indicated to the inspector that she was onto something.

"Ben loves... Loved Leah. He absolutely adored her. Oh God, what am I going to tell the kids?" Mary laid her hand against her forehead.

"Mary, could Ben have been seeing another woman? If there's anything, anything at all..." Theresa, sensing a breakthrough, made a mental note to drop the psychology course professors a 'thank you' note. "Mary?" she persisted.

Mary Munro dabbed her face with a tissue. She took a few breaths, then swallowed hard.

"A few nights ago, I dropped in at Ben and Leah's. I can't even remember why. She... She was out. Ben answered the door. I don't know why, but I just got the

feeling that he couldn't wait to get rid of me. He said
something about finishing off notes on some case that he
was working on. I got a feeling that he was lying. Normally,
he would invite me in for tea or whatever, wait for Leah to
get back."
        Theresa's mobile kicked off in her pocket. *Fuck!* She
reached in, felt the keyboard and expertly hit the off button,
catching it on the second ring. She had obviously done this
many times in the past. Theresa felt that she was close to
uncovering something here.
        "Go on, Mary," Theresa prompted.
        "Well, I went back out to my car and hung about for ten
minutes or so. Don't ask me why. I... I just thought
something was wrong. A few minutes later, a woman left
by the front door. It wasn't Leah."
        "Did you get a good look at her? Did they hug or kiss
on the doorstep?"
        "No, there was definitely no kiss or anything like that.
And yes, I did get a good look at her. There's another thing,
as well."
        "What?"
        "I've seen her before. I met her very briefly about two
years ago."
        "You're sure it was the same woman?"
        "Yes, I'm sure. She was sitting in Leah's kitchen, having
tea with her just like you and I are right now."
        "She's a friend of Leah's?" Bremner asked.
        "Apparently, but..." She stopped.
        "Mary?"
        "Well, she said the woman was a friend,— but I know
Leah. She was definitely uncomfortable around her. It was
as if she had dropped in unannounced. Leah definitely
didn't want her there. That was plain."
        "Could she have been a family member? A cousin? Even
a sister?"

"Leah had no family left alive, Theresa. I don't have a clue who the girl is."

"Okay. Anything else you can remember about the woman?"

"I never really thought any more about it. The next time I saw her was the time with Ben, recently."

"I need you to come down to the station— tomorrow, if you can— and give us a full description of this woman. A sketch would be fantastic. Maybe it's the same woman as the one who was seen with Ben in the restaurant." Theresa Bremner was scribbling notes in a little book.

"Of course. Anything. Leah? Is there any news on her whereabouts?"

"There has been a development." Theresa Bremner had one last thing to say before closing a difficult session. "Has Leah ever mentioned a man by the name of Thomas Mulraney?" the policewoman asked.

Mary, drying her tear-stained face with the palms of her hands, thought for a second before replying, "I've never heard of him. She's not mentioned that name, I'm sure. Why?"

"We have an eyewitness. She's a cleaner and says she saw Leah at Mulraney's works unit in the East End of Glasgow. The next day, she found Leah's purse lying on the floor of the unit. It was definitely hers— had her driving license inside."

Mary was turning the information over and over in her head. She shot the policewoman a puzzled look.

"I have no idea why she should be there. This man— Mulraney? Wh-what does he have to say?" Mary asked.

"We're looking into it at the moment," Theresa replied. She dared not discuss any more details of an ongoing investigation with a member of the public. Added to that, the news that both Thomas Mulraney and his Irish colleague had met a brutal and violent end in that very workplace, might not be something that Mary Munro's present mental state would appreciate.

Theresa had watched Mary very closely during their conversation. She would bet her mortgage that this woman was telling the truth. In her opinion, Mary Munro had not been involved in any of this.

Bremner's previous commanding officer at Randolphfield regularly had to reel her in, when he felt that she was getting too close to a case.

'Do your job professionally and subjectively, Theresa. Keep your emotions to yourself and you'll do just fine.' His words would come to the forefront now and again, especially when her work involved vulnerable women and/or children.

"Oh God!" Mary cried. "How the hell do I tell them what's happened?" She gestured towards the children.

Bremner racked her brains, searching for the right thing to say. "Is there anybody else who can take a turn looking after them? Give you a wee break?" It was all Theresa could conjure up.

Mary Munro shook her head sadly.

"Leah and Ben have no family that I know of. My parents are living in Australia and Will's father has Alzheimer's. He's in the loony bin. Fantastic, eh?" Mary fashioned a brave smile.

Bremner thought for a few seconds. She did not want to leave this woman all alone, especially not tonight.

"Tell you what. I finish my shift in an hour. I'll get us a carry out meal; Chinese, Indian; you decide. I'll give you a hand with the kids; stay overnight if you need me to. You must have a spare room in this mansion of yours." The kindly cop gently patted the back of Mary's hand.

"You... You'd do that for me?" Mary asked, tears welling up again.

"No problem. I'll call you in an hour," DI Bremner said,

this time obviously choosing to ignore the wise words of her former supervisor about getting too close.

*   *   *

Minutes later, Theresa was in her car heading for Strathclyde HQ. She wanted to bounce this latest information among the detectives. Maybe they would get lucky this time. Luck was certainly a commodity that was long overdue.

44

Bremner rolled her car into the spacious car park at the back of Strathclyde police headquarters in Pitt Street. She sat there for a couple of minutes, intentionally allowing the diesel engine to idle, warm down, before she got out. Theresa Bremner could best be described as a creature of habit; this motoring tip, courtesy of a retired police mechanic, was now part of her general, driving routine. The old friend had advised her that this simple exercise would add twenty percent to the life of the engine.

With the earlier parting instructions from Mason Blackwell— *Keep vigilant at all times*— ringing in her head, she would use the time to make sure that there were no suspicious characters in the vicinity, before entering the building.

On the way to HQ, Bremner had noticed a blue Renault taking the last half a dozen turns behind her. The Renault had hastily overtaken Theresa when she turned into the car park, accelerating away. Her spider senses were tingling big time, and she suddenly felt compelled to put her mind at ease; paranoia was developing with every moment, slight, but nevertheless apparent. It would drive her to investigate further.

She cut the engine and walked over towards the car park entrance, hugging the wall at the corner of the main street. Theresa peered around the corner and began to scrutinise parked cars on both sides of the road.

Around fifty yards up on the opposite side, the Renault was parked. It had obviously turned and was now facing back towards HQ. On the driver's side, judging by the height, Theresa could just about make out the shape of a man's head. She was too far away to identify him, needed to get a lot closer without giving the game away.

She became aware of heavy, deliberate footsteps coming up behind her. She turned quickly, the sight beholding her immediately giving her an idea.

She drew in a sharp breath and, with precision timing, slipped in just behind the couple, out for a late afternoon power walk. Clad in matching, shell suits and complete with hand-held water bottles, skip caps, bum bags, pump-up trainers, MP3 players and a little middle-aged spread, the pair's slow, tedious progress meant that Bremner did not need to work too hard to keep up. Impervious to their situation, due to the sounds of Abba's greatest hits invading their senses from the MP3s, the couple carried on with their routine, elbows flailing whilst they walked. Theresa even managed a smile, despite the tenseness of the situation; the stunted synchronisation of the walkers reminded her of her five and six-year-old nephews and their crazy, roboticmonster impressions.

Further on, breaking off from her human shields, Theresa bent low, her presence thankfully hidden by parked cars. She drew level with the Renault, stooping to pass between vehicles.

"Christ! Leave me a crowbar, why don't you?" she hissed under her breath.

The drivers of two bumper to bumper cars bore the brunt of her fury.

Still cursing, Theresa sidled carefully across to the opposite end of one of the cars. She sighed with relief; there were two and a half to three feet between it and the next. Almost on her knees, she moved stealthily between the cars, preparing to turn the tables on the voyeur. She let out a yell, nearly losing her head to a passing bus, roaring along Pitt Street; the shock dumped her unceremoniously on her behind, back between the cars.

Bremner thought that her heart would leap out of her throat as she sat there breathless, leaning against a bumper. She decided to stay put for a minute in case the man had heard her cries, although it was unlikely that he had, considering the thunderous noise from the engine of the bus as it flew past.

Theresa steeled herself to try again, craning her neck around the car.

Son of a bitch. Just what the fuck are you up to, DI Bremner mused. She had immediately recognised the driver of the blue Renault. She felt a distinct shiver fly along her spine.

Distracted MI6 agent, Andy Wells, was talking on his mobile phone and had no clue that the tables had been turned. Fearing detection, Theresa spun back into her original position. Eyes wide, her mind racing, she searched desperately for answers.

Similar to the way in which the experts might describe the visions a drowning person could encounter, Theresa's brain flashed up terrifying images.

Christ, this is an MI6 agent. Why is he following me? Could he somehow be involved in any of this? Is he one of the killers? Or is he some kind of sex maniac, stalking my every move? He's a government agent. He's carrying a gun!

An affirmative response to any of the above would not be a good situation.

Bremner quickly recalled how Agent Wells had apparently taken a shine to her during their investigation into the murders at Great Western Road near Clydebank.

Maybe he's a harmless type, just likes to watch, she

mused, not convinced in the slightest that this was the case. *If only it was that simple.*

Bremner heard a car start up. She held her breath, the Renault firstly pulling out, before braking sharply. Wells had stopped literally six feet from where she was sitting. All he had to do was to look down. Surely he would see her.

Andy Wells seemed to reach down into the side pocket of the car door; his shoulder leant against the window.

Theresa breathed in as calmly as she could, held it. She leant back hard against the car's bumper, almost trying to mould herself into the same shape. She closed her eyes.

Wells then yanked at his seat belt, clipping it in place before flying off— speeding along Pitt Street. The car swung right onto Sauchiehall Street and out of sight.

Theresa Bremner blew out her cheeks with relief. She thought it a good idea to wait awhile, in case the car should return, before heading along to HQ. In any case, she doubted if it would be wise to stand at that moment, given a sudden rush of blood to the head.

After a minute or two, Theresa got to her feet a little unsteadily, and calmly walked back along the road.

Her senses now razor sharp, she made her way, as per instructions, to the works entrance at the rear of the building. By now, confident that the threat had gone, she swiped herself in, using a card earlier supplied by Mason Blackwell. Theresa acknowledged the sentry on duty, before buzzing herself in to Blackwell's new, and hopefully temporary, office, a converted storeroom in the basement area.

* * *

Blackwell and Drummond were sitting on opposite sides of a huge, solid-wood boardroom table. Each had a little notepad opened up on his lap, police-issue biros hovering.

The top of the table was completely covered with all manner of documents: case file folders, ring binders, mug shots, scribbled notes.

Small, white, plastic cups, containing coffee remnants, randomly covered the surface. Even old school, Chief Constable George Drummond, had removed his jacket, loosened his tie. Perish the thought!

The 'late' Mason Blackwell's disguise— Theresa had jokingly referred to him as one of the Village People— lay neatly piled up on a chair. A hard hat, eye protectors, canvas gloves, boiler-suit, high-visual vest with Marshall Construction emblazoned on the back, and steel-toe-capped boots combined with a false beard— straight out of the BBC Scotland costume department— created the illusion.

"Oh, I'm sorry, Sir. I'll come back," Bremner said, noting the seniority of Blackwell's guest.

"No, Theresa. Please, come in. We were waiting for you. Take a seat," George Drummond replied, almost sweetly.

Before the incident at the crematorium, Theresa Bremner had met the newly appointed chief constable on a number of occasions, usually while attending training courses and seminars. Top policemen were often utilised in this way— to inspire and motivate. Bremner had initially considered Drummond to be a bit of a rough diamond, who could only get his way through raw fear and bombastic outbursts. In truth, that was a small part of the man's profile. The more time Theresa had spent in Drummond's company, in both private and professional capacities, the more she liked the man and his methods. She had seen him chew out the toughest and meanest of individuals with just a few carefully chosen words. His skill and choice of words when dealing with the media were legendary. And, this hard-bitten policeman could also mix it with the very best in the sympathetic, 'meeting victims' families' and 'delivering tragic news' modes, any hour of the day. The chief constable's 'Uncle George' type of persona was one with which Theresa Bremner could happily live till the cows came home.

"Thank you, Sir. Can I get anyone a coffee?" Bremner asked.

Both men screwed their faces; shook their heads as if they were heading for a caffeine overdose.

"Over there, Theresa. Help yourself." Mason Blackwell pointed.

She walked over to the small, tabletop cafetiere in the corner of the room, lifted the glass jug, felt the temperature and began to pour.

Blackwell and Drummond politely waited for Bremner to sit back down. Drummond handed her a notebook and pen.

"Will I go first?" Theresa asked.

"Fire away, Inspector," George Drummond commanded.

"Okay." She looked to the skies and began, "I spoke with Mary Munro at her home. Explained to her the situation with her husband. She's not stupid. She knows that he has to be kept as far away from her and the kids as possible. It must be hellish for her right now, especially as she has no one to help her with the kids. In fact, she's looking after four just now."

"Four? I thought the Munro's had twins?" Drummond asked.

"She's looking after the Vieri kids as well, Sir," Blackwell replied before Theresa could answer.

"That's right, Sir. There's no one on the Vieri side either who can look after the children, to give Mary a break," Bremner said.

"What about Social Services? Can't we give them a

call?" Drummond suggested with the air of a person possibly not in possession of the full facts.

Theresa Bremner rolled her eyes at Blackwell. It was obvious that she was not a fan of that particular department, having had a number of run-ins in the past with snooty, know-all officials. In her opinion, they were not in touch with the real world.

"I've offered to help Mary myself, Sir. In my own time, of course," she hastened to add, dodging any further debate on the subject of Social Services.

Blackwell lowered his eyes, expecting a verbal volley from the chief constable. Apart from a short, but gruff, acknowledgement, the statement was met with silence. Clearly, the young inspector had made quite an impression on the hardnosed policeman. Mason couldn't help thinking that anyone else would have had their arse put in a sling, if they'd ventured such a notion. He tried his hardest not to smirk, just about getting away with it.

"What was Mary Munro's take on the Vieri situation, Theresa?" Mason enquired, getting off the subject.

"What do you think, Mason? She's in bits. Her husband is being stalked by a hired killer. Her best friend's husband is dead and her best friend is missing," Bremner snapped at her colleague, obviously irritated. "Sorry, Mason. That was out of order," she immediately conceded.

"It's fine. Don't worry about it. I think we're all a bit on edge at the moment." Blackwell then glanced over at Drummond, as if trying to confer on the best time to break the news. He continued, undeterred, "Theresa, our forensics people couldn't find any evidence of Leah Vieri at Thomas Mulraney's unit in the East End. As a matter of routine, I had them go over to his scrap business and poke around for clues." He paused. "They found human remains at the site of a car crusher. Without going into too much detail, they only found some parts of the body. It was far too mangled for anyone to make a positive identification. They managed to extract some blood, enough for a DNA analysis. The bloods identified the body as female— something to do with hormones. I assumed that we would have to swab the kids, so that we would know for sure if the body belongs to Leah Vieri. I thought about that, and, out of respect, decided to go down alternative routes first. I wondered if we could maybe identify the remains from the database, without having to approach the kids. It all depended on whether or not she had a record. As it transpired, Kenny Tilton couldn't come up with Leah Vieri on the system."

"So, we have to get mouth swabs from the kids? Let me speak to Mary, maybe I can..."

"Not necessary," Mason cut in.

"But you said the database came up blank," Bremner countered.

"No, I didn't, Theresa. I said there was no Leah Vieri on the system. We did get another name, though. A Karen Richards."

There was a short silence.

"So the body isn't Leah's. Well, that's great news, isn't it?" Theresa asked, noticing the sombre looks on both of her colleague's faces. "Isn't it?"

"We dug deeper. Karen Richards disappeared off the radar a number of years ago. She'd been done for prostitution and small-time drugs; fairly minor stuff."

"And what's this got to do with Leah Vieri, Mason?" Bremner asked.

"A few years ago, Karen Richards changed her name by deed poll— to Leah Russell, who then later became Leah Vieri."

Theresa Bremner stopped in mid gulp, setting the coffee cup down gently.

"She wanted to clean up her act. Start a new life," she said quietly, her policewoman's training already searching for answers.

"Aye. We think so. Especially as Ben Vieri comes from an upper-middle-class family. Older parents who doted on their only child."

"She would obviously deny all connection with any relatives who linked her with the past. Oh Jesus!" Theresa suddenly barked.

"What?" her colleagues snapped in unison.

"You said Richards! Karen was the sister of Penny Richards!" Theresa smacked the flat of her hand down firmly on the table.

In their defence, Blackwell and Drummond had only just received the findings from senior CSE, Kenny Tilton. It was a flimsy excuse that they had been so wrapped up in everything that they had missed this simple connection. They both had. Mason sat back in his chair, slightly embarrassed, roughly running his fingers through his hair.

"Of course! We ran Penny's details through the database a few days ago. She'd a similar set of offences. Funnily enough, she dropped off the radar two or three years back, as well. She's either got smarter or cleaned up her lifestyle," Blackwell said. He tapped his chin with his pen.

"Mary told me that she'd visited the Vieri's about a fortnight ago. Leah was out and Mary suspected Ben of lying about what he had to do that night. She sat in her car outside the house for a while. Later, a woman left through the front door. Mary thought right away— affair. I think it could have been Leah's sister. Mary said that she had seen the same woman a couple of years before. This time, with Leah. She said Leah acted really uncomfortably around the woman. Said she was a friend."

"Do we have a photograph or identikit sketch of this Penny Richards?" George Drummond chipped in. "If Mary Munro or the waiter from the restaurant is able to identify her..."

"The waiter's given us a detailed description of the girl, Sir. Couldn't get anything going on the sketch, though. It happens sometimes; eye witnesses and artists can't get on the same wavelength," Blackwell said ruefully.

Drummond grunted an acknowledgement.

"Also, it was Mick McMenemy and Tam Watson who interviewed her when she came in here. They obviously won't be able to help. And I've never even met her," Blackwell mused, again cursing their luck. "No photographs; no prints; nothing," he continued, shaking his head.

"What about Will Munro? You said they used to be lovers, right?" Bremner asked.

There was a silence. Mason rolled his eyes, blew out his cheeks in exasperation. This case certainly was getting to him, another glaringly obvious fact lost within the smoky recesses of his mind.

"Do you think that he maybe has a keepsake or something?" Theresa asked, choosing to ignore the gaffe. "He could well have a photo? You did say that he was really mad keen on her at one point?"

"Aye. You're absolutely right. It's definitely worth a try. You'd have to go and see Munro, though, Theresa. Another shitty job for you, I'm afraid. By all accounts, Will Munro and Ben Vieri were really good friends."

"Great. Thanks, Mason," she stated sarcastically.

"There's nobody else I can fully trust to go and do it. I'll give you the address of the safe house. Just be careful and..."

"Keep vigilant, I know. And, speaking of that, someone was following me here today. I'm sure of it." Bremner had also nearly forgotten some more important details. What was going on in there today? Maybe complacency was heavy in the air.

"What happened?" Drummond and Blackwell asked in unison.

"A blue Renault took a few turns behind me on the way in. It sped past when I turned into the car park. I thought I'd investigate further, and walked back around to the front. I looked up the road. The Renault was parked; somebody was watching the building. I managed to sneak up and observe from the other side of the road." She paused.

The two men were hanging on her every word.

"It was Andy Wells, the MI6 agent."

"Wells? You're absolutely sure of it?" Mason demanded confirmation.

"One hundred per cent!" Theresa provided it.

"And he definitely didn't identify you?" George Drummond asked, so tight lipped that his mouth seemed about to crack into a thousand pieces.

"No, Sir. I'm quite sure of it," she also confirmed.

"I'm going to bloody sort this out right now!" Drummond stood, his huge hands grabbing the receiver of the phone. His fingers were already angrily thumping the buttons. Somebody at MI6 HQ was going to catch it, big style.

"Wait, Sir. Please? Let me try to find out what's going on first. I'll speak to Doug Mailer," Blackwell said.

"Let me do it, Sir. I think you're forgetting something else, Mason," Bremner replied, turning to her friend.

"What's that, Theresa?" Blackwell asked.

"You're dead, remember?" she replied, smiling.

"That would be a problem trying to explain," he admitted.

Drummond replaced the receiver and sat down again, his face like thunder.

"All right, Theresa. Get back to me as soon as you speak to him," the chief constable commanded.

"Of course I will, Sir. You want me to go and see Will

Munro now, Mason?"

"It can wait till morning, Theresa. I would go and see Mary Munro tonight. She's had a shitty day anyway. Might as well give her the news about Leah as well; get it all over with. Good luck with that." Blackwell felt really guilty for landing all of this on his friend. However, there really were no options. Mason Blackwell had to stay out of sight and Theresa Bremner was the next best person for the job. "Oh, and before you go, Theresa? Sign this, will you?" Mason produced a brown, reinforced mail bag, tearing off a white document, which had originally been stapled to it. He indicated at the place to sign.

Bremner looked puzzled, but still trusted her friend enough to sign at the 'x'.

Blackwell countersigned the form and picked up the bag. Tearing it open, he produced a small, black handgun in a shoulder holster and passed it over to a shocked Theresa Bremner.

"It's a semi-automatic, 9mm Glock. The best in the business. You have been trained in using it?" Blackwell asked.

Theresa had never seen him so focused.

"Well, yes, of course, but..."

"Then take it. It's time to even up the odds here."

Blackwell handed the gun to his colleague. Theresa Bremner felt her heart skip a few beats when she held the 'gift'. She glanced at Chief Constable George Drummond. There was a look of steely determination on his face.

I certainly didn't sign up for this, Bremner mused.

45

"Local Glasgow businessman, Frank Milligan, was killed last night in a shooting incident outside his home. The twenty-nine-year-old, who owned a number of businesses, including property letting agencies and a string of pubs, was found lying in the street in front of his house with fatal head and chest injuries. He was declared dead on arrival at the city's Royal Infirmary.

It is thought that Mister Milligan was discovered by his wife, Tracey, the daughter of Glasgow Cathcart Labour MP, Gordon Rennie. The couple had only been married for three months, their high society wedding attended by a number of celebrity guests including..."

Billy Buchanan hit the off button on his TV remote. He sat back in his chair, hands behind his head, in the private room of his pub, The Watering Hole. A smug look crawled over his face.

Buchanan had just been watching the morning edition of the local BBC news, and the lead story suited him just fine, thank you very much. Reaching into the bottom drawer of his desk, the borderline alcoholic produced half a bottle of Famous Grouse whisky, and cracked the seal, toasting his good fortune and the actions of the beautiful brunette, who had recently landed on his doorstep with an offer he couldn't possibly refuse.

The transaction had just cost him a hundred grand but it was well worth it. Billy was now ready to muscle in on the wreckage following the demise of the other three major players in his particular area of expertise— drug dealing.

Buchanan was a few things— ruthless, heartless, rich; one thing he was not, was stupid. In the last couple of days, since Penny Richards' visit, he had spent most of his time making sure that his business operations were whiter than white. Or as near white as he could get them. Probably a shade of dirty grey would be nearer the mark.

Buchanan knew that there would very soon be a visit from the police drugs squad, armed with a probable leading question— how and why would only three of the four 'faces' in the country be violently and brutally murdered within the space of a few days?

Worse, now there was a politician involved. A Westminster MP was lining up to throw his considerable clout behind the investigation.

Worse still, Gordon Rennie MP was the eternally grieving stepfather of a sixteen-year-old schoolgirl who had died under the wheels of Buchanan's speeding Diablo-red Ferrari, just over two years ago.

Rennie, a still practising, but part-time, prosecuting lawyer, was no match for the slick, but obscenely expensive, defence brief employed by Billy Buchanan.

Now, in a bizarre twist, Rennie's own daughter had been widowed at the tender age of twenty-five. Buchanan was firmly in the frame and the MP would surely stop at nothing to finally nail him once and for all. Billy had carefully weighed up the pros and cons before giving the green light for Milligan's execution. In his view, a multimillion-pound drugs empire was worth a little extra heat. The obscenely expensive defence lawyer had been alerted, already preparing for round two. *Let battle commence.*

"Boss, that's that big dame back in tae see you again!" The dumb barman dragged his knuckles over to his boss' door, shouting in.

"Tell her to come in!" Buchanan shouted back.

Seconds later, Penny Richards stepped inside, closing the door behind her. She smirked. Tweedledee and Tweedledum were sitting in their usual positions, as if they had been there since she last saw them. They even appeared to be wearing the same clothes.

Buchanan would, especially now, make sure that his bodyguard was shadowing him at all times. He was not in the habit of taking chances.

Penny smiled, nodded at the heavy; she received a cold, blank stare in return.

"I'm here for the rest of my money, Mister Buchanan," she said, coldly. Penny saw no reason for niceties. This was purely business.

"Have a drink first. We want to toast a job well done," he replied, again reaching into his drawer.

She screwed up her face. *Ten-thirty in the morning—don't think so.*

"No thanks, I haven't got time. And I don't want to hang about here too long. I assume you know that you're going to have visitors sometime soon?"

"Aye. I'm expecting them any time. Listen, when you're back in town, look me up, will you?" Buchanan invited, pulling out a folded piece of paper from his shirt's breast pocket. He tossed it over onto the desk in front of Richards.

Penny simply ignored his last statement, picking up the paper. She opened it up, studied it carefully for a few seconds. Her face softened.

"Thanks. I'll be on my way. Hope to be of service to you again." Penny stood, extending her hand towards Billy Buchanan. At the same time, her left hand was dropping Buchanan's receipt for the second tranche of monies— fifty grand— into her small shoulder bag.

The heavy at her side lazily dragged himself to his feet just in time to see the shiny, black handgun flash in front of his face.

The bullet entered just below the right eye. The big man fell face first, his head smashing sickeningly off the edge of Buchanan's desk, before he crashed to the floor. His flailing arms took some of the desk furniture with him, sending it flying across the room.

By the time Billy Buchanan could even think of reacting, he was taking the second bullet through the top of his head; blood and brain and bone fragments sprayed across the dirty window directly behind him.

Billy slumped heavily in his chair, his neck unnaturally bent over the back of it, eyes staring at the ceiling. Hot trickles of blood speared down his forehead.

Richards pumped another bullet into each body, lifted her bag and made for the door.

"Boss! You all right in there?" Knuckle-head had been drying glasses behind the bar, preparing for opening. Attracted by the commotion, he was now standing, nose pressed against Buchanan's door.

Two bullets ripped through the light panel of the cheap, 'egg box' door, one catching the barman's throat. The other slug rattled into his chest cavity, piercing the heart. He went over like a giant Redwood tree, his momentum taking him across a small, round table. The legs of the table instantly gave way; his limp body was left twisted and shattered among the resultant, tangled debris. A tiny fountain of blood coursed through the hole in his chest, each failing heartbeat making the fountain slower and weaker than the one before, until the flow came to an end.

Penny Richards allowed the dust to settle before slipping out of the fire exit door around the back.

At the front door of the pub, a small band of the local worthies was gathering prior to opening time.

Among them, waiting patiently, stood a couple of plain-clothed policemen.

Once again, the force had been beaten to the punch.

46

"Mason, I'm literally just off the phone with Doug Mailer. Can you talk just now?" Theresa Bremner was in her car, speaking via the Bluetooth earpiece.

She was on her way to visit Will Munro at the safe house on the outskirts of the city.

Theresa had made up her mind to be ultra cautious on every journey she took, periodically testing the following traffic with swift and sudden manoeuvres and lightning bursts of speed. The other road users' horns blasted in annoyance, as the very decent driving skills of DI Bremner were tested to the full.

"Aye, Theresa. Go ahead," Blackwell replied.

"There isn't much to tell. I told him what had happened outside headquarters yesterday. At first, he said that I must've been mistaken, and that he was working on a case with Wells at that time. When I gave him the make, model and reg of the car that I saw, he clammed up— wouldn't be drawn on anything else. He kept going on about Special Ops investigations and National Security and stuff— how he couldn't possibly comment."

"Aye, I'll bet. Mailer'll quote the company line all day. I would, as well, in his shoes if it came to it," Mason said, ruefully. "Did he say anything else, anything at all?"

"He knew that you and I were friends. Said he was really sorry to hear of your death. It gave me the creeps, to be honest."

"Okay, Theresa. Thanks for that. I'll pass it on to the boss. Don't know what he'll be able to do with it, but I'll tell him anyway. Good luck with Munro."

Blackwell rang off. He was sitting alone in his makeshift office, deep in the bowels of headquarters; to all intents and purposes, he was a dead man.

The silence was deafening. Theresa Bremner was right. It was eerie. Mason had been so busy since his 'death' until now. This was the first occasion that he had some time on his hands— for reflection. He didn't like being dead— didn't like it at all.

Chief Constable George Drummond had been called by the bigwigs to a hastily arranged, hush-hush meeting, to be held later that day in Edinburgh. Even *he* had no idea what it could be about.

Drummond and Blackwell had spent the previous day going over the fine details of their trap to catch a killer. Mason closed his eyes tightly, only too aware of the consequences of getting it wrong. He had insisted, through George Drummond, that Juliet Fields and Brian Wheldon accompany their boss to the meeting; that they never let him out of their sight, just in case.

As he began to get lost in the middle of the rehearsal of the plan in his mind, Blackwell came back with a start. His mobile phone, set on silent, was vibrating across the desk in front of him. He checked the display, smiled.

"Hi, love. Am I glad to hear from you! I…"

"Just shut up and listen good," the voice on the other end of the phone interrupted Blackwell's anticipated conversation with his wife.

Mason lowered the phone and rechecked the name in the display— Ali.

The three letters burnt like a brand into his brain. His breathing quickened. He could feel the thumping of his heart coursing through his head. Hands sweating and shaking violently, Mason's survival instincts began to kick in as he replaced the phone to his ear.

"Go on," he replied, his voice almost a throaty whisper.

"I have your wife. Unless you want selected parts of her posted to the police station, you'll do exactly as I say. Is that clear?" The voice delivered the lines simply and starkly.

Think! Blackwell reached for a pen and notebook, swapped the phone to his left ear. He began to scribble— Voice Disguised. Male. Trying To Change Accent? Familiar? Familiar? He underlined the last two words again and again, the frantic strokes of the pen taking it through to the next sheet.

"I said is that clear?" the voice asked again.

"I want to speak to my wife. Put her on the line," Mason replied, much calmer than before. *Find out if they, indeed, have a bargaining tool before proceeding.* He had read the words from some recent newspaper article, at the time concluding that it did seem to make sense.

There was silence for around ten seconds— the longest ten seconds of Mason Blackwell's life. *Please don't hang up. Please don't hang up.*

"Mason? Mason?" The unmistakeable voice of Alison Blackwell rocked him back to the living. Understandably shrill and panicky as it was, there was still no doubt that it was her voice.

"Ali, love? Are you all right? Are you hurt?"

"N-no, I'm okay! Please help m-" Mrs. Blackwell was then forcibly removed from the airwaves.

"M & D's, Strathclyde Park. Twelve o'clock. No police or she's dead."

"The funfair? It's a big place. How will I find you?"

"I'll find you."

The display then read 'call disconnected'.

Mason stretched his arms out in front of him, lowered

his head forward onto the desk and bumped his forehead on the surface repeatedly, but lightly.

He glanced sideways at the dusty clock on the wall— 10:15. His wrist watch confirmed the accuracy. Sitting again, he reached into his pocket, popping a couple of paracetamol capsules from their packaging. Mason downed them with a swig from a bottle of water. He studied the hand holding the bottle. Tremors, almost as strong as electric shocks, made the liquid lap violently up the sides of the bottle.

He felt inside his jacket, tapping a vital piece of equipment. Removing the 9mm Glock from its shoulder holster, Mason double checked the mechanism. He needn't have. The top of the range handgun was brand new and ready for action. Blackwell only hoped that he would have the chance to make sure that it got some.

47

DI Theresa Bremner had completed a number of laps in her car of the immediate area around Sampson Street, temporary address of accountant, Will Munro.

Satisfied that there was no tail, she decided to pull over anyway; sit for a few minutes, just in case. Theresa certainly would not want to be responsible for flagging up Munro's position to anyone. Especially since she had become friendly with Will's wife, Mary, and had begun to forge a special relationship with all four children.

Theresa had broken the bad news about the fate of her great friend, Leah Vieri; had been there for her as a shoulder to cry on.

She saw no point in highlighting the previously documented indiscretions of the dead woman. An impending criminal trial would definitely serve that purpose. In Theresa Bremner's opinion, it could wait until then. Mary Munro had already endured quite enough for now.

Understandably, Theresa had not slept well in the guest bedroom of the Munro house. The women had talked until two in the morning, and Theresa was relieved that she had heard Mary consider the possibility of adopting the now-orphaned Vieri twins. It meant that Mary was trying to accept the situation and was thinking of the consequences. Any further talk of adoption would have to wait, however, until the Munros were re-united. Which takes us back to the main reason for Bremner's restless night— she had to make sure that Will Munro was still in one piece for the long awaited reunion. Inside, she was secretly chuffed that Mason Blackwell had trusted her enough to provide her with the information on Munro's current location.

Theresa was on the steps of the tenement building, checking out every vehicle in the street. She had stored the position of each one in her mind. No movements in or out in the last ten minutes.

She stood on the top step. *Floor 3, Flat 1.* Bremner selected the correct button on the directory at the entrance.

"Hello," said a voice, cutting the silence.

"DI Bremner," she whispered, cupping her hand to her mouth as she spoke.

A buzzer, followed by the click of the door release, allowed the policewoman to enter.

On the third floor, Theresa stopped outside the door of Flat 1. She wheeled around to glance at the other three doors on that floor. No signs of life. Before she could knock, the door opened and a plain-clothed cop invited her into the flat. He duly scrutinised her ID, releasing his grip on his handgun when he had confirmed the identity.

"He's in there, Ma'am," he said, pointing to a room at the end of the corridor.

Theresa nodded, pushed her way in.

The flat was generally clean and tidy, if a little spartan. The living room consisted of a two-piece suite, nest of three tables and a cheap, MFI bookcase. A dozen or so paperbacks sat untidily on the shelves. The books had served their purpose— to go part of the way to quenching Will's insatiable thirst to read, which he had inherited from his father.

A rather bulky, old-fashioned, colour TV sat in the corner. Faded picture quality, it was set on BBC One, broadcasting   one   of   those   endless   property auction/renovation programmes that Theresa swore would frazzle the brain, if exposed to on a regular basis. Recently, back at Stirling, she had found herself actually watching, worse still, enjoying the drivel during some night shift weeks.

Sitting on one of the grubby chairs facing the TV, was a blond man, late twenties, piercing blue eyes, very good looking. Will Munro politely rose to his feet as Bremner walked in. Nervously drying the palms of his hands on his jeans, he extended a hand.

"You must be Inspector Bremner? It's good to meet you," he said.

"Please, call me Theresa."

"All right— Theresa. Please sit."

Bremner sat on the other two-seater chair, preparing to study the man, whom until now, she had only heard tell of. Tall, Nordic, lovely smile with a hint of five o'clock shadow. *If only I were straight,* Theresa pondered.

On the debit side, Munro looked a little gaunt and drawn; he was obviously under extreme pressure. It was clear that he was not used to receiving visitors. It was also clear that today he was expecting some news; good news he hoped, given the fact that DI Bremner's visit had been announced in advance. He was probably of a mind that he was about to be given the all clear to return to his former life.

Will Munro sat, any hopes of a quick solution exploding in front of his eyes. His face ran a full gamut of emotions, as Theresa slowly and sympathetically unravelled the horrors of the last few days. She elected to omit the part of the story regarding Ben Vieri's indiscretions, mostly due to the ongoing investigation, partly to limit emotional distress.

She found herself almost all out of consoling words, staring blankly at the TV screen, unable to concentrate, as the man opposite her cried like a baby at the loss of the friends, whom he and his wife had loved so dearly.

"I'm so sorry, Will. I know this is absolutely horrific, but I just need you to know— Mary's doing okay. I stayed with her last night. She's strong— I just wanted you to know."

Munro managed to fashion a sort of smile.

"Much stronger than me; that's for sure. Thank you for staying with her. I'm sure she appreciated it."

"No problem. I'm happy to help. There is one thing that you can do to help us," Theresa said hesitantly.

"Of course. Anything," he replied, still wiping away tears.

"We need to know if you have a photo of Penny Richards."

"Why? Who cares if that bitch's run off or not?" Munro suddenly snapped at the mention of his ex's name.

"She may be involved in the killings. Or her life may well be in danger. If we can find out where she is, I'm sure we can wrap the case up quicker." Theresa said her piece and waited, glancing over at him out of the corner of her eye.

Munro looked to the heavens, possibly for some guidance. He stood, dug into his trouser pocket. Unbuttoning his wallet, he produced a tiny, passport-type photograph. Will looked away as he handed Bremner the image.

She studied the photo. It was one of those small, booth-type efforts; the kind you might see at a train station or a post office. It depicted a young, carefree couple pulling faces at the camera. Luckily, the quality of this particular image was very good. The girl's striking features could be easily identified.

"It was taken a good few years ago. She was a brunette at that time; now she's blonde. Still as pretty." He choked a little on the concession. "Don't know why the hell I still have it. Hope it helps," Will said, more than a little embarrassed.

"Thanks. I'm sure it will." Bremner tapped the photo. "I have to go. The sooner we can distribute this, the more chance of a breakthrough." Theresa stood to go.

Right on cue, her mobile phone burst into life; the name, Mason B shone in the display.

48

Somewhere on the outskirts of Edinburgh

Some of the most powerful law enforcement officers in the UK were attending the meeting. Top policemen from a selection of the thirty-nine English, eight Scottish and four Welsh police forces were already seated around the table in the basement room of the small, insignificant hotel in the Dalkeith area of the city.

Secret Service agents swarmed around the town, blending in, mingling with the locals. They had been placed on amber alert.

The impending function, which could best be described as a terrorist magnet, had led to Edinburgh being chosen as host city. The choice was probably made due to the purpose-built, underground bunker in place at this, the unlikeliest of locations. The owner of the hotel, a former chief inspector, stood to pocket a right few thousand quid for the privilege. Some of the attending delegates had already openly debated the nepotistic nature of the choice of setting.

Chief Constable George Drummond was representing Strathclyde police force, the only Scottish member in the room. Detective Constables Juliet Baxter and Brian Wheldon had also travelled through from Glasgow with him, the reason, to them, unclear for now. Baxter, in truth, felt relieved to be able to take a break from her regular partner, Trevor Fields. She would wish him good luck in his, now solo, trawl through the department's seemingly endless, historic, crime cases.

Juliet much preferred field work. Fields, for his part, was a bit of a bookworm, who revelled in such assignments; the intense heat and tension of a field situation was not really his thing. Juliet had dug him out of a hole on a number of occasions. She kind of liked Trevor— that was clear to everyone— even to the point of having to endure idle and unfounded gossip around the station. The jury was out on the pair. Had they or hadn't they?

Brian Wheldon was as reliable as an old bloodhound, a real steady Eddie. Nearing retirement, he had become a little disillusioned with modern policing techniques. Brian was a clip around the ear, catch them young, kind of copper. Such attitudes, right or wrong, had undoubtedly contributed to him being perennially passed over for promotion. That said, Brian was never fazed by anything that the job would throw at him. Some people were cut out to be good, solid, respectable police officers, with little or no interest in furthering their careers. Wheldon was undoubtedly one of those.

Unaware of the fact that they had been handpicked by Mason Blackwell, Baxter and Wheldon had been ordered to hang around on the periphery, stay alert and question everybody and anybody who looked more than a little interested in what was going on. Worryingly, as far as both were concerned, they had also been gently coerced into signing acceptance forms to carry firearms. Wheldon had earlier explained to Juliet that, in all his years of service, this was only the second occasion that he had been asked to carry a gun. In addition, with the recent events that had taken place in Glasgow, and this hastily arranged meeting, Baxter and Wheldon were feeling more than a little jumpy.

Bizarrely, Drummond sensed the increasingly

heightened mood of his officers, and began to feel more and more at ease with every passing minute. He was a firm believer that a little rush of adrenaline would do no harm on such a day. It could provide the edge in a life or death situation.

It had been almost twenty minutes since George Drummond had filed into the meeting. Baxter and Wheldon, twitchy and tetchy at first, had begun to relax. The atmosphere outside and around the hotel was definitely low key— exactly the type of image top brass had been trying to project.

Drummond scanned the room.

Brian Hillhouse, commander-in-chief of the Metropolitan Police in London, was chairing the meeting. Hillhouse was old school, like George Drummond. Drummond and Hillhouse, having met on numerous occasions at meetings and policemen's balls and the like, had enjoyed a fair few drinking sessions at some of these shindigs. They would spend most of their time attempting to right the wrongs in the world.

George Drummond had heard that his colleague had not had his problems to seek in the last three years, battling alcoholism and family health problems— his lovely wife had been lost to cancer. The pair had exchanged a brief nod and a smile before the start of proceedings. Drummond felt that their next private conversation would be a sombre one.

On either side of Hillhouse sat a couple of dark-suited individuals.

Definitely Secret Service, thought Drummond. The older guy was around fifty, silver-haired, with a rough complexion. Although he was dressed immaculately with a crisp, white shirt and silk tie, Drummond pegged him right away as a field agent. The way he held himself, worked the room, there was no doubt.

The other man was mid thirties, slimmer, thick black hair; his voice came across as slightly effeminate. Drummond came to the conclusion that this man probably worked in the intelligence division. *The world's bad guys would have him for elevenses out in the field,* he thought.

"Gentlemen, thank you for taking the time to attend today's meeting. I'm sorry for the short notice, but, as I will explain, we have been left with little option." Hillhouse opened up the event. Standing, he reached into his pocket for his reading glasses. He perched them on the end of his nose and peered at a prepared speech, flattened out on the table in front of him.

There had been brief initial introductions among the police officers in the room. Drummond recognised Bill Hamilton from Derbyshire constabulary, Vernon Mattheus from Greater Manchester and Roger Tremell from South Yorkshire. The chief constable from Gwent in Wales had only recently been promoted to the position; a young and bright Ifor Lewis impressed the gnarled, hard-bitten Scotsman during a brief, two-minute conversation.

The two agents had made their entrance just before Brian Hillhouse stood to address the meeting.

"This is Special Agent Tom Lassiter. He is an experienced MI6 field agent, specialising in drug trafficking countermeasures," Hillhouse announced, motioning towards the older man. "The gentleman on my other side is Agent Bob Shanks. Agent Shanks operates out of the Intelligence Division at MI6 headquarters."

I can always spot them, Drummond mused, smiling smugly.

"I'm going to invite Special Agent Lassiter to speak to you first." Hillhouse nodded at the older man.

Lassiter stood, removed his jacket and placed it neatly on the back of his seat. He picked up a set of notes, and strode over to a specially prepared table at the end of the room.

A TV linked to a DVD player burst into life. Seconds later, everyone was staring at the face of a rather mean-looking character, black hair, black eyes, black moustache and beard; the kind of man you prayed that your daughter would never meet, let alone bring home.

"Gentlemen, you are looking at the face of Manuel Delgado. This man is responsible for the exportation of eighty percent of Colombia's drugs. He is head of the largest multibillion-dollar drugs cartel in the world, supplying to many countries." As Lassiter spoke, the DVD rolled images of how the various substances are made, grown, harvested and distributed, using a combination of child and slave labour. "The United States, Canada, Brazil, Australia, Denmark, Holland, Germany and the UK, of course. Their market here is second only to the States." Lassiter paused, slipped to the next page.

There were audible murmurings; the men exchanged short views on what they had just heard and seen. "Gentlemen, please. Hear me out. This is vitally important," he scolded. Mildly annoyed, Lassiter continued, "During the last few weeks, a number of high-profile murders have taken place throughout the country, most notably in Glasgow." He had spotted George Drummond's name badge, and nodded towards him.

Drummond sat forward as if hanging on Lassiter's every word.

"There have been incidents in London and Manchester." Lassiter went through the same procedure for Vernon Mattheus.

Drummond whispered oaths under his breath. He was becoming increasingly aware of the enormity of the problem facing them all. He had read well-documented FBI reports about the cartels. They were backed to the hilt by mighty powerful people; would stop at nothing to make sure that their poison got through. Drummond swallowed hard; the vision of his name written on Brodie Metcalf's hit list again came to the forefront of his mind.

"It appears that some of the police forces have been victims of their own success. The local drug pushers in each region have been squeezed to such an extent that their operations have almost ground to a halt. In the States, whole shipments from Colombia were seized before they even reached the docks— the result of good policing. Unfortunately, some high-profile officers who've been involved have been targeted— some have lost their lives," Lassiter said quietly.

The men appeared to bow their heads in unison out of pure respect. George Drummond nervously felt the back of his collar.

"MI6 has also received reports of the killing of a number of prominent, heavy duty crime lords who were running huge drugs empires in the cities."

"That doesn't make sense. Why kill the distributors?" Vernon Mattheus asked.

Drummond automatically assumed that the chief constable of Greater Manchester police had not heard or been aware of any similar troubles to the ones recently experienced in Glasgow, namely the murders of Vic Simpson and Thomas Mulraney. Drummond, himself, was not yet aware of the demise of the two next best, Billy Buchanan and Frank Milligan.

"We think that Manuel Delgado is going to put his own men in place. Ease them in. That way, the cartel is bound to get a bigger slice of the pie," Agent Shanks chipped in; his high-pitched, girly voice resulted in a few strange looks travelling around the room.

"Just who do they have doing the killing for them?" Brian Hillhouse asked.

Everyone agreed that it was a fair question.

"Contract killers, assassins. Delgado's prepared to hire anybody to make sure that his shipments get through. For every day the stuff lies in storage, they're losing millions. And there's the danger of them losing business to an influx of cheaper, maybe more dangerous alternatives. God knows what crap these people'll put into the mix," Shanks snapped.

The men murmured in agreement.

Agent Shanks began to command a certain respect. "Our FBI friends in the States have warned that key figures in the police departments there have been approached, even blackmailed," he said delicately. "The cartel is agreeing big payoffs for little favours; turning a blind eye here and there; re-prioritising an investigation or two— very tempting offers for the wrong man." Shanks paused to look accusingly around the room. At least that was how the action had come across. To be fair, that was probably not his intention.

"Okay, we're under threat. All of us. How is MI6 going to help?" Ifor Lewis, the new boy from Gwent, chipped in.

Drummond had been observing Lewis closely. He could almost see the cogs turning in the Welshman's brain. *Don't let the lilting accent from the heart of the valleys fool anybody*, he mused. Drummond could see exactly why Ifor Lewis had made the grade.

Special Agent Lassiter wheeled around, ready to pick and choose his words. Lewis stared him down. He wanted an answer.

"The law of the land forbids me from going into too much detail. Let's just say that we have people out there, actively working with... er, outside agencies to close down the operations at source," Lassiter declared, carefully.

"That would be the FBI?" Lewis asked.

"Draw your own conclusions." Lassiter's craggy face broke into a smile. "Like any organisation, MI6 is not immune from cutbacks, lack of funding. International terrorism and the drain on resources that go with it can also be factors." He was obviously referring to the Middle East conflict. "All I can say is that we have a presence in all areas. I would ask everybody to remain vigilant; keep doing the right things. Report anything unusual. We need to help each other," he said, quoting from the handbook.

That's fine, thought George Drummond. *I have plenty to report.*

49

Mason Blackwell checked his watch— 11:52 a.m. He was on a roundabout, near Bothwell, the exit leading off to Strathclyde Park. Situated between Hamilton and Motherwell, the park was used mainly for country walks and various sports, which took place on the impressive waters of the adjoining lake, stretching along the entire west side.

M & D's was a privately owned funfair and amusement park located in the centre of Strathclyde Park. Cheap, with lots of fun for the kids, it was flanked by fast food outlets, restaurants, a pub and a hotel.

Blackwell felt his heart thudding in his chest. Dry mouth, a wet moustache of perspiration on his top lip, his eyes were everywhere as he entered the park. In the distance, Mason could see a Ferris wheel reaching into the sky; he could hear the overbearing music blaring out from the rides and the arcades dotted around the complex.

The car park was maybe half full. By the time he had parked, Mason had scanned every car. A family had just arrived; the father, at one side of the car, unbuckled seat belts, unleashing children. The mother had the boot up; was erecting a buggy. On the ground next to the car sat a huge bag full of spare clothes and nappies that always seemed to accompany just one small child.

On the other side of the car park, an elderly couple were climbing into their Ford Fiesta, obviously having had enough of revisiting their youth for one day.

Blackwell glanced over at the main gate. He felt the gun in its holster; pulled over his jacket to make sure that it wasn't showing, and walked over towards the gate— 11:58 a.m.

The sounds and smells of the funfair filled the atmosphere. Inside the gates, the place was bustling; kids scampered in and out of the arcades.

Young teenagers screamed with delight as they were tossed about in rockets and cars. Browbeaten fathers, prompted by eager children, were forking out cash like confetti in their futile attempts to win cuddly teddy bears and goldfish. Overweight youngsters stuffed their faces with candyfloss and toffee apples.

In amongst all of this, there lurked a killer; a killer with a hostage— a precious hostage— 12:04 p.m.

Blackwell decided to walk over towards the entrance to the main building complex. It stood more or less in the centre of M & D's, a huge glass structure, which housed the many eateries and drinking areas in the park.

Blackwell's breathing quickened. Strained nerves made him feel a little faint, rubber-legged. Leaning against a glass door, he tried to put a stone support pillar between himself and MI6 Special Agent, Andy Wells. Wells had just come in the main gate. He was alone and he was definitely looking for someone.

50

Chief Constable George Drummond stood and gave it to them straight. MI6 men, Special Agent Lassiter and Agent Shanks listened carefully, as the experienced old copper provided the low down on what was happening back in Glasgow.

Detective Constable Trevor Fields, still firmly entrenched in case studies, had called the old man with the up-to-date news on the killings of crime bosses, Billy Buchanan and Frank Milligan. After informing Fields that he would no longer be required to trawl through case notes, Drummond had then delivered the news to the MI6 agents that Glasgow now had not one major player in the international drugs market. Apart from a couple of small timers, that was it. The city was ripe for a power struggle between rival gangs. With the Colombians poised to muscle in with their own men, Glasgow could soon be transformed into a bloodbath.

"If only they would just harm themselves." George Drummond's final statement to Lassiter and Shanks was borne more out of hope than good guidance.

Drummond said his goodbyes to his good friend, Brian Hillhouse of the Met. Delivering his sincerest condolences on the recent death of Brian's wife, George then wished his colleague all the best for the future and hoped that he would see him again soon. Empathy was possibly the most important word in George Drummond's political dictionary.

"Let's go back to Glasgow then, people. I take it all was quiet out here?" Drummond quizzed his bodyguards.

"Apart from his belly rumbling!" Juliet Baxter said, jerking her thumb at the slightly overweight Brian Wheldon.

Brian laughed, rubbing his paunch. "Skipped breakfast this morning, Sir. Trying to cut back a bit, y'know?" Wheldon explained.

"Come on, then. I'll treat you both to lunch. There's a little pub up the road just off the town centre. Let's go there. At least it's cheap," Drummond joked.

"I'll bring the car round the front, Sir." Wheldon eagerly disappeared into the car park.

"How'd the meeting go, Sir?" Baxter asked, a little tentatively.

"Aye, went okay. Cleared up a few things." Drummond was a master of keeping the cards close.

"That's good, Sir. That's good." Feeling the chill April breeze, Baxter rubbed her hands together for warmth.

Drummond glanced at the pretty detective.

"Is there anything on your mind, Baxter? You can ask. Might not get the answer you like, but you can ask."

She hesitated for a moment.

"Well, Sir. Wheldon and I were talking earlier. He... er, we are a bit concerned, Sir." She took a deep breath.

"Concerned? About what, Baxter?" Drummond played along. He knew where this was going.

"Sir, the incidents in Glasgow, and the deaths of the officers. And the guns." She tapped her left breast, on which nestled the 9mm Glock handgun in its holster. "Are we in real danger here?" she asked.

Drummond's face straightened. Baxter detected the strained look.

"Not if I have anything to do with it," he replied, sternly. His face then softened a little. "Look, love." He placed his hand reassuringly on her arm. "Just concentrate on doing your job. These are testing times, I can't deny that. But if you do the right things and keep vigilant, everything will be fine. I promise."

"Thanks, Sir," Juliet said, not entirely convinced. She pulled up the collar of her blouse; a stiff chill breezed up her back.

Wheldon swung the car in front of them, leaning over to open the door for his boss. Juliet Baxter climbed in the back, checking her make up in a little compact mirror. Wheldon spotted the show of vanity via the car's rear-view mirror.

"Not think you should get an estimate first?" he asked, a cheeky grin flashing across his face.

Baxter drew him a withering look, her free hand concealing a middle-fingered gesture from George Drummond.

There was a dull thump in the front. The car seemed to lurch to the side as Drummond got in. He slumped down violently on the passenger seat. George Drummond's head slowly twisted around to face a horrified Brian Wheldon.

A warm trickle of crimson blood was making its way from the small hole in Drummond's forehead and down the side of his nose. Eyes staring wide, he had drawn his final breath.

51

The oppressive sounds of the funfair rattled and banged inside Mason Blackwell's head. It was as if he were back at home, standing outside his teenage daughter's bedroom, pleading with her to turn the music down.

Blackwell had not taken his eyes off Andy Wells since he entered the park. Seeking refuge behind a stone pillar, Blackwell watched as the MI6 agent reached the front door of the building complex at M & D's funfair, Strathclyde Park. Wells turned to face the rides. His eyes were everywhere, nervously flitting back and forth between the amusements. Tiny beads of sweat were forming on his brow.

In true American cops and robbers tradition, Mason took off his jacket, draping it over the primed 9mm Glock in his hand. He stepped out of the shadows, prodding the gun into the small of the young agent's back, at the same time grabbing him roughly by the left arm.

"Looking for someone, Andy?" Blackwell had to raise his voice to be heard above the incessant racket.

"Blackwell. What the hell?" Wells barked, trying to free his arm from the grip, but to no avail. The cop held on tightly.

"I was just about to ask you the same thing," Blackwell hissed through clenched teeth. "Now where is she?" He wrenched again on the shoulder.

"Who? I don't know what you... Aaahhh!" Wells

yelped in pain as Blackwell tugged his arm painfully up his back.

"Wrong answer!" Mason looked around for somewhere to take the situation.

About ten yards away on the concourse, next to the flashing lights of an arcade, stood a bright, emerald-green tent— square, about the size of a small bedroom. Above the threshold the name, Gypsy Eva Petulengro, was displayed in sparkling letters.

"Over here, and no tricks!" Blackwell snapped.

The pair walked calmly towards the tent; Blackwell gave Wells little reminders, as if he needed them, that there was a gun to contend with in this particular equation.

Just as they got to the invitingly pegged back entrance to the tent, the pent up rage welled inside Mason Blackwell, caused him to roughly heave the young guy through the opening. Wells tumbled over a little table and chairs set, strategically placed in the middle of the floor space. The famed crystal ball really did lead a charmed life, rolling off the centre of the table before landing softly on a small, soft bag of shopping that was lying on the floor.

Gypsy Eva then appeared behind Blackwell. She was stuffing her face with a hot dog, a cup of steaming tea in her other hand. Obviously, she had not been able to foresee this slight problem in her crystal ball. She stood in the doorway, mouth agape.

Blackwell sensed the presence at his shoulder; glanced around quickly. He flashed his ID card at her.

"Police, Ma'am. I'll need to use this tent for a wee while. Sorry for any inconvenience."

Gypsy Eva said nothing, but grunted. He pulled the canvas door behind him.

"Right, Wells. Get up. On your feet, now!" Blackwell commanded, gun set firmly in his hand. He repeated the order. No response.

Wells had struck his head on the edge of the table on the way down.

Blackwell knelt, reached over to inspect the damage. Wells appeared to be out cold, a small patch of blood matting his hair at the front.

"Mason? Are you all right?"

The voice at Blackwell's shoulder gave him a start; a familiar, friendly voice that immediately put the inspector at ease.

"Doug? Am I glad to see you!" Blackwell turned to see Special Agent Doug Mailer standing behind him, holding up the makeshift door.

"What's going on here, Mason?" Mailer asked, stepping inside. He dropped the door behind him.

"It's Wells. He's involved in this. I don't know exactly how." Blackwell released his grip on the gun. "He called me earlier. Said he had Alison. I'd to meet him here at twelve or she's dead." Mason turned when he received no reaction. There was a stark look of resignation on Mailer's face.

"I know. We've been watching him for the past month or so. He's involved with a drugs cartel— been on the take, big time. We've copies of an overseas bank account set up in his name. Shed loads of cash going in," Mailer confirmed.

"I don't give a damn about that, Doug. I need to find out what he's done with Ali," Blackwell stated firmly.

"Andy's just come from a works unit in East Kilbride. I tailed him here," Doug retorted.

The friends looked at each other. It was as if their minds were now in tandem.

"Let's go! Get him up! I'll check his car first!" Mason shouted.

The pair dragged the unconscious Andy Wells to his feet, headed for the car park. The car contained no sign of Alison Blackwell.

The handcuffed Wells was then thrown, still

unconscious, into the back seat of Mailer's car. It sped out of the car park, bound for nearby East Kilbride.

"Doug?" Blackwell suddenly had a thought. He turned to look at his friend.

"Aye, what?"

"Don't you watch the news?"

"Eh? Oh, yes, you're supposed to be dead, aren't you?"

Blackwell nodded, never taking his eyes off Mailer.

"Come on, Mason. They don't call us Special Forces for nothing, you know?" Mailer joked.

Mason Blackwell did not exactly feel like laughing at that moment.

52

"It looks as if the shot came from somewhere over there, Sir. Going by the angle and position of the body." The detective sergeant pointed at a block of high flats just off the town centre at Dalkeith.

"You called the forensics team?" Detective Inspector Mark Brown of Lothian and Borders Police Force asked his sergeant.

"Aye, they're primed and ready at headquarters, Sir," DS Kevin Lindsay replied. "Just waiting for a body."

He turned to again check out the pretty Glasgow policewoman leaning against the back doors of the ambulance at the crime scene. It was as if she was standing guard, almost trying to protect the body of her boss which lay within. She looked haunted, staring into the distance. "Excuse me, Sir," Lindsay said. Kevin liked to think of himself as the chivalrous type. Walking over towards Juliet Baxter, he removed his jacket, placing it neatly over her shoulders.

"Thanks." She hunched the jacket in, and tried hard to smile at her colleague from the East.

"No problem. How are you holding up?" he asked, genuinely concerned.

"Not great," she replied, bordering on tears.

"Can you remember what happened?"

"We had just come out of a meeting— in there." She pointed over at the hotel.

313

"Aye, we had the heads up about that meeting. Not as hush-hush as they thought, then?"

"Obviously not," Juliet replied, a rueful look on her face. "Officer Wheldon brought the car around and the chief constable... er." She started to lose it, immediately trying to pull her senses together. She cleared her brimming eyes. "He climbed into the passenger seat. I was already in the back. I heard a kind of thump as he got in. Didn't know what it was, at first. The boss fell onto the seat. I... I think he was dead by that time. C-can you get me a drink, please?" Baxter asked. She already required a break.

"Of course. Don't go away." The 'white knight' left to pick up a cool bottle of Diet Coke from a little fridge fitted into the boot of his car.

Kevin Lindsay could most definitely be described as a gadget man. A bit of a computer nerd, he didn't get out much.

Fairly short, and handsome— to his mother— Lindsay felt a little self conscious around people— especially women. There was no doubt that he found Juliet Baxter attractive, very attractive.

A minor skin condition would, from time to time, prevent the married cop from wearing her gold wedding ring. Unfortunately, this was one of those times, and Juliet inwardly cursed her luck when she realised that this Lothian detective had become a fan.

It was not the first time that Juliet had been required to let some guy down gently. If she sensed that they were getting a little too friendly, Juliet would normally be able to delicately let slip the fact that she was married. Depending on the degree of persistence of the predatory individual, she was often heard to drop in an extra line or two, declaring her unfaltering and undying love for her eighth dan, karate instructor husband. Problem solved— most of the time. For the really, really infatuated types, the mere mention of syphilis had always been enough to do the trick.

"I think you have a fan," Brian Wheldon said, sidling up beside his partner.

"Hmmm! I know. That's all I need," Juliet replied, brightening a little.

"There's nothing we could have done, you know. It all happened so fast." Brian put his arm around her shoulder.

She managed a slight smile in response. "I know. It's just that we were supposed to be there to protect him. I've never felt so helpless," Juliet whispered.

The doors of the ambulance closed. Wheldon and Baxter stepped away from the back doors, turning to watch. They bowed their heads out of respect.

The driver started the engine, pulling out slowly into the traffic flow, bound for the local police lab.

Lothian and Borders would hold jurisdiction in this case.

"Come on, love. There's nothing we can do here. They want statements from us back at Lothian HQ." Wheldon took hold of Juliet Baxter's arm, opening the passenger door for her.

Seconds later, the car was gone.

Kenny Lindsay, the forgotten angel, returned, diet coke in hand. A familiar look crossed his face— the look of rejection. He dropped the soft drink in a nearby waste bin, sighed deeply, and turned to get on with the job. Maybe he could get things wrapped up and still have time to catch Juliet before she left HQ.

At least he would have an excuse to contact the pretty policewoman— she had left with his jacket still over her shoulders.

53

Mason Blackwell tapped nervously on his knees with the flat of his hands. He repeatedly looked over his shoulder, checking the status of MI6 agent, Andy Wells.

"Looks like he really took a whack, Mason." Driver Doug Mailer motioned towards the back seat.

Wells was still unconscious.

"How long till we reach this place?" Blackwell asked, ignoring the last statement.

"Be there in five minutes. Don't worry." Mailer floored the pedal, taking the last few turns almost on two wheels.

They ended up in the heart of a small industrial estate on the outskirts of East Kilbride, very close to Glasgow.

Blackwell was out of the car before it came to a halt, sprinting up to a double, glass door entrance. He drew his gun from its holster.

"Wait, Mason!" Doug Mailer shouted. "I'll check if he has a key for the door!"

Seconds later, the butt of a Glock smashed a small hole in one of the doors, near the handle. Mason reached in and flicked up the lever allowing him entry.

"Never mind the key, then!" Mailer announced, displaying more than a hint of sarcasm.

Gun straight out in front, Blackwell was in and out of the rooms on the ground floor in minutes.

"Ali!" he shouted ahead.

Three offices, canteen, toilets and cupboards. Nothing.

A door led into a large, open warehouse. It was an empty shell and Blackwell soon realised that there was nothing doing. He wheeled around, taking the set of stairs to the top level, four at a time.

At the top, Mason counted five offices, each with their doors closed. "Ali!" he shouted once again.

He managed to hold his breath, albeit for only a few seconds. The sound of his heart thumping was all he could hear. *Wait! Is that just...* Mason screwed up his face in concentration. He was certain he could hear muffled cries. Running over to the first office, Blackwell tried the handle. Locked. He backed off a few steps, flew at the door. It crashed heavily against the stud-partition wall that supported the structure. Nothing. Number 2 was kicked almost off its hinges. No result. Three opened up to reveal a young woman, gagged and bound to a chair at the far end of the office. Blackwell was there in a split second, his arms engulfing his wife. Both man and wife began to weep tears of relief.

"Oh, thank God I've found you, love! Are you hurt?" Mason asked, his expression changing for the worst.

"I'm okay. At least, I am now." She nodded wearily, blinking away the tears.

Blackwell had the gag and tethers off within a minute; the pair locked together in a seemingly never-ending embrace.

Mason felt his wife's body tense. He immediately sensed they were not alone; Alison Blackwell's blood ran ice cold.

"Honey? Are you all right?" he asked.

She tried to, but couldn't utter a single word. Blackwell eased his grip, turning around.

"Doug. You?" he asked, in amazement.

His old friend's normal, pleasant expression had been replaced with one of icy indifference.

"Aye, me, I'm afraid, pal," Mailer said softly, relaxing slightly on the grip of his Smith and Wesson. He noticed Blackwell checking the location of his own gun, which he had laid neatly on the floor, while he untied his wife. "And don't even think about going for the gun." Mailer reaffirmed his grip.

"But... But why?" Blackwell spat out the words.

"Just business, Mason. That's it. I wish to God it hadn't been you." Mailer paused, bordering on a show of emotion.

"Money? All this is for fucking money?" Blackwell snapped. He was working out a strategy, trying to buy a little time while he figured out how to get them out of this.

"I'd like to give you another reason, Mason. The truth is that some people are prepared to pay handsomely to have you killed." Mailer shrugged.

"Let Alison go, Doug. She's not a part of this. She..." Blackwell pleaded, squeezing his wife tightly to him.

She buried her face in his chest.

"You know that can't happen, Mason. Sorry." Mailer lifted his gun arm and took careful aim.

"I wouldn't do that if I were you, friend," a female voice rang out behind Mailer.

Blackwell closed his eyes with relief, receiving an acknowledgement from the visitor.

Theresa Bremner, alerted by Mason's earlier phone call as she left Will Munro's safe house, was standing, both hands gripping her gun tightly, aiming straight at the back of Doug Mailer's head.

"Drop the gun. Now, or so help me, I'll blow your head off!" Theresa shouted determinedly.

Mailer raised his hands in resignation.

"Put the gun on the floor and kick it over here. Do it!" she commanded.

"Okay! Okay!" he replied, lowering his gun to the floor

as he crouched. Mailer turned and leant over with his right hand, placing the Smith and Wesson on the vinyl floor at his feet. He gently pushed the weapon away from him.

At the same time, Mailer's left hand was slipping inside his right sock. A pearl-inlaid handled, silver Derringer was about to see the light of day. Before Bremner or Blackwell could react, the small gun flashed under the harsh, fluorescent lights of the unit. A shot rang out. Theresa Bremner's body stiffened against the impact. Her eyes glassed over. Terrified, she glanced across at Blackwell, almost apologising. Careering towards the dark void, Theresa's limp body slumped to the floor like a rag doll.

Mason was already on his way to the gun. He dived full length, scooping it up into his hand, turning and firing in almost one motion.

Unfortunately for Blackwell, Doug Mailer had squeezed a round off first, the bullet tearing into the right shoulder of the policeman, passing straight through and lodging itself in the prefabricated structure of the building.

Blackwell screamed in agony, dropped his gun to the floor. He stood defenceless, hand over the wound; the blood, coursing down his arm, dripped copiously from his elbow. A small pool formed in no time.

A shrieking Alison Blackwell instinctively ran over to her husband, forming a barrier between the two men.

Doug said nothing, hesitated, then took aim. A resigned Mason Blackwell closed his eyes, once again waiting for death.

Bang!

The sound of the gunshot resonated throughout the very fibre of the building. Blackwell drew in a tight breath. Through his arms, he could feel his wife's body shudder, as she pulled in oxygen.

There was a surreal moment of serenity within the unit at East Kilbride as the Blackwells found that they still retained the capacity to exhale— and inhale.

The pain that Mason could feel was acute enough— and localised— from his shoulder.

He stared at Mailer, puzzled. A slight smile appeared to force its way onto the MI6 man's face, before a small trickle appeared just above his hairline. His eyes rolled unnaturally in his head. The wet rivulet reached halfway down his forehead, as he dropped slowly to his knees, before crashing forward onto his face. Mailer's body smashed sickeningly into the floor.

Directly behind Doug Mailer, a still-handcuffed Andy Wells lowered his gun, before collapsing heavily to the floor.

Wells had somehow managed to get out of the car and make his way upstairs. He had then got into position, drawn his gun and fired accurately at his target, before again falling unconscious. The earlier blow from the edge of Gypsy Eva's table was obviously more serious than was first thought.

Wincing in pain from the exertion, Mason was at the side of his friend, DI Theresa Bremner, within seconds, hoping against hope that what he had witnessed had somehow not been real.

He turned the pretty policewoman over to face the ceiling, wiping away the blood from the side of her head, smoothing down her soft hair. He screwed his face in anguish. Things did not look so good.

Feeling utterly helpless, Blackwell lifted his hands to his face, as if trying to block out the events of the last two minutes.

Then, he felt a slight movement below him, a low moan. Excitedly, Mason held his hand lightly against Theresa's neck.

"She's alive! Ali, call 999. Police and ambulance. Hazelwood Industrial Estate, East Kilbride. Er... unit...

four... yes four!" He fumbled in his pocket for his phone, tossing it at the feet of his wife. "Theresa! Theresa! Can you hear me? Stay with me, love. Please!"

Mason tried to gently shake his friend back to life. DI Bremner's eyes fluttered a little, even opened for a few seconds. Blankly staring, bewildered almost, she seemed unable to register anything for the moment. Her mind, her being sliding away—unconsciousness then claimed her.

Mason again checked her pulse. It seemed strong for now. Her breathing was fine— as far as the layman could tell.

He turned to look up at his horrified wife, who was now standing at his shoulder. Her worried expression immediately swept the forced smile from his face. He swallowed hard, turning again to face the stricken Bremner.

"I know one thing. She's one tough bird," Mason said softly.

Alison bent down to kiss her husband tenderly on the cheek.

"Help's on its way, love. I'll go and check on our guardian angel." She looked over towards the figure of Andy Wells, still lying in a heap.

Due to his concern for Theresa Bremner, Mason had completely forgotten about the MI6 agent.

"Thanks, love. I think I owe that young man an apology," he said ruefully.

54

"You were lucky, Inspector. The bullet passed right through soft tissue. Right out the other side. The wound's been cleaned and bandaged. That's all we can do for you right now. I'd like to keep you in for a couple of days, though. Keep an eye on things. There's always a risk of infection." Doctor Richards delivered the news precisely and professionally.

"Thanks, Doctor," Mason Blackwell said quietly, a faraway look in his eyes. He wasn't really listening; he had other things on his mind. He snapped back to the here and now. "Is there any more news on Inspector Bremner?"

Mason had insisted on travelling to the hospital in the back of the same ambulance as his friend. He felt serious pangs of guilt. If he had not asked her for help in the first place, she would not be in this situation.

"She's still in surgery. That's all I can say for now." The doctor cut it short and sweet. He had been the first to see Theresa Bremner, checked her in. In truth, he didn't hold out much hope for her chances, but decided to keep his counsel for the moment.

"She'll be okay. I just know it," Blackwell stated firmly. He really tried to convince himself.

The doctor glanced over at Alison Blackwell. She'd hardly left her husband's side since he had burst into the room to save her, back at that works unit in East Kilbride. Alison lowered her eyes. She hoped that she and the doctor were wrong but...

"The other casualty, Andy Wells? How is he, Doctor Richards?" Alison asked, changing the subject.

"Oh, he's fine. A slight concussion. Might have a giant headache for a couple of days."

"I'd like to see him if that's all right, Doctor?" Blackwell asked, remembering some unfinished business he had with the young agent.

"Of course. I'll sort it with one of the nurses." Richards produced his finest doctor–patient smile, then breezed out of the room.

Just as he left, a strong hand caught the door, forcing it back against the closer. In stepped a rather sombre-looking Brian Wheldon, closely followed by Juliet Baxter.

Blackwell knew straight away something was wrong.

"Brian. Juliet. Where's the old man?" he asked, hesitating as he spoke.

Baxter stared straight at her feet, leaving Wheldon to make the announcement that he had been dreading since leaving Edinburgh.

"He's dead, Sir," he said quietly.

Blackwell leant back into his pillow, staring at the ceiling.

"Wh-what happened?" Mason asked, his voice wavering with nerves.

"There was a gunshot. The chief constable was getting into the car. We..." Baxter tried to make a contribution.

Blackwell shook his head, then cut in. "Wait a minute. You two were there to protect him. You had guns. How the hell could this happen?" Blackwell spoke slowly and concisely. He always made a point of never appearing to get mad. Mason's father had continually cited life rule number one to his only son— 'get angry and lose the battle'. He came close from time to time. This was one of those times.

Wheldon and Baxter chose not to reply, instead lowering their eyes, keen not to antagonise an already fraught situation.

Mason Blackwell studied the pair, like a mega-firm schoolteacher considering the concept of especially painful, corporal punishment. Alison, realising that the detectives had not exactly been out on the town living it up— they had obviously had a rough couple of hours— squeezed her husband's hand tightly in a 'cool it' kind of fashion.

Mason rolled his eyes skywards, cursing his stupidity under his breath.

"Listen. I'm out of order here. I'm sorry," he announced bravely. Blackwell was always big enough to admit his mistakes in public.

Who was he to criticise anyone daring to tangle with this American assassin, the most dangerous man he had ever encountered?

"It's all right, Sir. We couldn't possibly feel any worse, anyway." Brian Wheldon's statement said it all.

"Is there anything you want us to do for you, Sir?" Baxter enquired. Her voice had changed for the better, trying to sound more upbeat.

"Go home, both of you. Get some rest. You look as if you need it. I'll see you back at HQ in the morning," Mason replied, a renewed strength returning to his tone.

"Mason? The doctor said you had to stay here for the time being," Alison protested.

"I know, but we have no choice. We're just like sitting ducks to this bastard. I'll see you both tomorrow," he reiterated, despite her resistance.

"Right, Sir. And, Sir? We heard about DI Bremner. I really hope she pulls through. She's a really gutsy lady," Juliet Baxter said before leaving.

Wheldon nodded in agreement.

"Thanks. I'm sure she'll be fine." *If I say it often*

enough.

"Oh, and, Sir," Wheldon added.

"Aye, Brian?"

"Glad you're not dead, after all." Wheldon brought smiles back to the room.

"Me too," Mason Blackwell admitted.

* * *

"Agent Wells? Can I call you Andy?" Blackwell poked his head around the door before being pushed all the way in.

Despite the inspector's protestations, the nurse would, of course, get her way. She had volunteered to organise a wheelchair to transport Blackwell to Andy Wells' room on a ward at the other side of the hospital.

Blackwell had finally persuaded his wife to go home, tend to the kids. Reluctantly, she had agreed, but only when the children and their continuing welfare were mentioned as ammunition.

"Aye, of course. Come in, Inspector," Andy replied, fairly cheerfully. So far, so good.

"Thanks. And please, it's Mason." Blackwell turned to nod at the bossy nurse.

Stern faced, she eventually got the message, heading for the door. She decided to deliver a parting salvo before she left. "Twenty minutes. I'll be back to get you," she announced, a distinct lack of humour detectable within the recesses of her voice.

"*Sieg heil!*" Making sure the nurse from hell had left the vicinity, Blackwell performed a Hitler salute-type gesture, finger across the lip, straight arm out in front.

"Your rank'll get you nowhere in here, Mason." Andy Wells laughed.

"I think my wife's got them terrified. If anything happens to me in here, there'll be hell to pay!" Mason joked. He paused, cleared his throat. "I believe I owe you an apology." He was sincere, as always.

"Don't worry about it. I would have done exactly the same in your shoes," Wells conceded. "I'll tell you something, though." He rubbed the bump on his head. "You're a lot stronger than you look!"

"Ah, sorry about that, as well. How is the head, anyway?"

"I'll live. Listen, I heard about what happened to Chief Constable Drummond. I'm sorry. He was a good man," Wells said sympathetically.

"One of the best. He'll be a hard act to follow," Mason reflected.

"Is there any word yet on DI Bremner?" Andy asked, changing the subject back to the living, if only just.

"She's still in theatre. I've asked to be informed as soon as she comes out," Blackwell stated. "I'm sure she'll pull through." He stared into space, as if silently praying.

Andy Wells was sitting, fully clothed, on a chair at the side of his bed. It was obvious that the doctors were happy with his condition. He had spent the last two or three hours undergoing a number of tests, satisfying the medics that he was ready to go home and take with him the well-worn words— 'take it easy for a couple of days and come back in if you feel unwell'.

Andy stood a little unsteadily, stared out of the window of his room at Glasgow Royal Infirmary, his back to Mason Blackwell.

"I assume that you want to know about Doug Mailer?" Wells asked, getting down to business.

"The thought had crossed my mind," Blackwell replied, his face taking on a much more serious look.

"I know that you were friends, Mason. But I..."

"When he kidnapped my wife and tried to kill both of us, he became no longer a friend, Andy," Blackwell snapped.

"Good point," Wells conceded. "Okay, we, er, MI6 had been watching Doug for the last three months or so. One of our undercover men had identified him in London at the start of the year. He'd been meeting with underworld figures there— drug dealers, mostly. We had access to Mailer's bank accounts— he'd been receiving unidentified payments from sources unknown for the past three years or so. Then, a couple of months ago, he was seen attending a meeting with Manuel Delgado."

Blackwell shook his head, indicating that he had no idea who Delgado was.

"Delgado is one of the major players in the Colombian drug market. Our sources tell us that he had been chosen to lead a cartel that would muscle into every one of the main countries that suffer with robust, drug-running operations. Of course, the British Isles were a prime target. The cartel wanted to take out a number of prominent figures in selected areas of the UK police forces; replace them with, shall we say, less conscientious individuals, firmly on the drug barons' payroll. Not content with that, they've also started taking out the heads of some of the biggest drug operations. In Scotland alone, four were killed within days of each other— Vic Simpson, Tommy Mulraney, Billy Buchanan and Frank Milligan."

"So that's it." Mason Blackwell's mind was slotting the information into the appropriate sections.

"There's more. When the integrity of any employee of MI6 is brought into question, the intelligence department does a complete, warts and all, background check on the perpetrator. We received the final pieces of the jigsaw this morning. That's why I was tailing Doug to Strathclyde Park. Intelligence discovered that Mailer's mother had two families, the first here in Scotland. When Doug was young, she left his father, bailed out to the United States. She eventually hooked up with a man there, who was to become her second husband."

"I didn't know about that. He never once mentioned family in America."

"Nobody knew."

"So how does that explain anything, Andy?" Mason asked.

"His mother married a man by the name of Metcalf," Wells retorted. He stared over his shoulder at the policeman. There was complete silence for a few seconds.

"Oh my God! Brodie Metcalf and Doug Mailer are half-brothers?" Blackwell rested his back against the soft leather of the wheelchair. "Doug was taking care of the family's unfinished business— me!"

"Aye. It looks like it. I snapped him in a coffee house in the centre of Glasgow. We ran the pictures, but couldn't identify the other guy as an active drug dealer. We think now it could've been Metcalf, probably in disguise."

"So, if Doug was active here, then Metcalf was probably responsible for the killing of George Drummond," Mason deduced.

Wells merely nodded, an uneasy look crossing his face.

"What?" Blackwell asked, spooked by the agent's expression.

"There's no easy way to say this, Mason. This Metcalf— he has unfinished business. It's an unwritten code of conduct between killers— 'honour the contract'."

"It had crossed my mind, Andy. He's coming back for me, isn't he?"

Blackwell received the answer he had expected; Andy's eyes delivered the verdict.

"And he'll blame you for the death of his brother." Wells confirmed the killer's next move with his last statement.

"Alison! M-my kids!" Blackwell stuttered.

"I've organised a couple of MI6 agents to shadow your wife. It's just a precaution. I don't think Metcalf will consider going down that route. He'll want to move directly to go."

Mason swallowed hard. "What do you suggest?" he asked.

"MI6 has hundreds of safe houses," Wells simply stated.

"You think?"

"I think it's your only option. If you really want to protect everyone close to you?"

"Can you fix it, Andy?" Blackwell pleaded. He was now sold on the idea; potential danger to his precious family drove him.

"Of course. It's just a phone call," Wells replied.

Blackwell struggled out of the wheelchair, wincing in pain due to the hole in his shoulder. The men shook on it.

"Tell me one thing, Andy. How did you know that I was still alive? I mean, only a select few actually knew the truth," Mason queried.

"Because that's what we're good at!" the young agent replied, a cheeky grin on his face.

There was a knock on the door. The two men unwittingly took deep breaths, holding them as the door slowly opened.

"Inspector. Inspector Blackwell?" The voice preceded the individual.

"O'Reilly? Is that you? I thought you'd quit." Blackwell was pleased to hear the distinctive voice of Detective Constable John O'Reilly.

After walking in on the butchered bodies of Tommy Mulraney and Sean McGlinchey, O'Reilly had made the snap decision to call it a day. Mason Blackwell, true to type, had found time among the mayhem to try to convince the young detective that he had a terrific future ahead of him in the force. O'Reilly had given his boss a polite listening to, before finally deciding to go back to university to study politics or something else mundane. Or so it seemed.

"I went home, and thought long and hard about what you said, Sir. You were right. I... I was hasty. I do think I have a future here."

The words warmed Blackwell's heart; the only things that had during the past few weeks. For a split second, he was a normal policeman again— doing normal, mundane police things. For a full second, he longed for that feeling on a permanent basis.

"Good for you. And welcome back," Mason said, snapping back to reality and strongly shaking the young man's hand. "And what can I do for you, O'Reilly?"

"DI Bremner earlier dropped a small photograph into the station, Sir. She'd picked it up from Will Munro." He paused.

"Aye, I'd sent her to ask if Will kept a photo of Penny Richards," Mason replied.

"I hope you don't mind, Sir, but I took the liberty of running over the case notes from the file. I went to see the waiter at the restaurant where Ben Vieri was killed. He identified the girl in the photo as the same one who was with Vieri that day. It was Penny Richards, Sir," O'Reilly stated proudly, looking pleased with his work.

"Good work, O'Reilly. Now you can do something else for me." Blackwell turned him around and guided him towards the door. "You can go across to Ward 17 reception and ask for an update on DI Bremner's condition."

"I was getting to that, Sir. I was asked to tell you that she's out of surgery. What happened to her, Sir?" The young policeman, completely ignored, was left staring at MI6 agent, Andy Wells. Mason Blackwell was legging it, minus discarded wheelchair, over to Ward 17.

55

He could see the brightly marked police car in the distance, perched on the top of one of those raised, purpose-built motorway off ramps. Checking his speed— seventy-six miles per hour— he lifted his foot, just in case. By the time he sailed past them, the hired car, a Volkswagen Golf, was registering between sixty-five and seventy. The police car was another highly rated, German number, built for speed and endurance and Brodie Metcalf decided that it might be unwise to take on the Audi A6 so close to completion of his UK activities.

He glanced up at the motorway sign. Junction 40 was coming up fast. Brodie tapped the indicator, slipped off the M6 southbound and immediately took the first exit off the roundabout at the end of the slip.

The Lakes Hotel came into view, just as had been promised.

He selected a quiet spot at the far side of the car park, nosed in under cover of a silver birch tree; its branches reached over the car like a protective canopy. Old habits die hard. He checked his watch— plenty of time.

Metcalf sat there for a few minutes under the gathering gloom of a late spring day. He reflected on another job expertly done, recalling the moment that George Drummond had met his end. It had been so easy: the preliminaries; the hit itself; the getaway.

Brodie frowned. Under duress, he had agreed to allow

his brother to complete his initiation into the world of contract killing by taking out Mason Blackwell once and for all. But Blackwell worried the American. It was the first time in his career that he had come face to face with a mark and failed to complete the mission. Little did Metcalf know that Blackwell had previously outfoxed him— initial target Will Munro was safe and secure thanks to the policeman's quick thinking.

As the minutes passed and his phone still failed to ring, Brodie became more and more convinced that he had made a bad judgement call. Doug should have been here by this time. Or at least should have called in the hit. For the one and only time since the completion of his first contract, Brodie Metcalf began to feel the faint stirrings of an attack of nerves.

As if retreating into himself, his mind drifted back to an unhappy childhood. As a young child, and small for his age, Brodie had been a target for the school bullies. One in particular had taken great delight in relentlessly knocking the living daylights out of the younger, lighter student.

In later years, all-American, college boy, Brad Williams, had achieved everything that his doting parents had hoped and prayed for. Academically, he had gained a place at Harvard, destined for a top career in law. The University football team and a string of beautiful girls were to prove worthwhile distractions for Williams, and it seemed that life for him could not possibly get any better.

Payback time, however, would not be far away, and Brad Williams' former victim, armed with extensive training and knowledge in the fine arts of killing and torture, would finally get his revenge.

Metcalf would be fascinated and amazed by the human body and just how much pain and suffering it could withstand before expiring.

By the time he was begging— pleading for death— Brad

Williams had lost all fingers and toes, genitals, kneecaps and elbows. Revenge was merciless and complete. Furthermore, Williams' parents would spend the rest of their lives in purgatory. They would never be allowed to know why.

* * *

Metcalf had a decision to make. It was now gone 6:55 p.m. The meeting was set for 7 p.m. sharp and the link man for both parties, Doug Mailer, had still not arrived. The people making up the other party did not react well to changes of plan. Mailer had said so himself. Metcalf had a decision to make. He was staring at the mobile on the dashboard in front of him. Silently drumming his fingers on the display, he took a deep breath, bringing it up to his face. The light shone into his eyes as he scrolled through the menu. Reaching the name Wyatt in the display, he hit the call button. The entry was automatically preceded by the numbers '141', hiding the caller's number from the person receiving.

A few seconds later, a ringing tone cut the silence. Two rings... three... four... then silence— someone had answered the call, preferring to stay silent.

Metcalf put his hand over the microphone. He could hear the sound of light breathing.

"Wyatt?" He decided to go for it. No reply. "Doug? Is that you?" Still nothing. He hit the end-call button. "Fuck!" Metcalf slammed the phone down on the passenger seat.

At the other end of the line, Andy Wells continued scrolling through Doug Mailer's mobile directory, searching for any clues that may lead MI6 to the faceless people.

* * *

Metcalf feared the worst for his half-brother, but still was faced with a tough decision. There was a lot of money to be made from this cartel. He simply had to find out if they would deal directly with him. He checked his watch again— 7 p.m.

Two minutes later, Brodie Metcalf had enquired at reception, headed for the Penrith Suite and into the company of a Mister Horatio Wilkinson and his party.

56

"Theresa Bremner? I've been told she's just out of surgery?" Mason Blackwell panted heavily. He leant against the receptionist's desk in Ward 17, holding his aching shoulder.

After his obvious exertion, Mason was sure he could feel the beginnings of a warm trickle under the dressing. No matter. There were much more important things to consider.

"You must be Inspector Blackwell," the receptionist stated in a monotonous tone, bereft of emotion. "Mister Squires is expecting you. First room on the left." She yawned, pointing up the ward, never lifting her gaze from the paperwork on her desk.

"Thanks." Blackwell would normally comment on such slovenly behaviour. Right then, he couldn't have given a toss.

He rapped the door and entered, a nervous fluttering of the heart accompanying him.

"Inspector Blackwell?" The surgeon's voice was clear and precise.

Blackwell nodded.

"Please sit down," Senior Consultant Richard Squires invited the policeman to take the seat opposite.

Mason studied the medic closely. Late fifties, white hair, spectacles balancing on the end of his nose. He noticed how Squires' hands looked baby soft, his long fingers almost ladylike. Blackwell assumed that the man had never done an honest day's work in his life; never lifted a spade or a hammer. But how many lives had he saved? Had he become an instant hero to Mason Blackwell?

Blackwell knew one thing— Theresa Bremner's surgeon would make one terrific poker player. Mason had not yet received an inkling of how the operation had gone. He was only aware, at that moment, of the incessant thump of his heart.

"Looks like your wound's opened up." Squires was peering over the top of his glasses at a small red patch spreading on the gauze dressing on Blackwell's shoulder.

"How's Theresa?" Mason was finally forced to ask. The pain left him feeling a little irked, choosing to ignore the man's last statement.

Squires sniffed. He lowered his head, preparing to consult his notes. "She's alive— at least, for now," he conceded.

Blackwell pulled in a long breath. Hurdle number one had been crossed. Mason's pulse rate then began to settle down.

Squires closed his notes, removed his glasses. He leant back in his chair. Blackwell was certain that he detected the merest hint of a smile. The surgeon continued, "We managed to remove the bullet. It was touch and go for a while. Almost lost her on a couple of occasions. The truth is, Inspector— I don't quite know how she survived. She should be dead. The position of the bullet. The trauma it caused. But she's hanging in there, breathing unaided. She's alive." He paused to take a sip of Perrier. "Would you like a drink, Inspector? I've only water, I'm afraid. I'm not allowed to drink anymore," Squires said bravely, trying to smile. His craggy, lined face instantly lit up.

Blackwell felt like suggesting that he try to smile more often. He found himself warming to the man.

"Thanks." Mason reached across the desk, selecting a glass from a little tray at the edge. He turned the glass right side up and filled to around halfway.

"You know, Inspector?" Squires sat forward, lowering his voice as if providing a private consultation. "We doctors deal largely in facts— what you can and can't see, can and can't do. The books say there's just no room in medicine for spirituality and all that mumbo jumbo. I thought the same— used to think the same." He swigged another mouthful of Perrier, acting almost as if he was drinking whisky, becoming slowly intoxicated.

Mason, fascinated, never took his eyes off him.

The surgeon continued, "Sometimes we have people come through here; well, you just can't explain what keeps them alive. The nearest that I can get to it is the strong will of a person. A will that... That just refuses to let them die— you follow?" A serious look again crossed Squires' face.

"Aye. I believe I do, Sir," Blackwell replied formally, reflecting on the personality of his close friend.

"I had to remove the bullet. It was nudging the main cerebral artery. Just got her in time. If she had been left another couple of hours, the slightest movement would have killed her." He paused to take a breath. "I decided to place Inspector Bremner in what we call a barbiturate-induced coma." Squires paused for the question.

"A coma. Why?" Blackwell asked, worried lines returning to his forehead.

The surgeon picked up a model of a human head, which sat on the corner of his desk. He prepared to use the model to assist in his explanation.

"We're controlling her in a deep state of unconsciousness, using phenobarbital. The drug reduces the metabolic rate of brain tissue and blood flow. The vessels in the brain then narrow, lessening the room it requires in the skull." Squires indicated the relevant area. "This reduces the intracranial pressure. The theory is that, with the swelling relieved, the pressure decreases to such an extent that any brain damage is reduced or even avoided."

"Brain damage— there could be brain damage?" Mason's voice cracked a little.

"We won't know until she regains consciousness, I'm afraid. Sometimes the induced coma doesn't work." The surgeon always told the truth. He had neither the time nor the compunction to provide false hope to any of his patients or their families.

"How long does she have to stay in this coma?"

"A few days. If you're a religious man, Inspector, I suggest you send up a couple of prayers. The longer she's breathing, the better chance she'll have," Squires stated the obvious.

"Can I see her?" Mason asked rather impatiently, the pain in his shoulder now making him very uncomfortable.

"Of course. I'll take you over to her room right now. She already has a visitor. Her sister, maybe?"

"Oh, aye. That'll be it." Blackwell guessed that Bremner's visitor must be her long-term lover, Lindsay.

He decided that maybe the grisly old medic might not be ready for that kind of revelation.

"Then I'll have a nurse re-dress that shoulder for you, before you drip all over my hospital." The surgeon smiled, politely holding the door open.

"Thanks for everything."

The pair warmly shook hands before heading along the corridor to Theresa Bremner's room.

57

"Where is Doug Mailer?" he asked in a heavily accented voice.

The tall, elegant man stood to greet the latest visitor to the Penrith suite at the Lakes Hotel. Brodie Metcalf bravely strode forward, hand extended.

Two heavies— dark suits, expressionless faces— flanked the man, both leaning forward to halt Metcalf's progress. Brodie raised his hands in the air as the pair teamed up to roughly pat him down for concealed weapons and listening devices.

The bigger of the heavies indicated to the man that Metcalf was clean. They stood aside, allowing him to pass.

Brodie felt almost naked without his gun. He had made a conscious decision to leave it behind, safely concealed in the boot of the car. The actions of the bodyguards had proved that he had made the correct decision.

He scanned the room. Eight men sat around a conference table. Brodie noted the cut of their suits, the quality of their immaculate shirts and ties. He identified a couple of two-hundred dollar, hand-stitched, silk ties among them.

The main members of the cartel were indeed powerful, wealthy men. And from the information Metcalf had learnt from his half-brother— ruthless men.

A further two bodyguards stood in the background, each one occupying a shadowy corner at the far side of the dimly lit suite. Brodie had already identified the ample

339

bulges around the breast pockets of their jackets.

"I said where is Mailer?" the man asked again, glancing across at one of the heavies, as if inviting him to pose the next question.

Brodie got the feeling that the next question might be less than friendly.

"I've been expecting Doug to join us. He's been held up; has some unfinished business," Metcalf stated diplomatically.

"This is highly irregular. Mailer said that he would be here for this meeting. Wait here," Manuel Delgado replied.

Brodie caught a nod from him to the bodyguard, requesting that he turn the key in the entrance door to the suite. The second guard strolled over to the far end to join the other two. All eight VIPs stood, to a man, joining Delgado near the far corner.

Metcalf strained to catch a little of the conversation. He found himself racking his brain, struggling to recall if the native tongue of Colombia was simply Colombian or, like most of the adjoining South American countries, Spanish.

Brodie didn't need an interpreter. He knew exactly what was going down. Delgado was giving the members of the cartel the option to withdraw from their arrangements due to the absence of an obviously important piece of the jigsaw puzzle— Doug Mailer. If they decided to walk away, there would be no need to hire the continued services of an assassin for now. Furthermore, Metcalf had seen their faces— all of them. They would never have a better chance to take him out. He was unarmed and alone.

In Metcalf's experienced opinion, it was clear by the way that the conversation was going that the verdict would be close, hanging in the balance. A couple of the 'suits' were clearly hell bent on over-stressing their points. Brodie felt deep in his gut that this was going to go either way— too close to call.

Minutes later, the collective cartel was reaching the end of its discussion; the men repeatedly glanced over their shoulders at the little American, no doubt wondering from where his fearsome reputation had come. They would soon find out if they had made the wrong choice.

Brodie knew one thing: after the short meeting, Delgado would return to face the assassin before he delivered the verdict. Jack Feltham's training would always instruct his pupil to expect this from an opponent. 'Watch the eyes. They will tell the story'.

The assassin steeled himself as the group gathering came to an end. All four guards were in good positions for him; three standing together at the far side, one very close.

He had worked out his play:

Catch Delgado by the throat. Swing him around and use him as a shield. Stun the dumb guard standing at my shoulder with my free hand and snatch his gun as he falls. Take out the three guards still grouped together. Put a slug in the dumb guard's head. Snap Delgado's neck. Drop the body on the floor. See who else has the stomach for a fight.

Manuel Delgado strode back over with a purpose. Metcalf stared deeply into the Colombian's black eyes. He clenched and unclenched his hands in readiness.

Bring it on.

"We will continue with the plans, Mister Metcalf. Please, join us at the table." Delgado spoke softly, belying his reputation, and offered his hand towards the American.

Brodie glanced across at the guards in the corner, at the smiling VIPs now sitting in their original positions.

He hesitated slightly, until he was sure.

The pair shook hands.

The cartel had made its decision. A decision that maybe was not overly surprising. Millions were riding on it.

Manuel Delgado was the main player— the co-ordinator. He made it his business to know every finite detail within the process. The process that would help ensure smooth passage and safe, largely unrestricted delivery of the cartel's drug consignments.

Delgado had made a point of memorising all of Doug Mailer's contacts and responsibilities. And the identities of all the people throughout the UK, who had already lost their lives: in Glasgow— Simpson, Buchanan, Drummond and McMenemy; in Newcastle, Manchester, Birmingham, London— more casualties from both sides of the law.

Manuel Delgado was also aware of the calibre of the paid replacements, their locations, contact numbers and expected incumbency dates.

And, there was the small matter of Mailer's sizeable fee, which now looked as if it was about to be better spent elsewhere.

No doubt some of the cash would be re-routed to fund Brodie Metcalf's next list of assignments in the States.

*   *   *

Metcalf nodded politely at the men as he walked over to join them, dragging a chair out from under the conference table.

A slight noise outside the door made him stop, catch his breath. The unmistakeable click of a gun being readied had Brodie instinctively reaching for his own weapon. Quickly recalling that this was a pointless exercise, the assassin's next move was to make for the solitary window, a few feet from where he was standing.

Taking the rest of the occupants of the room by surprise, Metcalf made a dash for the window, hauling the trailing curtains off the wall. He clawed desperately at the handle.

The formidable sight outside of two Special Forces officers, dressed in full combat regalia, black as the night, had the American lift his hands in surrender.

Everyone, except Brodie Metcalf, jumped with fright as the door crashed off its hinges; the rest of the task force, numbering nearly a dozen, stormed the room.

Small, red laser spots filled the air, fixing brightly on almost every sweaty forehead. The cartel's bodyguards, who were obviously not fully equipped for this type of assault, had no choice other than to throw down their guns.

Metcalf offered little resistance as he was roughly turned around and handcuffed. This was neither the time nor the place for foolish decisions to be made.

The cuffs securely in place, Brodie took the opportunity to glance around the room. Feltham's choice words for such an occasion were— 'in the moments following an obvious set up, decide who looks a little short on the element of surprise'.

Metcalf found himself studying closely the expression on the face of Manuel Delgado.

58

The Greenacre Chapel of Rest, Chicago, Illinois.

"Such a beautiful service, Lonnie. It's so sad. He was so young." The old lady's voice trailed off.

"Thank you so much for coming, Rose. It means so much to us," Baltimore hissed through clenched teeth, the bile churning in his throat.

Rose Pattullo had been widowed for many years. Her late husband's firm, Pattullo Industries, dealt in the development and manufacture of synthetic skins for sausages.

Giancarlo Pattullo had also been solidly into racketeering, eventually disappearing one balmy summer's night, never to be seen again.

The cops knew who had planned and executed the hit. As usual, they couldn't prove a thing.

The fallout saw the old lady being coerced into selling out to the mobsters, but still walking away with a cool, ten million dollars for the business. She knew it was a fraction of its true worth but, quite simply, did not have the stomach for a fight.

Fortunately, Rose's husband and Longthorn Baltimore the First just happened to be great friends— both men as crooked as an eighteen-dollar note, and as loyal to each other as Lassie and Champion the Wonder Horse combined.

Baltimore and some influential friends then colluded to

systematically and brutally remove the heads of the offending family. The result of the cull left Pattullo Industries vulnerable and isolated, paving the way for a further takeover by a hastily organised consortium. The consortium, with Longthorn Baltimore at the helm, bought the ailing company for a million dollars, immediately selling it back to Rose Pattullo in exchange for the ten million she had received for it. With the help of the gangsters and some key individuals in strategic positions, Pattullo Industries' worth climbed to a stock market high of almost eighty million within two years.

Everybody won, except of course, the short-term owners. Rose got her company back in good shape; the employees got to keep their jobs, and the consortium raked in nine million dollars, and an agreed share of any future profits from Pattullo Industries.

Inevitably, there were some whispers of a romantic link between the widow and the head of the Baltimore dynasty. As Lonnie Baltimore was, at that time, in the running to claim a seat in the Senate, this notion was swiftly quashed. Also, there was the little matter of a so-called happy marriage and a couple of children to consider.

Some years later, at the funeral of Lonnie Baltimore the First, the unabashed show of raw emotion displayed at the graveside by Rose Pattullo, had served to confirm the new widow's fears. It was said by some that Imogen Baltimore, who passed away six months later, died of a combination of loneliness and a broken heart. In truth, cancer was firmly in the box seat. Son and heir, Longthorn Baltimore the Second, however, conveniently chose to hold the rich widow culpable on two counts— for the premature death of his mother, and for the unforgivable sin of leading his beloved father astray.

The thought of Rose Pattullo outliving Baltimore's son— her late lover's grandson— had been too much for the tycoon to bear.

In the days and hours leading up to the funeral, Baltimore had made a few calls, greased a few palms. Before this day was out, he would make sure that this despicable woman was removed from his life forever. What better day than the one in which his only son would be buried. An eye for an eye.

The service itself had been a grand affair:

Six horses, dark as night, drew a black, polished, oak-panelled coach; a pearl-white coffin dazzled among a bed of bright, pink carnations.

The setting itself was a stunning Italian-style cathedral, complete with hand-carved, finely detailed, selected figures of the Gods. The figures sat strategically placed on the many pedestals dotted around the interior of this vast building. Huge, brightly coloured stained glass windows, each one reaching from floor to ceiling, sparkled majestically under the soft lights.

An extremely well sanitised, Hollywood-type version of the painfully short life of Longthorn Reeves Baltimore III had resounded among the great walls of the cathedral.

The tall minister, resplendent in his fine robes, his all-powerful voice booming forth, had held the congregation in the palm of his hand. His performance was almost Shakespearean, shades of that great actor, Sir Laurence Olivier, drawing floods of tears from even the stoniest of faces.

At the end, as the congregation shuffled its way past the bereaved family, a faint smile crept across the debauched face of Lonnie Baltimore. His eyes followed the hesitant, slightly arthritic figure of Rose Pattullo. *Very soon. Very soon.*

A never-ending procession of gleaming, black cars followed the cortège as it made its final journey to the nearby cemetery.

In a beautifully secluded corner of the grounds, a towering, white marble obelisk bearing the simple inscription, Baltimore, reached into the cloudless sky.

The monument signalled the final resting place of six generations of the family. Most had lived long and healthy lives. The latest, and by far the most unfortunate, would soon be joining them.

A selection of specially invited guests stood around the grave, softly, correctly, dabbing their moist eyes. The coffin was lowered carefully into the prepared hole in the ground. One by one, the guests lifted a small handful of earth from the huge pile at the graveside, whispering prayers as they tossed it onto the coffin below.

The minister delivered an abbreviated version of his final thoughts, and the mourners left the scene, heads bowed.

Rose Pattullo was making her way back to her car with the help of the polite young son of one of her many nephews.

"I'll help you, Aunt Rose," he said, guiding her by the arm.

"Thank you, Aaron. You know, I think there's a change in the weather," Rose replied. She pulled her black jacket over her frail shoulders as the sun disappeared behind ominous clouds.

Small droplets of rain began to lightly pat the ground at their feet. Seconds later, the mourners were running at almost full pelt, jackets and cardigans over their heads; light rain suddenly morphed into a torrent of hailstones. The balls of ice relentlessly crashed down, bouncing around like tiny white bullets onto the previously sun-baked grass at the cemetery.

Half a mile away, on the roof of a luxury hotel, a high velocity rifle sat proudly on a specially made stand. The shooter had completed the final checks: stand planted securely; sights checked and tested; ammunition primed and in place.

The designers of the rifle had thought of everything. There was even a little canopy affixed to the structure to shelter below when it rained.

The assassin had decided to proceed with the hit, despite the change in the weather. 'This rifle could hit an underwater target.' The manufacturer's words proudly stated. It was now time to test that claim.

The telescopic sights swept the congregation. The cross hovered over the head of Rose Pattullo. The shooter drew in a long breath. *Hold it.* The forefinger tightened on the trigger.

The target's head jerked violently backwards, a huge, bloody spray exiting through the back, showering an unfortunate woman directly behind. The body slammed to the ground, staring, grey-blue eyes facing the sky. Piercing screams filled the air.

Penny Richards again used the scope to check the status of the victim. She smiled broadly at the sight of the stricken millionaire, Lonnie Baltimore. Penny was pleased. Another contract successfully completed.

Firstly approached by Baltimore's people to bump off Rose Pattullo, the young Scot had then received a second call from an unexpected source. She found herself in demand all of a sudden, negotiating a higher price from the latter. The added bonus for her new employer in this case— another of Brodie Metcalf's income streams had just been severed at the neck.

Slightly hard of hearing and seemingly unaware of developments, Rose Pattullo was climbing into her car, flicking melting hailstones off her new, black jacket. Then, inexplicably, the freak storm began to lighten.

As she watched the crowd gather around the unfortunate victim from the warmth of the limousine, Rose recalled the events of a couple of days ago.

A nice young lady with a Scottish accent had paid her a visit. The girl had told of the plot to end the old woman's life; of the cash she had been offered to take care of it.

A friendly chat over a lovely cup of tea later, the pair had become friends; Penny reminded the old lady very much of herself many, many years before. She reminded her of a steely determination and unstinting ambitions; of how she had bitten, scratched and fought to get ahead of the game; of how she had used and discarded the men in her life to put a great deal of money in her pocket; of how she had indeed cast a spell over Lonnie Baltimore the First, well aware of the consequences of such an action.

Ironically, it was that spell that had ultimately brought the assassin to Rose's door; it was also that spell that had now cost her ex-lover's son his life.

The old woman's pockets had been left considerably lighter by the experience.

Penny Richards and her shady broker had both bagged themselves five-figure sums for their troubles.

Rose considered the exercise well worth it.

59

Scotland Yard, London

"He hasn't said a word?"

"Nothing."

"How long?"

"Been here since three." He looked at his watch. "Six hours."

The dayshift policemen had just entered the interview room in the very heart of Scotland Yard headquarters. They were in the process of getting an update from one of their exhausted, outgoing colleagues.

Shirt sleeves rolled up, ties loosened and a collection of polystyrene cups, containing varying levels of cold coffee left behind; this was the total worth of their valuable police time.

The pair lifted their jackets from the backs of their chairs; scratched the stubble on their chins. They shook their heads at the lonely figure sitting at the little table in front of them, before shuffling wearily out into the corridor.

Detective Sergeant Carl Straiton followed them out, waiting until he was out of earshot of the prisoner.

"Has he been up all night?" Straiton asked, jerking his thumb back towards the room.

One of the policemen nodded, hardly breaking his stride. He carried on down the corridor, waving over his shoulder.

"What the...?" Weary cop stopped, peering out of a first-floor window. Even his dulled senses were telling him that a mob was forming outside the main entrance to the building.

On closer inspection, it became clear to him that they were media people— journalists and photographers.

A blue Ford Transit van pulled up on the roadside at the front of HQ. Although the road was clearly marked with double, yellow lines, the driver chose to ignore them, probably deciding that a parking fine was preferable to incurring the wrath of the under-pressure, executive news producer that he worked for. A television crew bearing heavy kit, spilt out of the van, heading for the front door.

"Must be some important people. Check this." Weary cop motioned at the mob before carrying on, then disappearing into the lift at the end of the corridor.

Straiton pressed his face against the window, trying to estimate how many people had been attracted by the recent visitors to the building. He counted at least twenty-five, maybe thirty. The TV crew were already getting down to business. Confirmed ladies man, Carl Straiton, checked out the pretty blonde boom-microphone operator below.

"Well hello, darlin'." Straiton gingerly stepped back from the glass, when he heard footsteps come up the stairwell next to him. He quickly hurried into the interview room for fear of his boss again catching him acting inappropriately.

Carl Straiton was one of the department's most talented policemen, but he was also running out of warnings, following his latest indiscretions with the pretty wife of a close colleague. It had been decided by the higher powers that it may be preferable not to mention the incident to the colleague.

The tough and uncompromising Northern officer, Detective Sergeant Brett Sadler, would be left in the dark for now, unless the act was to be repeated, in which case Carl Straiton may as well head for the hills and live the rest of his life as a reclusive fugitive.

Sadler wheeled around as his colleague briskly closed the door behind him. The look of fright on Straiton's face made Sadler smirk. He turned back, arms folded, to face the man, whom the pair had been ordered to interview.

Brodie Metcalf probably hadn't slept since around the same time the previous day. He was not unduly worried for now. Metcalf's body had been conditioned to withstand such punishment. At least it had given him time to think.

The look on Manuel Delgado's face came back to haunt Metcalf. During the nightshift cops' incessant questioning, Metcalf was sure that he had heard Delgado's voice faintly in the distance. He had glanced around the small room, finally decided that the voice was being carried through an air-conditioning vent high up on the wall. The voices from the nearby room had ceased around four hours ago; Brodie assumed that they had allowed the Colombian a few hours rest. He wondered if and when he would be afforded a similar courtesy. As far as Metcalf had been led to believe, the politically correct British would not resort to methods of torture as a means of extracting information. Maybe they did not count sleep deprivation among these methods.

"I believe you haven't exactly been a talkative boy lately?" Straiton enquired. He had quickly composed himself.

Metcalf stared straight ahead.

"Can I get you a drink? Coffee?" Straiton continued.

Brodie, handcuffs now heavy in front, reached over, slid an empty cup across the table. He glanced up at the silent DS Sadler. The big man uncrossed his arms, lifted the cup. He turned, made a face at Straiton before he left the room.

"I bet you'd like to go to sleep right now, eh?" Straiton dragged a small, uncomfortable chair over to face Brodie

Metcalf. He sat, made a face, rubbed his back, exaggerating the action.

Metcalf stared straight ahead.

"How long have you been up now? Twenty-four hours? More?" Straiton leant back, folding his arms. "Just think. Lovely warm bed; freshly laundered sheets; crisp pillows; duvet folded over. Calling your name, over and over again." Straiton's voice became almost a cruel whisper.

The briefest hint of a retaliatory smile crossed the assassin's face.

"You know what? You, my friend, must be a very important person," Straiton stated sharply, arms still folded.

The statement definitely provoked a slight reaction in the expression of the hit man.

The policeman leant in closer. "I hear someone from the FBI is coming to see you," he whispered.

DS Sadler came back in, placing the cup of coffee in front of Metcalf. He backed up against the wall, folding his arms, studying the prisoner.

DS Straiton adjusted his position on the chair, wincing a little as he felt a little sciatic pain flash up and down his legs.

"I hear that they want to take you back home. Have a whole list of charges to hit you with. Want to hear what they are?" he asked, lifting his eyes towards the assassin.

Still no response.

"Murder, murder and, oh yes, murder. I hear they have as much as eight charges of what they call premeditated murder. Great word, isn't it? In fact, it's two words joined together, yes? Pre-me-di-ta-ted." He exaggerated each syllable. "I take it you know what it means?" He paused. "The nearest I get to US law is on the telly, but, as far as I can make out, premeditated means the death sentence in some states." Straiton turned to glance at his colleague.

The look of bewilderment on the face of Brett Sadler made him smirk.

How the fuck is he ever going to catch me banging his wife, Straiton thought mischievously.

"As I said, some states in the US still carry the death penalty. Electric chair, gas chamber, lethal injection. The end result is always the same. Curtains." Straiton drew his finger across his neck. "The way I see it, if I wanted to bring somebody to trial, who I was in no doubt had committed the heinous crimes that they said he had, I'd push to bring the circus to one of those death penalty states. Wouldn't you? Texas is one, I think. Isn't it, Brett?" Straiton again squirmed in his seat, shifting his position.

Sadler shrugged.

Metcalf's eyes followed the policeman. Lifting the coffee to his mouth, Brodie took a long gulp, closing his eyes as the sugar rush hit him.

DS Straiton stood, turned his back.

"We know you've been busy here, as well. Glasgow, in particular. My boss would like to offer you a deal. This is a one-time offer only. If you give us the full bhoona— names, contracts and payments, etcetera, he'll make sure you get tried here in the UK, in Scotland. Now, Scots law is different from English. I dare say that they have ancient laws in place that protect the haggis or give bagpipes the freedom of the city. Who knows? But I do know one thing. They don't carry the death penalty. We'll guarantee that you'll do your time in the UK. And I believe the inmates rave about the conditions in prison nowadays. We'd make sure that you serve your sentence in one of those cosy, secure units. Much preferable to the US alternative, eh? So, what d'you say? Do we have a deal?" DS Straiton turned around, bent, and put both hands on the table. He stared impassively at the American.

Brodie Metcalf, ever silent, clasped both cuffed hands

together, bowed his head.

The big policeman straightened up, shot his colleague a look. The two men shook their heads in unison.

"Tell you what. We'll leave you for a few minutes. Give you time to think it over. I'll need an answer then, or the deal's off. C'mon, Brett. Let's get some breakfast." Carl Straiton delivered his ultimatum, leant in to release Metcalf's handcuffs and re-fastened them to his chair.

The two cops left the room; Sadler questioned the morality of his partner's last act as they headed for the staff canteen.

Brodie Metcalf took the opportunity of scanning around the room for a means of escape— any means of escape. He began to formulate the stirrings of a plan in his mind. Tugging at the handcuffs, he bent to study the make and type. His concentration was disturbed by the resumption of activities in a nearby room. Brodie was sure that the voices were coming from the same source as before, one of them from the same man—Manuel Delgado.

Metcalf had no chance of making out any of the conversations, no matter how hard he tried. In the tiled corridor outside, however, he could clearly hear the sound of footsteps getting closer. Three or four men seemed to be on a mission, and it looked as if the source of that mission was somewhere in Brodie's vicinity.

Muffled voices directly outside the room were followed by the tapping of the security code into the door opener.

Three men stepped in. One, a very pissed off looking DS Carl Straiton, no doubt irked at being deprived of his breakfast. The second man, DS Brett Sadler, tended not to give much away in the facial expression stakes. This was probably due to the fact that he did not possess the capacity to produce too many expressions.

Whilst lying in Sadler's bed with his partner's wife, Straiton often found it amusing to comment on his colleague's apparent dearth of brain cells. Mrs. Sadler also found her lover's observations cruelly comical.

In truth, Brett Sadler was definitely the kind of man who could be relied upon in a crisis. A big, burly, honest policeman who, despite his academic failings, had still possessed the gumption required to pass his sergeant's exam at the first attempt.

Carl Straiton's immediate supervisor, Chief Inspector Wilkins, had repeatedly warned him that he should underestimate his colleague at his peril.

* * *

The third man in the room was of average height and build. Dark hair with flecks of grey at the temples, Metcalf estimated his age to be around the mid fifties. He was dressed very smartly in a dark suit and tie with a neatly laundered, white shirt. His shoes were black leather Gucci.

Carl Straiton whispered something into the man's ear which was ignored. The man was carrying a black leather, zipped folder which he laid neatly on the table, his OCD making him immediately square the edges.

The man needn't have opened his mouth to introduce himself. The FBI screamed from his every fibre.

"My name is Doctor Richard Belzer," he announced, almost emotionless, or as damn near as anyone could get.

Metcalf noted the accent as originating from one of the southern states. Virginia, perhaps.

"I'm with the Federal Bureau of Investigation, based at Quantico, Virginia."

Brodie afforded himself the faintest of smiles at his accuracy.

"I head up the Behavioural Analysis Unit. You could say I was a profiler." He sat, omitting to offer a handshake.

In any case, Metcalf was not exactly in a position to

receive one. It was fair to say that the hit man was a little unnerved, but chose not to show it.

Straiton, still seething at being replaced by an American, backed off as per the last orders from his superiors. He and the 'easy either way,' Brett Sadler, stood, arms folded, as the FBI man attempted to sort out the situation.

"And your name is Brodie Metcalf, among others? Thomas Tremayne? The Viper?" Belzer queried, sneeringly.

Metcalf's mood darkened further. He did not like this man— did not like him at all.

"When the FBI got the call from Scotland Yard that you had been taken into custody, I volunteered to make the journey. I've been studying your movements for the past four years. I know about Jack Feltham, the heads of four 'families'. With a little effort— and a sample of your DNA, of course— I reckon we could link you with a lot more," Belzer announced in a clipped, voice-coached sort of fashion. He leant over to unzip his folder, producing a simple clipboard with several blank pages on it. "Gentlemen, if you would leave us alone for a few minutes? I'll give you a call when we're done," Belzer stated firmly, ignorantly refusing to turn around to address Straiton and Sadler.

"Sorry, can't do that. Against the rules. If the prisoner escapes..." Straiton protested.

"And just how can he do that, Sergeant?" the FBI man asked, obviously referring to the handcuffs.

"Let's go, Brett," Straiton whispered to his colleague. He decided not to push it, fearing further repercussions from his inspector.

The detectives had just been ordered to take a back seat and let the FBI handle the prisoner. Apparently, the Home Secretary had been involved in the decision. Enough said.

"We'll just be out here if you need us," Straiton conceded, closing the door sharply behind them.

Richard Belzer's dark eyes studied the prisoner closely. He picked up the clipboard, removing the paperclip that held the leaves of paper together. Placing the clip on the table, he bent to reach into the leather folder now propped against the leg of his chair. Metcalf never took his eyes off Belzer, as the FBI man placed a small, black box on the table. He took out an expensive, personalised, gold pen, clicking the top, ready for action.

Belzer leant back in his chair, crossing his legs, clipboard resting on his knee.

"Okay. Let me tell you what's going to happen here." He bent towards Metcalf, almost whispering. "Two FBI agents are making their way from Washington as we speak. They're going to escort you back there, where you will be held under high security guard awaiting trial." Belzer began to scribble on the board. After about thirty seconds, he began to fire out names at random. "Lyle Froggat; Guiseppe Manoli; Michael Van Zanten; Miller Pattison." He stopped, presumably to check for any reaction. He did not detect any. "You recognise some of those names? You should." Belzer slapped the clipboard on the table. "You were paid to kill every one of them. There's more: Allan Getz; Frank Di Carlo; Stevie Sonnbergh. Don't suppose you'd like to shed any light on any of them?" No response. "Didn't think so. No matter. All we have to do is get a sample of your DNA. A simple mouth swab. It can wait until we get back to HQ. You know the scientists say that a simple swab of cheek cells is usually enough to tell us the whole story? And you can just bet your bottom dollar that we are going to be able to match you up with something."

Metcalf lowered his eyes.

Belzer checked around the room, then leant in even closer, his voice barely a whisper. "I'm gonna make sure that you fry for what you've done. Jack Feltham was a great friend of mine. Helped me out a couple of times when

I joined the Bureau. The bastards fucking shit on him, forced him out, and called him a dinosaur. Then he gets stabbed in the back by a piece of crap like you," Belzer spat, unloading four years of pent-up frustration.

Richard Belzer sat up, glanced around the room like a naughty schoolboy who had just been rumbled. He straightened his clothes, patted down his hair.

Belzer gathered his papers together, leant across to pick up the paperclip he had earlier placed on the desk. A puzzled look crossed his face. It was not like the FBI man to be forgetful.

The unmerciful lights in the room highlighted a tiny flash of silver on the floor, which immediately caught his eye. He pulled in a long breath when he realised that it was the clip, intentionally straightened out to form a specialised tool.

A horrified Richard Belzer looked up to see Brodie Metcalf unclip the handcuffs from the frame of his chair.

60

Mason Blackwell was now at home.

He had stayed a while in the hospital room of his stricken friend, DI Theresa Bremner. Feeling completely useless, Mason had decided to make his excuses to Lindsey, Theresa's partner, and a second surprise visitor, Mary Munro. He explained to Lindsey that he would, of course, return to Theresa's bedside after he had made sure that his family were safely out of harm's way. Unsurprisingly, she had fully understood. The doctors had again stressed to them that every day that Theresa survived would be a bonus, given this induced, coma state in which she had been placed.

Mason had a dilemma. He did not want to send his family into a blind panic. At the same time, he had to stress the importance of getting everybody to a safe house as soon as possible. Two plain-clothed officers in an unmarked car outside the house made him feel a little more secure.

He was in the middle of explaining the slightly sanitised version of the master plan to his wife, Alison, when the mobile phone in his pocket burst into life.

"Hello, Andy. Is everything set?" Blackwell asked the MI6 man.

"Mason? You'll never believe it. We've had a break at last," Wells replied. "Metcalf's been picked up. A tip off caught him at a secret meeting with the drugs cartel. He's being held at Scotland Yard. My sources tell me that the

FBI's sending a team out to escort him back to the States. That's great news, isn't it?" Andy paused. "Mason? Are you there?"

"Eh... aye! I just had to sit down. Felt a little faint with the shoulder. Can't believe it, Andy. It's over then, at last?" Mason asked, the elation unaccountably draining the energy from him.

"It's over. So get yourself back to hospital. Take a couple of days rest. You deserve it."

"I'd love to, but I need to show face at HQ tomorrow. Even if it's just for a little while."

The statement drew a withering look from Alison.

Mason made a face at his wife before continuing, "I'm in charge after George Drummond's death, even if it's only temporarily. I've got to make an effort for the troops. They need to know that the system's still in place. And I'll need to organise Will Munro's release from the safe house."

"You're a regular saint, Mason. Keep well. I'll let you know about any further developments."

"Thanks for everything, Andy. I'll speak to you soon."

Mason Blackwell tossed the mobile onto the coffee table, sank into his favourite chair. The relief he was feeling was indescribable. The huge smile on his face was soon replaced by a sober look. "Just one thing to worry about now, Ali," Mason said quietly, furrowing his brow.

61

"How long's he been in now, Brett?" Carl Straiton again asked. Patience had never been high on his list of virtues.

Sadler pulled back the sleeve of his shirt.

"Twenty-five minutes."

The pair were standing outside the interview room at Scotland Yard, waiting for the emergence of FBI man, Richard Belzer, who had earlier requested a private meeting with assassin, Brodie Metcalf.

"What the hell's he doing in there?"

"Take it easy. The man said he'd call us when he was done. For fuck's sake, the prisoner's cuffed to his chair," Sadler snapped at his partner.

Characteristically, Straiton chose to ignore Sadler's observations. He pressed an ear against the door.

"I can't hear anything. Something's wrong, I'm telling you," he maintained.

Sadler was leaning against the wall on the other side of the corridor. He dragged himself back to the level, sauntered over beside Carl Straiton. Brett gave him the death stare on the way past. Pressing his ear against the door, Sadler listened for at least a full minute.

"See. I'm right. Yes?" Straiton declared triumphantly.

Brett Sadler thought carefully for a moment before taking the initiative. Tapping in the entry code, the heavy door then swung open.

"Jesus!" Sadler exclaimed. He couldn't quite

362

comprehend the scene in front of him. "Hit the alarm. Now!" he commanded his partner.

Carl Straiton flew into the corridor, slamming his fist against the panic button on the wall. The whole fabric of the building heavily reverberated with the invasive sounds of the recently installed alarm system at the Yard.

Brett Sadler was experienced enough to know never to touch anything at a crime scene. Rule Number 1: firstly, establish if a fatality has occurred. If so, lock the scene down until forensics gets there. Sadler could never be described as the sharpest tool, but even he knew when he was looking at a corpse.

FBI agent, Richard Belzer, was slumped untidily across the table, face down, his head turned to the right. Sticking out of his right eye was the top half of his gold-plated, personalised pen.

"Oh no! This isn't good! Wh-where the fuck is he?" Straiton blurted.

Sadler tried to remain calm despite his partner's ramblings. He scanned the room, his eyes eventually coming to rest on an area high up on the wall.

"The vent! He's in the air-con vent!" Sadler pointed to the spot.

The exterior grill, rectangular in shape, had been removed and presumably slid inside the ducting. Quite how the little American had been able to even reach the vent, let alone get inside, was mystifying. But unless he was able to make himself invisible, the ventilation system was exactly the method Brodie Metcalf had used to make his escape.

* * *

Inside the metal ductwork, Metcalf had both hands clamped over his ears. The shrill sounds of the alarm system seemed to have been amplified a thousand times in this metal prison, which he now found himself occupying.

Some minutes earlier, Brodie had been able to follow and close in on the familiar tone of a foreign accent.

Manuel Delgado could not possibly have been aware of the assassin lurking just above him as he endeavoured to spill his guts on the entire operation; from the cartel's plans and aspirations, the role of a certain Brodie Metcalf in the mayhem, the arrangements for Delgado's new identity and proposed new location along with a full amnesty. And last, but not least, the simple matter of five million dollars to be going on with.

The Colombian had sold out everybody, without exception. To be fair, Delgado had been caught red handed. It was deal or jail. The smart man had made his choice.

Metcalf seethed as he witnessed the men in the room below shake on the deal. The signing of the legal documents had been rudely interrupted by the untimely alarm. Delgado was asked to stay put in the room, while the rest ran to investigate. It was thought that the now precious commodity would be safer behind lock and key— and secret door code.

How wrong.

Brodie sucked in a deep breath before delivering a swift kick to the metal exterior grill above Manuel Delgado's head. The grill crashed to the floor below, the sound completely masked by the racket from the alarm.

Delgado leapt gingerly to his feet in fright, his eyes wide in anticipation. By the time he had figured out exactly what was happening, Brodie Metcalf was dropping down from the sky, like some kind of avenging angel, to stand directly in front of him.

There was a fleeting moment of quiet reservation, before the assassin flashed a short blow to the throat of the traitor, collapsing his windpipe.

Delgado's body shuddered and shook as he tried

desperately to fill his lungs. The Colombian collapsed to the floor in a heap, his survival instincts compelling him to crawl for cover under the interview table, to curl up into a foetal position. He began clawing furiously at his neck. Seconds later, he was dead.

Brodie Metcalf was already on his way back to his steel hiding place, courtesy of a sudden burst of speed and agility straight out of the armoury of former trainee circus acrobat, Jack Feltham. The hit man bounded against the wall underneath the open vent, twisting and bending in mid air. Both hands grasped the edge of the opening. With consummate ease, Brodie was able to haul himself inside, just as the panic alarm mercifully ceased. He rubbed both ears furiously; the increasing decibel limit began to really take its toll. The early stirrings of a headache began to form just above his eyes.

His hearing slowly returning, Metcalf was then aware of a low, heavy rumbling sound travelling along the ducting. He placed the flat of his hand against the metal, smiling when he realised exactly what he was listening to.

Brodie was able to move quickly and nimbly through the venting, the rumbling sound increasing in intensity as he crawled. Eventually, he reached the source. Peering through yet another grill, Brodie could hardly believe his luck. A huge, industrial tumble dryer groaned away in the corner of the laundry area at Scotland Yard. The suddenness of the alarm system had caused the laundry workers to immediately vacate the scene, leaving an unguarded chute to a possible basement escape. It would be a tight squeeze, but Metcalf wasn't exactly blessed with a whole world of alternatives.

He forced the fingers of one hand into the grill, delivered another blow with the heel of a shoe. Brodie pulled the grill inside the duct, poked his head out into the room. Coast clear, he was back on terra firma in seconds. He now needed another stroke of luck.

Here goes nothing, Brodie mused, disappearing down the chute, feet first.

*   *   *

Thirty minutes later, DS Carl Straiton and DS Brett Sadler were in the basement area at Scotland Yard. They had now ruled out the possibility that the silent assassin still inhabited the air-conditioning system. Especially since the introduction of a little tear gas into the duct. Everyone in the building had suffered as a result— except Brodie Metcalf. In hindsight, the panicky action definitely smacked a little of shutting the stable door.

After the discovery of the bodies of Richard Belzer and Manuel Delgado, Straiton, undoubtedly the more intelligent of the two policemen, firstly thanked the Gods that he was still around to tell the tale. Secondly, he sent up another Catholic prayer, hoping that he would never again set eyes upon this extremely dangerous person.

Carl Straiton deliberately held back as they swung open the double doors into the basement area.

"Police!" Sadler shouted. Bravely, he stepped into the room.

Deep in the bowels of the building, the lack of windows or sunshine meant that it was normally freezing in there in winter, cold in spring, cool in summer. The mid spring day was unusually mild for the time of year.

The basement was used only for storage. Freshly laundered and bagged bed sheets, duvets and towels lay in an industrial-sized wheeled bin, awaiting distribution around the accommodation areas of the building. The bin had been strategically placed under the chute leading from the upstairs laundry room.

Sadler peered inside, noting a number of burst and torn

plastic bags. Straiton followed his partner in, tentatively checking out the evidence. He looked up just in time to catch Brett Sadler glance up and down from the chute to the bin and back to the chute.

"Duh! That's right stupid! He was here!" Straiton said sarcastically in a Homer Simpson-type accent. His courage was returning now that he realised Metcalf was long gone. "And that's how he escaped." He pointed triumphantly towards a fire exit door at the back end of the building.

Brett Sadler chose not to reply, though his face reddened with fury. He strode angrily over to the fire exit door, roughly pushing the release bar across the middle. The back of the door crashed against the outside wall.

"What's up with you?" Straiton asked, a concerned look crossing his face.

Sadler still didn't answer. His only reaction was a dismissive wave over his shoulder. He walked out of the door and up a dozen steps to the car park compound. The area was security fenced with a ring of barbed wire across the top.

The car park benefitted from a couple of CCTV cameras. Sadler stood at the top of the flight of stone stairs. He quickly realised that there would be no real need to consult the cameras. Brett's face broke into a wide smile.

At the far end of the compound, a couple of heavy gates were lying flat on the ground. Part of the structure of the fence on each side of the gates had collapsed in with the impact.

Sadler, now doing his utmost to stifle a smile, stepped aside to allow his colleague to survey the scene.

"So what's the verdict?" Straiton asked, bouncing up the steps.

"Why don't you tell us, Clouseau?" Sadler asked, instantly wishing that he had a video camera to record the moment.

"All righty then— wait a minute." Emerging from the dark basement, Straiton's eyes had now become accustomed to the light. "Are you kiddin'? Obviously, he hotwired a motor and burst through the gates." He laughed, looking ever so pleased with himself.

"It looks that way, doesn't it?" Brett replied smugly.

The rage Sadler had earlier felt when he eventually found out about his wife's affair with Carl Straiton had subsided. From wanting to rip Straiton's head off and ram it up his arse, to complete and utter indifference. Sadler didn't love his wife, never had. There were no children involved and he had already made the decision to walk away, even before he knew about Carl Straiton's mucky involvement. In Sadler's view, the dirty bastard was welcome to that cow.

Little did both cheaters know that the 'dumb cop' had found himself a little gem of his own down at the local gym, where he worked hard to maintain his perfect physical condition.

Sadler watched as Straiton attempted to piece together the recent movements of Brodie Metcalf.

"Wait a fucking minute! Where's my Audi?" Carl Straiton shouted in anguish.

62

One week later

Mason Blackwell stopped outside the Munros' big house at Roman Road on the outskirts of Glasgow. Opening the car door, the inspector could hear the happy strains of children playing in the back yard.

Blackwell recalled that Theresa Bremner had detailed a similar scene a few days earlier.

"Inspector Blackwell, it's good to see you again. Please, come in," Mary Munro said cheerfully enough.

Mason had seen her last week at Theresa Bremner's bedside; her best friends' death and her husband's exile obviously weighed heavily on her mind. Dark, sunken eyes and a very pale, drawn complexion, Mary looked then as if her whole world was about to end. One comforting closure of a funeral service and a re-appearance of a loving husband later, and Mary's zest and resilience had returned to continue the fight.

She had applied a little makeup; her dark hair was scraped up into a short pony tail. Light blue T-shirt, joggers and trainers made her look and feel almost normal again. Her eyes were full of life, bright and sparkling.

"Mary, look at you!" Mason stepped in to give her a hug and a peck on the cheek. "You look really great, love. And please, it's Mason."

"Is this you checking up on us? If so, we're doing

okay."

"So I see," he replied. "I just came by to let you know that we haven't heard anything since we last spoke."

"That's a relief. Maybe that'll be the end of it," she said bravely.

"Looks like it," he retorted. He followed her into the living room, stopping to admire a tank full of tropical fish as Mary carried on into the kitchen.

Blackwell sat next to the tank, prodding the glass like a naughty child in a pet shop. The fish darted in and out of the cover of some ornaments and foliage on the bottom of the tank.

"Theresa? Has there been any news?" Mary asked. "I was at the hospital again yesterday."

From his seat in the living room, Mason could hear the kettle being filled. He got up and followed her into the kitchen.

"They're going to stop the drugs, day after tomorrow. The doctor says her brain should have had plenty of time to heal by then." He tried to stay upbeat. Truth was, with every passing hour that his friend remained unconscious, his once rock-like and steadfast optimism was being chipped away, little by little. "It's nearly time for her to wake up," Mason re-affirmed.

Mary noted his troubled look. She witnessed the cop's face run a full gamut of emotions. "That's great news. She's going to be fine, Mason. Don't worry." Mary put a consoling hand on the policeman's arm.

He smiled in agreement, his pulse racing.

The past week, since the shooting, had been a rollercoaster of emotions for Mason Blackwell.

He had received the call from MI6 agent, Andy Wells, who told him that the killer, Brodie Metcalf, had been arrested, was being held at Scotland Yard HQ. Then, almost with Andy's next breath, he was delivering Blackwell the news that Metcalf had somehow escaped, leaving a trail of death in his wake. The planned disappearance of the Blackwell family to a safe house had already been shelved, much to everybody's delight.

Accountant, Will Munro— the original target— had returned to his family, overjoyed and elated. The reunion of the couple, their kids, and the children of their best friends, had indeed been tearful and hugely intense.

With his next move anything but straightforward, Mason Blackwell had then decided to take a real chance with the lives of both families. For the following forty-eight hours, Blackwell had decided to do nothing. A pair of plain clothes outside each door— that was it. Mason Blackwell had decided that it was now time to stand firm. He was unwilling to deliver another downer for the families— to split everyone up once again. And, even if he were to do that— for how long would they be parted? Forever?

In truth, if Metcalf had come calling, it was unlikely that the token police resistance would have greatly deterred him. Mason was willing to bet that the assassin had had enough of the country. With a little luck, he would be recaptured. With a little less luck, the hit man would return to his homeland, at least for now.

In reality, it appeared as if option two had been the outcome; the discovery of the body of an airport security man, and the sighting of an airline passenger, bound for the States and fitting Metcalf's description, was enough to conclude the matter for the moment.

Both Mason Blackwell and Andy Wells had agreed, at the time of the escape, that it would be wise not to mention the fact to either family unit that the killer was again on the loose. Ironically, the media had later rather tactlessly taken care of that job; the news leaked out, despite efforts by the Secret Service to deny the incident. At the same time as the denial, a report that Metcalf had almost certainly fled to the

States was distributed by Reuters, much to the great relief of certain Glasgow residents.

* * *

Mug of tea in hand, Blackwell stood at the window looking out into the back garden. Both Munro and Vieri twins were playing happily on the lawn. Will Munro was also outside. He had been mowing the grass. Now he was in the middle of a game of commandos with the two boys. Mason smirked as the trio rolled around among the girls' dollies and toy picnic sets.

Will Munro sat up, cleared the loose grass from his clothes. He waved as he spotted the policeman through the window.

Seconds later, Will was in the kitchen, closing the door on the mayhem.

"Hi, Inspector. Didn't know you were here. How's the shoulder?" he asked.

"Oh, it's absolutely fine. The doctor says I should be able to ditch the heavy dressing sometime soon," Mason replied. "I see that you've got your hands full out there!" He nodded towards the children, who were, by this time, engaged in a full-blooded grass fight.

"Aye, you could say that! The good thing is, they all get along just fine. Thank God! Some minor disagreements, but, on the whole, they're just great kids— even though I say it myself." Will put a tender arm around his loving wife, kissing her softly on the cheek.

"Aye. They certainly are. Tell me, are you any further forward with the adoption process?" Blackwell asked.

Mary shook her head.

"Haven't had the time. So much has happened lately. But we're still here and that's the main thing." Mary's voice cracked; painful thoughts and memories of friends past flooded back. "I'm going to see a lawyer on Monday. Get the ball rolling on it."

"Look. Maybe it won't make the slightest difference to the outcome. If you need any kind of reference or recommendation, I'd only be too happy to fill out any form for you— if it'll help," Mason declared, sipping his tea.

"The thumbs up from a decorated and well-respected police inspector? I think it definitely will. Thanks, Mason," Will Munro said.

Mary leant over and hugged the policeman.

The quirky bass line from the start of *The Eagles'* song, *One of these Nights*, emanated from Blackwell's jacket. He plucked the mobile from the pocket, checked the illuminated display. He made a face, finding the number familiar. Stopping Don Henley in mid flow, Mason hit the green button.

"Hello?" he said sharply.

"Inspector Blackwell? Is that you?" The voice of Senior Consultant Richard Squires was instantly identifiable.

Mason's heart fluttered. "Yes. Mister Squires?" he attempted to confirm.

"It is. Inspector, we've had a development over here," Squires answered in a clipped, plummy voice.

"Theresa? Has something happened to her?" Blackwell turned away from the Munros and stared out of the window at the children. They were most definitely there, but he couldn't see them.

"I suggest you come down to the hospital right away," the surgeon replied, dodging the question.

The phone went dead.

"Is everything all right, Mason?" Will Munro asked for both of them.

"I don't know. The surgeon said I'd to go to the hospital," Mason replied, now looking extremely worried. "Mary, can you phone Theresa's partner, Lindsey? Tell her to go to the hospital."

"Of course, Mason. I'll do it right away. Good luck," Mary replied.

"Thanks. I have to go. I'll call you," the policeman shouted on the way out of the door.

63

Merry Hills Cemetery, Near Chicago, Illinois.

There had been a slight smattering of rain earlier in the morning. The newly cut grass all around the rolling gardens of this exclusive resting place stood to attention, as if revived by the life-giving water.

The facility's groundsmen, at least a dozen strong, immaculate in their logoed to the hilt, khaki coveralls, cut, planted, tidied and swept their way through another morning's work.

There were to be no new customers laid to rest at Merry Hills today, due to a local trades holiday. Almost everyone in Chicago and the surrounding areas marked the day in their calendar as one to be spent with their loved ones. Only some of the good people of the emergency services and the dedicated staff at Merry Hills would be expected to turn out.

In one of the most blatant pieces of copyright theft ever perpetrated, the owners of the cemetery would guarantee their clients that they would provide a twenty-four-hour service, with the heartfelt promise, 'we never sleep'.

The present owners of one of the oldest established companies in the US— the Pinkerton Detective Agency, with humble beginnings circa 1800s— had considered legal action to address the breach.

*   *   *

The grave of former FBI agent and hired killer, Jack Feltham, was sited in a leafy, secluded corner of the graveyard, overhung by a number of strong, young and healthy trees, including a cherry blossom and a weeping willow.

A sizeable hunk of the fifty grand that had been paid from Feltham's estate for the plot would guarantee to cover the costs of tending the grave forever.

The Merry Hills Company also owned an acre full of giant greenhouses in an adjoining field. Each year, hundreds of thousands of flowers and plants of all types and colours, were grown from seed to ensure that each plot would be lovingly cared for by the highly trained, caring staff.

The cemetery was normally a busy place on a holiday. Today was no exception; visitors, young and old, dressed in their Sunday finery, trudged in and out of Merry Hills, duly paying their respects to their loved ones.

The tall, slim brunette, dressed all in black, knelt by Jack Feltham's grave, her head bowed. The former Kelly Martin, left for dead four years earlier by Brodie Metcalf on that waste ground in Chicago, was again on her annual pilgrimage to pay her respects to the man she had loved above all others. She placed her own little posy of flowers at the foot of the headstone.

"Hello, Jack. How've you been? Can't believe it's been another year. The time just goes too quickly," she whispered under her breath, leaning closer to the ground. "It's a beautiful day, a little wet earlier, but then, you already know that, don't you?" She managed a wry smile. "I've just flown in from Scotland. There's certainly a lot to tell you. I just have to take care of one more thing. Later today, we'll have our justice at last, my love. I'll be back to see you in the morning. I love you."

Tears rolling down her cheeks, the young woman reached down, put both hands flat on the grass. Seconds later, she stood and started along the small pathway to the car park.

64

Blackwell reached the entrance to the hospital, took the stone steps like a chasing lion. He raced past the receptionist at the desk; respect for the infirmed within caused him to slow, almost mimic the technique of an Olympic twenty-five-kilometre walker when he hit the long corridor leading to Theresa Bremner's room.

Mason's leather-soled shoes clacked loudly against the highly polished, vinyl floor of the recovery ward.

As if theatrically staged, the target door swung open when Mason finally got there. Richard Squires, senior consultant, stepped out, a resigned look on his face. He stood aside to let the policeman enter, even though the notion to do so had suddenly left him.

Mason steeled himself, prepared for the worst.

Inside the room, the curtains had been fully opened, allowing the brilliant sunshine inside; hardly an appropriate scene, given the circumstances. Or was it?

Propped up in bed, obviously strained, almost managing to smile, lay the star attraction. Theresa Bremner held out her arms to her great friend. Her brave smile then vanished, replaced by a look of anguish.

The pair hugged for what seemed like an eternity. Theresa clung tightly to him, her tears staining his dark jacket. The tough cop drew the back of his wrist across his eyes, before cupping his hands to her cheeks.

"Welcome back, love," Mason whispered, kissing

Theresa tenderly on the forehead.

"Did you miss me, Mason?" she typically asked.

"Just a little. How do you feel?"

"As good as I look, no doubt." She pointed to her head, still bandaged, though a lighter dressing was now in place.

"You look great. Never better!" Mason laughed. "And early. That does make a change!"

"Early? For what?" she asked, concerned.

"We were controlling your consciousness, Inspector— with drugs," the man standing at the door answered.

Blackwell had almost forgotten that he was there.

Squires explained, "To make sure there was no swelling of the brain, which could cause irreparable brain damage. Apparently, last night one of the nurses omitted to administer your final dose for the evening. As a result, you came out of the induced coma early this morning, directly before your next dose." His tone was rather sombre, despite the outcome.

"Three cheers for the nurse!" Theresa replied, brightening a little.

"That nurse will be disciplined," he said, sternly.

Blackwell made a face at his colleague. "We were lucky. You were awakened sooner than we had planned. Your brain may still be slightly swollen. Tests will reveal if that is the case. Even if so, there should be no great problem at this stage, if you stay with us for a few days— for observation purposes?" Squires asked, smiling at last. He patted the back of her hand in a way that he must have done to other patients a thousand times before.

Bremner thought for a second, then agreed.

"Is Lindsey not here yet? I asked Mary Munro to call her. Oh, and Mary and Will send their best wishes," Blackwell said.

Theresa smiled at the reference to the couple.

"Lindsey left me a note, apparently. In case I woke up

early," she replied, a slight annoyance detectable in her tone. "Her mother's not too well. She should be home day after tomorrow."

"Don't be too harsh on her, Theresa. She's been here with you all along. She... We all thought you would be out for another two days or... What?" Blackwell had noticed the haunted look on Theresa Bremner's face. Her fragmented memory of the last moments of her previous conscious state was beginning to gel.

"Wh-what happened?" she asked, almost as if she shouldn't.

Blackwell glanced over at Squires, gave him the look. The surgeon took the hint, made his excuses to leave. Mason turned his attention to his friend.

"Doug Mailer's dead. Andy Wells saved our lives. MI6 think Metcalf is back in the States," Blackwell answered clearly and precisely. He had realised immediately to what she was referring, and decided to give her the facts without any fancy dressing up.

Straight talking was very much a huge part of their makeup.

"Another quiet day at the office, then?" she asked, deadpan.

65

Hotel Meridian, Chicago, Illinois

"I have a slight problem with my business. I hear you may be the one to see about correcting this problem?" The voice on the other end of the phone was definitely foreign.

"That would depend on what your problem was," Penny Richards replied cagily.

Eastern European, maybe Russian, she mused. She looked pleased. It would seem that her excellent work on both sides of the Atlantic had not gone unnoticed.

She now felt that she was the complete package. Since leaving London, the porn industry and her sister behind, Penny had travelled around the globe, falling completely by accident into the extremely dangerous, but highly lucrative world of contract killing. Her natural aptitude for, and fascination with, weaponry of all types had served her well thus far. Guns and knives had been the preferred options throughout her new career.

A chance meeting with a Japanese martial artist, with a penchant for swords and machetes, had resulted in Richards adding a new talent to her armoury. She had reserved these special skills for a few selected individuals— Vic Simpson, Tommy Mulraney, Sean McGlinchy.

Penny had the thought fixed in her mind that the unsolicited call was indeed coming from a Russian billionaire, desperate to ensure that nobody muscled in on his oil field. Within minutes, she had convinced herself that the Russian market was definitely the place to operate. And, with the country's rapid defection to Western ethos and values, why shouldn't this fiercely ambitious woman hitch a little ride on the gravy train?

"I would like to meet with you. I will make it very worth your while," the man said in broken English.

"I think that can be arranged, Mister...?"

"My identity is not important for now. What is important is that I have a job for you to do. A very urgent job."

Penny could hardly contain her delight. She tried her best to keep composed.

"Meet me at the Hotel Meridian, on the south side. Go to the reception desk and ask for Room 331. It's in the name of Abigail Clancy. One hour from now," she stated, succinctly.

"Excellent. I look forward to meeting with you."

Fifty-five minutes later, from her bedroom window, Penny Richards watched a long, black car purr into the car park at the front of the Hotel Meridian. The motor stopped directly below her bedroom window. She saw a man get out of the driver's door, crane his neck to look up at the impressive front facade of the five-star hotel. He was alone.

Penny reckoned that the man was around mid sixties with receding, grey hair. He was wearing a light jacket and trousers— not matching, with a black shirt and cream shoes; he was clutching a brown, leather briefcase.

She couldn't help thinking that the man's aura reminded her of a package-holiday tourist looking to splash out and spend some of his early retirement windfall.

Richards walked calmly across the spacious room and sat on a red, leather chaise longue. She made sure to hitch her micro-skirt up a little, crossed her long, slender legs. And for good measure, Penny hid a Smith and Wesson handgun below a cushion— just as a precaution. She took a couple of breaths to steady her nerves, and waited.

The ding of the lift arriving at the desired floor level broke the silence out in the corridor. A minute or two later, light footsteps could barely be heard outside the door.

"Come on in, it's open!" Penny shouted in reaction to the door chimes.

The old man entered the room, visibly double taking at the sight of the gorgeous woman in front of him.

"Please, may I?" he asked, nervously motioning towards an easy chair in the corner. "My legs, they are not so young as they used to be." The man slumped wearily into the chair, resting the leather briefcase at his feet.

Penny found herself warming to the sweet, old man almost immediately. She stood, pulling her skirt down as a mark of respect, covering her modesty.

"Can I get you a drink? I have whisky, brandy, and vodka." She once again opened up the minibar, doing her utmost to try to spend the hard earned blood money picked up on her most recent visit to Scotland.

"Do you have any mineral water, my dear? The doctors have told me to resist the alcohol— not good for my blood pressure, they say." He leant forward, his face breaking into a homely smile.

Penny suddenly had a déjà vu moment, fondly recalling a rare show of kindness from her own father, many years before.

"I don't suppose a little vodka will do any harm. I won't tell if you won't. Thank you." He sat back as she filled the glasses.

Penny emptied the last few drops out of a miniature bottle of whisky for herself. She made a mental note to phone reception to re-order.

She reached across, handing the glass to the old man. She walked over to the window, habitually glancing out as usual. Paranoia— one of the pitfalls of her particular profession was again kicking in. Her attention was taken by another car entering the hotel car park— a familiar car.

"So what is it I can do for you exactly?" Penny enquired of her guest.

Definitely pre-occupied, she was still watching the movements of the car below. A slightly bemused expression flitted across her face, as she recognised the driver emerging from the now parked vehicle.

The preliminaries out of the way, it was now down to business. Penny turned to face the ageing Russian, about to repeat her last question. She froze when she realised that they were not alone. Somewhere along the line, a gun— a semi-automatic— had joined the party, firmly within the grasp of the Russian. His smile had gone, replaced by a cold, soulless expression.

"Wh-what are you doing?" Richards' voice wavered with nerves.

He didn't reply at first, continuing to stare her down.

The old man reached up, his free hand firstly peeling away the latex skin on his head and face, then removing his grey wig. The process took around twenty seconds.

"Why did you kill Baltimore?" Brodie Metcalf demanded, the Russian accent deserting him.

"I... I don't understand. Who are you?" Penny blustered, confused by the developments.

"The question's simple enough. Answer or I'll kill you right now, right here," he said, ignoring her question. Metcalf lifted the gun, finger tightening on the trigger.

"Okay, wait! Don't shoot. I'll tell you." She began to edge over towards the chaise longue, and the Smith and Wesson, which still lay under a cushion.

"Stay there. Another inch and you're dead." Metcalf was too long in the tooth for such tricks. "You have five seconds."

"I was originally hired by Baltimore," she replied in a micro-second.

"Hired by Baltimore? Don't fuck with me!" he cut in.

"I'm not! I swear. Baltimore hired me to kill this old lady. At his son's funeral— I had to shoot her!"

"What happened?"

"I got a better offer. Someone else hired me to take Baltimore out instead," Penny announced, inexplicably calming. Her confidence was coming back— and with good reason.

"Who hired you?" Metcalf demanded to know.

"I did!" The voice came from behind him. "Put the gun down, Brodie," it commanded.

A bullet slipped seamlessly into the chamber of a gun.

Metcalf's expression suddenly changed; his face softened into a smile.

Richards, sensing Metcalf's hesitation, was at the chaise longue in seconds, snatching the Smith and Wesson, training it on him.

Brodie relaxed his grip on the gun, bent down to place it on the floor in front of him. He returned to his feet, hands in the air, still facing Penny Richards.

"I knew I should've finished you off when I had the chance," Brodie said, turning around to face Kelly Martin. Another tall, gorgeous brunette stood before him.

"You bastard. Jack loved you like a son, you know that? Why, Brodie? Why kill him?" Kelly Martin's contorted face bore years of hate, tears welling in her beautiful eyes.

"Money. It's always about money, Kelly. It's just the game we're in. You should know that," he replied.

"Nothing personal. Is that how it goes, Brodie?" she asked, blinking the tears down her cheeks.

"Yep, just business."

"I also have some unfinished business. This is for you,

Jack," Kelly said, almost in a whisper.

In a split second, Metcalf crouched low on his way to a concealed knife strapped to his leg, just above the shoe. Springing back to his feet, the blade left his hand, flashing across the room at almost the exact moment that the bullet exited the barrel of Kelly Martin's gun.

The heavy hunting knife slammed into her shoulder, the angle of attack causing it to bounce up and over. She fell in a heap, screaming in pain, the knife spearing into the floor at her feet.

Kelly's bullet had taken out part of Metcalf's right ear on its way to the defenceless forehead of Penny Richards. Penny was unable to react in time; the shock of the impact wrested the gun from her grasp. The gun clattered to the floor. Penny never stood a chance as the slug buried itself deep into her brain; her lifeless body shuddered for a few seconds before crashing earthwards.

Bizarrely, both surviving parties then took a moment or two to gather their thoughts. Metcalf was clasping his hand to his ear, blood streaming down his neck. He had his eyes on the Glock, which still lay exactly where he had placed it.

The former Kelly Martin, now known as Lindsey Wallace, was lying on her back, still bravely hanging on to the gun. She felt excruciating pain from her shoulder as she struggled to sit up, lifting the weapon to take aim.

Brodie Metcalf dropped to his knees, swept his gun into position.

Bang!

Both guns fired almost simultaneously.

66

Two months later

"Mason! It's great to see you! Come in, for God's sake!" Theresa Bremner threw welcoming arms around her great friend, pulling him inside the entrance vestibule of her Stirling town-centre, first-floor flat.

"You're looking fab, Theresa. How've you been?" Blackwell asked.

"Uh, y'know. So-so." Her smile waned. She turned, leading Mason into the living room.

"Sit. I'll get the tea on." Bremner disappeared into the kitchenette.

Mason sat in an easy chair. As if by habit, his attention was taken by the TV in the corner, one of those extremely tacky, morning reality shows bastardising the airwaves. The kind of programme that everybody denies actually watching but, when prompted, can accurately recount large portions.

This particular production appeared to highlight the problems of parenthood. Sat next to each other in front of a baying studio audience, was a normal, Joe Public sort of couple. Or so we were led to believe.

Mason studied the pair: he was about thirty-five, tattooed, shaven headed and massively overweight, with what Mason's granny would often consider a 'bad look about him'. To cap it off, the man was wearing a faded T-shirt with a Hell's Angel motif across the chest. Underneath the motif, a short message, probably bordering on the obscene, had been blurred out by the technical people on the show.

The 'loving wife and mother,' shoehorned into the chair beside him, had obviously forgotten to wear a bra, her ample bosoms heaving under a crop top, which must have been ten sizes too small. Her denim skirt had crawled almost up her backside as she tugged and heaved at it, struggling to cover her questionable modesty. Tacky earrings and the obligatory chewing gum accompanied her multi-coloured hairstyle, scraped back into an untidy ponytail. She looked as if she could spit a hole in a tin bucket.

The physical product of this pair was then introduced to the audience with the highlighted caption— 'I want to divorce my parents'— emblazoned at the bottom of the screen.

Mason's jaw nearly hit the floor when the fifteen-year-old daughter strolled out: tall, long blonde hair neatly tied back, no obvious signs of any makeup; a crisp, white blouse and pink cardigan, fashionable Gap jeans, and black suede ankle boots. She was slim, very pretty, with a winning smile— not a hint of either of the parents in her.

Mason found himself wondering if the girl had been the victim of one of those baby mix-up efforts at the hospital where she was born. No doubt that would be the subject for another day.

The girl, Britney, spoke eloquently and frankly about her desire to be forever free from the parents from hell. The father grunted, looked as if he would grab her by the throat at any minute. The mother posed, pouted and sobbed, unashamedly playing to the cameras.

How the hell can these people air their dirty laundry on national television? What the hell is that all about? he mused, shaking his head.

"Do you really watch this rubbish, Theresa?" Mason nodded towards the TV when Bremner entered the living room armed with teas and a selection of biscuits.

"What? Oh, no. I just put it on for background noise. Couldn't even tell you what it's about." Theresa set down the spread and picked up the remote from the table, choking the tattooed fuckwit, mid grunt.

Mason reached over and spooned two sugars into his cup. He sat back and sipped it slowly.

"When're you planning to get back to work?" he enquired.

"Monday. I've made up my mind. Got to get it over with sometime," Theresa replied philosophically.

"Get back on that horse," he said in a poor John Wayne drawl.

She giggled nervously. "H-have you heard any more news?" she asked tentatively.

Mason had expected the question. She had asked the same question each and every time they had met or spoken on the phone. He put his cup down, paused for a few seconds.

"The FBI has concluded its investigations for now. The case will never be dead, but new evidence will need to be introduced before they can reopen the files." He paused again before continuing, "They've confirmed that the other female body found in the hotel room was, indeed, Penny Richards. They also confirmed that Lindsey and Kelly Martin were one and the same. She and Brodie Metcalf were trained by Jack Feltham. Metcalf killed Feltham and Kelly... Lindsey, apparently went back to try to avenge his death. She nearly succeeded as well, by all accounts. The FBI found blood, lots of it, at the scene— from a third source. The smart money's on Metcalf." He stopped again, trying to gauge the level of her still-fragile state of mind.

"So she was some kind of killer, as well?" Theresa

asked, surprisingly calmly.

"In the States, at least, although there was no evidence of that kind of thing over here. I think that, after she met you, Lindsey decided to live a regular life— get a job, do the right thing." He reached over and patted her on the knee.

She swallowed hard and nodded. When the shocking news had finally broken about the circumstances surrounding the death of Lindsey Wallace, Theresa thought her world had come to an end. It was only thanks to the strong bonds she had forged with Mason Blackwell, the Munros and a select few at Central Scotland Police that she remained sane and alive. A psychologist friend had also taken the time to help her to come out the other side.

The friend had highlighted the fact that next Monday would herald the start of the rest of her life. And that time was the great healer. Clichés yes, but Theresa believed that both would be the rock upon which she would rebuild her life. The future, if not bright, was at least there to be striven for.

"The other girl, Penny Richards? Do they know why she was there?" Theresa asked.

Blackwell shrugged. "They're not a hundred percent. I have my own theory on it, but we'll never know, will we?" he replied.

"Theory? What theory?" She looked puzzled.

"Longthorn Baltimore, the father? He was killed at the funeral of his son."

"The drug dealer killed in Glasgow?"

"Aye. Well I think that Lindsey hired Penny Richards to kill the father before Brodie Metcalf could pick up his money."

"It was all about money?" she quizzed.

"Looks like it, love. And we now know for sure that Baltimore Senior hired Metcalf to kill his son's murderer."

"What a mess!" Theresa said forlornly. She rubbed her

temples, another headache forming. The doctor had told her that the headaches would subside in time. He'd said it was to be expected, given the circumstances.

"A mess, indeed. But, with the main players, apart from Metcalf, all dead, maybe the truth will never come out," Blackwell said.

"What about Metcalf?" Theresa asked.

"It's as if he's vanished into thin air. He'll have a new identity. We'll just have to hope the FBI eventually tracks him down. I know one thing."

"What's that?"

"Andy Wells told me the great news that these killers like to honour their contracts. As far as I can make out, there was only one piece of unfinished business over here; apart from Will Munro, that is."

"You?"

"Precisely. No, if that maniac appears back here, I'm definitely on the next plane out of the country!" Mason quipped, though Theresa could see in his eyes that it was not an idle threat.

She managed a kind of sickly smile, a little disappointed at her friend's flippant attitude.

"How are Will and Mary getting on with the adoptions?" She hurriedly changed the subject.

"It's nearly all tied up, as far as I know. At least they all have each other. Could've been much, much worse," he declared.

"Definitely," she concurred.

67

Somewhere on the outskirts of New York

Ryan Costello was sitting on his porch, another lazy day in the offing.

The housekeeper had cleared up the remains of his lunch— fruit juice, melon and sea bass— and excused herself for the day. Ryan wriggled down into his antique rocking chair, closed his eyes in peaceful slumber.

It was such a hard life being a millionaire.

The house itself sat in three acres of prime real estate. The previous owner had lovingly restored the dilapidated old abode, converting it from the haunted house in every local kid's nightmare, into a luxury mansion with a modern feel on the inside.

On the north side, near the boundary fence, the garden opened into a small, secluded orchard with apple and pear trees dotted around the perimeter. All manner of berry trees and exotic bushes lurked within, and young Ryan could often be found there whiling away the hours. Most of the young man's time would be spent writing crappy, science fiction stories or smoking joints with some of his ex-college buddies.

Costello was living every twenty-two-year-old American's dream. He was in the enviable position of being able to do exactly what he wanted, when he wanted. He could afford to employ a gardener and a housekeeper. He had more than enough money to see him out.

Two years ago, Ryan was living with dubious foster parents in a dingy, two-bed apartment in Queens.

One phone call from a top lawyers' firm in Manhattan later, and his life was about to change forever. The uncle he had only met a handful of times had passed away, leaving Ryan everything in his will. The house, the cars, the money, the stocks and shares, the wine collection— everything. Everything in return for a simple last request.

* * *

The man made a point of ignoring the sign instructing all visitors to 'please close the gate.' He jumped back in his car, trundled up the short driveway to the front of the house.

The visitor met the outgoing housekeeper at the front door. The woman dropped her handbag in fright, audibly cursing the intruder as she stooped to gather together the spilt contents. He bent down to help, immediately apologising, stifling a smile in the process.

The housekeeper just about managed to crack her face before taking off down the road, heading for her next job.

The poetic chimes of the doorbell announced his guest's arrival; Ryan Costello dragged himself lazily to his feet. He trudged through from the back porch to answer the door.

The glass of freshly squeezed, orange juice that Ryan was holding flew out of his hand, the visitor roughly heaving the door against him as it was being opened. The sound of the glass smashing over the wooden floor partially masked the thump of Costello's head against the solid brick feature wall inside the house's surprisingly small entrance porch.

From there the attacker grasped the neck of Ryan's T-shirt, dragging him along the wall and through the open door into the huge hall area.

The younger man spilled onto the floor, out cold.

Ryan Costello's eyes flickered. He was conscious enough to regain some feeling, move his hand to the back of his head. He winced as he brushed against the golf ball-sized lump, tightly closing his eyes in an effort to gather his senses.

"You've decided to rejoin us, then? About time," Brodie Metcalf said cruelly. He finished off the last of a diet coke, tossing the empty can into the corner. He waited for a reaction from his host, and laughed when he encountered none.

"Wh-who are you? What do you want?" was all the stunned young man could muster.

"Who am I? Who... am... I? Let's see now; I'm your worst fucking nightmare! That's who I am!" Metcalf hissed.

"I... I don't know what you..." Costello attempted to speak.

"Not another word. Now you listen to me," Metcalf commanded. He stood and jabbed a finger in Costello's face. "I was a friend, no, a good friend to Uncle Jack. Now exactly why he decided to leave all of this to the likes of you, we'll probably never know. I'm sure you'll agree that maybe the old man was rapidly losing it." He circled his finger around his temple. "I think it's only fair that you cut me in for a slice of the pie. How much are we talking about?" he asked, suddenly producing a gun from his pocket.

The action certainly seemed to have the desired effect. The sight of the weapon instantly drained the colour from Ryan's face; he drew in a long breath. It had been a while coming, but Jack Feltham's nephew steeled himself to carry out his uncle's final request.

"You must be Brodie Metcalf. He said you'd come,"

Ryan stated quite matter-of-factly.

The assassin was visibly taken aback - that was clear. He began to view the young man in a different light.

"Go on," Metcalf prompted Costello to continue before he would decide what to do with him.

Little did Ryan know, but his next few statements would be crucial if he were to survive the remainder of the visit.

"My Uncle Jack left something for you. It's in the study." Costello pointed towards a room in the corner, just off the main reception.

Metcalf flipped the gun over, motioned for Ryan to move his carcass. Brodie followed him in, close behind. The young Costello walked over to a large, walnut writing bureau; he bent down to pick up a small key from under the rug beneath his feet. He opened up the roller-front on the bureau, plucked a white envelope out of a solo compartment in the back.

As Costello turned to hand over the envelope, Metcalf snatched it from his grasp, a sneering look on his face.

The young man stepped back uneasily, unsure of his fate. And with good reason: Metcalf slapped his gun roughly down on the edge of the desk and began to tear open the envelope. He cursed when he found it double sealed.

Eventually, the envelope succumbed to his exertions. Metcalf shot his host a menacing look. Wisely, Ryan stepped back another couple of feet. Metcalf peered inside the envelope, reaching in to lift out a piece of white paper and a small, stainless steel key.

"What the f…?" He stopped mid curse.

Metcalf had opened up the note; the typed heading immediately caught his eye: 'to my great friend, Brodie'.

Metcalf's instincts made him check the position of Ryan Costello before continuing.

The fact that you are reading this letter means that I am no longer with you. In any case, I hope that you are fit and healthy.

I would like you to know that I considered the friendship we shared to be very special.

We spent some good times together and, for that, I thank you.

As a token of my appreciation for your loyalty and trustworthiness, I would like to reward you appropriately.

You will see that I have enclosed a small key within the envelope.

I have arranged for a safe deposit box to be set up in your name at the Bank of America on Jongleurs Boulevard in Chicago.

The individual code number for the box is 66769.

So sorry I cannot be with you, but I hope that the contents of this box do not disappoint you.

Yours forever,
Jack

"Well, fuck me slowly!" Metcalf laughed, shaking his head at his turn of fortune.

He put the note and key back inside the envelope, stuffing it deep into his pocket. As he picked up the handgun from the top of the desk, the barrel scratched deep into the expensive veneer.

Metcalf now had what he had come for, and, anxious to follow up on Feltham's note, headed for the door to the hall. He had almost completely forgotten about Ryan Costello, now looking absolutely terrified out of his wits— almost forgotten!

Metcalf reached the door, turning on his heels. He primed the gun, aimed it straight at Costello, picking out a point just above his eyes.

The younger man pulled in a short breath, clamped his eyes tightly shut. *Make it quick! Please!*

"Bang!" Metcalf shouted as loudly as he could.

He laughed cruelly as he left, almost taking the heavy oak front door off its hinges on his way out.

Ryan Costello looked down. A puddle was beginning to form at his feet.

68

Metcalf checked his watch: 2:30 p.m.

He was standing across the road from the Bank of America on Jongleurs Boulevard.

Following his recent escapades on both sides of the pond, Metcalf's name was understandably high on the most wanted lists of both the FBI and MI6.

The events that had taken place at the Hotel Meridian two months previously, had forced Metcalf into taking drastic action to ensure his survival.

The bullet that had almost killed him on that fateful day had passed straight through his body, somehow failing to connect with any major organs, arteries or blood vessels. Only the staining of his blood on the carpet provided any evidence that he had been there in the first place.

Clutching a hotel hand towel to his side, Metcalf had made his escape from the scene. The next few weeks had been spent lying low, self-tending the wound for fear of FBI detection. Luckily, infection had been avoided, and Brodie had grown stronger with each passing day.

He had wisely invested in another identity, as well as a change of hair colour.

* * *

For the past half an hour or so, Brodie had been observing the comings and goings at the bank, as well as studying the actions and movements of the people down on the street, going about their daily business.

The early signs looked promising to Metcalf— no sense of a set up. He could never be quite sure though, and unwittingly found himself, once again, following his ex-mentor's advice to the letter: 'Watch, listen, study. Weigh up the situation. If the potential rewards outweigh the risks'.

* * *

Metcalf followed in behind a group of tourists congregating at a pedestrian crossing. The green man flashed and the group crossed the busy road. Brodie checked all around for any sniff of cops or feds. *So far so good.* He broke off from the tourists' slipstream, pausing briefly at the bottom of some steps leading to the main entrance.

This particular branch of the Bank of America had only recently been modernised, and the brand new glass frontage allowed Brodie to spot the armed security guard standing just inside the door.

A coiled spring, no doubt, thought Metcalf sneeringly as he studied the poor posture and slovenly appearance of the man.

The guard stepped forward to open the door for the assassin. Metcalf noted that the man's handgun was securely buttoned into its holster.

I wonder how many times that gun's seen the light of day, he chuckled to himself, nodded his thanks.

"Excuse me, sir. Can I take just a few minutes of your time?"

The voice on his blind side gave Metcalf a start. Any other situation and the poser of the question would now be lying on the floor with a bullet planted in his brain.

Brodie turned to face a young, spotty, over-eager bank

worker, armed with a clipboard and pen. He looked as if he was about to launch into an interminable sales pitch. The last thing Metcalf wanted at that moment was to draw unwanted attention.

"I'm sorry. I have an appointment." Brodie attempted to brush him off gently. The lad had obviously been studying his rebuttal remedies and techniques.

"This will only take one minute, sir. I promise you."

"As I said, I have an appointment. In fact, it's right now," Metcalf stressed the point, tapping the face of his wristwatch.

"I'm sure a few seconds won't make that much difference to your day, sir. Now, if I can…"

The youth persisted until Brodie Metcalf casually leant forward, whispered something in his ear.

The bank worker, without another word, turned and proceeded to head across, post haste, to the opposite corner of the bank— as far away from this stranger as possible. He sat on a soft chair in the waiting area, clipboard across his knees. Nervously drumming his fingers on the board, the young man periodically glanced over at Metcalf, careful not to make eye contact.

Brodie glanced around the bank. There were six teller positions, all occupied. A bored looking waiting queue of people, eight in total, were standing in readiness, hands full of cheques, pay-in books and cash. One at a time they would glance up at a large clock on the wall behind the tellers, impatiently roll their eyes at each other.

Metcalf suddenly spotted the oasis in the desert— Customer Services— a sign, below which sat a pretty blonde woman of around thirty. Unbelievably, there was neither an organised queue, nor anybody waiting at the desk. Brodie strolled over. The blonde saw him coming, smiled sweetly as per the handbook.

"Yes, sir. Can I help you?" She flashed an even bigger,

toothier smile.

Brodie instantly recalled an article he had recently read, which described some public sector service workers as possessing 'too many teeth for any useful purpose'.

"Yes. I have a safe deposit box that I'd like to go and visit now, if you don't mind," he replied politely.

"Of course, sir. If you can fill out this form for me?" She produced a document from a drawer in her desk, laying it in front of him. "If you can complete the top section? Now I'll need to see some identification. A current passport or a driver's licence would be fine?" Blondie had adopted the everyday American habit of making a statement sound like a question— an occupational hazard.

Brodie reached into his jacket pocket, pulled out his passport. He placed it on the counter. Blondie opened it at the important pages, glanced from him, to the page and back, repeating the action. She smiled a little uncomfortably this time, probably due to the different hair colour, thought Brodie.

Eventually, she laid the document flat, noting the passport number on a piece of paper at her side. She handed the passport back to her customer.

Brodie completed the relevant sections, passed the form back.

"How's that?" he asked.

Blondie took the time to check the entries. "That's fine, Mister Metcalf. I'll just call for someone to come and take you downstairs to your box." She smiled again, almost dazzling everybody in the bank.

"Thank you." Brodie stood back, hands in pockets, studying the locations of the CCTV cameras. He would always do his utmost to provide difficult angles and positions. With the recent influx of digital, state-of-the-art surveillance gear on the market nowadays, it would be no mean feat.

A tall, silver-haired man in a pinstripe suit strolled across to Blondie's desk. He looked seriously pissed off, as if retirement couldn't come too soon for him.

A short confab took place between the two employees. The tall man then turned to face Metcalf, walked over, just about managing to stay pleasant.

"Sir, if you follow me, I'll take you downstairs to your box," the man said, politely enough.

Metcalf nodded.

The two men disappeared into a lift.

Downstairs, they had to negotiate a guard and a safety gate, before arriving outside the door to what looked like an enormous vault. The tall man hit the buzzer on the outside of the door. Seconds later, a voice replied.

"Can I help you?"

"Frank, it's Artie. I have a customer who wants to visit his box."

"Okay, Artie. In you come," the electro-voice commanded.

Brodie heard the enormous, computer-controlled mechanism slide the bolts across. Seconds later, the gigantic door began to open.

The two men stepped inside; Artie nodded at his pal, Frank, and another guard, who were sitting at a large desk just inside the door. Brodie noted their weapons, again buttoned into their holsters.

Artie handed Frank the paperwork. The guard then disappeared into an inner room.

"If you come in here, sir? Now I know it's a dumb question, but you do have your key, don't you?" Artie enquired. He led Metcalf into a small, private booth.

Brodie produced the key from a pocket, holding it up to Artie's face.

"And you do remember your five-digit security code? Can't get in without it, sir."

"Yes I do," Brodie replied.

* * *

Two minutes later, the guard appeared in the booth carrying the box. He set it down on the small, but obviously sturdy, table.

"I'll be right outside. If you press the buzzer when you're finished, I'll come and take your box back."

"Thanks."

The guard closed the door behind him.

Metcalf picked up a corner of the box, trying to gauge its weight. Or rather, trying to gauge how much money could be in it. He frowned when he was able to lift it quite comfortably using only one finger.

Brodie's expression changed. He reached into his pocket, opened Feltham's note. He tapped the five-digit code— 66769— into the numeric keypad on the front, placed the key in the lock.

The box sprang open.

"Jesus H. Christ!" Brodie Metcalf exclaimed as he realised that the box was empty but for a small envelope. "What the fuck is this with envelopes, Jack?"

He reached inside and snatched the letter out of the box. Instinctively, he held it up to the light, shook up the contents. Finally, he slid his thumb under the corner, ripping along the top with his forefinger.

No banker's draft; no share certificate; no bond note; no cash. Just another fucking letter! Brodie mused. He was now getting seriously pissed. God help Ryan Costello if Metcalf was forced to revisit New York.

The note was folded over three times. Metcalf cursed again as he fully opened it up, slapping it flat on top of the box. He began to read:

Brodie,

You are obviously now standing in one of the booths in the basement vault at the bank.
The contents of this box are perhaps not all that you expected. For that I am sorry.
In my previous note, I mentioned that you would be appropriately rewarded for your loyalty and trustworthiness. During the next few minutes you will discover exactly how.

Metcalf's face softened into a resigned smile. He continued.

Some time ago, I had the pleasure of working in the Middle East, in Dubai to be exact.

Brodie's mouth was dry, very dry. Small beads of sweat formed on his forehead.

The contract was very different from any others I had previously carried out. It called for stealth and silence. No guns, no knives.

Metcalf felt a slight flush come over him. He slipped off his jacket, laid it on the table, before continuing.

Dubai was where I met a remarkable man called Parwinder Singh. Parwinder worked in the same business as ourselves. The only difference between him and us were the methods.

Metcalf stopped reading. He looked down at his shirt. The navy fabric was sweat stained and dark as night. He flicked the damp sweat from his brow. He felt compelled to continue.

Parwinder's methods stemmed from a great knowledge of all

things horticultural...

Puzzled, Metcalf screwed up his face, tried to cough out the tickle forming at his throat.

He would create the most deadly of poisons from the most beautiful of plants. Biological neurotoxins entering the body through contact or absorption...

Metcalf drew in a sharp breath. He felt a tightening in his chest. His heart thudded heavily, as if the noise would soon surely shatter his eardrums. His eyes flashed back to the note.

...Would result in the victim suffering excruciatingly as the poison started to shut down his nervous system. A simple coating of the deadly mixture on a piece of ordinary paper was enough to guarantee the complete destruction of vital organs, followed closely by total and absolute paralysis, then...

Brodie was staring at his hands and arms. They were beginning to change to a pallid, yellow shade, his liver constricting, going into shut down. He could feel the vitriol rise in his throat, courtesy of his heart going into sudden shock. "What the hell is happening to me?" he tried to call out, the statement lost forever; his throat seized, strangling the words before they could come out.

Metcalf's entire body now racked with agonising pain, his legs were no longer able to support the weight. Buckling under him, they lurched sideways. He grasped furiously at the safe deposit box as he fell, sending it clattering into the corner of the booth.

Brodie Metcalf lay helpless on the floor, by this time almost completely paralysed.

The deadly note followed the box downwards, floating

like a feather on a zephyr breeze and eventually coming to
rest against the wall next to Brodie's face. His eyes widened
as he re-read the last line of the note.

...followed closely by total and absolute paralysis, then—
Death.
  See you in hell.

Yours forever,
Jack.

69

Scotland Yard HQ

It was now almost three months since the events which led to the capture of the Colombian drugs cartel, the subsequent killing of Manuel Delgado and escape of US assassin, Brodie Metcalf.

A high level meeting had been called by top brass. The venue: the scene of the above aberrations. The purpose: to provide affected police forces with an update on the current worldwide situation regarding the cartels and their efforts to reopen the channels necessary to flood in their deadly cargos.

The huge, purpose-built auditorium within the main building at the Yard was packed to the rafters; every police force in the British Isles provided at least one representative.

Detective Inspector Mason Blackwell, in the absence of a higher-ranking officer, was drafted in for Strathclyde.

A deputation of MI6 head honchos and chief constable of the Met, Brian Hillhouse, hogged the main place settings at the top table.

The meeting began with the formal introductions of Special Field Agent Tom Lassiter, Intelligence Agent and Spokesman Bob Shanks, and a rather delectable member of MI6 administration staff, Lucinda Williamson.

Lucinda's main function appeared to be the taking of

the minutes. Some might argue that she also fulfilled a more distractive type of role within the proceedings.

Mason Blackwell, sitting at one of the tables close to the beautiful blonde, smiled ruefully when he realised that he had just been introduced to the brand new girlfriend of MI6 Field Agent, Andy Wells.

Lucky bugger.

"Ladies…" Shanks nodded at Lucinda, the only female in the auditorium. "… and gentlemen. Thank you for attending this meeting today."

As before, at the earlier meeting in Dalkeith, some of the older, hardnosed policemen in the congregation frowned at the sound of Shanks' effeminate voice. A few awkward glances flew around the room. Shanks would have to try to win over a whole new set of colleagues. The challenge was nothing new for the openly gay, MI6 man. He was certain that he had the strength of character to succeed.

Surely the only thing that matters is whether or not I can do the job? Isn't that the only thing? Shanks would often run that question past his long-time lover. There would be no argument from him. He knew better.

"Those of you who attended the recent meeting in Scotland will have been horrified at the subsequent killing of newly promoted chief constable of Strathclyde, George Drummond," Shanks said rather formally and solemnly.

Blackwell lowered his gaze in respect for his former boss. Murmurings of agreement rumbled around the auditorium.

"Commander-in-chief of the Metropolitan Police Department, Brian Hillhouse, has expressed his desire to pay tribute to a fine police officer and a good friend. We shall hear from him at the end of this meeting," Shanks continued. "I would now like to ask Special Agent Tom Lassiter to address the meeting." He acknowledged his colleague.

Lassiter grunted his thanks, stood up to the microphone clutching a few loose sheets of paper containing some hastily prepared notes— out of character given his normally meticulous working methods.

"Good morning. Some weeks ago, I spoke to some of you regarding MI6's fears and concerns about the operations of a certain South American drugs cartel." Lassiter spoke clearly and confidently in his thick Lancashire accent. "I also highlighted the activities of contract killers working for the cartel. Unfortunately, this resulted in the slaying of a number of high-profile police officers throughout the country, most notably here, in London, in Manchester and especially in Glasgow." Lassiter acknowledged the attendance of Mason Blackwell.

Blackwell had worked with the highly experienced MI6 field agent a couple of times— once, in Aberdeen, during an investigation into why offshore oil workers were being targeted by a psychotic killer. The culprit turned out to be a disgruntled and obviously unhinged ex-employee of one of the multinational oil companies. Mason had received a special commendation by his chief at Grampian Police HQ for his unfaltering work in bringing the killer to justice.

The second occasion had taken place much more recently.

Fifteen months before, Tom Lassiter was standing in Mason Blackwell's office at Strathclyde HQ.

A number of known IRA terrorists had gathered for a meeting in the East End of the city. The force had received the heads up from one of Blackwell's informants. A quick phone call later to MI6 HQ had resulted in the arrival on the scene of Special Agent Tom Lassiter. It later transpired that the reason for the gathering had been nothing more sinister than the impending funeral of the father of one of the gang.

Mason had a lot of time for the straightforward,

uncomplicated Englishman. The two had got on like the proverbial house on fire, sharing a love for their respective professions and for golf. Both had been bitten by the golf bug at an early age. Both still played the game badly despite their years of experience and cynical single-mindedness to improve. And both would continue trying, pure dedication driving them on to do so. Matches between the pair tended to be close. They had played against each other eight times, each winning three, with two halved.

Lassiter continued, "On the credit side, some members of the criminal fraternity - the main drug dealers - were also taken out. We believed at the time that the cartel was about to slot its own people into important positions on both sides of the law. That way, they would have carte blanche— could do more or less what they wanted." Lassiter's stern face softened into a slight smile as he laid the notes on the table in front of him.

Out of character, he stuck his hands in his pockets before speaking. "As you will know, after a massive MI6 investigation, the main members of the Colombian drugs cartel were arrested and brought to these premises. It was our intention to 'persuade' the head of the cartel, Manuel Delgado, to assist us in bringing these people to justice— testify against them."

It was obvious to Mason Blackwell that Lassiter was choosing his words carefully. The policeman had already worked out that Delgado was to be paid off for giving up the heads of the cartel.

Lassiter continued, "Following the death of Delgado in custody..." He paused, glaring openly at the relevant commanding officer in charge. The recipient squirmed uncomfortably in his chair. "The case against the cartel fell apart due to lack of evidence. We had to let them go."

"So what happens now? They're surely going to come back at us?" Bill Hamilton, chief of Derbyshire

Constabulary, frowned at the thought.

"Well, the signs are good right now," Lassiter replied brightly. "The cartel had to abandon their immediate plans. The drugs, or at least most of them, aren't getting through here. The FBI has told us that the cartels have switched their attention mainly to the States for now. That's good—well maybe not for them!" he joked, again out of character. "The only downside to this situation is that, until the main players get their act together, the market will be flooded with cheap, dangerous imitations. In fact, we know that the sweatshops are working on it as we speak. The killings of the dealers have left huge holes in the system. The junkies still need their fixes," Lassiter said sadly. "If we can shut down the new operations before they can establish... you never know. Maybe we can save some lives," he stated thoughtfully.

Lassiter gesticulated at his colleague, Bob Shanks, to take over.

"Gentlemen. I've taken the liberty of printing off copies of the information that we feel can be of help to you in your fight against the drug dealers. It goes without saying that this information is highly confidential and care must be taken to ensure that it does not fall into the wrong hands." Bob Shanks quoted the company line.

Blackwell could have said it along with him.

"There's one for every force. The names are on the top left-hand corner. Lucinda? If you could do the honours? Thank you."

Lucinda stood up from the table, picked up a heavy handful of the bound and sealed envelopes, and strolled around the auditorium, laying one beside the name-plate of each constabulary.

Every pair of male eyes in the place, except maybe those of the gay Bob Shanks, followed her every move with interest.

70

An exclusive suburb of Glasgow was hosting a special gathering.

Mary Munro was sitting out on the back lawn. Husband Will was tending the barbecue. Their four children, the Vieri twins now formally adopted, were amusing themselves as most children their age would— in their own company.

The Munros had invited some people over— some very important people.

Detective Inspector Mason Blackwell and his wife Alison, Detective Inspector Theresa Bremner, MI6 Field Agent Andy Wells and his lovely new girlfriend, Lucinda Williamson.

The womenfolk sat together, nursing white wines, chattering about fashion, the weather, and children, of course.

Theresa was standing close enough to express an opinion, fussing like a mother hen over her chicks. She was positioned directly underneath a wooden climbing frame, poised to pluck from mid air, any falling children happily playing above.

Mason and Andy were standing in the shade near the back door of the house. Both men sipped cool Budweisers, laughed as they surveyed the happy scene in front of them.

"Lucinda's a really sweet girl, Andy. You're a lucky guy," Mason conceded.

"I do like her, Mason. In fact..." Andy paused, mid sentence. He couldn't believe he had nearly uttered the L word. He had obviously quaffed one or two Buds too many, before deciding against completing the statement. Mason read the signs. "How long have you been seeing her?" he asked.

"About a month." Andy felt even more foolish after confirming the timescale.

Mason smiled. Not because of his friend's almost frank admission. Unwittingly, he had been watching his wife closely for the past minute or so.

His face took on a more serious expression. With all the happenings of the past few weeks, Mason had not had the chance to tell Alison just how much he loved her; tell her exactly how beautiful she was. And she certainly was beautiful. He continued to watch, almost mesmerised.

Alison was wearing her gorgeous blonde hair piled on top of her head. A couple of wisps had worked loose, fallen down, one on each side of her face. She would nervously scrape the hair back behind her ears with a forefinger. Mason would often tease her about the habit.

His mind went back to their university days— to the pretty medical student with the gorgeous smile; the smile that had left him hopelessly in love.

His eyes worked their way down his wife's body. She was wearing a long, low cut, powder blue dress, hugging closely at her slim waist and hips. The dress split at the front, her sleek, tanned legs protruding, revealing from above the knee. He smiled again as she discreetly pulled the material over to cover the naked flesh.

* * *

The women's keen conversation somehow stalled for a couple of seconds— only a couple of seconds— Alison

Blackwell seizing the opportunity to check the whereabouts of her husband. Not in a checking up sort of way, mind you. The incidents with Brodie Metcalf and Doug Mailer had had a profound effect on the young wife. She had come close to losing her main reason for living, aside from her babies. If she could somehow shrink Mason and keep him safely in a matchbox, she would.

* * *

Double taking, Alison caught her husband staring at her.

'What', she mouthed, wrinkling her brow.

'I love you,' he mouthed back at her, a cheeky grin on his face.

'Love you, too.'

She went back to her conversation. Mason just couldn't take his eyes off her.

At Alison Blackwell's right hand sat Andy Wells' new girlfriend. Mason's eyes eventually drifted towards her. She stared coldly back at him. For a fleeting moment, he felt sure that he had seen something familiar in those icy blue eyes.

Maybe not, he thought, her face easing into a polite smile.

Mason Blackwell returned the favour before Lucinda Williamson, younger sister of Doug Mailer and half-sister of Brodie Metcalf, rejoined the conversation.

END

9 781616 671754